ALIEN HERESIES

Alien Heresies

Diplodocus Press
Bangkok, Los Angeles

Trade Paperback: 978-1940999-52-4
Hardcover: 978-1940999-34-0
First Edition

10 9 8 7 6 5 4 3 2 1

Alien Heresies

SCIENCE FICTION STORIES BY

S.P. SOMTOW

and the drawings of
MIKEY JIRAROS

diplodocus

CONTENTS

A Word....

This is a fairly comprehensive collection of my science fiction stories ... from the very first one I sold, in 1977, to more or less the present. It spans several decades in which I was first a science fiction writer, then a fantasists, then a horror writer, a magic realist ... and finally an opera composer.

There are some well known stories—"world's best" selections, Hugo nominees and such—and some extremely rare pieces that haven't been seen in an age. They are presented in "sort of" chronological order, more or less—at least, the earliest and most recently published are in their respective places, so we have alpha and omega but what's in between is about as well ordered as my mind is these days.

I've tried to not use stories that are parts of series, so there's an Inquestor story but it's the original non-canonical version, there is the original *Aquila* story before it was ever dreamt of as a trilogy, there are no *Mallworld* stories because you can find them all in the *Mallworld* collection.

I've also used this volume as a way to showcase some bits and pieces from my son (or daughter) Mikey's sketchbooks.

This is a huge—nay, *massive*—collection of art that keeps growing and growing—Mikey seems as prolific, as versatile and as febrile as a young Picasso at times. At first I was planning to ask him to illustrate the stories themselves, but his English might be a bit of a problem. Instead I'm chosen from these hundreds of pieces of paper lying around in his studio images that seem to complement or contrast with the stories themselves.

This retrospective only takes us up to 2007—so there's a thirteen-year gap between now and this book coming out. The last story in the collection, *An Alien Heresy*, was written when I was having a severe sleeping disorder and had to take a break from running the opera for some time. As always in my life, music and writing are a refuge from each other. When one overwhelms, I seek solace in the other.

I have taken advantage of another enforced sabbatical, a world-wide one brought on by the latest biological scourge, to assemble this collection.

But it's also enabled me to work on other writing, including a new Inquestor novel which has just come out. I'm thinking I may relaunch my science fictional voyage—as I'm in the Third Act of my existence on earth right now, it may be that this will be the mythical journey to the west.

I would like to say that doing everything myself, and often reach out to my readers in person, messaging them on a one to one level, is an exciting new experience. What I don't enjoy is discovering that my level of concentration isn't what it used to be and the number of dropped words, errors, missed typos and so on has become quite irritating. I think that the core of my thinking burns as bright as it used to, but there's a few layers of dust it has to work through to be able to shine again. I hope that my return to publishing will enable me to hire someone to do a lot of the copyediting and proofing that seems to slip my mind. I'm great at doing it for other people's work, but you know how it goes....

What is great (and onerous) about Diplodocus Press is that it's straight from me to you, no middle men. In my twenty year absence from the publishing field a lot has changed. We've gone technologically so far forward as to have returned to an earlier time, when a writer *could* put out his own books and have a small circle of friends and readers and be a *real writer.*

Sure, I'm not going to be able to sell 100,000 copies of anything anymore, but I figured out that reaching out in person to a few hundred has its own satisfactions.

Last year I had a new novella in *Amazing Stories*—it is not in this book because I am saving it for a parallel collection of my fantasy stories.

Having chosen to work mostly in opera in the last twenty years I have found that I can finally start stitching together my fractured career. Opera lets me do *all* the things I love in one go—from words to music and everything in between. I'm not going to leave opera and go back to just words or just music. But I do need to keep words and music going.

Science fiction is more special to me than any other branch of literature even though I've become more known for, and made more money over the decades from, horror and fantasy. Why?

Well, this is very much about my childhood in the 1960s and about the circumstances of my becoming a science fiction writer in the 1970s.

In the early 60s we were "home" in Thailand for the first time—we had been wandering the earth since I was born—and I was a stranger in a strange land though it was my native land. I couldn't speak Thai yet.

The Bangkok Patana School had a small bookcase in my classroom, a private classroom library. Since this was a small English-speaking school in what was then sort of a backwater, expats returning to their native countries would often donate books to the library and it just happened to have a small trove of science fiction books.

The contents of that library are essentially what made me who I am today. The first stories I remember *clearly* are "The Skills of Xanadu" by Ted Sturgeon—*clearly* the influential force behind my story "The Thirteenth Utopia" and thus the real origin of the entire Inquestor series. *And* "Placet is a Crazy Place," the novels *A Case of Conscience* and *Methuselah's Children*. Oh, the Madeleine L'Engle books were there too, but even then I realized they were not quite in that particular nerd-geek mainstream.

From James Blish I learned that science fiction is a vehicle for complex philosophical thought. From Heinlein I learned that science fiction inhabits a future that boys fantasize about, the widest frontier of all. From Fredric Brown I learned whimsy and weirdness.

Around 1978, burned out from trying to revolutionize music in Thailand after a couple of wild years when I had returned from school in Europe full of passion and fire but not full of any long term plans … I ran away to America and started writing to clear my mind out of a musical burnout. What did I turn to but science fiction?

My first stories were imitations of what I had read as a child in the classroom library at Patana.

I don't know *who* donated those books to the classroom, but they made a *huge* difference in at least one person's life.

I'd like to dedicate this book to that person.

If only I knew who it was!

Alien Heresies

Sunsteps

… highway seems to go on forever.

I'm alone on the gold throne of the nine-seater, nestling into unaccustomed softness. Cushions stuffed with rose-petals.

Such luxury is reserved for the ones who feed the gods.

There is a glass divider. But in the driver's mirror I see his eyes, crystalline and impassive. I see black, leather-gloved hand resting lightly on the wheel, a blackness of face and hair and raven-feather cloak.

It all flashes by, the cliffs, the sky. Three days in this car! I can't describe the bleakness of it. The Sacred Highway is quite empty. Naturally: its only purpose is to bring me speedily to Tezcatlipoca and to death.

Don't you think I haven't agonized over this decision, I'm not old. Forty. (I still see the puma eyes of my wife Takl, disillusioned, as I tell her, "They'll take care of you," I say. The show of indifference wrung from me; I speak with an unwonted harshness. With start, I recognize the emotion behind her dead stare. I don't think she believes, I think she is a skeptic. I hate her because her emotions touch an unacceptable resonance in my own soul.)

The images flash by. Yet occasionally I fancy I can see her eyes still, harsh as ever, suspended like twin ghosts over the accelerating scenery. The fields, the valleys.

But there is the God. The Sun, mystically rekindled by the blood of dying victims. It glares down on me now, it blinds me when I turn to face it.

For now I am the sun, I am the God to whom even the Emperor-Dictator of the world must bow. To me alone belongs the knowledge of my humanity, the privilege of doubt.

I'm also a scientist who has asked a forbidden question. I want to be cynical, intellectually objective about why I have offered myself. But finally all my thoughts begin to sound so poetic, so mystical, that the scientist in me would rather think nothing at all.

The forests, the beaches. It's the fourth day without refuelling. It occurs to me, sometimes, that this searing isolation must be *some* ultimate test of my divine composure. It's all so oppressive, this paraphernalia of godhood! This coronet of solid gold, this dazzling cloak of quetzal-feathers covering a full-length robe of cloth-of-gold. These clothes are six hundred years old. And it's this weight of time, of distance, of divinity, of loneliness that drives away my logical doubts, thrusts me towards the inescapable conclusion that—

I am the God.

Involuntarily, in a moment of exasperation, I cry aloud: "Why did I choose to die?"

The lakes, the deserts.

The driver does not respond; in spite of his uncanny

humanness, his intellectual programming is too limited.

***

My eyes are closed. This must be a dream, and yet—with a surpassing vividness, I see the past unfold …

Summer, the Year One of the reign of the Emperor-Dictator Montezuma XVIII. Prosperity in all the world. Praise be to the Sun!

I shut out the Antarctic blizzard with a flick of a switch. The triple doors swing to. Takl, my wife, looks up briefly, a plain brown face framed in fur.

I pick up a little aluminium stool, set myself down rather ceremoniously.

" … His Imperial Dictatorship-Divinity Montezuma XVIII today issued an edict banning all scientific research," the radio whispers. They are all listening, four or five of them at the Antarctic Research Station, tense in the unnatural warmth. Takl pulls off her fur cloak, but I don't think of taking mine off. I am sweating.

" … His Divinity said that further knowledge is unnecessary. We stand at the center of the created cosmos, the Sun deigns to shine, the world is good and plentiful. Remember the old legend about the conquest of China, seven hundred years ago, how they with their ungodly knowledge loosed their terrible inventions on the People: gunpowder, writing, rifles, cannon. Remember how knowledge foments war.

"For the peace of the world, for the glory of the Sun. Given at the Throne at the foot of the Sacred Mountain Popocatapetl, on the twelfth day of the first year of His Divinity the Emperor-Dictator Montezuma XVIII."

Click.

Everybody starts talking at once.

Takl says, "It's all right. They've made an exception for

us. The Emperor *has* to understand the nature of the Sun, so as to serve Him."

They stop talking abruptly. Then they turn to look at their leader.

"Well, I did know about it," I admit. It's an uncomfortable moment. "I think we should try to understand His motives," I continue. "He must know. You've seen this, otherwise you wouldn't dare to be here. Simple extrapolation shows that the world population will be down to one million in only eighty years. Within His Divinity's lifetime, I'd say, given regular transplants. It's His problem, He knows it."

"But what will happen then, Professor Kuzdai?" the assistant asks. Her complexion is delicate, like polished wood. Takl glares at her.

Sighing, I state the obvious, dreadful reality: "Without food, the Sun will die. The Universe will come to an end." She quickly controls herself. To the best of my knowledge, the fact has never been stated so baldly amongst us …

And I cannot even imagine it: total ending! Total destruction! No. Now there is truly a dead silence in the room, and I can feel the bitter deadness of the freezing waste outside, pressing relentlessly on the metal walls, you can feel a desolate coldness the heart penetrating the artificial warmth. Here we are so from the sun.

"Science has gone far enough, though, hasn't it?" I go on earnestly, wanting to hear anything, even myself, rather than the iciness of the silence. "Look, we've got cars, airplanes, every kind of convenience. We've pushed down to the very limit—hypothesized the indivisible atom. It's only right that everything should now be channeled towards a single end, saving the world.

"We know that human sacrifice is the only way of keeping the sun burning." I begin to relax into the familiar cadences of my standard pep talk. "But if we discover just how the mechanism works, if we can unleash this undiscovered force in those bleeding, plucked-out human hearts, we can perhaps—"

"Learn to synthesize the power," Takl says. It's a familiar speech. I let her go on for a while; I'm a compromiser at heart. Locust, the stupid little assistant, says, "It's almost like a kind of sacrilege."

There is another protracted lull. I can't stand the tension —we've been together like this now for four months—so I turn abruptly on my heels and stomp toward my own lab, slamming the door.

It is because of the potential accusatIon of sacrilege, of course, that we are banned to such a remote part of the world.

My laboratory has no windows. Carefully I close the door behind me and walk over to the only table. I'm experimenting with various tissue types, trying to get a statistical correlation between the predominant sacrificial type and the brightness of the sun on any given day.

It's annoying work, very detailed, very fidgety, especially with the ban on writing. I have to cassette all the experimental results. I feel too morose to do anything, so I sit at the table, watching the automatic burette dripping accurate amounts of cell suspension into little conical flasks. The results will probably be negative, as usual: I have begun to think that the divine must be beyond scientific consideration.

A timid knock. "Kuzdai, come quickly, come see."

More steps, the door is flung wide. Locust is beckoning.

"Outside, out of the sky, a fireball!"

I follow her, confused. Up the escalator to the top level, where there is one room with a small window.

We're all crowded around the small round pane, sweating together, and all at once I see the fireball, burning high against the white sky. You can't tell earth from heaven, it is all one integrated whiteness, the sun is behind us and there is the one unearthly object, fiery, gracefully dropping on us.

Well, I think, with a sudden surge of exaltation, living so close to the secrets of Divinity, one is bound to experience these supernatural events at times. This is a very beautiful one.

"A piece of the sun!" my cold wife exclaims, catching the heady exhilaration from the rest of us. It seems that the Sun is going to give up its secret freely, by revelation. We should have trusted!

We're all talking and laughing, and my wife says, "Let's go," with unexpected enthusiasm, so we don't even bother to grab our cloaks as the three doors swing open and we all rush like children into the cold and the sunlight. I'm practically naked. Our bare feet slop into the new-fallen snow. We keep on laughing together; the whiteness around us goes on and on, out to the horizon, up to the zenith.

Locust finds the ball, gleaming in a pit in the snow. It seems to smolder for a while, there is a cloud of steam, and for several minutes after it burns out, no one dares to touch it.

***

It's in my lab now.

The uncanny, eerie feeling of total joy has passed, nobody is quite sure what to do or say. The ball is on the table. We've cleared everything away. The ball—about a foot in diameter—sits there, its surface perfect like the sun's. Takl and Locust, the two women, are hypnotized.

Breaking the silence as always, I say: "Well. I'm puzzled.'

"Won't it communicate with us?" asks my dour, dark-faced second. I don't answer, as it seems rather a fatuous question. Elation is replaced by a growing irritation.

"Leave me alone," I growl. They disappear quickly, responding by habit to my frequent touchiness.

The globe sits on the table.

I pick it up. It's perfectly spherical, sun-shaped. It must come from the sun, because we make no spheres, in case we accidentally draw away some of the vital force from the sacrificial altars of the world. The globe hardly weighs anything; its metal is unfamiliar to me, a little brighter than silver and quite unmalleable.

As I clasp the object in my hands, I hear an alien voice stirring in my mind. The revelation!

"Do you come from the sun?" I ask out loud.

"Be patient," comes the ghostly voice, an inner whisper all the more spine-chilling because it sounds so uncannily familiar. "I am going to ask you the questions. I am a provoker. I awaken dormant possibilities."

I nod to myself, An idea familiar in our myths, though it feels il strange in reality. But our work brings us close to Divinity.

Abruptly: "What is that object?"

I look at the tubular metal device lying on the workbench, bewildered, wondering why it hasn't been put away.

"Why," I whisper—I don't want people to think I'm talking to myself! —" it's a telescope. Comes in useful sometimes, if one of us gets lost in the snow."

"Why don't you point it at the sun?"

Disbelief. I shudder. What sort of voice it this, that dares so casually to suggest the unthinkable? But I realize that I've often wondered why science has never considered dealing with the sky. Sacrilegious thoughts, always instantly curtailed. Because we have always known all the facts about the heavens, science is supposed to uncover new things, not truths as old as man and older even …

But when a voice from the Sun itself has suggested it… .

Working feverishly, I take a pile of photographic negatives the drawer, tape them one by one over the end of the telescope frame. The others are in the lower level, noisily eating the evening meal.

I tiptoe back to the only room with a window; the Sun has set to the west—it is not quite the time of the midnight sun— I know that if I raise my instrument to the skies I will see the face of the God himself.

I do so, trembling. In that moment, I discover two extraordinary new truths.

One: my eyes do not smart, I have not been blinded.

Two: the sun has spots.

I am back in the lab again, sitting at the table alone with the celestial object. My fists are clenched, sweaty. I am fighting the growing realization that the sun is really weakening, that this is really the brink of the dreaded holocaust. The image that would not burn out my eyes has burned itself into my mind, the glowering glory of the sun, hardly muted by the protective negatives ...pitted with tiny flaws.

As the only person in the station with access to all the data cassettes, I know that the number of sacrifices has dwindled to a trickle, a hundred thousand a year at best, all over the world. And so it has begun.

"Are you sure you are jumping to the right conclusions?"

I push the cassettes into the machine, one by one, Listening, I note that there has been no fall in the average world temperature.

Perhaps the spots *have always been* there?

But if you can accept that, you must be drawn to accept even stranger things. The structure of truth disintegrates.

There is a secret doubt within me, never acknowledged, deep-dungeoned and concealed. Not understanding it, I still feel it gnawing inside. I think of Takl for a moment, Takl who has always been cynical, whose reasons for joining this project are almost certainly heretical. though she is a thorough, careful researcher. I think that she has planted within me this seedling doubt.

The object says nothing all this while, and I dread the coming of its voice, knowing my beliefs will be tested to the utmost. Why does the voice sound so familiar?

The regulated night-chime sounds; I go to Takl.

I do admit one appalling heresy: I keep a diary. I *write* in it. Writing was an art abolished when the People overcame the barbarians. You scratch little marks on paper, and lo! they become words! It smacks of heathen magic, but I cannot help myself, because my diary is me, I don't care to reveal its contents to anyone.

That night I bring it out. Takl is waiting in the bedroom level deeper; I make some excuse and go to my lab, unlock bottom drawer.

In it I write down everything that has transpired today. I do it by candlelight, since night and day are regulated automatically. Suddenly there is someone in the shadows behind me.

It is Locust.

"What are you doing?"

She is suddenly so desirable, this lovely little girl who naive, embarrassing questions!

I have been caught red-handed. But I don't think she will turn me in. "Marks on paper," she whispers. She looks over them casually, not, of course, understanding anything. We look at each other in the candlelight. There is a moment of yearning sexuality, but it subsides. I must go to Takl, waiting for me with feigned passion in the artificial heat, in the artificial night.

***

Wakefulness.

The car, the robot driver .

…We are stopping. Drowsily: " …Tezcatlipoca?"

"No, Your Omnipotence," says the driver in his mechanical, precise voice. He does not look around. "It is necessary to refuel. If Your Omnipotence has no objection—"

"No; why should I? Where is this?"

"This place is called Louisville, Your Omnipotence. It was ancient capital of subject peoples known as whitemen."

…The Feeder Center! I sit up, look around. It is a inoffensively pleasant terrain, very ordinary looking. The pulls into a refueling station that seems to be the only building miles around.

An old man is leaning against the fuel pump. I do not see his face as he comes over, bends down with his hose; as I look over him through the rear window I glimpse only wisps of white hair.

He looks up. I am stunned.

He is a whiteman—old, obviously past fifty. But they're always given to the sun before their late teens, I think, while still traight and golden and superb in their sunlike beauty. *Why is this man alive?*

He glares at me fearlessly, so that I am taken aback. For the past year I have met only humility. Here is a look of hatred so intense and concentrated as to ruffle my schooled composure.

Behind the hatred, I feel, is pain; and behind that anguish is some certitude, some knowledge about me, that I cannot grasp, that makes me tremble.

I want that knowledge.

"Let me talk to him awhile," I command the driver. The car has already started up.

"Your Omnipotence, time is short."

"I will come down for a moment. I *will* rest."

"Your Omnipotence—"

Desperately, "I'm famished!"

"Very well, Your Omnipotence. You may stop here for a while and avail yourself of the pump attendant's hospitality."

The car door opens. I step out gingerly, unsure of myself. The old whiteman prostrates himself, and now I see why he has been chosen to survive: there is a reddish, blotchy birthmark on his back, just by his left armpit. Imperfections displease the Sun.

Two boys, young, laughing, run out of the building, stop, look at me shyly. Their golden hair is beautiful, the soft fair down on their naked bodies is beautiful; they are the image of the glory of the young sun.

What a beautiful people! What a splendid life, I think, to live so perilously near to the God, to know that one will die for the Sun, that the obsidian knife will inevitably fall. These children, for instance; they are truly close to Divinity, their every breath is a rapturous urgency in the face of destiny.

I'm jealous. At a word from their father, the boys retreat into the building. The old man rises, beckons to me.

There is a small throne room behind the refueling station. Wordlessly, as they have trained me, I walk up the ten or fifteen steps and seat myself. There is a smell of disuse about the place; am I the first Living God who has deigned to stop here?

A dumpy, unlovely whitewoman comes in and prostrates herself beside the man. He dismisses her. "I am hungry," I reiterate. I realize it is true: I have been fasting for five days. Then I wait in silence.

Eventually the woman returns with a golden platter. To my dismay I recollect that as the Living Sun I am only officially allowed one kind of food.

As the platter is passed up to me, I see two human hearts,

raw, bloody. I hesitate briefly—but I have been well schooled. Not wishing to offend, I devour them greedily, making the requisite noises of gluttony and delight. Soundlessly, the takes the platter from my lap and leaves the room, abjectly, arthritically.

The old man sits on the floor at the foot of the steps. We alone in the small throneroom. It is quite dark; the only comes from two candles at my feet, mounted on skulls.

Again I think about the beauty of his people, how blessed they are in the Sun's divine love. They are really the Chosen race: go to the Sun every year in their tens of thousands, chosen from the Feeder reservations, they all ascend the golden escalator into the sky ..., I see that the man is gazing at me with that same look hatred. It is incomprehensible, for I am wearing the benevolence of the God who has eaten his fill. I wave my hand in blessing, to be answered by the relentless look of hate.

"Why do you hate me?" The scientist in me is forced to the surface.

"You ask why I hate you!" he grates. "You, the lordly one, symbol of tyranny, whose whim raises us for slaughter."

I am thunderstruck. This interview is not going at all as: expected. "What do you mean?" He is bitter, I reflect. because he is too imperfect to have been chosen.

He can hardly control his rage. "This 'religion' of yours," scoffs. "You know it's an excuse to enslave us!"

"What do you mean, 'religion'? The People are enlightened, we go by scientific principles and axioms." I struggle to rernain calm, because I feel the dormant skepticism in me stirring. "It's your unfounded 'cults' that are 'religious.' Why, when we conquered you, you were worshipping some unfortunate criminal tied to a tree!"

His raving is lunatic. All too clearly I see the totality of the flaw that must have barred him from union with the Sun.

"Don't think you've brainwashed us all, you so-called God! You are Professor Kuzdai from Antarctic Research. We send our children to your training schools, where your priests knock elevating thoughts into their heads about divine destiny—but we are there too, with the truth!"

"But I am going to die, too," I protest unconfidently.

"You *chose!*"

My hidden skepticism whispers that a precious illusion is being shattered, for the good. But I make an effort to combat the thought, to see the madman for what he is. "So what can you do about it?" I say, petulantly. "You will die anyway, 'truth' or no 'truth' …unless you fall short," I add, looking at his birthmark with distaste.

"For a God, you're not particularly omniscient," he sneers. "So I won't enlighten you about the hidden armoury, the secret army, the Messiah or leader that is to come."

I have had enough. "I bless you, madman," I intone, my Divine voice tinged with irony. He rises, shaking his fist at me, and leaves the throne room.

The driver comes to fetch me. The sun is setting; the grass is blood-red, the building and the gas pumps are a gloomy black against the red sun-glow.

I see the old man cowering in the shadows.

I am filled with great compassion. His imaginary world moves me, with its armies, its fighting, its Medieval revengings. I don't stop to ask myself why I feel for him so strongly, knowing that it might be the darkness inside me that answers.

I don't want to leave so abruptly, so, in a kind voice, I try to ask some meaningless, trivial question: "Where are the children?"

To my astonishment, the old man breaks down, he crouches, clinging to his fuel pump in a hideous parody of a lover's embrace, sobbing uncontrollably, despairingly, into the dusk.

I cannot understand this. I am powerless, though a God. He lashes out at me from a face distorted with unspeakable grief: "You ate their hearts!"

***

Monotony, monotony.

So easy to slip back into the past ...

The radio has stopped functioning now and won't let itself be fixed. So we have become truly isolated, a self-sufficient island universe in the Antarctic waste. It has been many weeks since the object spoke to me.

I am too terrified to go into the laboratory alone now. When I am there I talk incessantly—my new volubility is much commented on, especially by my wife.

"Can't you shut up? I can't think."

I stop talking for a moment, but without even looking at the object I can sense the vague stirring in my mind. Quickly I go on talking about this and that, joking about the state of putrefaction of this or the other tissue sample, remarking on how this flask is more congealed than the other, just the usual laboratory small talk. And suddenly I'm alone.

But here I am at that same stool again. I don't think I can keep up these defences much longer, I'll go crazy.

Question pops into my mind.

"Why don't you do a spectrographic analysis of the sun?" *Analyze* the sun? I am tempted. The awareness of makes me shiver, though, in spite of the stifling warmth.

Nervously, I fumble with the sun-disc clasp of my bearskin The ghostly voice is silent, leaving me without an external object on which to project my inner conflict.

A few days later, I discover the composition of the sun. It been very simple to design the equipment, given one awesome leap of imaginative thinking—to *look* at the sun. It's hardly a device, using the tell-tale lines in a spectrum—Ixtyl's cassettes are almost a hundred years old.

It is all hydrogen, a trace of helium. Elements you can find on earth—the lightest ones, strangely but plausibly consistent with known scientific theories.

What of the divine matter then, that all the ancient cassettes sing about? Everybody knows what the sun is made of, what the readings may say …

I have seen the results with my own eyes, my scientist's eyes. Another shattered illusion. Days later, another question: "Where do all the elements come from?"

"I'm tired!" I shout to the empty room.

Here I am, toying with the clasp again, and I'm dog-tired. The others have all gone with the huskies to the nearest supply station. For a while the blizzards have abated; it's the first opportunity.

I don't want to communicate with the object again. starting to regret not going along, and yet I seem to have manipulated staying behind. Sweat glues me to the stool; I lay open to temptation again.

I am in two minds now. The questions have set up radical new trains of thought, seditious, positively evil, but undeniably logical. Why doesn't the object talk to anyone else? Is the object talking to me at all, or is it some repressed inner self that is using the object to express its ungodly being?'

The new question, now: automatically, I fall to thinking. Hydrogen is the simplest element, and the others have bigger atoms; atoms are surrounded (according to the recent hypothesis) by energy-shells that are the basis for electricity and chemical reactions. But atoms don't come *from;* they are. I fail to see the point of it.

The sphere gleams quietly in the shadows. Wonderingly, I pick it up—I am not now so sure of its celestial origin—and I gaze into it. Another question comes: a whisper, resonant, insidious.

"Is the atom indivisible?"

"Yes, of course, by definition!" I blurt out. The question irritates me by its illogicality. I slam the object down on the table; it rests, unperturbed.

"Is the atom indivisible?"

Why, if it weren't, you could synthesize other atoms by pushing together hydrogen atoms! Why, why—my mind is racing with unheard-of extrapolations. Have I been drugged, is the object some diabolical mind control device? But if the Sun is all hydrogen, and helium is the next highest element by weight, then couldn't the atoms be so crushed together in the sun that they fuse together—at some terrific, unimaginable pressure? And then wouldn't this tearing up of atomic structure release enormous amounts of power— more then electricity, much more?

It would explain the burning of the sun, the creation of all other elements! I see a vision of earth as a conglomeration of heavy atoms thrust out from the sun in some fiery, grand agony of birth.

Then, logically, there are some stupefying conclusions:

The human sacrifices have nothing to do with the sun's energy source—And the sun is only a mechanism, not a God!

My world comes tumbling down.

I get up reeling from my stool, pace frenziedly up and down the corridor, my steps echoing metallically in the emptiness. I try to calm down. Why, I have the secret of everything in my hands, it's only another step, a matter of time, from knowing how it operates to being able to reproduce it... .

The tension cracks.

The object gleams seductively, but I am numb.

I find myself in my seat again, scrawling the theory in my

diary. It's only a theory, I keep writing, logical, but it contradicts all known realities.

Obviously, I tell myself, this continual isolation, this constant sexual tension between me and Locust and Takl, has damaged my capacity to reason. I'm mad, this is all madness. They say the midnight sun gets to you, the continual exposure to God, enveloping you, penetrating walls of solid steel. I'm not pure enough to be here, my heart conceals some secret darkness.

I calm myself with a superhuman effort. I look, feigning impassiveness, at what I've written in the diary. It is in ludicrous. Analyzing myself, I note the beginnings of a dangerous megalomania. "Secret of everything," indeed! Carefully I diary away in its drawer. If I don't look at it, it can't damage mind any further.

I need to see a priest, to leave the station for a while. Nervously, I unclasp my cloak, try to clamp down the noisy chattering of my teeth.

Resolutely, I say to myself: This excitement is unwarranted. I'll simply call the Ministry of Science—what's left of it—and ask for a brief vacation.

A chilling gust of wind and Takl is there. I imagine her to pounce on me, like a tigress. Paranoia.

We stand, face to face, a few inches apart. I am about to speak.

"Why, what is it?" she demands, shoving the door closed. She does not seem concerned.

I tell her I am going for psychiatric counseling, probably: . the home Temple at the city of Nefertari. in Egypt. I explain briefly: "The sun-sphere: I keep thinking that it's talking to giving me strange, corrupting notions."

"Oh, it's been talking to you too?" she remarks.

I can only gape. They're all in collusion against me!

"You're a fool," she says. "And a coward. There are

changes afoot, you can't just cling to the old ways."

Chillingly I realize the extent of her irreligiousness. Yes, they're all in it together, they, the sphere, the ungodly people, they probably planted the sphere to delude me, to drive me to despair.

Paranoia is inevitable, I keep insisting to myself. Must get a grip on myself.

"Pack," she tells me, and walks away. I follow her into little bedroom, and she has already started to sort out the clothes. She is well experienced, since this is my second nervous' breakdown.

I let her do all the packing. I'm completely disoriented, I wander in a daze, succumbing to an unnatural feeling of entrapment, the new thoughts continually stealing into my consciousness. I don't dare to acknowledge the crucial conclusion, so I try to banish my thoughts by humming and mumbling to myself.

Now I'm in the lab. It's all so unreal, so out of focus ..., vaguely I see the shifting shapes of the flasks and bottles, I glance at the torn poster of a pregnant whitewoman gazing raptly at the sun, at the stool which I have kicked over at some point. My travel satchel is in my hand.

Locust is watching, strangely, as I carelessly load the gleaming sphere into it. She doesn't ask me why, and I am hardly aware that I am taking my temptation with me.

The thoughts again.

God is God! I repeat over and over in my mind, as though to drown out anything else. I long for some proof of God. You cannot gauge the profundity of my despair... .

We are rapidly approaching the heartland of The People. There are deserts and more deserts, and then the highway broadens. The driver slows the car for the last few hundred miles: the triumphal progress through the Seven Cities of

Gold.

Dots on the horizon grow into great pyramidal ziggurats that line the road, some of steel and concrete, others half-crumbling stone, relics of the past now veined with shrubbery. In between the pyramids, a forest of statues—squat, grimacing fertility gods, bloated war gods from forgotten war-torn antiquity, red paint still lurid on their lips, fallen statues of dead heroes and kings, arms and heads half-buried in the sand.

My lips tighten. I must prepare myself for what is to come.

First there is a distant hum, inoffensive, like lowing cattle. Steadily it grows, and there are people everywhere, yelling the names of the Sun, waving, prostrating themselves, on either side of the highway. Zetsoc is one of the great cities of the world, with 200,000 people …

A mother, laughing, lifts up her gap-toothed child to see the God. An ocean of faces washing the windows, old men are tearing their clothes and throwing them at the car, the streets are strewn with feather headdresses, bowler hats, confetti.

The roof of the car opens, my throne rises slowly, and I sit, my arms upraised until they ache, ascending into the sun's oppressive glare.

The throng is hushed. Still I rise, then lifting my ceremonial obsidian knife I point it at my breast, my left arm pointing towards the sun.

At once there comes a surge of yelling, fanatical screaming, for the Sun has shown his willingness to die so he may feed on himself, for the sake of man. And first an old man comes running and throws himself prone onto the highway; the car speeds up a little, I feel the crunch as the tires crush him, and then another one immolates himself, becomes one with the chariot of the another—and still I rise hydraulically, majestically into the sky, my face masked into the appropriate expression of otherworldly strangeness; blood splashes the tires and spatters the and so we go on through the city, like a surfboard battling the tide.

Never have I felt such power. The grandeur of my gestures, the sense of eternity in these ancient postures, as I become, I *am*, all who have preceded me!

There is a coldness in me, a sense of immense distance.. My mask of indifference becomes real; I really am unmoved.

Now I can truly say I am the God. In Louisville, two boys for me. In Zetsoc hundreds give up their lives, too frenzied to feel pain, squelched into laughing death, extinguishing their being at the very source of their being.

***

Sitting there, with the sunlight on me, I lose interest in the screams of the dying. I am recalling how I came to be here, in former incarnation as Kuzdai, the neurotic scientist… .

I have come home. Takl has come too; she insists I am too sick to be alone. She does feel a kind of love for me, I think.

We live not far from the great Pyramid of Khufu. You know the story—or any child could recite it to you—of how the Emperor came to conquer Egypt. It was Montezuma II of the of the great ships. When he saw the Pyramids he wept; amid these alien peoples they were so familiar, so sun-blessed. And—so the story goes—the Emperor fell to his knees, disregarding the hot sand blowing in his face, gazing for hours at the marvel antiquity. He laid his weapons down (muskets or swords—the oral tradition is vague, since at the time we hadn't even discovered, let alone banned, the 'writing' of the whitemen.) He spared the People and sailed home west, into the sunset. Egypt is that sort of place; very holy, very contradictory—after all. why are the Pyramids there at all, when the people themselves were not The

People'?

I drive to the Pyramid, where there is a small psychiatric center. Its two red-brick stories are deep in the pyramid's shadow. I park the car.

My priest-counselor receives me: tall, pale, almost whiteman-colored in his complexion. He has kindly eyes, surprisingly large and young-looking for his age. We sit and talk in one of the sound-proofed cubicles reserved for the mentally ill.

"Well," he begins this final session. "We've progressed quite I think; it seems, after all, to be only a conventional aberration, remarkable only in its extremity.

The memory of my extravagant heresy is warning. I keep the object in my car, these days, daring myself to face its blandishments, but it has never spoken in the two months since my return home. I associate my confusion with the blizzards, the isolation, the bitter cold.

"Do you feel healed?" he asks me gently.

Emphatically, I reply "Yes."

"I think not, though; there is an inner core of—something analysis hasn't penetrated at all. But I think you must find the way yourself, from now on. All I can suggest is that you go out for a long while into the desert. Seek communion with the Sun. Your spirits will be lifted, perhaps your religious crisis will be blown away."

When I leave I feel dissatisfied. I start to drive away. On impulse, I leave the highway, thrusting out into the directionless sand. I want to be alone with the sun for a few hours. Perhaps the priest is right.

I go on and on into the monotonous yellow expanse, suddenly becoming aware of the resemblance between the two wildernesses, the desert and the freezing wilderness where it all began. The sun beats down on me—the car is roofless—the heat is as extreme as the cold was, the yellow like the white, stretching forever. I feel confusion again, and glance at the sphere that is lying at my feet.

A dune looms up: behind it, an array of parked limousines and tethered camels. I curse misanthropically; I did not expect to stumble onto other people.

A brass band is playing, French horns and Tibetan trumpets. There are about two hundred cars dotted about, and, as I should have realized, it is the Sphinx in its newly moved location in the middle of nowhere. A golden escalator has been added up the creature's flanks and all the way to its back, where an Altar to the Sun has been built, a gaudy, feathery outgrowth of the animal's back.

There is the Sphinx, superb, incomprehensible. I note the new nose done like a quetzal-beak, the neon-blinking sun-disc halo above its head.

Priests are singing softly. I get out of the car and start trudging towards the celebrations. It is quite a long walk and when I arrive I am exhausted, burning.

People are clustered round, singing in unison. Some are wearing outlandish costumes of the subject peoples—tuxedo doublets, grass skirts. There are long tables for the ensuing feast, laden with suckling pigs and champagne machines.

A girl emerges from the house between the Sphinx's paws.

She is surrounded, jostled by priests with their peacock-feather-topped staffs and heavy robes, and she herself is naked. They a crowding her, but she is far away, like a slide projection, not quite real.

She smiles.

I push myself up to the front of the crowd, she walks past me and her arm brushes against mine. The serenity of the smile! The steadfastness of the walk! The sun plays on her long golden hair, gentle on her, while savagely scorching the crowd. Her eyes are cold like the Arctic Sea, already turned to the God.

She has the peace I long for. I crave it. As she passes me, the singing swells, an ancient paean in the old tongue, and I join them; I'm carried away with my sense of belonging to the one People:

Now she has reached the escalator of gold. For a moment she pauses—an instant of frail humanness!—then she goes to the Sun, standing stock-still on the moving Sunsteps. The priest high above us raises the knife. It flashes dazzlingly in the sunlight and you can see nothing else for a moment. One with the crowd, I am: dizzy with joy. The priest—he is a robot-rips open the girl's chest; accurately he finds the heart and tears it out, lifts it, still bloody, to the i sky.

The heat, the heat! I am dumbfounded by the outpouring of energy, of benevolence, from the sky.

And I *know*.

Of course! There is something that can purify my mind, cleanse me, wash my iniquity from me.

How did I ever waver? How could I ever have conceived that the Sun is a mechanical object? It's all so logical. Joy is in the people's hearts as they sing, it *must* stem from a fundamental reality. Joy isn't founded on a lie.

And I can become part of it. I am singing as I walk back to the car, the sun bores into my pores and the sweat gushes out, my feet are burning as they tramp into the hot sand.

I see the globe glinting in the car. Suddenly: "You wish to extinguish yourself for the sake of a known untruth?" But with a rather self-conscious sense of symbolism I pick it up and dash it hard against the sand. It rolls in the direction of the Sphinx, out of sight.

I am still humming the hymn to myself as I pull into the center to volunteer as the one yearly Victim chosen from the People to play the role of the living Sun.

When I emerge, Takl has come to meet me from the

supermarket. We are standing outside the Temple gates. When I tell her, she looks right through me and says—as though to herself —" Do you know? The object only asked me one question. It said: 'What would the sun be if it were a trillion trillion miles away?'

"It obsessed me, that question. For of course, the sun would be a star. It's a crafty object, that sun-sphere. Because it was only logical for me to turn it around, to realize that all the stars are suns, and if there can be other suns, there must be other earths.

"Kuzdai, we're not the center of the Universe! The source of the sphere is not the Sun. And there is more to come, I know, much more. "You're not going to accomplish anything by dying—you're merely pandering to your own selfishness."

It stings me, that she cannot understand the simplest of motives. Quietly, I try to disillusion her: "But by dying, I'll preserve the whole structure of our beliefs—my beliefs. The world will be sealed into its true course, since only I have conceived of these ideas and they will die with me."

"A martyr complex! They haven't healed you at all!"

"What are you worried about? They'll take care of you," I counter, with a nonchalance I do not feel. I stalk away to the car. This is the essence of my transcendent revelation: I never looked at the sun. I never made the spectrograph. Vain fantasies, delusions of loneliness that have been dissipated by the sunshine, like the night by the day.

Then why am I speechless with rage as I drive away? Why does Takl's meaningless accusation provoke me?

***

We've arrived.
The holy citadel on the high mountain.
Night. Gloom.

They have left me alone in the cavernous marble hall. It is so dark that the room seems endless. Quiet sounds: cicadas, distant hymning to me. No wind to touch the stillness of it.

Footsteps. A barrage of artificial light. A palanquin approaches, covered with purple silk veils, billowing as the bearers sway.

They set it down. It is a splash in the marmoreal whiteness. I ascend my throne. A bearer partially lifts one veil; out steps the Emperor-Dictator, His Divinity Montezuma XVIII.

Now he is just a form prostrated at the foot of the throne. I survey him, my expression haughty. "Oh Sun! I come to pay Thee customary homage before Thou returnest to the sky, and to bring Thee Thy bride."

It is a clear voice, dispassionate. I bless him, smiling benignly. The Emperor humbles himself still lower. I feel pride that the Emperor kneels to me! He dismisses his retinue. The lights are dimmed as he rises, obscuring his face. We are alone together in the gloom, the only light the flickering of an incense-burner, blue green, smoke—healing, and fragrant.

"A clever way of arranging an audience," he says, fingering the flashing medals on his military uniform. "You might as well stop this charade now, Kuzdai. God, indeed." He snickered unpleasantly.

He has confused me. I come down from the throne. I do no see his face because it is in the shadow; he seems like a talking uniform, decapitated by the darkness. I think there is a penetrating stare. Curious? Quite a calculated risk, Kuzdai. But do you think you could be allowed to die, after *this*?"

He thrusts something at me. Involuntarily I catch it with both, arms. It is the diary. "How-?"

He disregards my question. " 'The secret of everything.' No, Kuzdai. You will not die; a robot will be killed in your place. It's been done before."

"What!"

"I want you to help me," he says wearily. "You say there is a possibility of making the power, of imitating the sun. Without the tyranny of the sky, civilization will push forward, nobody will die needlessly again."

I can't believe my ears. "You're mad," I gasp, realizing with a shock that His Divinity has read the diary, that he has allowed his position to be polluted by an obscenity. "No, Kuzdai. This was planned. There was a fireball that fell into my garden, whispering strange thoughts to me. I didn't want to hear them, but I became more aware of the nature of responsibility. I allowed your research to continue because of it; and you saw through to a solution I didn't envisage, but nevertheless a solution."

I am terrified. "How can the Emperor be a heretic?" I blurt out, my mind awhirl with contradictions. "How can you stand here and say this in front of your God?"

He laughs, quite warmly. His mood becomesmore patronizing. "It's all right. It's not a trap, Kuzdai. I'm a ruler, and a ruler is by nature a skeptic.

"You're a traitor!" I feel my convictions strengthened. I am the God, tomorrow I will die and it is not for nothing. "I can feel your dishonesty, your political ambition, perverting your sense of reality. You can't change facts, and I'm not going to change them for you."

His Divinity says, grimly, "This play—acting has gone to your head, Delusions of grandeur. Remember, the real power is mine, yours the illusion."

"No! I've raised myself up from confusion, I've absorbed the truth. I'll not go back into the darkness that the sun has wiped from my mind. There is an almighty battle between good and evil to obtain my soul, and if you win, the Sun will not shine tomorrow."

"Tomorrow," His Divinity muses, "I could have it announced by radio, all over the world, that the Sun is not a God, that millions have been sacrificed for nothing. I could proclaim a new era of life and mercy—I'll find someone else to do the research, create the energy, if you die."

"They would not believe you."

A pause. "I know," says the Emperor. A tremendous sadness emanates from the shadows where he stands, and the voice rings hollowly in the huge chamber.

Finally, he asks me in a formal voice: "Living God, what dost Thou desire?" So I have convinced him, cured him. "To die," I declare. Fervently, firmly, according to the ancient formula. The god has conquered temptation! "For the Sun will not rise tomorrow, nor the warmth of the Sun descend upon the earth, unless I return to my celestial abode. I am the heart of life, and I offer unto myself my own living heart, for the sake of my servant Man.

"Thus I speak those words in the city of Tezcatlipoca, where my rays first struck the earth a thousand years before the coming of Man."

"At least give me the book," the Emperor—the incarnate trickster-god—pleads.

"No," I say, tossing it into the flames of the incense burner. The blue-green fire devours the pages, flaring up for a brief moment.

"Ah well," the Emperor-Dictator sighs. "There is but one more formality.

"I must bring Thee Thy Bride. And she is here with us, Princess Hatakatl, my sister."

He steps aside, and another figure has stepped unnoticed from the palanquin.

When she comes to me, naked and lovely, I understand many things have come to be; the feigned stupidity, the questions that ferreted out necessary truths, the night my

was seen by another. She was no fool, this girl Locust.
***

Before the Dawn that is not to come..... .

No crowds, but an endless staircase of rough-hewn rock. Two priests only for this most private ceremony, the Emperor and his sister on their thrones, torchlight.

Theatrically, a shaft of light bursts onto a golden escalator next to the ancient staircase.

The two priests motion me to ascend.

"It is not my wish."

Brief consternation.

"I choose this ancient staircase where I first ascended."

All are relieved, except the two royals, who sit without apparent emotion. I begin the ascent. Each step brings me nearer to God, to myself. The peace comes to me at last. Robes weigh down on me, seven layers of ornate cloaks and coverlets. The golden crown presses down tight around my skull and still I climb to spite it; it is so dark that I cannot see to the summit of the pyramid, but I climb on.

At each step the heaviness lifts, the robes grow lighter. I am loftily at peace, alone, giving up everything and gaining everything. I'm dying for the pump attendant with his bitter delusions, for cold Takl, for warm Locust, for the skeptic Emperor-Dictator.

Immortality!

I climb. The air becomes harder to breathe, but I am indefatigable. My passion and death are in the old manner- no escalators, no machinery to mar the perfection of my sacrifice.

Will they never end? Step follows step, I never stumble, though the steps are steep and treacherous. Now the pinnacle is in sight. The clouds are dark. I am one, alone. I begin to sing softly to myself.

And then—
***

Abruptly, the sky bursts into flame! I jerk up my head to see a million fireballs raining from the sky. There is a thunder like gigantic war-guns, the sky is brighter than day. I cover my eyes with my hands, I try to climb on regardless, but I am rooted to the spot. Again and again there are explosions in the sky, and then comes a huge voice pounding into my brain, reverberant, soul-shaking …and I sense that the others far below are hearing too, that perhaps everybody on earth hears.

"The truth is painful. but necessary.

"There are other earths. We are from such another earth, and we have come to help you solve your problem of self-annihilation.

"Direct intervention now becomes necessary to save the life of one Kuzdai, who we have selected to help lead your People through a perilous ordeal of re-orientation into a productive way of life."

No! My illusions are having one final try at claiming my soul! No, I order these visions to desist from tormenting me, I order with all the force and the power and the majesty of the Sun whose incarnation I am!

Wildly, I scream out: "You can't take choice away from me! I make myself free of you!"

And I wrench myself away from the spot, I run up the last hundred steps, my eyes closed to the tumultuous burning of the sky. I reach the altar, carelessly I fling down my robes and offer myself, knowing full well that the robot priest is not programmed for such a contingency and has no choice, while I am a man and must choose.

So I am lying on the altar and the sky is burning before the dawn and I can taste the lips of Locust on my lips and the obsidian knife flashes and rips into my entrails with a messy splat.

   ***

Time runs backwards.

Agony! My heart flies back into my chest, the blood races from the stone steps into my arteries, with a searing pain my wounds close tight together.

It is day. The fireballs are rapidly shrinking into brilliant dots against a cloudless sky.

On the altar there is a single sphere. It speaks to me, its voice no longer ghostly, but a voice of reason and authority.

"I am sorry. But you never had any choice," says the creature in my mind. "You see, we have power even to reverse the time flow locally, to alter the continuum to a small extent."

"So I was wrong."

" ... not exactly. You were chosen. Our agent placed no ideas in your mind that were not latent, ready to pop out if you only let them. You have a strong sense of right and wrong—that is necessary too. You were willing to die for it."

"In the end, it was only selfishness."

"Not exactly; you were demonstrating something for the whole species—in the end, you died for the sake of individuality. Those were your final thoughts. And we will not tamper with that individuality, we promise."

"Why did you not just reveal yourselves, take over?"

"We do not tamper. The voice you heard was your own voice, scientist's voice."

A pause, then: "I am sorry it became necessary to intervene because now we have thrust you, willy-nilly, into the galactic community. I think only a few like you possess the imagination to prepare people."

It seems, then, that the real power has finally come to me.

It is too soon, I think, to measure the full impact of coming: especially the knowledge that they will be here with superior to us, for a very long time.

Is it possible we have merely exchanged the tyranny of own misconceptions for the tyranny of aliens?

From this height I can see the whole city, a cluster of houses; I can see the twin royals still unmoving on their thrones the foot of the broken steps. A strong damp wind strikes my face." makes me shiver, and I gather up my discarded cloaks.

Sunrise has come, and there has been no sacrifice.

—Bangkok, 1977

Cruise Eternity

They pulled him out of amniosis and into the briefing room. A friendly robot with emerald bug-eyes told him that Rosalind was dead.

"I want out!" he said at once. "Rosie was the reason I took this cruise in the first place. It was our honeymoon."

The room was swimming. Through the drug-drenched haze he could see dark walls. No windows. Of course there'd be no windows. Too much to explain. They'd have to give you a full rundown before unleashing you on the future.

"I sympathize with your momentary discomfort," said the robot soothingly from across the coffee table, "but unfortunately, David, some people just don't take to amniosis. You saw the contract. Think of the future."

"You don't understand! I wouldn't be here if it weren't for her."

"David, she's been dead for a hundred years."

He was shaking. "I want off. I want off. You hear me? Off. Off. Off."

But the robot merely shrugged—fairly convincingly at that—and said, "Oh, David, we wouldn't do that to you. Abandon ship here? You wouldn't like it here. America's a totalitarian police state—1984 and all that—you'd simply hate it, and we'd never forgive ourselves."

"But we were promised utopias! Get the long view, the brochures said. Take Cruise Eternity down the road to the gleaming future. Spend a week in every century, see the human race's dreams come true... ."

"Now, you're simply getting overworked," the robot said. Its voice was pitched at optimum tranquilizing level, but David didn't feel like being tranquilized. "You're not taking the long view at all, David."

"At least let me see her."

The robot sighed. It rose from its floral loveseat, wiggling its tentacular arms in a sidewise gesture, half wood-nymph, half movie monster. "I've been trying to tell you. She's been dead for a century. A century, David. You'll be indemnified, of course. Add that to the compound interest on your initial deposit, and—"

"But the dreamstone," David said. He remembered placing it around her neck before they sealed her into the amniosis chamber. Into the coffin. The dreamstone sparking against the warm slender neck. "Didn't you keep the dreamstone for me?"

"Her personal effects were inherited by a younger brother. Who is also dead."

David sat back in the armchair. It was a perfect copy of the Naugahyde monstrosity in his New York apartment. As his vision cleared he saw more: his father's little league photograph, quaintly two-dimensional, on the wall; he hadn't seen it since he'd been a kid. Books peppered with dust on the antique twentieth century coffee table. They weren't real books, of course. When David looked at them closely he could see the glimmer of the hologram field. They'd plucked things randomly from his mind to make him a little home environment, a cocoon of ancient history that could travel along with him, untouched by time.

Out there, beyond the walls, beyond the familiar objects, lay their first port of call: A.D. Twenty-one twenty-seven. The future.

"It's not worth it without Rosalind," he screamed at the departing robot as a hearty American-style breakfast materialized on the coffee table.

"Time heals all wounds," the robot said at the door, selecting, doubtless, from its encyclopedic store of fortune-cookie aphorisms. "Oh, and your private briefing will begin as soon as you're rested."

It vanished. He touched his throat. His half of the dreamstone was there still. He unclasped the alien jewel. His hand closed around it. He breathed in its fragrance: jasmine, roses, dying leaves. Rosie's scent.

"I'm alone!" he shouted in the empty room. "Alone—stranded in the future—and everyone I've ever known is dead!"

Wildly he contemplated getting off the cruise right then and there. But the robot was right. He hated totalitarianism. Next stop, though! he thought. Next stop I'll skip the cruise and go back to timeslugging. Next stop, next stop.

   ***

They had met in front of the Cruise Eternity building in New York. He was on his lunch break. He worked as a program-debugger for the fiction-writing compusystem at Shameless Romances. He was depressed as he fled his privy-sized office cubicle, depressed as he threw on his smogcloak, depressed as he emerged from the subtube and mounted the plexitunnel skywalk that spanned the upper city, threading the hundredth-story windows of the better side of town. He had been tinkering with the program for weeks, trying to sweeten the plot-twist-potential algorithm, only to get found out by a fink of a coworker, raked over the coals by an officious robot, and summarily commanded to degauss the entire subsystem.

"And next time," said the robot, "we'll degauss your brain, too, David."

That had always been his hobby, trying to sneak a little imagination past the formula-prone parameters dictated by the powers above. Twenty years before, he would probably have been a writer; he had always thought of himself as having been born in the wrong century. Like someone from the past, he was ugly, too, lopsided; he had never bothered to fork out for the orthosomatic treatments that simply everyone underwent. He didn't look like other people and he had no debts. A freak on both counts. David didn't belong.

He brooded about his not belonging as he sailed over the city on the plexitube's airstream. Around him, buildings vaporized into imitated sunlight in the wake of the urban renewal that would soon convert Manhattan into the shopping annex of the local launchport. The sunlight stung his eyes; they never seemed to get it right. Some days you might as well have been on Mars.

He forked off from an express tube into a local and swung down over Chelsea. That was when he saw the line, and her standing, waiting. Actually it was the dreamstone that he saw, a momentary firedart that dimmed to a dull spot on her neck. He saw the line from his vantage point—snaking around corners, zagging through parts and in and out of the crushed houses that poked from the rubble like broken winebottles. The dreamstone blinked. It seemed to draw him downward. He didn't even realize he was hopping down at the nearest chute, holding up his palm to be debited by the overhead monitor, racing down the wind-tunnel towards her like one of the heroes of the very videos he programmed daily.

Not that the wearer of the dreamstone was that remarkable. She had sharp features, long, scraggly hair, a small, wrinkled mouth, a one-piece fur-stocking garment out of some order-by-number vidmall. But there was the dreamstone around her neck, an alien artifact, perhaps an organism, they'd picked up somewhere out there among the azroids. He could smell it even from where he was. David knew all about them. When they were first discovered, they became a big fad, and every romance he programmed had had a dreamstone as a love pledge or an ancient alien curse or a gage of feudal fealty. They drew color and sustenance from the sunlight …sometimes they would divide in two, so there were a lot more of them now than when they'd first been brought to Earth. But still, they weren't *that* easy to come by. No one went into space anymore. It wasn't that interesting a place; no money in developing it. And the aliens? An ancient race …long dead …vanished galactic civilizations …all very romantic, now that men couldn't afford the stars anymore.

David found himself elbowing his way toward her.

"Who are you?" He had almost collided with her. It was then that he saw her eyes: wild, driven, a startling blue that matched the highlights of her black hair. And the dreamstone.

"I'm David."

She shrugged, smiled a little; he wondered at his own forwardness. In Chelsea it was not customary for strangers to address one another.

"What's the line?" He wanted to keep talking to her, desperately wanted the moment to continue.

She pointed. Up ahead, a silvery phallic edifice pushed up out of the sea of dirty buildings. Lights flashed:

cruise eternity

cruise eternity

cruise eternity

"What does it mean?" said David.

"You don't know much, do you?" the girl said irritably. "Cruise eternity ...gateway to the future. You know?" She recited the slogan in a singsong voice, sure that David would recognize it. He didn't.

A voice behind them launched into a raucous rendition of the entire commercial spiel. "Become godlike! Get the overview ...the long view ...the ultimate perspective on history. Journey with man through the most exciting voyage of all time—*through* all time! Spend a week in every century; sleep through the horrors of the world's petty day-to-day affairs in amniosis, the new hibernation breakthrough!"

"He's certainly bought the hype," said David, "but what's someone like you—"

She said, "This is the lottery line. They give out a few free tickets every day. And I want to go. Bad. Real bad."

"Why?"   But David was already beginning to understand.

"I don't like it here. I want to be a streaker. I need to be. I need—I need—"

"You need out." She doesn't belong, David thought. Like me. Born in the wrong century, the wrong timeslot.

"But I can't afford the regular fare. You have to be worth so much to get a berth on Cruise Eternity ...they invest it and you're guaranteed some huge income every time you wake up… ."

"That's crazy!"

"Not crazy. It's—it's the human dream!" Her eyes danced. David wanted her suddenly. "Tomorrow I'll be in amniosis maybe …then when I open my eyes you'll have been dead for years and so will the rest of this fucked-up society! But you're a timeslug. You wouldn't understand."

Timeslug! That's what they call us, David thought. We're slugs and they're streakers, zipping down the ages while we turn to dust. But something wasn't quite right about her. "If you can't afford a ticket to never-never-land," David said, "how come you have your own dreamstone?" He touched it. She flinched. It sparked up. He snatched away his hand.

"Shh," she said, "it's pregnant." She cupped her fingers around it. She looked away into the distance, and it seemed to David that in spite of the surging crowd, in spite of the thrum of distant atmosphere-generators and the hubbub of expectant conversations, she was quite alone, far from all of them. And David wanted to be with her in that bubble of solitude. He had never felt this way before. "My Dad was a spaceman," she told him, not looking at him. "Now he pushes paper for a robot."

"I sympathize," he said. "They have all the best jobs now."

"Maybe you should get out too."

"No," David said. "Nothing doing. I've got a great job … I've got credit stashed away, coming out of my ears."

"You push paper for a robot too, don't you?"

"Yes. I'm at Shameless Romances."

"And you hate it."

"Not at all! I don't hate it! It's a fabulous job—low hours, wonderful benefits—"

"You hate it," she said, but with a half-laugh on her

lips.

And he knew that it was true. She had no right to know this about him, no right to see this despair that smoldered inside him, far from his conscious thoughts. She had only just met him. He didn't even know her name.

She looked right into his eyes and said, "I think you're one of us, David. I'm never wrong about these things." And she smiled at him and it seemed to David that the dreamstone caught fire from her smile and illuminated the hidden beauty in her hollow cheeks, her somber features.

One of them! David thought. People who want to throw everything away ...their lives, their friends, their position in the here and now ..."I'm not one of you," he said, realizing abruptly that he had no friends, no life, no position... .

"You are," she said firmly. David almost believed it at that moment. Then she unclasped the dreamstone and held it out to him. It was shivering, living. "Aren't we lucky! It's going to divide."

David looked into the stone. Their hands touched, palm to palm. The stone was milky white, shot through with glitterstuff. It shook and shook and then, all at once, it was two of them.

"They say the dreamstone only splits in the presence of true lovers," she said.

"Superstition." One of the half-stones fell into his palm. It burned and he yelped. "You'll ride off into the sunset and I'll stay here ...each of us clinging to this tiny remembrance of what might have been—"

"You've been reading too many Shameless Romances!"

It was true, David thought. It was getting to him. He needed a vacation. Maybe a week alone in a holiday bubble drifting across the Pacific. Maybe a few days in a brothel making love to a phantasm of latex and cold metal.

"I think," she said, "that you're in love with me." And she looked at him quite seriously, without even the ghost of a smile, as a flock of wintering birds crossed the face of the simulated sun.

David couldn't bear to look at her any more. He looked at the ground.

Above them, robots dangling from ornithopters bellowed out lottery numbers. The crowd surged like a hungry serpent.

"Be quiet!" a woman yelled at the screaming baby in her arms. "We have to hear the lottery numbers!"

David and the woman stayed until long after his lunch break, waiting for her number to be called. Streaks of sunset striped the tumbling husks of skyscrapers and burnished the pylons of the soaring plexitunnels. The rubble reddened as the rays of digitally matched color crept across the ruins. The crowded had melted away after the last number. She's going to cry, David thought. But no, she was stony-faced, hard. Dry-eyed. He held her in his arms.

"I guess I'll kiss the future goodbye," she said softly.

"Isn't there any other way?"

"Money."

"I have money," he said.

A pause. "What do you mean?"

"Money. I have it. We could both go."

"What are you talking about? Program-debuggers don't make the kind of money that—"

"I have that kind of money," David said. "Because I'm a misfit. Because I've let myself stay …lopsided."

"You don't even know my name," said Rosalind. And then she began to cry.

***

He went to the observation deck to meet his fellow travelers. The deck was surrounded by screens that endlessly replayed the highlights of the last hundred years. A gaggle of screeching women in gaudy clothes sat in deck chairs, commenting lasciviously about the dead. David did not feel one of them at all. He found a table, had the robot attendant bring him a drink, stuck a disk in the stereo and saw the same pictures, in miniature, projected into the air above his drink.

"Look at that!" It was a bearded man with a mohawk, wearing ecclesiastical robes. "Just look at that! My word, aren't we lucky—if we'd stayed back in the past, we'd've been plunged into the Dark Ages in only twenty years!"

David fast-forwarded through the holograms. Dictators were marching through Middle America at the head of high-tech troops. A slogan-slinging mermaid, six-inches tall, danced inside his bubbling alcosynth sour. "The name's Lavin," said the bearded man, "Professor Quentin Lavin, Ph.D., chair of history, University of Michigan. What splendor we're living through!"

"If you can call it living."

"Look over there," Lavin said, pointing at one of the giggling tourist women, indistinguishable from the others. "You know who that is? That's Melinda Maledicta, the notorious poetess of 'found invective'. Strings together the chance insults that she hears in the street into short lyrics of profound and startling beauty."

"How did you get a ticket?" David said. "I thought the University of Michigan had seceded from the union."

"Well, yes, but they're paying my way, you see. And I have dual citizenship—got my green card just before they shipped me to New York. It's the Californians they're trying to keep out, not the independent university-states.

I'm working on a book, you know. Half the people here are. You a writer too, I take it?"

"Sort of." He couldn't bring himself to admit that he programmed romances for a fiction-writing computer.

Suddenly Melinda Maledicta rose from her deck chair and began to declaim; her friends watched her with singleminded idolatry.

"Turds!" she shouted. "Daughter of a she-camel—

Yo' mama perfidious insect bad bad."

Lavin stood up and began applauding enthusiastically.

I want to go home, David thought. Maledicta stopped as abruptly as she had begun, turned to David, and said, "Wanna fuck, sailor?"

***

David stepped out of Cruise Eternity into the rain. It was the last day of the stopover in the twenty-second, the first time he'd felt any curiosity about the future they were visiting.

"They keep it raining," the robot had told him in the briefing, "because it keeps the people too miserable to complain."

"Forget the tour," David said, "I'm going out on my own."

"All right," the robot had said, "but don't lose your boarding pass."

David was looking at it now, an identidisk welded to his hand, beaded with waterdrops. So this was the twenty-second.

The streets were the same, more or less; if anything they were more rundown. Water sluiced down garish murals depicting some glorious revolution. Here and there, among the wreckage, a gleaming chrome building sprouted. David didn't know what he had been expecting, some glittering science fiction book cover he supposed. He hadn't been expecting this drabness.

People here and there in gray, darting, never walking, from building to street ...frightened-looking. David saw why. There were metal eyes in the sky, giant eyes, hovering, weaving in and out of the nimbus web. He shuddered from the cold and from the fear.

A man looked up, clenched his fist, shouted something ...lightning struck him. He shriveled, charred, melted into the driving rain. David was afraid but still he walked on. He only had the day in which to find Rosie's descendants. It was to be short layover; the Cruise Eternity tourists were not well liked in the twenty-second.

It was easy. There were no secrets in this future. David found a walk-up information tower. A machine burped out an address; they'd never changed the street names. David walked. Cruise Eternity still dominated the skyline, even after he'd followed all the twists and turns of the alleys that were shadows below where the plexitunnels used to fly. There were apartments, vibrant primary colors slapped down over rust-eaten walls, slogan-filled posters disguising the boarded-up windows.

David stood weeping in the rain.

There was a woman in a hallway. Gaunt, dressed in a shapeless gray mantle. She had Rosie's eyes. Their eyes met for only a moment before she looked away, stared at the wet ground, not acknowledging his existence.

"It's cold," David said. "Ask me in."

"You're a streaker." She wouldn't meet his gaze. "You don't understand our customs. You aren't liked here. They'll kill me."

It was then that David saw the dreamstone at her throat, catching the glimmer of distant killer lightning. "I have to be at the factory," she said.

"But I'm David! I was Rosie's lover! You have something of mine that I want back, you don't know how much."

"I know who you are."

Could it only have been a week ago, when the dreamstone shivered and became two, when he had cashed in his whole life and walked into the amniosis chamber hand in hand with her? They had not even made love yet. They had been saving it for the first layover. They had loved each other like ancient innocents, like the protagonists of those endless romances his company churned out to dull the minds of the masses, to distract from the petty horrors of synthetic food and sunlight and of kowtowing to officious robots. "If you know who I am," David said, "you must have heard of me from someone … you must understand how much it means to me… ."

"I am Janine, the granddaughter of Rosalind's brother. My grandfather talked of you sometimes. He gave me the dreamstone. You were not regarded with much fondness, David."

"Why not? I gave her what she wanted."

"Don't you understand? You stole her from her family. Oh, they tolerated her waiting in line at the lottery day after day …it bought us time. They could have worked it out. You murdered her!"

Her outburst took him by surprise. The downpour continued. Warily, Janine looked left and right. There were no metal eyes cruising the alley. "You look strange," she said, as she looked him over for the first time. Had there been no pictures of him in her grandfather's house?

"I'm lopsided," he said. "That's how I could afford Cruise Eternity."

"I don't mean that. Everyone's lopsided now. Before the revolution the robots dictated everything …even the perfect measurements of men." She sounded as though she were reciting from a schoolbook. "Now we are free of the tyranny of metal over flesh."

"I don't think so," David said. "I've seen metal strike flesh dead, again and again, since I left the cruise ship."

"The metal serves the revolution."

How could she mouth such terrible things, she who looked so much like Rosie? Did she share nothing of Rosie's visions? But David wanted so hard to cling to her, to this last shred of remembrance. He ran after her as she turned away from him.

"It's forbidden!"

He thudded against an invisible barrier. She was talking to him still, but he couldn't hear her anymore. He pounded soundlessly on the forcefield. "This is no life for you …I've got a spare berth on Cruise Eternity for you! I could give you freedom, save you from the endless gray rain, from the drudgery of the factory …God, you look so like her, you're wearing her dreamstone, our dreamstone, the dreamstone that split for us, the dreamstone of our love… ."

The insubstantial wall between them shimmered a little. He could see that she couldn't make up her mind. "Dissolve the barrier," he said, battering at it. Suddenly it melted. She was in his arms. He saw her embarrassment at the unexpected intimacy.

"Please let me go."

"Listen to me!" He could smell her scent now, the scent that came from mingled dreamstones. He was mad with grief. "I'll save you from all this …from the eyes in the sky …I'll love you the way I loved her …just say the word and I'll—"

He kissed her. She pulled back, wiped her mouth with the back of her hand, told him it was the kiss of death.

Miscegenation with the streakers was bestiality.

"Miscegenation? We only—"

We began to weep. Rosie would not have done that.

"I'm not going to let you die because of—"

The eyes were gathering. He held her tight and held up his other hand with the identidisk. The eyes backed away, hovered, shielding them from the rain. They were safe from the eyes. As long as he held on to her so that if they tried to kill her the lightning would vaporize him too. Streakers had immunity; he had his boarding pass, his transit visa. They had to leave him alone.

He led her through the skein of tangled streets. A flock of eyes followed them. Lightning grazed them. Those who stared too long fell dead. They ran.

Inside the Cruise Eternity ship, David told the emerald-eyed robot that he was giving Janine Rosie's ticket. "It's paid for," he said, "I can assign it to anyone I want."

The robot shrugged.

They prepared for amniosis. Our berths were side by side. David thought of Rosie. The girl wasn't really Rosie at all. He knew that now. Her cheekbones are wrong or something, he thought. But she has the dreamstone, and it shines for her as well as for me.

"I don't want to be here," Janine said. "I'm afraid, I don't want this."

"You have to want it!" David cried out. "They were going to kill you!"

"*You've* killed me," she said, "just like you murdered my great-aunt Rosie."

He was seized by the dreamless sleep before he could reply.

   ***

The twenty-third was a wipeout. They never left the

ship. They sat in the first class café facing in opposite directions. Tourists dashed in and out with their trinkets: talking baseball cards, shrunken heads, antique telekinetons, nude reproductions of the Statue of Liberty.

They overheard talk of aliens. Aliens who knew of the source of dreamstones. Aliens had been sighted. There was an alien embassy. They were at war with Earth. They were at war with someone else. They were godlike beings who were incapable of conceiving war. They were here to stay. They were here for only a few weeks, on their way to some outpost in the Magellanic Clouds. No one knew anything about them, except that they had somehow brought the 150-year-old revolution to a standstill and balkanized the world into a thousand fractions almost overnight.

They sat at the table farthest from the window. Janine cried; David sat writing in a notebook, attempting to revive the dead art of the poem.

"Just as I thought!" It was Professor Lavin, who had come in on the arm of Melinda Maledicta and another friend of theirs, a cyborg. "You _are_ a writer!"

"You have to join our poets' roundtable," Melinda said, winking at Janine.

"Is this your …your …passenger?" Lavin said, eying her with undisguised interest.

"I see the word has been spreading, David," Janine said. "Everyone's pretty anxious to look at the new freak." She avoided his eyes.

"Cruise Eternity is a very small kingdom," said Lavin. "It's kinda like one of those ancient city-states, you know? Abundant slave labor—all done by robots—a decadent aristocracy that has nothing better to do than gossip and seek new thrills—not a bad deal if you ask me."

"But who is the king?" said David.

"Why," Melinda said, "we all are! That's the beauty of it! And the timeslugs are the circus of eternity."

"Not eternity," said Janine. She did not, David noted, address her remarks to him, but stared steadfastly at the floor. "We all have to die sometime. This thing doesn't make anyone live any longer. It just …stretches them out thin, like an elastic band."

"How profound," said Professor Lavin, as he casually injected a neon pink liquid into his arm. "May I quote you on that?"

***

Only on the last day of the stopover did they speak directly to one another. At least it was David who spoke, never quite knowing whether she heard him. He talked about Rosalind, mostly. How she wanted to cut away her past like a malignant tumor. How she talked earnestly about different futures, new technologies, other worlds. How she dreamed of living through Cruise Eternity until the end of the world and beyond. A century was five thousand years in Cruise Eternity, and who knows what life-prolonging methods they would have in five thousand years' time? She could not imagine an end to her future. She felt she could outrace time itself.

At last, Janine said, "But you never think about the future anymore. You're lost in the past yourself. You're a timeslug after all, David. Like me."

David didn't believe her. She'll learn, he thought. In time, she'll take the long view.

\#

The twenty-fourth was a utopia, it seemed. The Cruise Eternity ship still stood, a lone structure in an ocean of knee-tall grass. Its metal walls were gauzed over with vines now. "The wars," the robot told them, "have been over for some time now. The world is sparsely populated, its high technologies concealed in subterranean control centers."

What wars? David wondered. What about the aliens?

There was a museum, the robot told him. The aliens had long since gone away.

There was no money in this new world; David's credit account, and all its accrued interest, had been converted into a stockpile of metals for barter: uranium, titanium, palladium.

For the first time, Janine showed an interest in leaving the cruise ship. So they walked out together and stood just beyond the shadow of Cruise Eternity, contemplating an emptiness neither had ever experienced before. Surely, David thought, she could feel what he felt. "Nature and man blending, harmonious, healed," he said softly. They walked on through the wind-tousled grass. "I had an daydream of a place like this sometimes, sitting in my cubicle at Shameless Romances, trying to program the parameters for domestic tranquillity and relationship dynamics. I almost feel like settling down."

But she was timid; she hugged her chest; she was afraid of the wind. All she said was, "I wish I could go back."

He said, "Go back? To that gray place you called home, where if you made a false step the wandering eyes would burn you up ...where you worked all day in a factory and brought home nothing at all?"

"I was comfortable with the police eyes," she said defiantly. "I knew how far I could go. I want to go back," she said.

Time only moves one way, he thought. "We're above all that now," he said, "we're streakers. We get the overview. We see the future stream by, witness the human dream, we are like the gods." Were they his words or a garbled memory of Rosie's? Was it himself speaking?

"Advertising slogans," Janine said, and David suddenly remembered waiting in line at the Cruise Eternity building with Rosie, and the man behind them chanting the phrases from the commercial as though they were great poetry. How pathetic David had thought he was, standing there drowning in a pool of computer-generated hype. When David and Rosalind left the line, the man had still been standing there, his tattered clothes flapping in the breeze of the artificial night.

"There's a lot we have to learn to forget," David said.

She kissed him lightly on the cheek. It was a cold, comfortless kiss. He knew, from the pre-debarkation briefing, that in her long-dead society people did not kiss in the open. He said, "Wait. Give me time. I'll open your eyes, I'll love away the prison bars around your soul." Even as he said it he knew that he was still in the grip of Shameless Romances' programming algorithms.

She laughed. "So I can be like my great-aunt Rosie."

That hurt him. She walked farther out into the field. She stood timid, alone; she didn't like the grass snagging her mantle. The wind sprang up and made her hair fly. She cried out in surprise. She ran. David thought: She looks so much like her. And ran after her. They reached a stream—a real stream, not a hologram—he caught her, held her, kissed her. And she cried softly, saying only, "It's forbidden, it's forbidden."

"What's forbidden?" he said. He could feel her heartbeat.

"The procreation police." She disengaged herself from his embrace, looked wildly around at the expanse of grass. Cruise Eternity peered from the ocean of green.

"I don't want to procreate," he said, "I just want to make love with you."

She did not understand him. She came from a future—
no, it was a past now—where such things were rigidly
controlled by the state. He was going to have to
deprogram all her repressive conditioning. Who better to
do this than a program-debugger for Shameless Romances?
David had executed this loop a thousand times in his office
—the alien princess/Indian maiden/Edwardian housewife
raped by an irresistible stranger—degraded at first, the
heroine comes to love the mysterious lover from across the
sea, from the wrong side of the tracks, from the country of
the enemy …from another time. He didn't balk anymore.
He seized her, kissed her hungrily, hardly pausing to
breathe. At last he felt the warmth being returned …
tentatively, inexpertly. Her mouth tasted like Rosie's. Or
was he kidding himself.

No, he thought, as she twisted free and ran lightly from
him, and the wind played with her hair. She was meant to
be a new Rosalind. Rosalind had come back to him. She
was never dead. It was a cruel trick …an entertainment
devised by the robots to amuse him on his cruise. He
imagined her pulling the plastiflesh prosthetics from her
face, popping out the colored contacts, laughingly telling
him that the rumors of her death had been greatly
exaggerated. Just testing you, she'd tell him. When you
have the long view, you play new games …you tune
identities in and out like viewing a novel, like muzak.

He caught up with her. They made love. She lay on
the ground like a dead woman. At the end she whimpered
a little. He saw blood on the grass. He looked at her face,
lost in some private anguish, and knew that she was never
going to transform magically into the woman he had
loved.

That had been three weeks ago. Three centuries.

This woman was a stranger.

"I'm sorry," he said. He couldn't look at her anymore. "I made a terrible mistake." Is that all I can say? he thought.

"There's nothing we can do now. Let's make the best of it."

"Yes," he said.

Their dreamstones began to shimmer suddenly. Sparks flew between them. Why? he wondered. What shared emotion had they picked up? It occurred to David that the dreamstones might have their own agenda. Like the aliens, who had come and gone during the brief subjective night they'd spent in the sleep of amniosis.

***

The aliens came back in the next few centuries, but there was no real change for hundreds of years. Gradually David and Janine drifted into a semblance of what David thought their relationship should be; but even when she seemed most passionate, he could tell that she was trying to be someone else for him, following the path of least resistance. They made love, they exchanged pleasantries.

In the twenty-ninth, spoken language had been rendered unfashionable; people communicated large concepts by gesture, nuances by blowing smoke rings in different shapes and hues through a mildly narcosis-inducing prosthetic implant just behind the lips. The aliens were the only ones even interested in talking to the streakers. Mostly, the aliens worked as janitors and fruit-pickers.

There were no animals anymore, and few machines; the technology of Cruise Eternity seemed quaint and decidedly vulgar. Fruit was all they ate in the twenty-ninth, though some of it had been engineered to a passable imitation of a rare filet mignon.

After a day of orientation, the two of them went exploring. There were fruit trees everywhere. Even the buildings were a kind of mega-tree, with natural chambers floored with interweaving branches, ceilings of shivering foliage. Now and then a human being would float by in a puff of rainbow-colored smoke. You could spot the aliens easily enough; they were the only ones who looked the way people used to look, the only ones engaged in menial tasks. They didn't, of course, really look like people; that was an illusion projected from a little box they wore strapped to one of their pseudopods. But to Janine and David they seemed far more like people than any of the human beings who drifted past.

He began to believe she might be changing.

Hand in hand, they came upon an alien picking fruit. Gnarled branches twisted above them and let in a few strands of sunset. The alien rode a mechanical harvester that zigzagged through the gaps in the foliage, jogging the fruit free with a butterfly net. He dressed like a late-twentieth punker and spoke with the kind of stilted gravity that David's compusystem always attributed to the aliens of romantic fiction.

"Ah, tourists. Ah, perhaps you would care for a ride, your reverences?"

Brought up as he was on the twentieth-century myths of advanced alien species with super-science, David felt uncomfortable with the alien's obsequies. When the alien identified himself as Lyndon Baines Johnson, he felt even more disoriented; but the joke was lost on Janine. Where she came from, all history had been erased by the revolution.

The alien was only too happy to drop what he was doing and fly the two of them around on his harvester, stopping now and then to pluck a few delicacies for them.

A kiwi fruit that yielded a delicate sushi melée; a pineapple with compartments for five neon-colored liqueurs; leaves that sprouted chocolate-honey locusts. Now and then the alien adjusted a fertilizing device or pruned a few twigs.

"The food is …different," Janine said. On Cruise Eternity she had ready access to the nutrient mush that was all her people ate, and she had found it difficult to adjust.

"Ah, we take pride in our work, your reverences," said the alien, and bowed gravely.

"I want to know," David said, "why you're here, why you're content to do these menial tasks, what you find interesting here… ."

"Why," the alien said, and his hands trembled—was there a glimmer of the pseudopod behind the projected icon?—"why, it is because of *you* that we are here. We are interested in *you*."

David saw the dreamstone glitter madly against Janine's neck. She cried out from the warmth of it.

"Why us?" David said. "Are we so fascinating a species?"

"He doesn't mean the human race!" Janine said. "He means you and me." And he felt the warmth flooding his own throat, and saw the sparks flying between the two stones, and felt her grip his arms in fear.

"The dreamstones!" David whispered.

"Our children," said the alien, "our gods."

"What do you mean?" Janine said.

"In time you will learn," the alien said, and did not raise the subject again, though they spent the entire day flitting from orchard to orchard, and the dreamstones never stopped twinkling.

***

That night they made love in an arboreal cocoon. Through chinks in the foliage above came faint lines of moonlight. Cold fire from the dreamstones, hung up on a twig like lanterns, played over Janine's face. She had never seemed more like Rosalind. "I love you," David said.

"Never say that," she said, and turned away.

"But it's true."

"What do you know about truth?" Janine said. "All you understand is what you've paid for."

David stared at her. The light from the dreamstones danced.

"Let me tell you a story, David. A story from the gray time, when I was still a human being with a place in the world. My grandfather used to tell me about Great-aunt Rosalind: about her crazy fantasies, her colorful dreams. She used to kid her family about running away to join Cruise Eternity, but her parents knew it was just her way of telling them to snap out of their complacency. And it worked. Until you came and bought her soul, and the next day she came back to our apartment in a silver-lamé sack with a bill from the undertaker. You stole her from us! Did you know my grandfather lost all his money trying to sue your estate? You slept for a hundred years while my family fought you! You and your fucking long view of human history. You should have seen what the worm's eye view was like! It killed my grandfather, did you know that? He couldn't stand it anymore. He raved about Rosalind and drove my parents crazy. One day he just plugged himself into a sex interface and fucked himself to death. I was five years old. There was nothing we could do. He smelled of shit and come. It was before the revolution, before they banned all those things. *You* killed him, David! You killed her too. And when you found out, you didn't think about how much you had hurt us ...all you wanted to do was go out and get the best substitute money could buy."

"How can you say these things?"

"You never even loved her. She never loved you. You both had selfish needs and used each other! You're using me too, trying to stretch out the illusion—"

Speechless, David found himself hitting her in the face, in the chest. Blood spurted from her nose, her lips. She did not protest. She did not even cry out. It was as though he were only doing what she expected of him. At last he turned away from her and wept bitterly. It couldn't be true. It had to be untrue! They had met …it had been chance or fate …a whirlwind passion …a tragic hero …a vulnerable heroine who yearned for hope …suddenly he realized those were all phrases from the lexicon of Shameless Romances' fiction-writing computer.

Through his tears, the dreamstones glittered, brilliant, burning his eyes.

They returned to Cruise Eternity, and the robot patched her up. They did not speak to each other for the next five hundred years. David heard—one could not help hearing —how she was shacking up first with Professor Lavin, then with Melinda Maledicta the poetess of obscenity. He himself had tried Melinda once or twice; there was a certain piquancy in the way she interleaved her thrustings with scatological remarks. He tried to write poetry again. He sometimes met Janine in the corridors of Cruise Eternity. Once he was sure he had seen Rosie. But it was only his imagination. The world was expanding with very century they traversed; how was it that he felt such claustrophobia, such helplessness?

***

In the thirty-fourth century, he came upon the alien

again. There was no more earth; a war had rendered it uninhabitable, but it did not matter, since no one who was anyone was living there at the time. Cruise Eternity had been moved to Mars, where it floated, surrounded by a simulated terrestrial environment, inside a bubble of force that dangled from the orbit of Phobos.

It was in a museum on the planetary surface. He came upon the alien methodically removing graffiti from the walls of the lavatory.

"Where is Janine?" said Lyndon Baines Johnson, looking at him with dull eyes set in a simian face.

"She's back at Cruise Eternity," he said. "We don't go places together much anymore." He wasn't sure who this was or why he should know his identity. But sometimes the figure blurred against the whitewashed walls, and now and then a gelatinous appendage emerged from the well of illusion. Suddenly he knew who it was. "It's been five hundred years for you, surely," he said. "Unless you go to sleep, like we do, for a century at a time."

"Ah," said the alien, "for every long view there is a longer view."

"What does that mean? Do you live forever?"

"If you can call it living," said the alien. "There are many of us who do not. It is hard for me to judge; I am insane."

***

David returned to Cruise Eternity. Janine was in the coffee shop, having her hair sculpted by an attentive robot, sipping a tall glass of artichokes' blood. She looked at him with studied indifference; he looked away.

"I've seen the alien again," David said.

She nodded. "So have I."

They parted. That night, to his surprise, she was in his

cabin waiting for him. They made love without speaking. Once Janine cried out; it was not a name he had heard before. Always the dreamstones glittered. Each day David visited the museum, and each day the alien was waiting for him with a new piece of the puzzle, more tantalizing than the last.

   ***

Attempts to terraform had been abandoned; pockets of the mother planet had instead been enclosed in forcefields and strewn across the polar surfaces. No illusions masked the sky's unfamiliar azure or the rocky redness of the landscape.   Within the forcefield, fountains played, rosebushes bloomed, and David watched the alien as he fastidiously worked over the Venus de Milo with a feather duster.

"What did you mean," David said, "when you told us that the dreamstones were your children and your gods?"

"Just that," the alien said. "First children, then gods. And in between, madmen like me."

"What do you really look like?"

"Ah," said the alien, "but you already know."

The dreamstone shivered; the cold made his throat tingle, stole down his esophagus, tickled his stomach a little. "Something to do with the dreamstones, isn't it?" David said.

The alien shimmered. There were tentacles. There were pseudopods. There were antennae. The alien was none of these things. All were illusion. The alien smiled and went on with his dusting. An overpowering sadness emanated from him. He's lost something, David thought. He's lost a piece of himself.

He saw Janine behind the rosebushes. She didn't speak to him. She was waiting for him to go away, waiting her turn to question the alien.

She was waiting for him in his quarters. The Naugahyde couch had been replaced with a levitating palanquin, and there were a few real books next to the holographic ones, and a couple of souvenirs of the eras they had passed through, but otherwise the room still mimicked that apartment in long-ago New York.

The dreamstone lay on the coffee table. She squatted in a corner. She was shaking violently. He hurried to her. The sadness he had felt with the alien was here too; the air was heavy with it. Some pheromonal thing, David thought.

"Try to take it off!" she screamed. "Try to fling it from you as far as you can!" He clutched his dreamstone and tried to yank it from his throat, but the sadness swooped down on him, battered at his mind ...he knelt down beside her. She was wracked with sobs. "They're parasites," she was saying, "eating away at us somehow ...we've become addicted to them."

"Is that what you learned?" She nodded. "I learned something too. They're just like the aliens ...only different ...an embryonic form maybe ...they're all of them linked together somehow... ."

She managed to wrest the dreamstone from his neck. She thrust it from them. It was an arc of stardust in the air. It landed on the coffee table beside its twin. David felt it all at once: an icy terror, a desolate emptiness ...the silence between the stars ..."What's happening to us?" he gasped, and the two of them drew close.

The dreamstones flew together and became the alien.

"You rang?" said Lyndon Baines Johnson. "Ah, I cannot hold this shape too long."

"What are you doing to us?" David shouted. The terror

gripped him. The alien shimmered with dreamstones' fire.

"Why do you reject me?" the alien said. "Ah, we cannot live without each other. Do not, ah, turn away from destiny. In only a few millennia we will all be as one."

And vanished.

"Don't you see?" Janine cried out. "I've known it since I started wearing the dreamstone, since my grandfather willed it to me. It's changing us into itself." She got up, went to the coffee table, picked the stone up and put it around her throat. All at once, David saw, she seemed more tranquil.

"Those thing are dangerous!" David said. "Maybe we shouldn't wear them anymore."

"I need it," Janine said. "We *belong* together."

That was how they were different, she and he. I don't want to belong to anything, David thought, but she makes a fetish of belonging. She's never going to become a real streaker.

He looked into her eyes. He wondered how he had ever dreamed that this woman could be like Rosalind. She said to him: "You and I belong together too, you know. No matter how it happened. I think, David …I think I <u>am</u> starting to fall in love with you a little."

It was true. They made love that night for the first time in many centuries. She was bathed in the dreamstone's glow; its iridescence had seeped into her very pores. She's becoming an alien somehow, he thought. They made love on the floral loveseat, amid the relics of an antique time.

***

Quentin Lavin knew all about the aliens. He had been putting together a chart. David found him poring over it on the observation deck. The big screens were recapitulating the entire history of the human race up to that point, accompanied by a bombastic score in the serial maximalist mode which had been composed for the occasion by one of Melinda's friends, who was even now conducting the robotic orchestra from his icon console. There was no one watching; everyone was at the picnic that had been organized by the Martian tourist board; a new canal was being unveiled, complete with a singing, dancing chorus line of little green girls. Janine had gone; she had been energized by last night's lovemaking, while David felt completely worn out.

"Boy," said Lavin, as he guzzled, snorted and shot up at the same time, "this is just about the most exciting thing! Wait till the boys back home ...well, they're dead now, but you know what I mean... ."

"You're working on your alien discovery charts."

"Oh yeah. That's why I joined the tour, you know. I wanted to find aliens. Been a historian all my life ...it's all the same no matter how far back you go. Repeat, repeat, repeat. But aliens ...they could be different, see? Especially these aliens. They don't have time, you see."

"You mean, they're outside time, somehow?"

"They don't perceive it in a straight line. And there's really one one of them, a hive mind sort of. And the dreamstones are a highly concentrated form of them. You might call them larval, except they don't go through stages —they're all their stages at the same time. It's all so deliciously non-linear, so, so, so *alien*. And those humanoid hallucinations, those auditory illusions that make us think we're talking to your average Smiths and Joneses—"

"Do they want the dreamstones back?" David said. "Is that why they keep hovering over me and Janine?" Maybe if we just return them, they'll leave us alone, he thought.

On the screens: the mass exodus from earth ...the cities

vaporizing one by one, a chain of fire across the continents …tsunamis, volcanoes, earthquakes …the music solemn, recursive, knell-like.

"I don't think they want them back as such," Lavin said. "But they want you to want to give them back. Maybe they want you along with them… ."

"Like parasites?"

"Who knows? Gosh, it's exciting though. Real-live aliens—I haven't slept in a couple hundred years."

He showed David his chart. There were balloons containing key phrases like "morphological integration" and "is morphology integral?" and arrows pointing wildly every which way, and corkscrew lines connecting crossed-out mathematical formulae.

"I can't make head or tail of it," said David.

"Oh, and …I can wait for the big shindig they're having two thousand years down the road… ."

In a few millennia we will all be as one… .

"Yeah!" said Lavin. "Some kind of cosmic confluence …time flowing backwards as well as forwards for them … they all turn into their dreamstone form and throw themselves into the sun, I gather …ritual of rebirth or something …using the stellar graviton field to propel them into the next dimension …something like that. They do this every few eons. Maybe that's why they're after your dreamstones, huh."

David didn't think he would give up his dreamstone. It was all he had of Rosalind. It was his anchor to the old reality.

"Tell you what I think, David," Quentin Lavin continued, unplugging his umbilicord from the pheromone dispenser, "this is …what …I …think!"

"Huge epiphanic revelation coming up, huh," said David.

"Yeah! It's this ...you and I and all of us, we think we're riding this sleek shiny rocketship to the future, we're the tourists and the whole universe is just one big sightsee-o-rama, right? Wrong. We're on a one-way ticket to death. This thing just gives us the illusion of being like the gods, see? But the aliens ...to them, you and Janine, you're no more than sleek shiny rocketships yourselves. They're just catching a ride on you, nibbling on your minds as they travel towards their mega-great-big harmonic convergence or whatever the fuck it is. They think of you as nothing more than a vehicle—not even a souped-up time travel machine like this cruise pretends to be—more like an oxcart or a bicycle, because they're crazy aliens and they like to take the slow scenic route."

"I'm not going to let it happen to her," David said slowly.

"You know how I know all this shit?" Lavin said. "She let me wear hers once. It was awe-inspiring."

David hadn't worn his dreamstone since the night she'd told him she loved him. "I never got any information like that from it," he said.

Lavin shrugged. "Gotta see with the right eyes. Samadhi. Perfect inner tranquillity." He tapped his forehead.

"Sure," said David.
***

Centuries passed. Mars was terraformed, became in turn a paradise, a garbage dump, a suburb, a retirement haven. Cruise Eternity went on. They shopped. Redecorated, threw our their quaint and ancient-seeming furniture, covered their cabin walls with simulacra of remote planetscapes or etchings of lost Earth cities. They grew used to each other and, in their own fashion, fell in love.

One day they found themselves back on Earth; Cruise Eternity had flown there during amniosis; they were to watch the first stages of the world's rehabilitation. Professor Lavin could scarcely contain himself as he and his friends—David and Janine tagged along for the ride— took the auto-palanquin down to the local village. They toured the marketplace the first day and found picturesque natives in bright costumes, mutants, many of them. The aliens owned the best restaurants. The whole planet was being renovated as an entertainment for the streakers; The Cruise Eternity corporation had bought the land cheap a few hundred years before.

Melinda, declaiming from the back of an elephant, was scattering coins to the mob. The professor was lecturing in endless detail about how society had been reconstructed with a hierarchy of mutants. Janine and David stood apart from the others. "The streets," she was saying, "the streets still have the same names… ."

It was true. The muddy avenues bore signposts: Lexington. Broadway. David said, "Perhaps they just want us to feel more at home."

"We *are* home!" Janine said. It was true. David could feel it. They had brought Cruise Eternity right back to where New York had once stood. David could see why right away. It would be time for the nostalgia buffs to go crazy. Perhaps a giant walking, talking Chrysler Building would be their guide; perhaps they could have private banquets in the decapitated head of the Statue of Liberty. "I want to see where I used to live," Janine said. They started walking.

"Will you know the way?" David said.

"Can't you feel it? Something …calling us." Her dreamstone blinked rhythmically, hypnotically. David rarely wore his now, but for some reason he had put it on today; perhaps it was because this was Earth again, because he too was succumbing to the nostalgia thing.

As they walked, he could see ghostly shapes of his past rear up from the muddy streets and thatched hovels. Ruins and tall buildings and plexitubes that sutured the cityscape like a pasta surprise. "How are they doing it?" he mused aloud. "They must be generating the images somehow from the cruise ship's memories ..."

He pointed out a convoy of ornithopters to her, winging across the bright sun. She couldn't see them. "Wandering eyes," she told him. "Gray rubble. Rain. Nothing but gray."

They were walking side by side in separate universes.

On a platform in the distance, Melinda Maledicta was declaiming to a rapt audience of dwarfs and two-headed women.

They walked on, hand in hand, for a long time. They were approaching the street where Janine had once lived ...Rosie's old neighborhood. He could see it, see the way it all used to be, more and more clearly ...but somehow, mixed in with the images of his home time, there were also bits and pieces of Janine's past: here a wandering eye peeping from a burnt-out, graffiti-strewn wall of gray stone ...here a patch of gray in the sky. I'm getting double vision, he thought. Her universe is leaking into mine.

What could it mean?

And then they stood in front of the doorway where they had first met. He saw her standing there: proud, unreachable, as on the first day. Their pasts intersected. He saw her standing, haloed by the dreamstone's glow, full of anger and undiscovered love. His viewpoint shifted. He saw himself through her eyes. He saw himself as her grandfather had seen him, the man who had murdered

Rosalind and escaped into dreamless sleep.

He touched her. Sparks flew from dreamstone to dreamstone. She was changing. The aura came from her, not from the stone alone. Light was bursting from her pores. Her eyes were alien. "What are you becoming?" he said, bewildered.

She said, "We're changing. We're going to go with them. Don't you see, David? You wrested me away from everything I belonged to, but now I've come full circle, I belong again, I'm whole again… ."

"Not me," said David angrily.

She gripped his hand. There was warmth and love … and he knew that if he pulled away there would come terrifying loneliness …"You want to go with them? Get yourself catapulted into the sun, into a new dimension you can't even imagine?"

"You're the one who were always going on about the long view …you're the one who kept feeding me the hype …well, there's a longer view than yours. I'm going to merge with them, I'm going to share their consciousness …"

"You're going to kill yourself," said David. "That's what it means. You're going to degauss your soul."

"You can be with us too, David," Janine said softly. The stars in her eyes were real. "They came to us. We are special to them, we're chosen, we're the new life that will seed a new universe… ."

"You're raving! They're parasites …you've become addicted …it's all in your mind… ."

Still she did not let go of his hands. He saw all his pasts at one time, coexistent, through the mind-matrix of the dreamstone: the desolate Martian desert mingled with the lush holographic landscapes of his youth …there was Rosalind too, standing where Janine stood, calling out to him ...only a tiny part of him still rebelled against it. An image flashed through his thoughts: Janine's grandfather, plugged into the sex interface, orgasming to death. The dreamstones were like that. She was turning into the very thing she feared the most! He had to resist or he would relinquish his very identity.

"No! I'm not going to do it! I'm not going to let myself get sucked into an alien intelligence! I'm not going to die!"

She smiled. "No, David, you are going to die. Cruise Eternity is an illusion. You don't live any longer than your natural lifespan. I'm the one who's never going to die."

"But what about me? Don't you love me?" he cried. The universe revolved around them. The planets sang. Joy engulfed him, bittersweet, intoxicating. He wanted to stay this way forever.

"I do love you, David," she said. "But this is greater than love and stronger than death."

He twisted away from her. He tore the dreamstone from his throat and hurled it into the mud. All at once the world became narrower, more confined. The color drained from the air. He was cut off. Loneliness tore at him.

The street was just the street. There was a shoddy reproduction of Janine's old apartment, and a sign announcing to passing tourists that this was the place that the star-crossed lovers, David and Janine, had first met, as portrayed in the world-famous epic poem by someone David had never heard of. A mutant stood at the corner hawking holograms of David and Janine with idealized features; the fantasy-David wasn't lopsided anymore. The alien appeared on the doorstep next to Janine.

"Hello, David," he said. "We're converting this little old, ah, trysting place of yours into a cozy little restaurant."

She was cocooned in light. She was a hair's breadth away from him. She was unreachable.

"The romance of the ages!" the alien rhapsodized. "That's what you are to these miserable, ah, mutants. I bet you never thought it could happen to you when you were programming those fiction-writing computers with those idiot plots."

He turned away from her. He was tormented by an overpowering sense of loss. But he knew he could not be with her.

"If you don't come with me," she called out after him, "I'll become the streaker and you'll be the timeslug. Don't let that happen, David ...please."

He stepped away. Strode furiously into the crowd, bursting with grief and anger.

***

In a thousand years they learned a great deal more about the aliens ...the alien. A continually shifting lattice of quadrillions of interstellar viruses, some called it. Some questioned whether or not it had consciousness at all, or whether its blandishments constituted a mere simulacrum of consciousness. Many pondered the relevance of such speculations. But some things were clear. It didn't exactly exist in spacetime as humans understood it, but a little askew of the continuum. It was capable of assuming many forms, and of mimicking humans fairly closely. It was big, ancient, and extremely bored. It was approaching the end of some great cycle at the end of which it would vanish, taking along its conquests—or converts, or trophies, however you wanted to look at it—into some kind of sideways-parallel universe.

There was a farewell party for Janine on the eve of the great sun ceremony. An alien ship was parked beside Cruise Eternity, poised for takeoff, ready to take her away at the stroke of midnight. Melinda had composed an open-air opera for the occasion, or rather had written the words for one and the music randomly generated by Cruise Eternity's central entertainment computer. There was a huge turnout for the party, from the ship as well as from other Cruise Eternity subsidiaries. There were a lot of alien —at any rate, the alien had come as a lot of different people.

New York was completely abandoned, submerged beneath the rising poisoned sea, but an exact reproduction of the twenty-first century city floated on an artificial island, and as far as the eye could see, everything was the same; the whole journey might as well have been a dream.

He sat next to Janine at the opera and they picnicked on obscure extraterrestrial delicacies.

The dreamstone was in a little lead box to protect him from its influence. He took the box from the picnic basket. He opened it.

The dreamstone shone. He was filled with inexpressible longing. He thought he had grown used to the sense of emptiness, but now, in the presence of the dreamstone's radiance, he almost could not bear to part with it. But he knew what he had to do.

"I want you to take this with you," he said, "I never want to see it again."

"O piece of shit," sang the bloated robot soprano in the Valkyrie costume as she drifted across the stage on a motorcycle. "I shall not soon forget thy perfidy."

"What a pity," said Lyndon Baines Johnson. He looked up and saw the alien hovering over him. He had wings now, and his robes fluttered behind him though there was no breeze; in his arms he held a harp on which he strummed discordantly now and then. "We were hoping for a matched set."

Professor Lavin, who had joined them and was dosing

himself intravenously with booze from a wandering cocktail dispenser, said, with intense interest: "Is this a Noah's Ark kind of deal? Universe going ka-boom and all that?"

"Something like that," said the alien, smiling. "But you won't be around for it. It was millennia ago. Or hence. It's hard for me to keep linear time straight. It's going on now, of course, but you can't see it."

Lavin looked at the alien with such longing, such hunger. David took pity on him then and said, "Here, you take it."

"You mean it? You really really mean it?"

There was a moment of terrible inner anguish. He felt that he was being torn limb from limb, physically, emotionally. And then there was nothing. A kind of relief, almost.

Janine smiled a wry smile. "Looks like I'll have another human being for company after all, then."

"Whoopee!" Lavin jumped up and down, ripped the cocktail tube from his arm and sent the dispenser scurrying away to find another customer. The ersatz sunset filled the air with a thousand recreated hues of purple pollution. "Merging with the ultimate all-in-oneness! Nirvana! The ultimate goal of humanity!"

"Suicide," David said, and shook his head.

Janine began to glow. Streams of light poured from her dreamstone and wrapped themselves around her in a tight net of radiance. Her eyes shone. She stood up. The alien strummed; no longer dissonant, it was an ethereal heavenly music that enveloped them, harps and celestial choirs and beneath it all a hint of distant thunder.

"Ho-lee shit!" cried the professor.

Janine spread her arms wide. She stood in a shaft of light. A high wind rose. David smelled incense.

The opera went on, but no one was listening. David could see Melinda stalking about on the makeshift stage, haranguing the performers. Lavin fished some ear muffs out of his caftan. "I hate opera," he said.

Shimmering metallic steps appeared in the air. The alien starship rumbled. A doorway opened at the pinnacle of the ship and the stairs rose up to meet it.

"What about _your_ ships?" David shouted at the alien, who was fibrillating wildly.

"Ships? We don't use ships," said Lyndon Baines Johnson.

"Come on, professor—or you'll miss the boat," Janine said softly. She turned, began to ascend the golden stairway.

David felt the old emotions stir inside. "Wait!" he shouted. "Think about everything we've lived through together—"

He began to run up the stairway. He collided with a forcefield. He pummeled the empty air with his fists. "Let me in! Look at me!" he screamed, but already the dreamstone's influence was draining from him; already he could sense that its vampiric energy had found a new focus. He ached with the love that he had felt for her. But the passion was fading fast.

She turned.

He heard Janine's voice, though her lips did not move, inside his mind: "I belong to something now, David. Don't hurt yourself by trying to get me back. There was a kind of love between us, and it was a beautiful thing. But human love is transient. What I belong to now is forever. I am eternal."

"You're just going to be sitting around in a zoo or something." It was an old argument and he repeated it knowing already that their minds would always be apart on this. "You'll always be at their mercy. You'll always be helpless, like you were in that faceless gray world I plucked you from."

"It's what I'm used to," she said. Lavin ran past him through the barrier of force, waving his arms and shouting. He beat at the shield again, until he could feel the blood trickle from his clenched fists. "Goodbye," she said.

"Goodbye," he said, and kissed the emptiness where he could still see her lips.

   ***

A thousand years went by, and another thousand. The tourists partied. They visited a hundred societies: they viewed ages dark and renascent, free and enslaved, human, alien, and cybernetic. They partied and traded souvenirs and sat in their cabins poring over old holograms. Although the big bad alien had long since left the universe, there were other aliens to be encountered; some of them had much more in common with the humans, others were so alien that one could no more communicate with them than with rocks or clouds. There was never a shortage of things to see, even in the depressing epochs.

In a thousand years, he grew accustomed to the emptiness; in a thousand more he began to heal; a thousand more and David finally started his novel. It was, as all first novels tend to be, heavily autobiographical. He knew that it was probably not terribly good, but it was better than pushing paper for robots in the twenty-first.

One evening before amniosis he lay in bed in Melinda's arms. "I'm tired," she said. "I think I'll get off soon."

Many of the guests had abandoned Cruise Eternity to start their own private utopias. There was a new one opening up, a commune that was planning to revive the prehistoric principles of Jesus, Karl Marx, and Shri Bhaktidass. There were still a few places available.

Melinda said, "Why don't you come with me?"

David was tempted for a moment. So few of the original travelers remained. Even Melinda had changed. She hadn't said a bad word in five hundred years, and she had given up the arts completely. There had been so many universes to choose from, all of them lost in the irrecoverable past. Perhaps it was time for him ...but how could he ever know whether the next world might not be better? Getting there is half the fun. He smiled to himself, thinking of that ancient adage.

It wasn't some alien force compelling him to throw aside his whole world and follow a strange woman into times unknown. It was just himself now. The emptiness was still there, but at least it was his own.

"I'm not ready to belong yet," he said. He kissed her as she slipped from his arms.

"By the time you wake up I'll be long dead," she said. "Are you sure you wouldn't rather ...explore our relationship a little longer?" She opened the door.

He got out of bed and reached for his notes. "I'd rather take the long view," he said softly.

—Los Angeles, 1990

I Wake from a Dream of a Drowned Star City

ONE

In Dreambreak we say that the stars begin at the sea. But that's only at low tide when you can if you're lucky catch sight of the drowned star city. At high tide the sea covers the first three stories of my father's kingdom and we are isolated except for one skywalk that joins the seventh floor to the easternmost of the derelict palaces maybe a half-mile to the west at the edge of the kingdom we call Savage-is-Speared. That's once in the daytime and once in the dead of night. That's when you can smell the fish. The fisher families hang long nets from the windows and before sunrise there's a curtain of wriggling fish plastered against the walls of the first three floors and they are prying them loose with forked poles, their ragged kids laughing as they balance on the broken sills and do their baby-fish dance, dangerous as death. Sometimes a kid tumbles but he grabs the net with his toes and monkeys up, catching three, four, five fishies in his mouth so he can barely laugh: in winter the nets are slippery and they sometimes fall.

The smell is so strong it makes you sick.

I was not supposed to play with the fisher children. But it was difficult for me not to. I was always tempted. The princes' dormitory was on the twenty-seventh floor of the kingdom. In summer they ripped down the storm windows and used them to shrinkwrap extra rations of fish, the monster catches from the Mutant River. Nights were so bright they burned my eyes when I tried to sleep. The wind from the sea was drippy with the smell of fish.

I shared a room with my next-up brother Skart. He was the only one of my relatives who talked to me. The others, of course, did not. Now and then at High Court my father used to address me in the third person but I was never surtt,it was me he meant unless he used my name and he always attached some qualifying epithet to it, like he would say, "Morry the Magnificent," or more often "Morry the Lazy,"

"Morry Who Won't Amount to Much,"

"Morry Who Is Too Short," and the worst was "Morry Memento," because it'd make everyone laugh, all around the courtroom, and I didn't know what it meant but the only one who never smiled at that joke was Anskowl, the hereditary Picklemaster, with his ceremonial flask of embalming fluid. So I knew the joke carried some doomladen undercurrent Well any other time only Skart would say anything at all to me. As before we fell asleep I'd hear his dreamy voice say, "Morry catch a fish for me Morry Morry."

Was it this that gave me the courage to sneak out past the

dorm sentinels? But they were only statues anyway.

It was stupid to be afraid. They were there to protect us from magic and superstition. My father would often murmur some ritual formula to ward off magic and superstition, and the whole High Court would sigh piously. The statues stood guard over the elevator that linked the royal palace with the rest of the kingdom. They looked like me and my brother and my sisters and my four mothers and my father. But you could pass your hand right through them and they were fringed with prismlight. Their eyes were red and my attendants would stare at their feet avoiding their gaze while they waited for the elevator to come for maybe a half hour. I was more scared of the attendants than the statues. But at the other end of the corridor was another exitway and a winding metal staircase that clanged and echoed so I'd have to tiptoe, barefooted, quiet, holding my breath.

My brother Skart was like a mirror to me but older though not by much. We shared a scarred sofabed beneath the window so when it was opened for summer the wind came roaring in and ruffled our hair while we slept, the wet and fishy wind I spoke of. For most of my childhood I didn't know why we were kept together. I knew about me, it was that I wasn't a man yet. But him, I had another brother who looked no older but I'd see him outside all the time and he sat beside my father in the High Court and spoke his mind, and when he didn't know what he was talking about they shrugged and waited it out. And one of the mothers (his special mother) Smiled, half-sad, half-laughing.

But they treated Skart like they treated me. They never spoke to him. Except for the servants, and for our tutor, but he was an alien and didn't count. But Skart was like me, a prince, but penned up with me and willing to talk. He also wrote poetry on pieces of toilet paper that he saved. Everything I knew or thought I knew I learned from him, really, or from the alien.

Once in the summer before we slept I said, "Skart, why?" And he said, "I knew you'd have to ask. Why did you have to ask? Fuck you little brother I say fuck you."

I said, "I don't know why I'm not supposed to ask you. I'm only twelve years old and you're the only one who speaks to me."

He sat up and looked seriously at me in the full moon. "Face to face, we're mirrors," he said. His eyes (my eyes) a gold-flecked mauve. His eyes (my eyes) always drew and draw attention. The eyes, the face of the House of Draus. The face too: his face (my face) high-cheeked with a hint of an angled muscle twitching, his (my) mouth thin, his (my) hair white as the foam-caps of the sea. "We are carbon copies. That's good. You have a habit of asking dumb questions. One day they're going to kill you just like they're going to kill me, you'll see."

"They can't kill you, you're a prince. And you're the only one who talks to me."

"Morry. Grow up." He stood up. Went to the window. In the moonlight his hair seemed like strands of a precious metal. I don't think that I loved my brother. He was cruel to me and he beat me sometimes. But he was the only one who talked to me.

He rested his elbows on the sill. "Low tide. Look, the drowned star city." He pointed. I sat up on the bed and looked far to the east. "It's a special place. Do you ever dream of it?"

"No." But I was lying and he knew it.

It rested (and still rests) on a bed of saline mist. It is a nest of rust-mottled metal needles or reeds that spring up from the black water. Beyond it skeletal skyscrapers hulk up, domes caked with seaweed haunching from their sides. Maybe the domes are starships or the wombs from which they sprang. (In the winter it frosts over. Then it looks like a high-tech helmet with electrodes dangling, or like a glazed porcupine. It is less interesting then, because it is all white, and you cannot spend hours separating out all the hues and textures. One summer my brother Skart did that for a whole week, and catalogued it all on scraps of toilet paper which he carefully shrinkwrapped in a piece of loose window and hid under the mattress of our sofabed.)

"Our kingdom is so well-named," my brother said softly, "Dreambreak. Dreambreak. The easternmost point of the world. Just shy of the drowned star city. Where the human dream is shattered. Dreambreak. Dreambreak."

"Skart," I whispered, easing myself up behind him with my arm between his sharp shoulder blades and feeling his smooth skin damp in the wind. "Skart, where *did* they all go? The people out there. They must have gone somewhere. Skart, Skart?" I stuck my head between his right arm and the chill patinaed window frame.

"We're on the outside looking in, looking in," said Skart. "Just before dawn when you hear the squalling of the baby-fish dancers from below you'll see the morning star, that's where they are, they terraformed it and now they're gone and we're still here."

"How'd you hear that?" It sounded dubious to me. I couldn't tell if he was putting me on.

"The alien told me." That was that.

The starlight drizzled (and still drizzles) onto the sea. The full moon wakes the phosphorglow. "Ghostlight," my brother sa+d. There was a fever in him. I wanted him to sleep so I could go exploring. I didn't want him to know. I didn't trust him. He was the only one who spoke to me. But what if he spoke to them, too? "You want me to fall into bed and start to snore," he said. He always read my mind too well. I think he had pieces of my mind on those sheets of toilet paper tucked under the bed. "But I can't let you go yet. You asked the question tonight, that question, the one I've been dreading. Fuck I say fuck!"

I ducked. A look of impregnable fury in his face. "Come back. I won't hit you." I came back. He slapped me hard across the chest, harder than usual, not playfully at all. I started to cry. He laughed. "You asked the question, Marry. Look at me, look into my eyes."

I obeyed him. Maybe I *did* love my brother. There was no one else to love.

"Face to face—" he said.

"We're mirrors." I was tired of thinking that. He curled his lip. Unconsciously I curled mine.

"But back to back—"

He turned his back to me. In the moonlight his skin was almost green. "You can't see your own back, can you, little brother? You think we're mirrors back to back? Have you ever seen any of our other brothers naked?"

"No." They always carne to the High Court in various ritual garments. All the garments had this or that meaning, usually to do with the three Gifts of the House of Draus. I touched his back with my forefinger.

There was a patch of shadow in the small of his back like a baby's fist. I always used to jab at it. It was like a map ofsome romantic island like maybe on the morning star. I prodded him there again, as usual, being playful.

My brother said, "That's where we're not mirrors."

"So what!" I was puzzled. "But everyone in the House of Draus is exactly the same. That's why—"

"That's why we rule! That's why we're perfect! Male and female we were cloned, before the art was taken to the drowned star city and carried to the sky and lost! But for that one chromosome we're all identical! That's why we rule, that's why we are only allowed to have sex with each other.

That's why I'm imprisoned here with you, that's why I'm not allowed to see any of our mothers and sisters!"

"What are you talking about!" I said "I've never heard of any of this. And I want to be exactly like you, I don't want you to be different. You're my next-up brother, Skart." It was unthinkably upsetting to be different from my brother. I always thought I must have an island on my back too, though I'd never seen it. (I remember when I was five years old closing my eyes and feeling my back and knowing it was there and navigating a broken fingernail around its perimeter and wishing it was lifesize so I could have adventures on it.) "Skart," I said, a bit desperately, "I don't believe you."

He punched me in the face. "I hate you little brother I hate you," he said. Whenever he hurt me I knew that a thing was true, and important. "Leave me alone. It's almost dawn. Don't cry. I'm sorry." Then he hugged me and that felt good. "It's not your fault. Today in High Court I saw ~kowlthe Picklemaster staring strangely at me. Swirling the flask of embalming fluid. He's getting ready for me. I know it."

"They're not going to kill you. I'll stop them!" I said fiercely.

"How? You? Don't make me laugh." He didn't laugh.

"I will use the Three Gifts," I said.

Now he laughed.

He said, "It's almost dawn. Go, sneak down the back way, play with the fisher children. The tide' II be in if you don't hurry. I'm not supposed to know, remember?"

"How do you know, next-up brother?"

"Before you were old enough to talk to, Morry, I found the exitway too. What, you think I'm stupid?" His confession filled me with excitement. We were alike then, even more alike than me and my other brothers who wouldn't speak to me! What difference did a discolored patch of skin make? It was frightening and exhilarating to imagine my brother tiptoeing down those metal stairs, alone, scared, while I slept. I felt an overwhelming sense of kinship to him, I was ready to explode with pride, but I couldn't let him see all that. I think he would have been angry. I couldn't understand why he thought they would kill him and what it had to do with me.

Quickly I went into the changing room and dunked myself in body grease and dusted myself with white powder. I kneaded the white into my hair. Then I painted myself with streaks of fluorescent orange, green, turquoise. It wasn't a well-equipped closet and there was never anything I could do about my Draus eyes. But I wanted to be as inconspicuous as possible among the dregs of my father's kingdom.

TWO

Past the glowering sentinels and past the long gray corridor of the princes' dormitory where the doors were mostly laserlocked or ironbolted. Cold light from the zebra phosphors tripes along the ceiling. In a way I groped my way to the exitway though I could see it clearly enough. I imagined dimness and danger though there was none to me. I was my father's son. I was a high Draus and born with all three Gifts and able to rule all Dreambreak. But it was not fun to think of being king. My father never smiled and all his jokes were at other people's expense and everyone laughed hard, too hard at them. My mothers hovered around him. All of them my mirrors, mauve-eyed, but they made themselves different by painting their bodies and covering their privates with costly codpieces of feathers and leathers and tumbled glass. And behind my father the tall Picklemaster with his flask and sometimes with his deathmask. The High Court was a cold place. It still is.

I longed to dance in the fishy nets. But more, I longed to climb in the drowned star city. How to achieve that? Childish, my brother always told me. Enough to dream of it. But once when the full moon came out one night I saw him wadding up a sheaf of toilet paper and on it he had scratched the words *MO'rry …star city …Morry … star city* over and over with a graphite stick. It was more evidence of how alike we were, that's what I was thinking when I slid from banister to banister, the greasy metal cold and stingy on my ass.

There was no light in the back staircase in those days. If you walked you were ankle-deep in mush. Seaweed slithering between your toes. Here and there a dry patch. Or a cluster 'bf phosphor-bearing weeds, a glimmer, a memory of light. The walls: if you ran your finger along them they were gritty, the concrete chipped and sometimes worn bare to its metal skeleton, and a soggy dank smell like the breath of a carnivore. It made me afraid, but I went on and I counted the steps aloud to myself, thirteen for each landing and two landings for each floor. Third was what I wanted. There it was. A crack of light beneath the door. I heaved. It gave, squealing, enough for me to squeak by. I was slender then.

Huge bay windows facing seaward. The fishers everywhere, milling about, yanking at the nets. So low down in the kingdom the view of the drowned star city was bad. It barely grazed horizon. More, the tide was coming in. A man shouted: "Why are you loafing, kid? Get out there." I slipped into the sea of bodies greased with fish grease, slathered with fluorescent bodypaints. They wore the grease against the chill before dawn. They wore the colors so they could see by the light of their bodies. I elbowed past them to the edge of the window.

A hand brushed my hand. "You act like you're new. You hitching from upstairs? You a tourist?"

I could only tell she was a girl from the paintless vpatch on her crotch. Elsewhere she was striped in red and green and around her eyes she wore circles of cadmium yellow and her hair stood up in spikes. She was maybe a year or two younger than me, she had no breasts. "I'm not a tourist," I stammered. "I'm not afraid to do the baby-fish dance."

She giggled. "You are. Look, you splashed that crimson all over your dickie-bird. You should have left a blank circle. Like my triangle."

"Shit. Forgot," I said.

She giggled. "Come on."

Led me to the edge. I felt the whipping fish wind. I looked down. Down! The nets stretched down maybe fifty, sixty feet, black or dark brown. The fishers were tangled up. They shivered all silvery like twinkling stars. "Forget who you are," she said. "There is magic in this dance."

"Magic's a bad word," I said softly.

"Wow, you must be from on high. Maybe you're a librarian or an artist or maybe a fighter yes a fighter, I see your lean muscles under the paint, but remember that everyone has to eat and food is magic." To hear the word magic used lightly always made me uneasy when I was a boy. I didn't know then how thoroughly magic had infiltrated my father's kingdom. After all, I had been educated by aliens. Aliens do not believe in magic. "Scared?" she said, misinterpreting my hesitancy. "Go back upstairs, boy with the scarlet dickie-bird!" She laughed and I blushed and got angry. I thought if she knew who I was she wouldn't laugh.

"You lead, I'll follow," I said.

She screeched and leaped from the window and caught the net one-handed and dangled with her foot pointing at the sunken star city. I eased myself over the sill grabbing the nets in both fists with the triple-twined seaweed of the ropes biting into my palms. The wind blew me against the concrete. I gripped tightly gritting my teeth from pain and heard her howl. She twisted the net-strands around her ankles and dropped head first to stare me in the eye upside down. "Now dance," she said, reaching for fish and throwing them up at the window where the grown-ups gathered them in. There was one! It flapped between our cheeks. She grabbed it in her mouth with a twist of her chin. "Be right back." And clambered up to spitting range of the great window, and sent the fish flying, and returned.

"How can you do thatt" I said.

"And you say you're not a tourist."

"I'm not."

"Follow me."

I kept up with her, barely. She maneuvered downward where the reek of the sea was stronger. Fewer kids down here. Above I could see by the wide open windows the fish pelting upward from the fists and mouths of kids that glowed against the black walls.

"Come down, hurry, hurry, it's what you came for isn't it?"

She swung hand over hand and sometimes somersaulted and sometimes did a tornado twist with the ropes around her ankles, pushing against the wall for leverage when she tossed the fish thirty feet up. I tried to do what she did. There was a rhythm in it when you were used to it. Fist down, leg forward, roll, roll. The sea, below, was lapping at the first floor where the windows are boarded and where the dungeons are. Sometimes you could see where a face had been sticking in the window, stretching the window fabric out into a pointy funnel. I saw a fish impaled on one but couldn't reach it because she was already far ahead and I wanted to catch up. She threw a handful of fish to me and taught me how to aim, arm straight, eyes focused sharp on the crowded windows. I held them in my mouth like she did. The scales abraded my tongue and inside of my cheeks. We hung upside down and eye to eye and I could see countless little pit-scars trailing from her lips, one going all the way to her ear like the tail of a comet. I could see it even through the fluorescent paint, a stippling effect.

She saw me stare and shrugged self consciously. An upside down shrug is strange, it sort of shudders through the whole body when it is tensed against the nets.

"Do you have a name?" I said, because I didn't know if the fisher folk were allowed to have names.

"Why, do you? How many do you have?" she said. She seemed angry. "I only have one. My mother calls me Jonellys. " She went on staring. "Horny?"

"What is horny?"

"Fuck I say fuck, you make me wonder. Come let's right-side-up and go down lower. By the water's edge."

Lower now. Water licking my soles. "No, lower, lower," she said. She whispered now though the nearest other kids were out of earshot. "All the way down." We sank into the water neck deep. Then I felt her hand teasing me, running down my chest, my belly, my flat hairless pubis.

"Let go," I said, I was embarrassed getting all stiff and the water was'lchilly though I barely felt the cold through the coat of bodygrease.

"Let go? Let go?" She looked me in the eyes, her own eyes wide and solemn. "Don't you know what I'm doing? Doesn't anyone ever do"—she cupped it in an oily fist—"this to you?"—and ran a calloused finger up the inside of my thigh.

"No one." (But, I remembered vaguely, sometimes my next-up brother Skart would kind of do something when he thought I was asleep. But I knew that was something to do with them keeping him away from my mothers and sisters. I would let him do it whatever it was and close my eyes and think of exploring the drowned star city. It was good I guess because afterwards he wouldn't hit me for several days.) "No one," I said more firmly.

"No one taught you about sex?" she whispered.

"No. I have been taught entirely by aliens."

"Then you *are* a prince."

"I—" How could I deny it? I possessed the Gift of Honor.

"I should always have known. Your eyes give you away. Your name is Draus. I think you're the youngest male. But you all look exactly alike. By magic."

"No, technology," I said, protesting. Suddenly I remembered the island of discoloration on my brother's back.

"Shall I teach you?" And she teased me even more down there. And it was like firework heat, bursting from down there and racing through my nerves. And teased me again. And let go of the net entirely and ducked into the water so all I saw were the spikes of her hair like a clump of stiff seaweed, and wrapped my legs around her face.

"The water's rising. The tide will be in soon." I looked far out to sea. The drowned city was gone. I spoke to the clump of seaweed at my crotch and was answered by bubbles. "Come out of there, how can you breathe?" I said, grimadng at something I couldn't tell was ecstasy or embarrassment. My penis was straining hard against something mostly soft but here and there sharp and maybe pointed. I kept looking for the drowned city, not looking down.

She came up for air. The sweat running onto my lips tasted of raw fish, sweet and oily. "I can go on if you want. It's better than catching fish any day. We always come down to the first floor in the hours before sunrise and play sex."

"The tide! Shit, I have to go." I didn't look at her. At that moment I wasn't sure if I should ever come down again in case I saw her again knowing she knew who I was. I started to climb up using the technique I'd learned from her, fist over fist straight up.

"Come back, don't you like me?"

I did like her but I was too confused to answer. I tried to blank it out as I clambered along the ropes, thinking about the dream I used to have where I parted the sea and forged a hi$hway to the star city and stood before a crowd of a millron people and shouted, "The dream is no longer broken, once again the stars begin at the sea." And thought of Skart scratching on sheets of shit-paper. I could sense her right beside me, sometimes just beneath with her stiff hair tickling the soles of my feet and even that made my penis harden. I vaulted clumsily over the sill. The sun was almost up and the sea was crimson and it was warming. It seemed I had barely made it because the water had almost reached the window and the kids who liked to wait till the last minute were cartwheeling over the window ledges and some of them were bobbing up and down in the water with their bright hair flapping like garish flowers in the red-gray water.

The adults were stuffing the fish into baskets now, sorting them out by size and species and throwing the mutants back into the sea, misshapen things, blobs or weirdly colored. I pushed my way past them and made for the exitway which was part open and lightly burnished by the red of the dawn. It would be safe once I got there. I would shut them all out and run to the top and be safe in the palace and the dormitory where no one but my next-up brother and the aliens would talk to me.

But as I tugged at the door to get it to screech wider I heard her call my name out sharply: "Morry Draus," she said with a voice that rang in the corridor. And the crowd parted like the sea in my dream of reaching the drowned city and bringing it back to life.

She stood in the pathway between the halves of the crowd. The paint had faded from her skin and clung to her in flecks and I saw her supple body wet and shiny in the morning sun. I heard the people all whispering my name and staring at me with awe. I looked at myself, at my arms and chest and legs. The white powder and the lurid paint were mostly worn away. I was thinking of how she had made me all excited with her teasing hands and tongue. I was ashamed. I turned my back on them. I overheard one of them say, "He will be great, because he has slipped down the back stairs in secret to play with our own children. In humility there is strength." But another voice said, "They always sneak down here, all of them, when they can't hold it in anymore. They like to fuck like anyone else." Another voice: "I think this one is different though."

I didn't want to hear. It was easier to talk to aliens. At least when you didn't know what they were talking about you could say well, they're aliens. I ran and clanged the door behind me and started to grope my way up to the royal palace.

THREE

Even before I unlatched the door of our room I knew that something was wrong. There was an odor in the air, acrid and acidulous. I knew my brother had never gone to sleep at all. When I went inside I saw him crouching beside the bed with his pheromone synthesizer in his lap. It was one of the toys he had hidden in the closet under the bed. The closet was out now and unfurled across the bed and I could see the blipping hieroglyphs that the aliens use to catalog the contents. My brother was deeply absorbed and wore a mask over his head and he cradled the synthesizer with his right hand lazily rippling over the keys and his left hand jamming down the intensity control. I said (I knew he couldn't hear me) "Skart, you know we're not supposed to have that in here," and I ran to the bed, picked up the closet and started to roll it up.

The icons flashed one by one: toilet paper wads. My seashell collection. An encyclopedia. A pair of skating gloves. A cache of bulbs and fermented soymilk. Half a fish uneaten. I pushed the picture of the soymilk, reached through the fabric to drag it out from the folded space inside, took a swig, threw the bulb back through, flattened the closet so I could roll it up. Then I stuffed it under the mattress. The sun was almost all the way up now. My brother sat in shadow sucking up pheromones. Gray light crossed the bed. I sat on it kicking Skart gently trying to nudge him out of his trance.

He ripped the mask from his head. I saw that he was angry, so angry. "You're so fucking stupid," he said, "you smell of fish so bad, your whole body is slick and stinky with fish oil, I know where you've been playing."

"Skart, this girl—"

"This girl!'l This girl! I hate you little brother, I've been sitting here piaying the smell of our mothers and sisters when they're aroused, their cunts smell like fish oil, did you know that did you know that? Don't talk about girls." He stood up, his hands twitching, cuffed me across the bed so warm blood spurted from my nostrils and gelled into the sweat and oil. "Look at you. Fuck you I say fuck you."

"Why are you so angry, Skart?"

"You fool, don't you know yet what's coming?" He slapped me when I tried to speak again. Then he pinned me down on the bed and started to thrust at me with his thighs slipping and slithering against mine drenched with the fish oil and the bodygrease and the fading swirls of the fluorescent paints. "I got a right to live too," he said.

"Of course you do, Skart," I said, I could hardly whisper because of the pain. It must be important because he'd never hurt me so hard. I knew he was doing something he'd never done before except when he thought I was asleep. And it made me think of the girl, the girl. "What's wrong, Skart, what's wrong?" I said.

He didn't speak but slammed his whole body down on me so I rolled off the sofabed and smashed the synthesizer that lay still purring on the floor.

A fog from the pheromone synthesizer. "Quick, stuff it back in the closet before it makes us crazy," Skart said. I scurried, pulled out the closet and unrolled it again, picked up the instrument and pushed it into the surface of the fabric until I could feel the space-folding trigger lock on, then I watched it disappear through the waferthin cloth into the empty space on the other side. "Put it away," Skart said. I shoved it under the bed.

But all the different smells were already hitting us both and I felt the skin of my balls tighten and the skin of my arms bursting out in goosebumps and sweat running down my face and my spine prickling, all at once. There were real pheromones and artificial ones in that synthesizer, it wasn't a professional model but plenty powerful, not exactly a toy. I'd heard the royal orchestra play brain music before but not like this, all chaotic and sexual. I could see that Skart was affected too and I tentatively reached up from the floor to touch his ann and recoiled from the burning as he sat on the edge of the bed breathing heavily and staring into my face as ifhe wanted to kill me.

He grabbed my arm and wouldn't let go. The melange of smells swirled around us both. "Fish, fish," he said. "My next-up brother who has never talked to you at all, Marry, he taunted me, he said it smells like fish. Now you smell like fish, little brother."

Slowly I said, "You can do anything you like but don't hit me. I know there's something in you I can't touch, something frustrating, something to do with not being allowed to see our mothers and sisters and I don't understand it yet, maybe because I'm too young or something. I don't know why it makes you hate me. I don't want you to hate me.'\

He said, "I can't help it."

I could feel his middle fmgemails dig into my forearm. Maybe there was blood. It was all wet anyway with sweat and oil.

Slowly he pulled me up and then I think he kind of raped me. But I don't know because I was thinking of the girl on the nets and I could hear her laughing at me gently while the water licked the sales of our feet. My mind was far away. I think his was too, he was thinking of the mothers and sisters. I understand it better now, but then I didn't understand at all. He was grinding away at an object in his mind and I was there and for some reason he chose to hate me and it had something to do with the patch of skin on his back that was the wrong color. It was different from the once or twice I'd pretended to be asleep, maybe because the pheromone mist was battering at our brains, maybe because of the young girl on the fishnets over the sea. He was crushing me, I knew he was driven by anger mostly, I could feel the knuckles in his fist kneading the small of my back and making wedges of sharp pain. But I couldn't be mad. Oh I was far away, far away, like lying on the concrete on the pavement outside the kingdom's gates and feeling the tide lap in slowly, dragging me under. Then when I was ready to burst it was like nothing I'd felt before and I imagined it was me and the girl jumping from the nets high high into the leaping rockets of the star city brought back to life in the time of heroes. It was gooey and fiery all at once and sticky stuff was spurting all over and matting the two or three hairs of my stomach.

I just lay there panting for a long time (the sunlight was streaming in now) and didn't notice that Skart was no longer beside me but standing against the wall. Until he said, very slowly, "That was it. You came, I witnessed it. That was my death sentence."

I sat bolt upright. "Why do you keep talking about death, Skart?" I said.

"You selfish, self—absorbed boy, you are so fucking unobservant. Don't you know that's the only reason they kept me alive, to make sure you attained puberty according to the proper signs and exhibited no imperfections? Why do you think I hated you so much? You can answer that yourself."

I looked at him. I couldn't believe it. "You're my mirror," I said. "Your eyes, my eyes, mauve and goldflecked. Your hair, my hair—"

"Snow-pale. But my back is wrong. I can never be a true prince of the House of Draus. I can never be king. Instead I must be watchdog over the one who will replace me. If only there'd been something wrong! We could have gone on, you and I, until our mothers had another son. We could have watched him grow to manhood. And maybe we could really have been like brothers."

"Skart," I said. I went up to him where he stood out of the swath of sunlight, his face deep in shadow. "Skart, I don't want you to die. I never wanted you to hate me. You're the only one who ever talked to me. You're the only brother I've had to love. That's why I didn't mind all those times you hurt me, really I didn't."

"I don't want to die." I was only a few inches away from him now. I saw for the first time that he was crying. I had never seen him cry before. "My brother." I wanted to hug him but I was afraid he would rebuff me. "Why must it be this way?"

"Ask the aliens. I did. They'll tell you about how the first Draus became king and cloned his successors, made them different only by sex so he could enjoy knowledge of himself, and how the science of cloning became first a lost art and then officially magic, and how they decreed that the Drauses should be pure for all eternity, as long as Dreambreak should be a kingdom."

"It's stupid! It's fucking stupid!"

"Don't say things like that! Or they'll say you have a mental deviation from the nonn, and they'll kill you anyway."

"We won't tell them. About this." I swabbed at the come on my thighs with a finger. "They'll know. When we're in school, every day, a sentinel comes in and analyses the bedsheets."

"I didn't know that."

"You never know anything!" he said harshly. "I hate you and your point nine nine nine soma and your protestations. You've reached puberty and it's time for me to die. That's how it was and is and ever shall be."

"No!" How could I prove to him that I was different? How could I be different without being killed myself? It was so much to have to learn all at once. Love and death and honor all in a few hours. But those were the three gifts of a member of the House. "We'll clean it all up. There must be something in that alien closet of ours that our tutor gave us, some kind of selective vaporizer or something."

"It may be star-technology, but it's not magic," he said.

"We've got to do something!"

"We! We!" he said scornfully. "It's not your problem! I will die properly and with honor, the way I was taught."

"I'll make them free you!"

"Don't make me laugh."

"I'll petition the High Court, I'll fall on my knees before

our father the king! If it's true that my childhood is over, then I am free to use the three gifts of the House of Draus."

He laughed.

I found the vaporizer. It was in the eighteenth screen of icons that I called up on the closet. I cleaned everything up as thoroughly as I could. I matched the selector with a sample of my caked semen and played it over everything in the room and made the stains disappear, humming a soothing melody as it worked, some alien song where the notes twisted and turned in ways I couldn't understand.

Skart just watched. In the end he asked for the wadded toilet paper sheets he'd written his poems on, and when I retrieved them from the folded space he went and sat in a dark corner of the room leafing through them again and again. And murmuring quietly, words as incomprehensible as the tune of the alien song.

When I was sure that there was no trace left of my abrupt awakening to manhood, I crawled into bed. As I drifted into dreaming I felt him creep in beside me. We pulled the darkscreen over our heads to shut out the bright sun. I turned up the air cushion and we lay beneath a dome of darkness, though the light still penetrated it sometimes the way you can see through your eyelids if you squeeze them tight shut and tum your face to the sun.

I dreamed of the girl on the fishnet. When I woke up my thighs were all stained again. They had already taken my next-up brother away. The poems were scattered all over the floor. I collected them all. I didn't read them, but ripped off a flap of the window, wrapped them up again, and threw them back into the closet.

My feelings were so mixed up. I felt a terrible guilt, but also a kind of exhilaration at cOming into my own. They were going to speak to me now, my brothers and my mothers and sisters and maybe even my father. And Skart, I was sure that I could save him, now that I was to be powerful. I told myself that again and again. A fine spray-mist still hung in the air from the shattering of the pheromone synthesizer, addling my emotions still more.

A note lay beside me, in the warm hollow where his body had lain. I picked it up. The paper spoke to me in a hollow, expressionless voice.

It was a summons from the king.

FOUR

But the High Court was not to meet until evening. I still had my school to go to, and then I had to do something about Skart. Though I didn't know where he was, or whether he was already dead. I don't know whether at that moment I loved my brother. I only know that I didn't want my life to be sectioned off into separate universes (like the world inside and outside a closet) but to have something continuous in it. I was afraid to go on by myself. It was preferable to have Skart even if he hit me over and over.

The tutors' wing was one floor below. I took the elevator then walked to the room where Skart and I had been schooled together for as long as I could remember. I burst in, I shouted: "Skart, where's Skart, I want Skart!"

I looked around. The room did not face the sea and the drowned star city. It looked west, toward the Mutant River, and over the neighboring kingdoms of the delta, from Savage-is-Speared to Zoo to the tenements on the right bank where the aliens lived, next to Lepers' Desert.

"A special day for you, Morry-Draus-come-Prince?" My alien tutor looked at me through bulbous compound eyes, eternally sad. I went up to his plinth and stroked his bottle idly, my face glued to the glass which, curving, showed his form distorted: an indeHnite number of limbs, scaled or furry, dull green-brown, a pale face veined with blue like a leaf. Sometimes he appeared completely different, like a Hne mist, once even like a beautiful woman, the day he taught me about sex. Today he looked as he most frequently looked but I knew that that too was an illusion. The swirling nebula of dust was closer to the truth. He liked to play with our perceptions. Sometimes he used to look like one thing to Skart and another to me. He did it by fiddling with our minds.

"A happy occasion," I said without much enthusiasm. "I ejaculated and they took away my brother."

"Do not be sad." His voice emanated from the speakjewels embedded in the bottlecap. "I am still with you, no? I am here to tell of countless truths. Of realities within realities."

"You are here to lie to me. There's never anything in what you say," I said bitterly.

"Come, lift me up and take me to the window. Today, on the agenda: geography, history, comparative linguistics—"

"First tell me where Skart is."

"Not privy to such info. You must ask the king."

The windows were tightly flapped down and fastened at all four comers, closing out the wind. Right of the window there was a folding screen in four sections. One was just a closet; I could see the icons blinking, but beyond the symbols for simple household objects like vaporizers and fishhooks there were many hieroglyphs quite alien to me. Two more sections were spacetime windows of some kind. Sometimes he would use them to show me vistas of other worlds, but I wasn't really meant to see them, because he would just let me glimpse them and then sternly switch the scene to something more prosaic. They were blank now.

The fourth section I'd never seen before. It seemed to be

not an alien artifact at all, but just paper. A painting. Pastel pigments. A woman was depicted, a woman with the Draus hair flowing behind her. When I moved my head the eyes seemed to follow. I realized suddenly that the eyes of the painting themselves were empty, that the eyes I saw were human eyes peering through eyeholes, and that they were eyes like mine.

"Someone is behind the screen," I said. "Someone watching me. Is it Skart? Tell me. It's just a trick, they didn't take him away at all."

"Come, you know better."

Aliens do not have names. Not this kind of alien anyway. And mostly this was the kind that hung around our kingdom. "What will I call you today?" I said. It was a game we played a lot. If we played it for a while he seemed less inclined to cram me with facts.

"Today you may call me Carnifract," he said, purple teardrops running down his cheeks. "Excuse me this show of emotion, but I am sorry to see you growing so fast, frankly." The tears crystalized instantly and clinked as they hit the floor of the bottle, which was littered with tiny faceted gems of many colors, the results of many previous outbursts of emotion. I lifted him up and placed him on the window sill.

"How can you stand living in this bottle?" I said.

"Back home I had far less to call my own."

"But isn't it cramped?" I glanced nervously at the eyes in the screen, which had blinked.

"It's like one of our closets," Carnifract said. "Space is all folded up inside them. I commute to your schoolroom every morning from the alien quarter across the River and I never leave this bottle. Bet you'd like to know how it works."

I was intrigued. It was a way of forgetting what had happened and what was still to come. I knew it would be an ordeal.

"You are almost twice as tall as this bottle now," the alien said proudly, as if I was his son. "So how does it work?" I felt the eyes again. Who was it? It had to be Skart.

"Ah, what was on today's timetable? Linguistics, geography, history. No mention of transdimensional physics or superspatial mathematics?"

"What, magic words?"

"You know that aliens do not believe in magic. Perhaps one day I'll teach you these things, my boy. But you people (I use the term loosely) don't have the sort of minds that can encompass *grand* thoughts. Having gone native all my life, I understand you, you see. Back home they'd just think you were all insane."

"Well," I said, miffed because he had dangled forbidden knowledge in front of me and then yanked it away, "teach me whatever it is you plan to teach."

"Yes. In capsule-sized tidbits. Pick a subject, any subject, one of the three."

"Geography."

"Look out there. What do you see?"

I looked. There is a skywalk that joins us to the mainland, the only way across during high tide. It leads to an upper level of the complex of ruined palaces. That kingdom is called Savage-is-Speared. The natives are wild. At night they dance and set fire to the tops of the palaces. We call them Fire-eyes, because their eyes are always bloodshot from something they drink. Beyond their kingdom is Graveyard, where they are all sorcerers and like to fuck corpses. The right bank is not connected to Dreambreak at all, though at low tide the river is easily forded. Lepers and aliens live side by side. Beyond the aliens' colony is a tall building called Cruise Eternity. It is shaped like a starship from the time of heroes, but it seems anchored to the ground and flightless.

"Did you know that this was all one city once," the alien

said, "and that the city was one of a hundred cities and not even the greatest of them, and that that city was part of a vast kingdom, and that kingdom not even the greatest of kingdoms?"

"Mythology was yesterday, Carnifract," I said. I regretted reminding him, though, because I loved his fairytales the most. But I wasn't a child anymore, right? I had better steer him back on course.

"No, no, this is history now. I realize it's almost the same, boy. Pay attention!" But I kept looking behind and being wary of the eyes.

"Where was I? Today's capsule geography combined with history: subject: Cruise Eternity. Built some three thousand years ago at the height of human prosperity before the Decades of Ennui, Cruise Eternity represented a particularly decadent way out for those who were too refined to accept the decadence of the period. Those who subscribed to the cruise were placed in a state called amniosis. They would be woken up once every century for a weeklong tour, and then put back to sleep again. It is now operated entirely by robots. Their sales department is still open twenty-four hours a day and new clients are accepted either upon payment of the appropriate fee or as a result of lottery drawings. This lesson is particularly apposite because the next big revival is, I believe, scheduled for four years from now."

What to make of this? "Your stories are really stupid today, tutor. Why would anyone pay to be salted away for a century at a time? He'd have no anchor in life." suddenly thought of Skart and about how I'd maybe lost my own hold on my childhood. I'd be like one of those drifters through time if I couldn't save him. "It's just the same as dying!" I said.

"Today's linguistics lecture," he went on without stopping to let me make any comment, "is about the role of personal pronouns in the dialect of the Fire-eyes. The Fire-eyes are also known as the Velk. Adapting to changing sex roles over the last four hundred years, the natives of Savage-is-Speared now speak only in the third person. The three pronouns that in conservative dialects such as that of Dreambreak represent gender differences are used instead to represent an individual's status within the social hierarchy. To address a person as 'she' being honOrific, 'he' neutral, 'it' pejorative. In this regard the dialect shows the influence of some old Asian languages. Of course, you don't even know where Asia is, but we'll do that tomorrow under pre-holocaust ethnology. The Fire-eyes also make frequent use of the subjunctive, I might add—"

"What the fuck use is this information?" I shouted. "You sit in that bottle all day long telling me useless facts. I don't have any way of proving them or disproving them. They're probably all lies. I'll never talk to a Fire-eyes anyway. Maybe I'll kill one or rape one, but not talk."

"A king must know such things," the alien said mildly.

"A king!" I froze. I felt suddenly cold all over. I had to look at the window to be sure it was still sealed tight. "You shouldn't say that. That's treason."

"It is not," said a voice from behind the screen. A quiet voice, but resonant: familiar, as from a haunting or a repressed dream.

"Who are you?" I whirled around. Then I took the bottle in my hands and started to shake it angrily. "What tricks are you playing now?" I could see the alien's cheeks throbbing regularly like the gills of a fish out of water.

"Put your tutor down," said the voice from the screen. I obeyed. As I did *so,* the apparition in the bottle turned into a cloud and vanished. I saw clear through to the other side, all the foreign kingdoms bending and blending in the bottle's refraction.

"See, you frightened him, you made him run off home."

"I didn't mean to." I went up to the screen, wondering whether I should fold it up and reveal who it was. It wasn't Skart's voice, but who else could have such a familiar voice? Maybe he was speaking through an encoder or something.'

"Go on. Don't be afraid."

I put the bottle back on its plinth, and then I went up to the screen and folded the painting-section behind the closet-section.

There was a woman sitting there. She was masked. Otherwise she was naked except for a triangle of beaten bronze that formed the woman-V over her crotch. Above the mask I could see the hair (my hair) fleece-white and soft. The mask was of bronze like the triangle and represented a wolf. The hairs of its face were carefully chiseled. The teeth were sharp and probably deadly.

"You may not yet see my face," she said, "until tonight But I just had to see you. You don't know how terrible it was to wait these twelve years, not knowing if you would come out whole. But here you are."

"You're my mother?" I said.

She held out her hand for me to kiss. "Your special mother," she said softly. "The mother whose womb once sheltered you." I knelt before her. Her hand trembled against my lips. Or was it my lips? I could not tell.

"The alien was not completely wrong to mention kingship to you, my son. Your father is old. You are the last of his brood, and I think you are the most true to the mold of the House of Draus. And the title of king always falls to the one closest to the original Draus. That's the law. But as you might guess, that's not really how the succession works."

"How does it work?"

"Shush! Your questions are too direct. Like the way you treat your tutor, so direct! That might be interpreted as a character defect. Maybe a mental deviation from the norm, in which case you might follow your brother—"

"Where is he? Where is Skart?" I demanded. "Forget him, Morry. Together we must plan for your rise to power. It's time for a new beginning."

Humbly I clasped my mother's knees. "Do I have to, Mother? Why does it have to be this way? What if I don't want to rise to power?"

"Then my twelve years of waiting will have been in vain! And your sequestering will have been wasted!"

"You're a stranger to me," I said. "It's my brother Skart I want. Tell me where he is and I'll listen to you and obey you. Just tell me if he's dead or alive."

"He's in the basement, of course! Where he belongs."

The basement, I thought. Where they keep the prisoners. Only last night I'd seen them staring at me and Jonellys while she teased my scarlet dickie-bird. The basement, the domain of Anskowl the Picklemaster. My prospective elevation tasted bitter in my mouth.

"Don't try to see him," my mother said. "It's not that it's forbidden, it's just that I don't want you to be hurt. Come, embrace me."

I stood up and gave her a perfunctory hug. Her breasts against my chest made me uneasy. They were dry, like lizardskin. She held me closer. The metal of her mask chilled my cheek.

"Until tonight," she whispered. "So much time to make up for, my son."

"Tonight," I said, not daring to meet her gaze. Instead I looked way past her out into the kingdoms beyond. The tide was ebbing, and already I could see the lepers fording the river to trade with the Fire-eyes and to buy fish from our people. And I saw the distant tower of Cruise Eternity, the starship that led only to a kind of death. And thought also of the drowned star city, of the dead starships.

Cruise Eternity, I thought. A kind of death.

I turned around to address my mother again. Suddenly I had so many questions to ask her.

But the screen with the painting was back in place now, and the eye-holes were empty.

FIVE

The elevators of Dreambreak do not go down as far as the basement. The control screen shows a number of icons beneath the symbol for "lobby," but they have not worked for a hundred years or more. Instead you must get out at the lobby and obtain clearance to pass down further. A robot scans your retinas or thumbs and either lets you pass or sends you back. The robot is rooted to a plinth just in front of the elevator doors, but if you try to evade it, it summons sentinels from below. And those below belong to the Picklemaster, body and soul. I think even my father would have thought twice before crossing them. And I was a young prince of twelve only just come into manhood and already unmoored from all he had thought true. I was afraid when I stepped out and stood for the robot to lock eyes with mine. But I was angry too and that made me less fearful. I stood there dumbly for a while, my gaze wandering to the fluted columns set into the walls, the peeling mural of a funerary ceremony, a sick-sweet odor of embalming fluid.

"What do I do now?" I said, uncertain whether the robot had released me from its scrutiny.

A voice from further beyond: doorways behind doorways: darkness. "Come, Morry Draus, if you dare. Do you dare? Come. Come into Anskowl's kingdom."

"There is only one kingdom here," I said hotly, "my

father's. You defy him?"

"Silly boy. Come forward, come, come, come. Some kingdoms are of this world and some are not. Mine is neither. My kingdom is a kind of stopping-place, a respite in the long journey toward eternity."

I stepped forward. Darkness swooped down and caught me. Had I stepped through a closet-field like the kind the aliens did? Steps now. I descended the narrow , space between two rows of skulls painted with brilliant blue phosphor, the only light. Damp and dank. Somewhere water was running. We were beneath even the low tide here. Murmuring, the water seemed to flow above my head.

"Anskowl?" I said.

Skowl-skowl-skowl-skowl-skowl.

Dank. Damp. I reached the bottom of the steps. My feet touched water. Cold. A stench of rottenness was everywhere. At last I saw the glimmer of light on the water. Here and there the wavering light fell on reeds or the arms of skeletons floating on the water. The light came nearer and I saw that it emanated from a raft that hoverskimmed over the flooded passageway and that the walls were embedded with human skulls. Once the walls had been white I think but now they dripped with sewage water and were almost black. A tall figure sat in the raft on its only seat with his bony fingers jabbing at the control screen. His other hand held the ceremonial flask.

The raft stopped where I stood. Anskowl beckoned me. "Ah, you are here for the tour," he said. "Very good. This is an auspicious first day for your coming to manhood. Since you've escaped me, you naturally want to get a whiff of what you've escaped. Come on in, my boy."

I stepped onto the raft. Like every other member of the High Court Anskowl had never spoken to me directly before. His body was painted completely black, even his face, except for the phosphorescent circles around his eyes and some ornamental cheek-scars in scarlet. They made his face even more pinched and sallow. A black robe covered his loins and trailed down into the foul water. We entered a mist, laced I think with pheromones of fear, though my father had forbidden their use outside the legitimate dosages used by pheromone bards. I trembled as we passed through, but forced myself to be strong. "Good," he said, arching one eyebrow as he looked me over. "But then, you have no cause for fear."

"I didn't come to take the tour," I said angrily. "I came to find Skart."

"Skart! Now who might he be?"

He lifted his hand from the control screen; I saw the icons shift. "You know very well. Skart, my next-up brother. He was taken away from me before I woke this morning."

We turned a comer. The channel broadened. On either side were caves or grottoes. In some of them skewer-sharp railings prevented their inhabitants from jumping into the water. Others were open, but the people in them were chained to pillars or nailed to the concrete floor. "Skart is in this place?" Wildly I thought, is he being punished for all the times he hit me? But he never did anything to deserve it. But for the past twelve years he's known he would come here. And he still lived with me and sometimes he didn't hit me at all. Though I still didn't know if I loved my brother, I knew I wanted him back.

"I tell you, there is no Skart here. There are no names here at all."

"No names." i heard moaning from the torture-grottoes. But mostly they were all silent and staring, subdued by the mere presence of the Picklemaster.

"You think a name is so important, my boy!" Anskowl chuckled. "You think everyone has to have a name. Why you have two names and most people must make do with one, have you never thought of why that is, have you have you?"

"No."

"Disturbed are you? If they have two names on the top floor, why should they have any names in the basement? Even I who am master here and giver of life and death, I have only a single name and am theoretically your servant. Theoretically!" He laughed again, almost doubling over the blinking screen.

"A wall!" I screamed as it veered up ahead and I saw another peeling funeral mural showing the tossing of a fisherwoman into the sea.

"What wall?" We passed right through it. It was of the same substance as the sentinels that guard the elevators upstairs: a trick of twining lasers. "This labyrinth is full of illusions, no? Here we must park the raft. Help me to tie it to that post." The post was a pillar on which hung a young girl with no eyes.

I knew that girl.

"What are you staring at? Come away, come away, I must show you the sights." He stepped out and was already starting down the passage, the wet end of his robe slopping against the gravel of broken concrete that bit into the soles of my feet.

"You knew," I shouted after him, accusing. "That's why you took this route!"

The girl moaned. She was not dead. She said (her voice rasping through parched lips) "I hear you. I wake from a dream of a drowned star city and I hear the voice of a boy I almost loved."

"Jonellys."

"He remembers my name."

She had been strung up above floor level. Her crotch was about level with my face. Her clitoris had been burned out with a triangular brand. I couldn't look. "Why?" I screamed. "Why is she here?"

"How should I know?" Anskowl shrugged and came back to fetch me. "Well, speak to her, ask her!" He was lying.

"What are you doing in this place?" I said, remembering that I had been thinking of her when I first felt the wetness bursting from me and later in my dream too.

"I dared to touch the body of a Draus, and to look boldly at him, though I'm only a girlchild from the third floor," she whispered. "Don't go away, Morry. It was worth it. You were beautiful. Beneath the tacky paint and under the scarlet of your dickie-bird you were a prince and a perfect one. ah, it hurts. They'll kill me soon." Still I could not stand to look at her.

I turned on Anskowl in a fury. "Let her go," I said.

"Go where? She has no eyes. Soon she will have no tongue. That has been scheduled for tomorrow. Afterward she will go to the Lepers' Desert. Touching you unbidden is not a capital offence." I knew from this that he had always known and that he had placed her in my path to torment me, though I was technically his master.

"I want her down, now."

"You want to break the law?"

"I command as Draus!" It was the first time I had even uttered those words. But I had heard my father speak them and seen people scurry to do his bidding.

"Well, since you put it that way," Anskowl said shrugging. "But take care, little Morry. You are not the king yet. If you show too much compassion or if you show a bad temper, beware that it does not get reported as a mental deviation! Then you will end up as *mycreature*."

He clapped his hands and Jonellys crumpled to the ground. For a second I glimpsed the eyeholes crusted with mucus and congealed blood. Then Anskowl kicked her face over so it lay in the mushy concrete. It was not really a kick, it was a motion far idler and more dispassionate.

"Now what?" he said.

"I don't know," I admitted.

"Well. You don't know. I'll have her sent to your chamber after she's been cleaned up a bit. And now, if my Lord would deign to follow me? This is a long tour and it's got to be finished before the High Court meets."

I followed, leaving the girl whimpering on the prickly concrete. I looked after her a few times. She was still and didn't cry out anymore.

"Is she dead?" I said.

"Don't dawdle, boy!" said Anskowl. "She'll be all right. Now, you are to look at the family vault. By your father's command, I may add, so don't you dare try the Draus-words on me, or you'll be guilty of a breach of the Gift of Honor."

We stepped through several more illusory doors. Finally we reached a hall so long I couldn't see the end of it, and it was lined with glass urns, each one about man-high, and dimly lit from above and below with phosphorstrips. I was about to ask Anskowl what it was, but he shushed me. The first few urns were empty. But soon we came to urns that were occupied. Each contained a man or woman like myself, a Draus, each naked, each white-haired and purple-eyed. But sometimes I saw one that was a hunchback or an albino. One with two heads. Now I understood. "These people are the failures," I said.

"Keep walking."

"You kill them and you preserve them in these jars and that's what you're going to do to—"

At last we had reached the end of the corridor. And passed through another doorway. A large room now. Lined with more urns. And in the center a large rectangular tank. An old man in it. I recognized his eyes, my eyes. And a woman beside him. Expressionless they floated in the embalming fluid. "Look your fill," Anskowl said. "These two are the ultimate cause of your good fortune. You are born of their genes. They are the john and jane Draus," h€t said, calling the two corpses by the epithets used only of a house's ultimate ancestors. "Because of them you are blessed with the material of kingship." A hint of longing in Anskowl's voice. Did he envy us, he who was entrusted with executing our imperfections and torturing those who transgressed against us?

I looked hard into the faces of the john and jane. An unbearable emotion filled me, a big thing that I couldn't understand.

"Because of them you are pure. Your seed is never to be mingled with that of any other house. And you will have a chance to be king over all the houses of Dreambreak."

So that was why my brother dreamed endlessly of my mothers and sisters yet was forbidden all communication with them. There was cruelty in it but also terrible grandeur. The big emotion overwhelmed me and I fell on my knees before the embalmed bodies of the john and jane. It was as though they were somehow still alive and their inner light shone on me but I could not say whether it was benediction or anathema. The light was cold and burning. "What if I am not selected to be king?" I said, still prostrate on the hard cold floor.

"You fool! Have you no eyes and ears at all, that you must ask such obvious and painful questions? Have you never wondered why you have mothers and brothers and sisters and only one father?"

This confirmed what I had already divined from the words of my mother. But if this was simply the way things were, why did I feel such wrongness in it? Was this an instance of some mental deviation? I had to lock these thoughts up deep inside myself. I didn't dare get up from my prostration. I didn't want to see the eyes of my ancient ancestor on me and have him know I was thinking such traitorous thoughts.

At last the Picklemaster raised me up and said, "There is still much to do before the final rituals of your first day of manhood. You must go now."

Suddenly I realized I had forgotten why I had come down into the basement. "Skart," I said. "I must see Skart."

"He must die," Anskowl said, almost tenderly. "Don't grieve, my boy. Go on now."

"I don't care if he has a patch on his back. I love my next-up brother, Anskowl." It was the first time I had ever said it, and the first time I ever knew that it was true.

"Love?" He smiled ruefully. "That is one of the first things you will learn to give up. But you will see him in due course."

"I command as—"

"No!" He put his hand over my mouth so that I would not finish uttering the words that might cause in him an unthinkable clash of loyalties. "Oh, say it. What do you know? You don't even know who really runs this kingdom," he said. "You think the rituals are the reality! You foolish boy!"

I turned and ran with his laughter echoing behind me. At the mooring post I realized that I would have to wait for him to come and operate the raft. I looked for Jonellys who had lyeen lying blinded and half dead by the water's edge. But they had already taken her away.

SIX

I found Jonellys lying on the sofabed in my room. They had swabbed her completely clean and she smelled of disinfectant. She heard me coming and she moved her head in my direction. I saw her closely and in sunlight for the first time. Some tiny smears of blood remained on her cheeks. She had probably bled since they cleaned her. The wind from the sea blew strongly scented and moist. Her hair was damp and hung like seaweed on a scalp scabbed like a barnacled rock poking from the sea. Eyeless she seemed lifeless like a zombie in a horror symphony like the kind the fighters loved to watch in smoky rooms permeated with low-grade pheromones. But I knew she was alive because she propped herself up moved toward my voice.

I said, "Fuck it I say fuck it this should never have happened it's all my fault."

"No," she said softly, "never blame yourself, Morry Draus. I was the one who chased you knowing the consequences."

"You knew what might happen?" I was incredulous.

"It was a risk. I've never been caught before. I've chased many Drauses. I am bold." She tried to laugh but couldn't hold her cheeks wide without pain and instead cried out.

"Why?"

"The Gift of Love is in your power. It is sacred to dare to touch the Drauses that sneak downstairs in the middle of the night, sacred to risk all for desire, sacred to accept the Gift of Death. You are perfect. That's what my parents taught me. We are not worthy of the three Gifts, but we can aspire, dream, try to grasp! Oh Morry, I love you."

Slowly I said, "I don't think you can know that." . "I've been taught to love you all my life, seed of the john Draus and the jane Draus."

"It's only been twelve hours since we last met," I said. "Look," (no, I had forgotten myself) "I will look for you, the tide is out again. I see the star city." It flamed on the water and its towers were like burning arrows that the sea thrust out at the sky. "I hate me," I whispered, "because just by existing I'm hurting people. My brother. For twelve years I loved him. And you. You say that all your life you have loved me."

"And I will be twelve soon," Jonellys said.

"I will give you sight, turn back time."

"How?"

"Come, I'll take you to my tutor, to the alien."

"Aliens! Magic."

"Aliens do not believe in magic. But there are things they know. Even if they usually lie to me."

I took her hand, hard, calloused from fishnets and from scraping on the scales of the fish. Even through the disinfectant they smelled faintly of fish. I led her to the schoolroom. The sentinels turned to stare, their heads wagging in perfect unison. But they did not dare challenge me now. Already I was learning to walk proudly as a prince must walk. I laid her on the plinth in the schoolroom. The alien's bottle was empty.

I took it in my arms and whispered into it: "I'm sorry, tutor. I didn't mean to scare you before. Come back, please, come back? I need you. Oh, please." I rocked the bottle like a baby.

The bottle misted. The swirling took shape. "Carnifract," I said.

"That's not my name anymore," said my tutor who had taken the shape of a fiery amphibian. "I wish to be called Amaday."

"Why is it so important?" I said. "It's just a game. Please, you have to help me."

"It's not just a game to me. To be named is to continue to live. Truth is ever-changing. Rebirth is the only birth."

"Can you help me?"

"The girl," Amaday said, regarding Jonellys with ever larger and more mournful eyes. "I shall need a different name."

"Please. It's so frustrating."

"You may call me Eristradu. Then I will help you, I think." He did not wait for me to call him by his new name, but simply said, "You are looking for eyes, no? I have eyes. There. In the closet." I went over to the folding screen and looked over the blinking icons. "Nothing there? Call up the next screen." I did. I saw a hieroglyph of an eye. "Reach inside."

I did. Three wet glutinous balls appeared in my hand as I pulled it out.

"Three!" my tutor said. "They won't be the right kind of eyes. Show me." I held them up. "Infra-red, mostly. Better than nothing, though. I don't know why I kept them around. You can throw one of them back in, any one. Now, the optic nerves are intact? Otherwise it's useless."

"I don't know," I said. I stared at the two eyes left in my hand in disoelief. They felt well refrigerated. I knelt over Jonellys and tried to soothe her. The eyes looked fairly human in front except that they had no whites at all, they seemed to be all iris. The eyes had a fuzzy kind of backing. When I looked at it closely it looked like velcro. Except the little fibers seemed to be capillaries and nerves and tiny tubes.

"Well, hurry up," said Eristradu. "One size fits all, they just glide in." I tried to stuff the left eye into the socket. Jonellys moved and stifled a moan. "Quick," my tutor said. The eye was malleable and I was able to squeeze it in. I heard a sizzling, hissing sound as the eye became activated and nerves and vessels writhed around in back hunting for connections.

"Tickles," Jonellys said, and closed her eye. I think she was afraid of what she would see. I put the other eye in. Itslid in easily. She was more relaxed probably. Both her eyelids closed by reflex. I waited.

"Am I supposed to kiss them open?" I said.

"No. I can manage." She was weeping. "I can see even with them closed. But it's different." She got up. "Where your voice is coming from it's like a boy-shaped blur. I see your racing blood like the veins of a leaf. And rainbow-fringed patches where your lips should be, and your heart, and your genitals. I see a big square of nothing behind you, like a hole in my vision." That was the window, I guessed. It was closed and always cool to the touch and stole the heat from you when you went near it. "It's mostly dark and vague. It's like I was still down in the basement, Morry."

"You're not. And the sun is shining. It's an alien eye you're wearing."

"No it's not," Eristradu said suddenly. "Made right here on earth. I got it while moonlighting among the Fire-eyes." It was the first time I had ever thought that my tutor might want to visit any other kingdom than our own. How eccentric.

"You're lying," I said.

"You know, that's why you're my favorite student," he said (probably a lie too.) "The others just accept halfdozing. You tell me I'm lying even when I tell the truth. You *care,* Morry Draus. It'll probably kill you though. That's the only reason I'm bending over backward to help you."

"I'm grateful," I said, as Jonellys stood up and gazed around her. Everything she looked at was something to wonder at.

"Now what are you going to do with her?"

"Do?" I had no idea. "I suppose she'll serve me somehow."

She started to cry. Her tears were mixed with blood, I suppose because the eyes hadn't quite taken yet. Suddenly I saw what it was. I hadn't noticed before because the triangular scar of her burned-out clitoris had been so horrifying I hadn't wanted to look too closely. But now I saw thft they had sewn her vagina shut. "And inside?" I said. '

"Inside? They've taken it all out. I'm already dead, worse than dead. Give me the Gift of Death, Morry Draus. It's the only proper thing to do."

"Fuck I'm furiOUS," I said. "Isn't there anything we can do? In that closet of yours—"

"Sorry," my tutor said. "But you might be able to get help where those eyes came from."

"From the Fire-eyes? That would be magic. My father would kill me. Whatever I do I seem to get in deeper and deeper!"

"Magic is relative," said Eristradu. "Well, I am out of names today, so I can't help you anymore. But I can give you hints. Everything you learned in today's lesson is a clue to what you have to do with your life. I've told you how to save Skart and I've told you how to help this girl."

"What? You're lying again. Today we did capsules on linguistics, history, and geography. There wasn't anything on saving anyone. Besides—I turned on his

II bottle suspiciously. "You didn't even know any of this was going to happen. Or did you?"

"I subsist within a transdimensional interface, II the alien replied enigmatically. "In certain cases, the future can be considered the past. II

The girl was sobbing loudly now. She hardly seemed to be the same girl who had laughingly seduced me among the weeds and fishes. I did not know enough to comfort her. I knew so little of how my own society worked. Even a girl from the third floor seemed to know more about how I was supposed to act. "What do you want me to do?" I said, exasperated. "Didn't I do the right thing by saving your life?"

"Shame on you, prince, II she said bitterly. "You have commanded me to go on living, and I must. I must go on living with infra-red vision and no cunt. I can stay here and be laughed at for the rest of my life or I can go to Lepers' Desert or I can run away to the Velk and ask for help. Maybe they'll give me a velcro cunt to go with these velcro eyes?"

"I thought you loved me," I said helplessly.

"Of course I do!" she screamed. "That's why I'm acting this way." She rushed at me and pummeled me weakly with her whip-scarred elbows. Then she spun around and fled from the room leaving me with my mouth wide open. I listened to the uneven patter of her limping feet.

"Don't go after her," said my tutor. "You don't have time. You have to go and get ready for this evening, for the final ceremony of your coming-of-age. The first day of your manhood is almost at its climax."

"Do you think I'll last a whole day?" I shouted. I lifted his bottle and started to fling it across the room. Then I thought better of it and set him gently down. He was the only one who could still help me. I couldn't lose him too. I tried to calm myself and to apologize, but midway through I saw that I had been talking to an empty bottle.

"I don't want to be a man," I said to myself. "I think I'd rather die."

SEVEN

My room in the early twilight: the girl sat motionless and hunched up in a corner. She had painted herself completely white like a corpse. She had whited out the woman-V of her crotch so that everyone could see she had become a neuter. She sat there pinked by the evening sky. For about an hour I had been watching her, not knowing what to say.

Finally I gave up, pulled out the closet that used to contain all my and Skart's belongings, and rolled it out on the bed, and ran a finger along its slippery-smooth surface. With a fmgemail I drew lines from icon to icon and made imaginary constellations. At last I realized I hadn't shit all day. If I was supposed to see the king tonight I'd better not slip up. I reached through the closet for some toilet paper and unfolded it, pushed the closet out of the way, spread out the toilet paper on the bed and sat down on it. As the field focused and locked onto my inner cavities, I suddenly noticed that Jonellys had started to laugh. I was alarmed. I had almost forgotten she was there.

She said, "You rich people and your alien technology. On the third floor we had to shit and piss out into the ocean. We didn't have little pads that are sensitive to dead organic matter and can dump it into another universe."

"You can see that well with your new eyes." I saw that her eyes (they were you remember without whites) had started to glow and because her whole body was covered with the pearlwhite pigment she seemed almost like one of the Fire-eyes, though I had never yet seen a real one.

"I see an outlige," she said. "Your body shimmers and palpitates, more than mine, it exudes a rainbow of heat. Your metabolism must be superfast. Does it embarrass you if I talk about shit?"

"Most people carry a sheet of toilet paper on them and

are capable of using it discreetly," I said. "It's not *niceto* talk about it."

"I remember when I was very young, my friend across the hallway said, 'You know, the aristocracy doesn't go weewee like we do, they shove their shit into vacant universes.' I told her she was lying. Later I thought there must be a planet out there somewhere in that vacant universe where the shit of the rich is falling out of the sky."

I laughed. It was an image that had never occurred to me. "But it is clean, and completely thorough," I said, protesting, "and unmessy." I pulled the sheet of alien fabric out and started to put it away, when I noticed that there was writing on it. "Fuck it's one of Skart's poems," I said. I held it up to the dying light. The scratches were faint now. I used the twilight to highlight the contrast and held it to my ear. The toilet paper whispered to me in a voice that cruelly imitated the voice of my next-up brother who maybe was even already dead.

It said:

To my little brother Didyou know? I touch you all the time.
I think you are asleep. You are all I have.
I want to ram and slam into you but I don't want to wake you.
Why not? I hate you enough.
But not as much as I hate mefor not being you.
Do you know what I'm doing?
Forgive me.
Ifonly we were Velk, it would all be different.
Instead you will be king and I will cruise eternity.

"It's terrible," Jonellys said. "Is it poetry?"

"It wasn't meant for your ears." I wondered how she could hear what to me was the ghostliest whisper.

"My hearing has become much sharper even in the last few hours," she said, "because of the way I am forced to see. Morry, kill me now, I beg you." She looked straight at me in her colors of death.

"How strange," I said. "Today's capsule lessons from my tutor. The Fire-eyes are also called the Velk. Why?

Because of their velcro eyes? What else? My tutor taught me how their pronouns had changed from changing sex roles. Why? And he also taught me about Cruise Eternity today. And it's all in the poem."

"You're not making sense you've gone mad you shouldn't dwell on it, shouldn't brood. This is the way things are."

"Says who?"

"How should I know? Ask the alien in the bottle."

"No." I knew that the answers must rest somewhere in the clues I had already been given. There had to be a way of salvaging the mess. Other than turning my back on it. Anskowl had told me that love would be the first thing to go. But,I didn't want it to go yet. I wanted to \

cling to it for at least a few more hours. I had only just discovered it after all. Was every tiny move I made from now on always to result in death and maiming and torture? Something in the alien's clues. Something! Clues were all he could give, I knew that. Something to do with "xenological non—interference," whatever that was.

I sat thinking for a while longer while Jonellys relapsed into silence. But just as I began to see an inkling of a solution, attendants came to fetch me to my father. I had to be bathed, my body greased again and dusted with fine white powder and delicately painted, and the circle of manhood had to be carefully drawn around my pubic area and the white within it scraped clean with a strigil. Then I was covered with a cloak woven from dried and beaten seaweed. A lotion was rubbed into my hair that made it billow of its own accord, and even when they sealed the windows my hair danced to a private wind that no man could feel.

As I left I heard Jonellys say, "They have coated you over

so many times. Your inner heat has been masked from me with cosmetics and garments. You are chill now. You have gone dark to me, Morry Draus, quite dark."

EIGHT

It was the most solemn of processionals with some of Anskowl's apprentices banging on huge humanskin drums and conches blaring. Outside the big east suite of the princes' dormitory there was an exitway to a staircase that zigzagged all the way up past the king's quarters to the roof and reached all the way down to the basement level. A sign said "Fire Escape" in the old writing (it could not talk however long you stared at it or even if you shone a flashlight right over it) but it obviously wasn't a fire escape, there were never any fires, it was a flood escape so that if the tide came bursting in too fast the fisher people could climb up for a temporary shelter.

The procession wound slowly up the outside of the building. I looked down and saw that the tide was high and the people were casting the nets and the drowned star city was totally submerged except for a single spire that jutted black in the mid-distance like the fin of a giant shark. After several robot security checkpoints I realized we were going all the way to the roof. They were going to hold High Court in the highest of high places where they made electricity. I had only heard about it in servants' gossip and in the intimations of my alien tutor.

At last I saw what I had only seen in dreams. A flat expanse of flagstones veined with moss and weeds. At one end of the roof stood about twenty windmills with their blades churning in the salty wind. Some servants were unrolling a length of window and setting up a transparent barrier between us and the wind. My mothers sat on chairs beneath the windmills and wore masks of rare animals. I saw my special mother Sitting at the right hand of my father's throne, but the throne was still empty. In front of the throne w.,ere two booths set off by alien closet screens so you couldn't see inside. The procession took me to the very foot of the throne. I saw my assembled brothers and sisters for the first time, in concentric ranks around the throne. I fell prostrated.

Then I heard the voice of Anskowl behind me, addressing my father's empty place. "A soul has been plucked from the genetic ocean, O king. A soul raised up and saved for a span from the final drowning that is the fate of all. A fish thrust up and not thrown back into the sea. O king, behold your son!"

My face was still down on the flagstones with the smell of moss earthy in my nostrils.

The king's voice: "Look up. Let's have a look at you." There was a gruff kind of mildness in his voice. He sounded old, as though the original john spoke through his lips. I raised my head. I saw him closer than I'd ever seen before. His face (my face) was lined but I still knew it for mine. He was sitting on the throne. His body was painted in broad strokes of gold and silver, and a pale purple ointment had been rubbed into his cheeks to pick up the color of his eyes. "Don't be afraid, Morry," he said. "No one's going to eat you now. Well, perhaps one of your mothers will. But it's something you will enjoy, I promise." Something like a lascivious leer crossed his face. But the weight of the face paint was such that he could not smile for fear of cracking the designs on his face.

"And now, O king," said Anskowl, "you shall say farewell to that other one, born to be guardian of this one who bears the blessing of the john and jane Draus."

There was a scuffling noise behind me. One of the two booths was being opened up. A gasp from the audience. I couldn't help turning around. It was Skart.

He was crouching fetally in one of the glass urns. The embalming fluid was about up to his calf and dripping slowly down from a siphon that had been installed at the neck of the urn. He was conscious. He looked at us. His face was contorted by the curvature of the urn but I could see the anger in his eyes and in my mind I felt his fists clubbing me and then the sweat of him running down my back and also, sometimes, the strained warmth that he had in him for me, that I saw in the poems on the sheets of toilet paper. "Skart," I whispered, "my brother." remembered I had great plans of saving him from death.

But now that I saw him in his urn and I saw that the eyes of the High Court were all on me and I lay at the feet of the king, I was frightened and alone and tongue-tied. In the end it was the king who spoke.

"Come to me, Morry," he said. "Don't be afraid. You are angry now, and you think that it's terribly unfair." He beckoned to me. I went up to him. I had never been so close to the king before, and I know I was trembling like a strand of seaweed in the wind. He held my cheeks between hands that were greased and scented from the pigments based on fish oil. Suddenly he hugged me, this old man, weeping. "My son, my son. Must I always lose a son to gain one? How I have loved you these twelve years. For twelve years I have slept with a hologram of \

you by my bedside. Now I shall throw it into the sea. Don't grieve for your brother, son. Rejoice in your new status. The past is in your next-up brother. We must accept that there is pain in the past. He will die in pain, I'm afraid. I've watched so many fall victim to Anskowl and all the Anskowls before him. The last hurts as much as the first.

Believe me. But your destiny will be as magnificent as your brother's is ignominious. And he has served his purpose well." Although the words sounded noble and almost made me think it was all right to kill Skart I still felt sick to my stomach about it and I was still cursing myself inwardly for not being able to speak up. The king motioned to the assembly. "It is time. The feasting and the music." My special mother was still wearing her mask of the wolf. That was how I knew who she was. She nodded to me but I was too overwhelmed to reply yet.

The king made me share the throne with him. I could see now that we royals were flanked on the left by a small consort of bards. Arlyn, the king's master pheromonist, was sitting at a synthesizer whose keyboard was inlaid with tumbled stones that caught the moonlight and stippled the flagstones around him with spots of reflected light. I could tell that they had already started to play, because there was something in the air, not even a scent yet, but a kind of prickling sensation at the ends of the nerves of my outermost extremities. I looked at Skart. The level of embalming fluid had not risen much yet. He would not really suffer until it reached his face and then I knew he would start to scream and then it would slowly seep into him and pickle him gradually, almost with tenderness. Behind me the windmills had begun to chum frantically. The wind must have risen but we were protected by the invisible sheets of windowstuff. Now there was a faint tang in the air and I could feel a tremor in my heartheat and a tickling at the base of my penis. And suddenly I was all excited. I barely noticed that the food was being served. There were platters made from stretched out skins of stingrays piled high with seaweed and chopped fish both raw and cooked and sprinkled with rock salt and great bowls of a broth thickened with sharkfins that had been braising for weeks. The smell of fish masked the subtle sex odor that the orchestra was sending out. The sex feelings were interspersed with episodes of other emotions. There was a note of bloodlust in every phrase of the music. The background aurals heightened the tensions with steady urgent ostinati in the deep bass that made my whole body tremble. And the king whispered in my ear: "A wonderful wonderful music to fuck by, my son, not so?" and I could only nod dumbly as the feeling swept over me in black waves now as though I were hanging from the nets and letting the tide batter me against the slimy gnarled walls of the third floor.

My special mother rose up and came to me and took my hand. She still hadn't removed her mask of the wolf. She said to my father, "As special mother I ask of you the privilege of bestowing the Gift of Love."

The king said, "Rejoice."

My mother led me to the second of the two booths, the one still enclosed by the alien closet screens. As I turned to face my father, the music still pounding inside me, I saw who it was who sat on the side opposite the musicians. It was a group of twelve extremely old men and women. Only their heads appeared, for every inch of them was covered with a billowing cloak of seaweed like my own. "Who are they?" I whispered to my mother.

"They are the Tribunal of the Three Gifts," she said in a diSmissing tone, "who decide on the interpretation of the finer points of the Drauses' code of behavior. But they needn't worry about you. You're above all that now."

"What do you mean, now? Was I subject to them before?"

"They also interpret the mystic DNA charts of the House of Draus," she said.

In that case, I thought, they must have been the ones who decided that Skart's deformity had been too much.

"Will we consummate openly? Or do you want privacy?"

said an official who appeared in front of the booth and bowed to my mother.

"Alone," I said. I didn't want the whole court staring at me. I didn't want to see Skart and I didn't want him to see me. Even though the music was sending the blood rushing to engorge my penis and making me shake all over with desire, I still felt the guilt of it. Deep inside. "Alone," I said again.

I think my mother was a little upset by my reticence. She'd wanted a triumph before the whole court. But she would have to be content with a secret triumph. "Let the boy have his way," she said, since I had already commanded and it would look silly to disagree on so minor a point of protocol.

And so we stepped through the screens. And were in a chamber far bigger than the booth could possibly have contained. I knew then that we can come through one of those folded space contractions of which the aliens are so fond. We had entered a bedroom in some completely different part of the palace. Though I didn't think of it then, it occurs to me now that the room could just as easily have been on some other planet. If so, it was the only time I ever left the earth.

"Kiss me," said my mother. But she made no move to take the mask off.

"Your mask," I said.

"Kiss me! For twelve years I have prepared myself for this moment!"

I steeled myself for my lips to encounter cold metal. But as they touched the mask the golden wolf-face melted and my mother's face resolved out of blur. The screens had not shut off the music with its chemicals of arousal. They seemed amplified here. Everything about her was hot to the touch. Her lips burned. I threw myself into her arms and knew that this was the moment for which I had been born and for which I had endured so much pain.

NINE

After the first kiss I backed off, scared by the magnitude of all that had happened today. I tried to make her face out in the room's dim light. I thought that she must be old, disfigured by time, to want to conceal her face under that mask. But she was not. She was firm-bodied and her cheeks, beneath the luminous white of her facepaint, were unlined. She said, "Come to me, Morry, why do you wait?"

But I just stared at her and said, "Your face, your face."

"Mirror to mirror. Oh, Morry, I was twelve years old like you when my womanblood first came and they brought me to this place and your father came to me and it was beautiful so beautiful. But I had Skart. Anskowl tried to have me banished, did you know that? But the Tribunal intervened. And the king said four words: 'She is still young.' Those words saved me from the water of death that runs in the basement of our kingdom."

I wrapped my seaweed cloak tighter around my shoulders, wary suddenly, embarrassed. My special mother laughed gently and said, "You're not cold, are you? No. Just a little timid. Tell me, did you ever go downstairs to play with the fisher children?"

"No." I couldn't help lying. Something (the pheromones maybe) were blocking off my memories ofJonellys. I knew she didn't believe me.

She took me in her arms again. And kissed the thin seaweed of my cloak again and again so that it began to dissolve in her mouth and I began to feel her tongue moist and warm as it moved teasing up my arm and down the center of my chest and then I pressed against her hard my head nuzzled in the gap between her breasts and her fragrance melding with the wild arousal of the artificial pheromones that wafted in from outside and I wanted so much that I could barely yet understand I wanted so much so much. And her hands dug hard against my sharp shoulder blades and her fingertips counted the vertebrae one by one slowly slicking them with spit and sweat and she pushed my head down down until my lips met the hot and pungent lips of her vagina and the oily hair bristling in my nostrils and choking me with the perfume of desire and as she ate away at my cloak her tongue was flecked with green.

She stopped suddenly and said, "What's this? A sheet of paper secreted in a fold of your cloak."

"I'd forgotten. Toilet paper. It's nothing."

"There's a poem written on it." She held it to the light The paper spoke again. Its voice was even fainter than before. But it was still recognizable as a mechanical parody of Skart's voice courtesy of alien technology.

When it was over my mother thrust it from her in a fury.

Then she began to weep appallingly and disconsolately.

"Why, mother?" I said. I tried to comfort her.

"No, don't give me platitudes. It's my son out there, too, dying. Don't try to tell me it's destiny."

"I'm not. I want to save him."

"How can you?"

"I think that all the answers are in the poem."

"Forget. Forget, Morry. For so long I've struggled to forget. We must make love now. Urgently and passionately and completely unmindful of the world outside. Because you must complete the ritual. Because you must be king. Only then will Skart's death have any value."

"No!" I was angry too now. "Skart will not die!"

And I seized her the way Skart had seized me earlier today and pinned her down and threw myself on her and thrust again and again more with anger then desire at first. There was magic in what we did and magic I knew was evil. But desire overcame me. I rose high high high on the current of pheromone paSSion. My vehemence astonished her then won her over and we were riding the wave together now and leaping and bucking the way whales make love, frantically swimming to maintain their balance in the swell of the sea. Then we switched sides and she reared above me a sea horse whinnying. Oh she smelled. of the sea with the wind high and the fish silvery in the nets. Oh she held me clasped me close as a starfish cracking a clam. Oh we burned we were on fire on the water. She contained me utterly. It was love as I had never known it consuming and consuming until at last at long last when I could bear it no more I burst I spurted I screamed out words that made no sense and we lay suddenly still.

And then after a time I felt her moving in my arms. The taste of greasepaint and her sweat was on my lips. "You love me," she told me. "We will live for each other now. We will thrive. One day we will rule." And I could only smile and agree because she spoke of things outside the realm of my understanding and because I was overwhelmed by the afterglow. I had not known before that quiet joy could follow such violence. And so I only smiled. We stayed almost completely still I don't know how long. Until I realized with a start that I had almost forgotten about Skalt-i 1

"Don't try," she said. "Don't ruin everything. If you undo one tiny element of our heritage, the whole may come tumbling down."

"I don't understand these things, Mother," I said.

"You must!" she said peremptorily.

I only smiled again. She was relieved, thinking I had acquiesced. I let her think so. I didn't want her to think me ungrateful, or worse still a freak, a mental aberration from whom the right to be Draus might be withdrawn.

Then we emerged, our bodies smudged, the paints all running into each other, hands held tight, to rapturous applause. I clutched the balled-up toilet paper in my fist.

I faced the king. The king beamed with pleasure, and I ran up to receive his embrace of welcome.

TEN

It was my special mother who first spoke the words which I came to know were a ritual formula for this occasion: "Your son is a man and more than a man. I declare that he is a true vessel of the seed of the john and jane of our house." Her voice rang out on the rooftop where they sat, the tribunal and the mothers and sisters and brothers. Now I saw that they had rolled up the walls and canopy of windowstuff so that the wind would dissipate the leftover chaotic fragrances of the pheromone recital. It was time for me to be bold. My mother had announced to the whole house that I was a man and more than a man. I approached my father confidently and though I fell prostrate as was the custom I did not bend my head quite so low and I looked up at his face, my face.

My father said, "I'm proud of you. I think the tribunal will agree with me that your performance has been exemplary. I'm supposed to grant you a wish now.

Anything at all. Within the limits of the law," he added. I knew then that it was useless to ask for Skart's life. But I had a plan. "What is that in your hand?"

"Just toilet paper, Father," I said.

"Well, fold it up and put it away, son. This is a solemn occasion. I want you looking splendid. Nothing slapdash."

He turned to clap his hand. An attendant came forward with another cloak. Mine was in tatters from the predations of my mother's desire. I took the cloak from him and threw it over my shoulder. "That's my son," said my father. I turned away from him. I looked out over the sea. The tide was out now. There it was. The sunken city reborn from the sea and awash with moonlight. Sp it was that I knew twenty-four hours had barely elapsed since the time I decided to sneak down to the third floor. And then I saw Skart. The embalming fluid was maybe up to his waist now. I steeled myself to look. I had to look. I turned to my father again and even he recoiled from the blaze of anger he saw in my *eyes.* I saw him flinch. I knew even then that he was not omnipotent.

"You will not ask me *that!*" my father said. Whispering in the aisles. The wind rose. I felt bold, I who had come to know my mother and fulfilled my brother's broken dream. But I knew I could not demand Skart's freedom. My mother had taught me the first lesson of my maturity. I must not break the fabric of our society right away. First I must try to bend it. Drip, drip, drip, the fluid oozed into Skart's urn. No one looked at him. They looked at the good things: my father majestic on his throne of power, my mother proud in her holographic mask of a she-wolf, me lithe and young and already strong with my Draus face framed by the flapping cloak and the wind-whipped milk-white hair. I must speak quickly before the fluid reached his face and suffocated him. Already the fumes must be intolerable. His eyes were glazed and his skin seemed like rubber.

"I do not ask for my brother's life," I said. I could feel the shifting of feet and the mumbling of the courtiers. I spoke more softly now because I wanted them to strain to hear me. "But since I now possess the three gifts, I ask that I be allowed to bestow the Gift of Death. Father, let this be my first act as your son."

The murmuring came louder now. I scrutinized my father's face. If it showed anger I was doomed, Skart was doomed, maybe even my mother, whose name I did not even know yet. My mother's wolf-mask seemed to become more intense, more shiny. She had turned up the field to deflect as much as possible from her face. My father held up his hand. Silence fell suddenly and all I could hear now was the wind howling and the rhythm of the windmills' wheezing. The tension was intolerable. I knew that the crowd was as hungry for my death-sentence as it was for me to be proclaimed the next of the Drauses.

It was then that I noticed that the king was holding back laughter.

Now it burst. The court was catching his mood, laughing too. My father took my shoulders and lifted me to my feet and embraced me and said in a loud voice, "My new son is compassionate. He understands pain. He doesn't wish his brother to suffer, and has offered to name himself the manner of Skart's death. What a heart! Of such a ruler Dreambreak will be proud."

A hush fell over them, for my father had as good as named the next king. My blood ran cold. I had to speak now, while the embalming fluid had still not reached my brother's face and had not seeped too deep into his pores. "Father," I said, "I want Skart to be sent to Cruise Eternity."

I couldn't even hear the wind. It had died down just for that moment. A gasp from my mother's throat. I knew she saw it all draining into toilet paper, all her aspirations and dreams of controlling the throne.

"Irregular," was all my father said. For the first time he seemed displeased. Abruptly he turned to the tribunal and said, "Verdict!"

The oldest of the Tribunal of the Three Gifts rose and said, "Cruise Eternity is not death, king. The young prince must name some other penalty."

The king turned back to me and shrugged as if to say that it was out of his hands, there was nothing he could do.

The crowd started to murmur again, thinking the brief confrontation over. Then I pulled the toilet paper from my cloak and thrust it at my father. "They're wrong," I said. "Listen to this poem my brother wrote. He uses Cruise Eternity as a metaphor for death. He will not wake up in our time." I lied a little there, because I remembered that the alien had taught me that Cruise Eternity was due for revival in only four years. That was when the time tourists would be let out to gawk at what the world had become in our century. "He will be frozen in a state like death. If it is death to him then it is as good as real death. Poetry is truth, isn't it? Any pheromonist will tell you his concoction's not only as good as the real emotion, it is the real emotion." And I held the paper to my father's ear. When he heard the opening words he blanched and then became visibly angry.

"This is nonsense," he said. "Continue the execution." I turned to the tribunal, my hands upraised in appeal. I had far overstepped myself. Perhaps I was guilty of a public breach of honor, in which case I might as well join my brother now, for I would never be king.

The fluid was on the brink of touching my brother's lips.

The Tribunal of the Three Gifts was conferring in whispers. The old man got up again and said in a faint voice, "King, we find that the prince's request is within the bounds of the Three Gifts and may, if you wish, be granted. It is consistent with the spirit in which the Three Gifts were conceived."

The king sat heavily on his throne. "Why do you have to put the burden on me?" he shouted at the old man. "It's up to you to decide, not me. I uphold the law, I don't make it." A long pause. Then, "Oh, very well, have your way. You're my son, I'm proud of you, it makes no difference anyway, and you deserve a little slack after all you've gone through today. Release him," he said, pointing to the urn.

And then I saw Anskowl's face and I knew in the deepest part of me that this was my enemy. We exchanged no words but said it all in silence. Hate tastes like a fish bone in the throat.

But for the present Anskowl obeyed my father. He moved swiftly across the flagstones to where the urn rested and waved his hands over the spigot of embalming fluid and muttered some secret words. It looked like magic but could not be, of course. Perhaps the mechanism was keyed to his voice. He drew a piece of paper from a pouch (it was like toilet paper but silvery in color and texture) and'ldropped it into the urn. It drained away the liquid almost 'instantly, no doubt consigning it to the same planet in some other universe where the shit of us royals constantly rains from the sky. Then he took a little awl from the pouch and tapped the urn lightly with it. The glass shattered and my brother stood before us naked and shivering with the cold. I ran to him, almost forgetting the gravity of what I'd gotten myself into.

"Here," I said, "take the cloak, I don't mind." I tore it off my shoulders and threw it over him. He made no move to fasten it.

I waited eagerly. I think I expected gratitude, I expected some maudlin show of emotion. Instead he looked at me first in astonishment and then with utter hate. I think it was hate because it was like the way Anskowl had looked at me seconds before, and I knew that was how I had glared at the Picklemaster.

My brother said, "Can't you leave anything alone? You've stolen from me even the dignity of my death. I'll never forgive you. When I wake up a hundred years from now or whatever it is you'll be dead and I'll still hate you."

"I thought, I thought, you'd, no, it's not gratitude I expected but I thought I should do something because you'd lived all those years with me knowing this was coming and not telling me and," I said, "and, and, and."

I didn't get to finish. I couldn't have said anything coherent anyway. I didn't know what I was thinking or what I was supposed to think. I wanted to somehow redeem myself by saving Skart but he wanted nothing to do with it. Before I could try to get my thoughts together, the king spoke again.

"So now you know, kid. What it's like. To fool around with customs that have been established since time immemorial, to try and tamper with the way things work. I understand, Morry, believe me. But now," he paused so that the whole court could hear the import of his words, "you must do a small penance for interfering with tradition. Cruise Eternity is far from my kingdom. It is some miles upriver. Since you have decreed Skart's fate, you will lead the expedition to Cruise Eternity. I'll have this done in style. I'll not have my flesh and blood waiting in line to get in. Before you go you'll select some gems and cowrie shells from the treasury so that you can pay the robots who run the thing. Consider this a diplomatic mission, Morry. I'm raising you to ambassador for the duration. But you will relinquish that rank as soon as you get home, it's just to make sure you're not attacked by anyone from the other kingdoms, since they all honor the pact. And, one of my daughters will travel with you. Someone expendable." He pointed at my mother, who stiffened and bowed down to him. "Take good care of him," he told her. "I love my son."

No one knew what to make of it. In the same speech he had both condemned me and raised me to the rank of ambassador. He had berated me for my stupidity yet said with simple candor, "I love my son." The pundits would be interpreting' his utterance for weeks or maybe months, trying to figure out how I stood in relation to the succession and how much deference to give me. I was to learn this later from my mother.

He wasn't quite finished. "Now listen, my boy," he said, this time for me alone, for he lowered his voice so that only those closest to us could hear. "You've really been indulged today. I want no more irregular behavior from now on. Especially I don't want any breaches of honor or invocations of subtle interpretations of the Three Gifts. You'll get no more leeway, do you hear? Sure, you're allowed one mistake. But fuck I say fuck, the next mistake will get you kicked out of this kingdom. I mean it."

"Yes," I said, "Father."

Then he said, for all to hear, "Enough of weighty matters. Let's go back to feasting!" There was a burst of reticent but heartfelt applause. Fresh food was being carried in as I turned to find my brother. As usual I was too late. They'd already taken him away. I would have to wait until dawn.

My mother was beside me now. "Do you want to eat, or?" she said. "I think we should get out of here. You've gotten us into enough trouble already."

"Are you angry?"

"Yes. I am so fucking angry I could pitch you over the side of the kingdom." She took my hand. We walked away from the festivities. No one noticed. Or if they did, thought nothing of it. The spectacle of my defiance was over. We reached the edge of the roof, the edge that faced the sea.

"There are no pheromone symphonies playing now," she said, "nothing to whip us into a frenzy of lust. Do you still feel anything?"

I looked out at the drowned star city. "Why is everyone so angry with me? I did what I thought was best."

"The city is beautiful," she said. "Do you often look at it?

I haven't, not for years. But now that I have loved my son, I see it—"

"With new eyes?" I thought ofJonellys, waiting for me downstairs in the cold room. It must be completely dark to her now, since the chill night had begun.

"Yes. Yes."

She pulled me close to her. Again I kissed her, chastely at first. But I could not stop at that. It had not been just the music that had given me this desire. Again we made love, and again. It dulled the edge of my grief. Then we cooled off in the wind, the starlight soft on her features which were mine.

ELEVEN

The drowned star city wavers in the sea that is cloaked and choked with mist. The drowned star city bums in the dawnlight copper gold sear vermillion streak the dying sea oh drown, oh, drown. Oh, drown, it is a dream because the drowned star city hovers toylike in the palm of my hand and my hand itself is the fire that surges out of the dead waters, surges surges. Could the drowned star city undrown itself, unplunge from the dark dread salt, unfall, unravel the killed past, undie?

How can I know? It must be a dream.

At last in my room I slept.

And woke.

I shook Jonellys who lay at the foot of the sofabed. "You have to come now. Come. Now."

She followed me. I looked only briefly at dawn that had broken over the sea and only for a moment sniffed the wind. We took the elevator to the seventh floor, a bleak and plaster-peeling floor where no one lived except the robot sentinels, cyclopeans with ever-whirling floodlit eyes. The skywalk that crossed over to Savage-isSpeared was heavily guarded.

"Jonellys! Tell me what you can see."

"Not much. Rectangular patches. Something bright."

They were the bay windows that overlooked and overlook the Mutant River. "Little round fuzzy things, receding. " The eyes of the sentinels. "Where are we?" Then, "No!" We had reached the balcony where the catwalk began. "I know this is the seventh floor because we're out in the open but it doesn't sound like we're below, it sounds high up. You're banishing me, aren't you?"

Her directness mafes me want to evade. But I can't evade because I hold the Three Gifts. "Don't think of it as banishment. Among the Velk, a refugee from the other kingdoms is welcomed." This is what the alien had told me. "They'll fIx you. You'll see again. You'll love again. You'll forget," I said, knowing she would not because the things fIrst fIxed on never leave men's hearts.

"You're going to cut me loose? With my inhuman eyes and all? Morry, why?"

How could I explain to her what kind of a vision I was having? I barely understood it. What could the dream mean and how could I dream of dragging the drowned star city back to the sky? But I knew the Fire-eyes would undo the damage done to Jonellys's body. It was magic but I was already beginning to learn that magic was relative. Maybe it was only magic because we didn't understand it. It was a subversive thought and I didn't dare say it aloud. So all I said was: "Go! I command ...as ..."

"Don't say it." She lifted a finger and found my lips somehow perhaps from the aura of my cold cold breath. "Please don't. Don't say that I'm leaving behind my home and my people and everything I know because you command as Draus, royal words, four tiny empty words. No.

Say I go of my own free will because" (she could hardly speak the next few words) "I love you."

"I will see you again." I couldn't believe it, didn't dare to.

"Yes." I heard the hope in her voice. I couldn't bring myself to dampen it. I held her hand as we walked to where the skywalk began. It was covered and cool. Ahead at the end of the tunnel I could see a small circle of light (I knew she could sense it too) and she was already moving toward it without help from me. I tried to hold her back in fact but she was already slipping from my hands like salt water sliding through a clump of seaweed.

And halfway over she stopped and turned to look. I don't know ifshe saw me. I was standing away from the midmorning glare.

"Goodbye, Morry Draus."

Her voice barely sounded above the whisper of waters. I didn't answer her. I had a grand scheme. To find her and pluck her back from among the Fire-eyes with her body made whole by magic yes and to force the king to bestow legitimacy on her, yes, yes, after studying the interpretation of the Three Gifts carefully, or becoming king myself, yes but that was only the edge of the grand scheme. There was a wrongness in my kingdom but to change the kingdom I would have to change the king. Become the king.

Become the king!

From child to king was a tremendous leap of the imagination. I'm a fool, I told myself. The dreams are already evaporating with the dawnlight. I went to find my mother.

TWELVE

On the morning after the day that everything changed, we cast off from the riverside pier. My mother and Skart and my alien tutor, who had come to lecture me on the sights. And robot rowers who couldn't speak and a herald who stood in front and now and then blew three long notes and hit his drum to show that we had diplomatic immunity. I had never left the kingdom. The only one among us who had was the alien.

My brother was handcuffed to the stem. He was the only one of us who wasn't masked. My mother sat on a low table with her green cloak billowing behind and touching the water. Already the woven kelp was becoming waterlogged. I wore only the body stripes of an ambassador, and a red circle around my heart and my genitals to show I was unarmed. Dawn. The kingdom was completely an island.

I was the last to step on. The hoverengines hummed and the rowers clanked and cranked themselves to action.

"Skart," I said. "Skart, Skart."

He looked steadfastly out over the river. The water was black and littered with dead fish and disused magical devices. I went up close to Skart so that no one would hear me and I whispered, "Skart, Skart, it's all a ruse, you'll only be in amniosis for four years, and then they'll let the time tourists out and then you can escape and I'll be waiting for you."

But he didn't answer me.

On the right we passed the Lepers' Desert. The lepers stood by the bank with their bodies rotting and they jeered as we drifted past. This was the place Anskowl had chosen for Jonellys after she had been tortured to the brink of death. I ha£ never seen so many people in one place, and all of them deformed, twisted, and most not twisted by nature but by the hand of Anskowl and Anskowl's people.

On the left rose the ruined palaces that ringed the kingdom of Savage-is-Speared. My tutor summoned me to raise his bottle up so that he could get a good view of what lay ahead. He changed his name whenever we passed a new landmark.

"Here is the beginning of a lake of glass," he would say, "and my name is Irk-me—not. It was a beach once, but it became fused."

I saw it only vaguely through the mass of stilted huts that rose from the river. Children stared with big eyes in long faces. Sometimes they dived naked into the water and swam behind us. They were not much different from our own, who danced and dance nightly on the fishnet in the sea.

"Look!" he said again, "while I change my name to Strachamonda! Up there! Ahead! The tower of Cruise Eternity can already be seen. Do you not see it? Shaped like a starship in a dream. No true starships have ever looked like that, sleek and silvery and many-finned. True starships come shaped like an octopus or a discus or a drowned city, not as the concretization of men's phallic thrusting toward uncertain futures, no, no, no. This is the starship of fantasy."

And this is what I saw rear up sheer-flanked and glittery from the pubic fuzz of a shantytown. And my brother looked and for a moment and a moment only his eyes came to life but when I tried to draw him into conversation he murmured only, "Puck I say fuck and let me die."

Cruise Eternity is not within a designated kingdom. The shanties are the homes of the world's refuse. The street that leads to the gates of the starship winds uphill a little, but the hill is a hill of dead metal things, and inside the dead metal eyes that watch out of cavernous darknesses and creatures that flit. In the shanties they remember the future and forget the past, because remembering what cannot be is all that is left to them.

The herald walked ahead. I clutched my tutor and my mother followed me, and last of all came Skart, cuffed between two robots, half-walking and half-carried. A final robot carried the payment for Skart's voyage, two sacks of predous metals salvaged over centuries from the flesh of dead fish.

We reached those gates. I read through the papers, signed them with a glance at the retinal scanner. Watched them unmanacle my brother and walk him into the silvered shadows within. We exchanged no more words.

"You are angry," my alien tutor said as we turned back.

"Yes!" I said. "I've lost my soul. You have to tell me if I can ever get it back. You know all the answers. You're an alien. You've been up there and breathed an alien air and touched an alien soil. You have to know."

"But only if you call me Upside-down."

"What kind of a name is that?"

"Look to your dreams. To commoners, dreams are but idylls, but the truth can come to kings in their dreams."

We walked back to the skiff and I fell asleep once more as we turned home, rocked by the rhythm of the rowers and tasting the music of a lullaby in my nostrils as my mother's plectrum picked at a pheromone koto.

And this is how I dreamed.

I will part the waters! The stars will begin once more at the edge of ocean! I am the one who will break and remake, the perfect molding who will shatter the mold! Oh, such a potent dream for a powerless child, who has tasted in twenty-four hours love and death and betrayal and kingship and rebirth, oh, who has lived the world's history in the span of a day. How can I dream these things?

I stirred. The arms around me were my mother's arms. The pheromones of night wafted over me and returned me to slumber however hard I forced myself to open my eyes.

"Sleep, sleep, Morry, sleep," she whispered.

I see the john and the jane smile down at me.

And another piece of the great plan falls into place as we reach the dock that leads back to my father's kingdom and I wake once more from my dream of the drowned star city.

—Los Angeles, 1985-1991

The Last Line of the Haiku

Spring, 2022

The million-year silence between man and the whale was. first broken on April 3, 2022. This did not result from the painsJ taking teamwork of cryptolinguists and zoologists, for humanity; had for the most part given up such lines of research as did not meet its immediate and very urgent needs; nor was it some lone, half-crazed genius, struggling for decades to communicate with the great aliens who share this planet, who was first to stumble upon one of the most well-concealed secrets of the universe ... Instead, this story deals with a young, mildly attractive girl on her first journey abroad, aboard an insignificant fishing vessel (one of the few remaining of its kind) that set sail from Beppu, the City of Seven Hells as the long dead tourists called it, which is a port in the shadow of the volcano Asoyama, on the startlingly." bright green island of Kyushu, a surprising jewel erupting fromil the poisoned Pacific.

Ryoko was alone on deck when it happened. She was following her father's command, which was always to keep

her eyes and ears open: *for there are whole continents outside Japan, my dear.* She had laughed inwardly at his solemnity, but went, an obedient girl.

They were far too respectful of her, though since she was Minister Ishida's daughter, and so she had been lonely almost all the time. The first weeks she was sick every day and stayed in the vessel's one minimally sumptuous cabin, which they had set aside for her. When she was better, they wanted to show her everything. The boat was powered by sail in the ancient way, and sometimes by electricity. It was, of course, no longer used fort fishing. How it worked did not interest her, and she only wanted to see land again and not have to stand on a ground that swayed to a timeless music not of her choosing. So they left her mostly to herself.

Turning from their work, they would sometimes see her pass by, one hand caressing the soggy railings, humming some wailing melody from the classics, for she was quite a scholar, or she would be staring, hypnotized, at some imagined strip of land just beyond the boundaries of her vision.

This time she had been standing for nearly an hour. The boat was hardly moving. She stood stock still, like a statue, her mind lulled by the patterned dancing of light on the water. It was almost evening when the sea crashed open and a great black island stared back at her.

She started.

It was a whale.

She could not tell which species, for so far as she knew all of them were virtually extinct. She saw only his hugeness— he was big as the boat at least—and how he thrust the water from him with such terrible force, how he sprang imperious from the swirl with a movement so charged with life that it seemed to fling aside all the hopelessness of the times.

She loved him, then; she was terrified of him, too; and she feared for him, knowing that the oceans were seething with radioactive poisons. And she remembered the sad haiku an old monk had written at the close of the last century, after the

Treaty of San Diego:

> *Oh, Oh, the darkness!*
> *The fishes have left the sea*
> *in the midst of spring.*

and because she was bereft of words she began to hum quietly to herself, and because she was lonely she hoped he could understand her.

But then the whale spoke to her, calling her by name: "Ryoko." It was a liquid murmur that seemed to emanate from the water itself; totally inhuman, rich and elemental. It called out to her as from an unremembered past, and dispelled her terror.

"Ryoko," the water said, and Ryoko was reminded that before the Millennial War there had been scientists who had concluded that the intelligence of whales might be far higher than that of humans ...but who's to understand what it thinks, then? she thought. It's an alien, there are no common referents in our environments, probably not even space and time.

"So why are you speaking to me?" she ventured, "and why haven't you communicated with us before?"

He disappeared from sight, and the empty waves whispered: "The first is simple. I am creating sound waves by telekinesis. Our intelligence is not one of hands or tools. To the second question: you do not know what you ask."

He rose again from the depths, shadowy and shapeless in the twilight. Telekinesis, she thought: then why didn't they command the harpoons of the ancient hunters to fall useless into the sea? "It was irrelevant!" the water thundered.

"On our history tapes I saw my forefathers killing yours by millions, in the days before the Millennial War."

"Child, oh child: you are mayflies that fizzle in the

sunlight, cherry blossoms that sparkle when their corpses litter the grass. Your conceptualization of death is so innocent; you do not understand it as I do, and your people's reaction to it is rooted in ignorance and emotional immaturity. No, life is not one of our primary pursuits. A beautiful death is the supreme joy, the supreme achievement of intelligence; life only exists as a necessity for it."

Ryoko's heart leapt with understanding.

"We consecrated ourselves to death many millennia ago, Ryoko. It was a game."

I know about this death, she thought. It is what makes us different from the other races, it's why the whale has come to one of us. My people worship death: the beautiful suicide of young lovers, the noble death of a warrior in the spring. It's the ultimate beauty that pains the heart.

"Child, we must help one another, now."

A breeze came, a sudden chill. There was, almost, no sun.

"Help? How?"

"It concerns survival," said the whale. "You humans have not played fairly in the game of life and death.

"We thought we had outgrown our desire for life. We had set our thoughts on eternity, on breaking through the barriers of the material. But when the survival of *all* came into question—well, even we have not the all-embracing wisdom to accept this. We are, it seems, still mortal, still bound by our animalness—" he seemed to hesitate. "It is difficult to communicate this to a creature without the concepts …

"Even you will not survive, and most of the animals are already dead."

"No, no," said Ryoko. "My father says some of us will survive." But she thought: Survival is relative. And the whale—again he seemed to have read her thoughts—said, "Yes, and we shall all survive, if you do as I say."

"You ask *us* to help you; your killers."

"Yes, yes, and you shall know why, when the time comes, later."

The whale paused; in the darkness she heard water churning, and she wrapped her arms around herself to ward off the cold. She sensed the compassion in him, and loved him still more.

"But what must I do?"

"Tell your father that he and his cabinet must come to the harbor at Yokohama in six months' time. We will meet there, to discuss what they are building."

"Building? What could my father be building? And don't you have the power to control matter? If you need something built, can't you build it yourselves, even without tools?"

And she knew the answer even before it came.

"We are not builders," said the whale, "but dreamers." And he dove into the dark water and was gone. For a long while she stared after him, shivering a little.

"Miss Ishida?" came a voice, startling her. She whirled round. It was only the captain, telling her she would be ill if she remained. At first she did not answer him, and because he was sorry for her, he stood beside her and showed her the stars, giving them fanciful names out of old myths. She looked up politely, not wishing to offend, and pretended to be impressed at his knowledge, but she knew also that some of the stars were artifacts from the past, still directing their lethal radiation at long-perished targets.

Afterwards they went inside, and she found herself of a surprisingly friendly disposition toward the crew, and they sat talking of little things; but she mentioned the important thing to no one.

From there it was a month's journey to Hawaii, where Ryoko saw enormous charred skyscrapers, black skeletons of hubris bloodstained by the setting sun, and also a fused sheet of glass many kilometers long that dazzled her eyes and brought the tears to them, and she visited the hall where the young mutants lived and the hospitals where they lay dying. Their deaths were not beautiful. She also saw the great crater inside Halemaumau, the one not put there by nature, and the cliffs that had been ripped asunder. She had never understood these things; it was all before she was born. But she began to realize why her father had sent her on this journey, had insisted that it would make her ready for life.

She heard that Hawaii was nothing compared to the devastation on the American continents, and on the way back when they were in Shanghai for a few days, she saw a level desert that stretched in every direction, and then was jostled by beggars whose faces were torn to the bone, and glimpsed a few of those others, those who had grown fat on forbidden flesh. She understood despair for the first time, and clung ever more fiercely to the whale's enigmatic promise of hope.

At night she would sometimes come out on deck to watch for him. He never reappeared to answer the hundred questions she had for him, but occasionally she would hear the high whinings, the reverberant hummings, the throbbing deep tones that were the whale's song, sounds alien and compelling, like the music of the old *Noh* plays. But usually there was nothing; no gulls cried over the waters.

She became aware that because of the things she, had seen, she would be returning to her father no longer a girl.

Summer, 2022

Her father always used the diminutive with her. "Not a word, , Ryochan," he said, "not a word until I've looked my fill at the Fujisan …no, no, not a word."

He took her hand to steady himself, bent to unbutton his archaic tweed overcoat because of the heat, and allowed her to lead him across the flags toned plaza, past the grandiose, disused marble fountain into the disheveled shade of a cluster of trees. Ueno was still a comparative oasis in the clutter of Tokyo; somehow the great Quake of '89 had left it alone. There were low buildings on all sides of the square, seventy or eighty years old,) which seemed not to belong to the present, but to emerge out of a trans-temporal haze; moss-veins had fuzzed their outlines, and the torrid sunshine would not lighten their gloom.

Ryoko noticed a big signboard to her left, where patina'd metal gates had been clumsily boarded over. It was written, not in the usual roman letters, but in the elaborate ideographic kanji of the twentieth century:

Notice: Ark Project.

Ueno Zoo has been closed. owing to the recent decision of the Survival Ministry to ship the animals to an environmental reconstruction project in Kenya, American East Africa. Your patience and forbearance is craved.

Signed:

Akiro Ishida, *Minister for Survival*

"A new project, otosan?" she asked him. although she did not wish to talk of generalities, really; she was full of the message she must give him, and for a moment the roar of the waves was vivid in her memory. but she sensed the time was not quite ripe. Better to let her father relax. see what he had come to see, first.

They stood in front of the sign. Someone had scrawled, beneath the signature, in roman letters: "I can't read this old writing!"

"Well," Ryoko laughed, "after fifteen years of Back to

History, people will still be living out their Americanized fantasies of progress."

"Let's go," said her father, "it's hot, a very hot summer. The museum might be air conditioned by now …"

"Well, perhaps it was an immigrant," she said to herself, her eyes lingering on the sign. "It was a wise plan of you Ministry's, father, to strengthen our survival by reviving our Japaneseness, to conjure up the past when we haven't much of a future."

"Oh, it didn't work, Ryochan," her father mumbled, "and the animals are all dead in Africa."

"Everything is so beautiful now, father …do you remember the cherry blossoms on the drive to the park? It must be the impending world-death, heightening everything …"

"The new mutated plague-virus got them when they arrived, we hadn't counted on it reaching Kenya from across the Atlantic so soon …" He saw they were not communicating, and began to walk—quite briskly for his age—across the street to the museum which had been one of the world's wonders in the twentieth century.

But before they went in he turned to her and said diffidently, "I am sorry not to have seen anything of you or talked to you since you came back. I'm glad we can have this time together."

Ryoko suppressed a twinge of impatience, and appraised him silently in return: an old man, a wisp of a man, a small man, an unsteady man, a man of power.

They walked past interminable corridors, past listless guards with stiff hands and dead eyes, and he chattered on about this and that, so that she sensed beneath his well-schooled superficiality some unspoken disquiet.

He needs me, she thought: but he would lose face by saying so to me, a woman, his only child.

Fujisan stood by itself in a glass case. It was a brown, blotchy vessel irregularly streaked with a dull white; misshapen, crooked, by any conceivable non-Japanese standards-ugly. It was—and remains—the ultimate teabowl: the supremely perfect imperfection.

When the two of them had gazed for several long moments, they were overwhelmed, close to tears.

And after, in a little coffee-shop called *The San Diego Treaty.* which served a passable synthetic coffee and had its waitresses charmingly attired in pre-war two-ply polyvinyl tunics. they each had a cup of "blue mountain"—whatever the name. it all came from the same laboratory—and Minister Ishida listened to his daughter's story. He heard the whole thing out, without interruption.

"What strikes me now is that the whale was so Japanese, h spoke about death the way a Japanese might. I'm sure he would understand Fujisan, too, and the tea ceremony, and all the things the old gaijin experts found so bafflingly alien about our culture … Father, you don't believe me."

He sipped his coffee. "Did anyone else see it? Was it not a hallucination, a dream?"

"No! …you don't believe me."

"Ryochan—" he lowered his voice. "Our ministry's Back to History proclamations, the cultural revival programs, the renascence of the old life patterns … what do you feel about these things?"

"What does it matter, father? Oh well; these things may amuse the people. What few remain of them. I see there was another suicide wave in my absence." Then she said slowly: "Our culture has never been significantly influenced, even by the surface Americanization of the old days. I don't think what your Ministry is doing is really relevant, otosan."

"Your trip has cleared your mind, I think. You're right, our entire program is a coverup. Despite our support for every form of suicide, especially the traditional forms like seppuku, we really are working for another kind of survival …a nd there is no way, of course, short of totally altering the environment, before the great plague takes us all."

With a flicker of earnestness, he continued: "So we have to find a new environment."

And I know, thought Ryoko, what that environment will be: the land of shadow. Honor would survive identity. So she said, "The whale came to the right source, then. He knew things I did not know."

"Yes."

"Still, you don't believe me."

"Your mother came back from Hokkaido a fortnight ago, Ryochan, your mother whom you've hardly seen since I divorced , her. She has caught the plague—there isn't a town in the North without one or two cases."

Why did he not concentrate on the subject? "Father, I'm sorry," she said, not without irony. Somehow he seemed so spent, so ineffectual. But the memory of the whale was vivid to her, and she could only feel an annoyance at him for not reacting with the proper urgency. He was avoiding an answer, he did not believe her. Well, she would withhold her sympathy.

"You don't believe me," she said, edgily.

"What choice do I have?" her father said, suddenly emotional. "How could my own child lie to make me lose face?"

Her hand shook. She drained her cup and set it down. Her father was paying the bill—six million yen—with a ten million credit note, and was getting up without waiting for the change.

At the corner, the chauffeur, an American immigrant, was holding open the door of the black electric Toyota.

They were silent on the drive home. They passed

immaculately desolate streets, past the empty department stores and the blind traffic lights, and she began to suspect him of knowing much more than he had cared to say. He had seemed so unsurprised at it all.

There were still three months left, before they would have to face the whale again, together.

There is a little island, thought Minister Ishida, pushed out of the sea by a volcano, twenty, thirty years ago, several hundred kilometers north of Hokkaido. On what happens there, everything depends, everything.

The driver took them up the ill-kept ramp on to the Shuto Overpass. The Minister sat well back as the car rattled across cracked pavement and clumps of lichen. He felt his daughter's presence: pensive, quiet. She had grown very comely; in her classic kimono, she was almost beautiful. He loved her, though he could not bring himself to say so.

She is wise, he thought; in the old days when they had computers and universities, she might have made a talented poetess, an observer of truths. But the sea has returned her to me a stranger; not soft as before, but strong-willed, a little alien, even. Today, she defied me, challenged my belief in her.

If she were not telling the truth, she could not have changed so much. So I believe her.

I was over fifty years old when she was born. But I could swear that her thoughts and attitudes come from a more distant past then I can remember. She's so quintessentially Japanese, so much that she doesn't understand what I mean by *survival*.

She thinks that our *survival* is really a euphemism for death, and that my Ministry, like the other two, is' essentially a religion.

But why don't I want to die? he thought ...like the others? Am I too Westernized to feel the need to take. in honor, the consequences of mankind's evil?

There is an island, though …

His mind wandered; age was beginning to touch him at last.

They had come to a cleared up stretch of the Overpass, and Tokyo's clashing garishness kaleidoscoped about his eyes, even through the smog.

Not *spiritual* survival! he thought, Corporeal, factual, *literal* survival.

My hopes are on this island alone, this secret island, where they are building the tall spacecraft, this island from which one day they will burst into the sky to rendezvous with an abandoned prototype starship of the Russians that has waited, passengerless, in orbit for forty years to begin a journey of four thousand years, where the arrivers will have no memory of the departers, nor of earth.

What could the whale want with me? He knew it must concern his project.

The intelligence of whales came as no surprise to him; but why would they take the trouble to make contact with man? It violated the purity of his image of them—for he had never seen one, nor even a photograph, and they were to him like dragons or phoenixes, creatures of dream and myth—and he was sure that they were meant as creatures apart, ineffable, beyond man, living amidst events and emotions as transcendent as they were incommunicable.

And now, they wanted to do something to his spaceship.

He turned to see his daughter speaking with him, but he heard nothing at all, because the silence tablet he had swallowed earlier was beginning to take effect.

Autumn, 2022

They are, Ryoko thought, like three pathetic old women, parasitically consumed by their glitter—heavy ceremonial robes.

Her father was there, and Kawaguchi, the Minister of Comfort, and Takahashi, the Minister of Ending, patron of suicides. Their oversized robes flapped against their chests and billowed out behind with the strong wind from the sea. They were abrupt splashes of color in the ashen expanse of sand, sea, and sky.

Ryoko watched them carefully, but as was seemly for a woman, she stood some distance off, not intruding on the men.

There were some others, too, on the beach: a dirty old beach scavenger, tethering his rickety boat to a post; two little girls, kicking a rusty can; a mangy cat, sniffing among scatterings of refuse … but all the images were lost in the grayness, and all the sounds dispersed in the slow susurration of the surf.

Behind her, far behind her, broken warehouses of worn concrete, a century old.

She heard them softly bickering; not indecorously, but with undertones of menace. "Has he perhaps brought us here for no reason?" Kawaguchi asked.

The Minister of Ending, tall and sacerdotal in sacramental mitre and in purple and gold, looked steadfastly at the sand as he declared: "I have no opinion; I have come as a favor to Ishida." Clearly, this was untrue; he had come to see his colleague lose face.

"But might this not be ridiculous?" came Kawaguchi's feeble, edgy tenor. Minister Ishida remained aloof. After all, he was the only one with anything to lose. If the whale doesn't come, thought Ryoko, my father may have to kill himself.

They waited.

Until evening fell again. Then again the water burst asunder in the mid distance, and the blackness loomed out of the water, distorting all perspective. The three Ministers gaped in unison. The old scavenger, gripped by terror, whimpered quietly. Only the two children were unconcerned, and went on kicking the can.

Ryoko felt a surge of tremendous love for him, and she trembled at the grace of him, creature of twilight, leaping from the dark water in a perfect poised arc that mocked gravity for a moment. There was pain, too, with this joy, this beauty made unbearable by its transience. And the bittersweet pungent wavewind swept her face, and she yearned to be like him, to live with his intensity and fierceness, a life-force battling inexorable death.

The same voice came to her that she had heard from the ship half a year before, but amplified, like thunder and a waterfall. *Come! Come!* it cried.

She heard Kawaguchi's voice: "The whale does not speak, Minister Ishida."

Ishida: "Wait." The first word he had spoken.

"But I hear him!" she said.

Come! Come! the voice sang, and it was whale-singing mixed with the music of Noh and Kabuki and Bugaku, eerie; and hypnotic, and she felt herself yielding, yielding beneath its spell, her body moving of its own volition towards the soft water …

Kawaguchi said (she heard him only faintly) "The whale has not spoken, Minister Ishida. I think we may leave."

A shriek: "Your daughter! She'll drown!"

"But I hear him, but I hear him, but I hear him," she screamed desperately, as the others' voices faded into the roar of the waves.

"My daughter!"

"Old man, old man, lend us your boat, quickly!"

"B-b-but—"

"How dare you argue with the Minister for Survival?"

"*Hai, hai, irashaimasse,*" a frightened old voice, remembering his place and remembering the ceremonial forms of address in time ...

She gave herself into the arms of darkness. The whale's consciousness touched hers, led her into the warmth. A lone gull cried above the thunder. The water parted for her like blankets.

There was no cold in the water, only a profound joy, a release from turmoil, a peace, a foretaste of death.

She was a tiny consciousness enveloped in vastness. She emerged, standing on the waves, buoyed up firmly by an impalpable force ... as from an immeasurably distanced vantage point, she perceived the wetness of the waves and wind which never touched her. The mind in which she had become imbedded was a cavern, an abyss, a cathedral dome, full of compassion and mystery.

Her voice sang out the whale's thoughts.

For some moments, she struggled to regain control of her body; but she gave herself up to the joy of helplessness, like a child on a plummeting rollercoaster.

" ...she's walking on the water!" a tremulous old voice. The little rowboat came into view, the three Ministers huddled together with their robes in disarray and the old scavenger pushing the oars. It was a kilometer from the shore.

Don't be afraid, she heard herself say. A voice strangely like her own voice, but more sonorous she realized, for she could be heard above the howling of the winds.

I am holding up your daughter telekinetically, Minister Ishida. She is unharmed; do not be afraid.

I am sorry to possess her body in this way, but I cannot

otherwise communicate with you; to find one such as Ryoko, with the clarity of perception to tune in to and comprehend even some peripheral aspects of our thoughts, was no easy task.

She saw her father stand up even as the boat rocked wildly to face the creature as a man should; but the others remained in a bundle together, terror-frozen.

"You want to claim our starship? To ask our help in leaving the planet we have made uninhabitable for your children?" Ishida asked.

"Starship?" Kawaguchi stammered through his fear. "What's going on?"

What could I want with your starship? Its dimensions are wrong for me, its environment is wrong. How could a whale travel with you, in a voyage of generations?

The two other ministers were glaring at Ryoko's father with anger and incredulity.

"Ishida, you lied to us!" whispered Takahashi. Ryoko perceived directly the meanness of the man, the self-aggrandizing pettiness of him. "What is the whale talking about?"

She saw in her father's mind the picture of the starship in the sky, the desperate hope that he clung to, and understood him, his image of survival.

Ishida said to the whale: "We will help you; we owe it to you."

Ryoko was moved towards them, across the turbulent waves. She came like a ghost in a *Noh* play, her dry dress fluttering a little, her face chalk-white and blank, masklike, serene.

Take the girl. Soon she will seem as if dead. Hospitalize her; remove her ovaries. You will find, in them, fertilized ova; they are my children. They are in psionic stasis, and will not begin to divide until you arrive at the end of your journey. She carries, in her mind, instructions for your scientists, so they will know how to make them grow when they arrive. Is it too much to ask?

"No," said Ishida. "But it is a great thing, a strange thing, that we should meet like this and exchange small favors on the verge of the great ending."

"Ishida!" gasped Takahashi. "You are polluting the purity of the Ending, destroying honor! Have you no Japaneseness in you at all?"

Softly, Ishida said: "Perhaps honor is only earthbound. I do not think it will matter to the stars."

Kawaguchi: "I shall die, though, when I have done my duty. I am not a coward; and your scheme will fail."

Bitterly, Ishida turned to Takahashi: "And when do you plan to die? Are you not Minister of Endings?"

Stiffly: "I remain as long as possible, sacrificing my honor for those who want death, to facilitate their passage into beauty."

Ishida laughed quietly, without rancour.

Help the girl into *the boat,* she heard herselfsay. She reached out her arms, of her own accord, and clutched her father's hands-how dry, how papery—alien! something inside her whispered—and was eased on to the boat. They were all cramped together. Hardness of wood, she thought. Wet splinters against my hands.

The other two Ministers were protesting in their own ways.

"A hoax," said Kawaguchi, "there's been no spaceship research' for 50 years!"

"Man isn't supposed to overreach himself," Takahashi~ rasped. "You're violating the purity of Ending. Haven't you learned anything at all from our past? You're tampering with truth, trying to find loopholes in it that can't exist …"

Ryoko felt her father's disregard for them. He was looking only at her wonderingly, the way he had gazed at Fujisan in the museum, with awe.

Her voice said: *You are wondering why I ask you these things. Perhaps you imagine me some great ancient of the waters, able to communicate with you from the supreme wisdom of my old age.*

You delude yourselves, if so; I am a young whale. I have not yet learned to love death; and my request is not necessarily that of the others.

Look! The wind subsided. The not-quite night became clear. Misted in distance, great whales clove the air in a frenzied dancing. There were a hundred of them, perhaps more, and they were leaping in unison and falling slowly in intricate symmetries, to crash heavy against the water.

Ryoko felt their surging ecstacy, and how the others were feeling it too. The whales seemed near and far, outside concepts of dimension, as she perceived them from her perspective of immensity.

It is the death-dance. It has always been said that men will never see it. Nevertheless, Ending draws near, the rules are changed.

They leapt and then they died, some of them, from sheer exhaustion, and Ryoko touched the edge of the extinguishing of a gigantic consciousness; how they were released from life, how they were all compassion, like Buddhas. The air rang with strange music, *Gagaku* music, apprehended neither as motion nor stasis …as dead bodies slapped against the sea.

See them. Hear them. They will never communicate with you. They are in love with death, and their lives have become pure music.

As though from a great height she could peer into the others' minds, and she saw her father's wary exaltation, Kawaguchi's grudging acceptance, and the untouchable darkness that was the soul of Takahashi, Minister of Ending. There was the mind of the old man, too; small, frail, timid.

The images faded. The death-dance was far out, beyond

the horizon, but its realitv had reached them through the mind of the whale. And now he had disappeared beneath the water.

Takahashi, seeing him gone, spoke more boldly: "Why do you believe we will do you favors? Is it not human nature to be treacherous?"

Then the voice of the young girl revealed the great secret that had never been spoken since speech began ...

We have among us a myth, which it seems is founded in truth.

We have no names—the concept is alien to us—but there was once a great dreamer to whom we gave a name, Aaaaaiookekaia, gene-changer. She dreamed a great dream, about planting her own children among the primate-sentients on the dry land. They do not think she reflected, but they have the potential to be great fashioners of tools. It we could only join forces.

She summoned a thousand thousand others from all over the waters-we were millions, then—and they dreamed the great dream with her, dreaming with such power that new zygotes were created. Aaaaaiookekaia struggled on to the dry land to give birth, and abandoned her children there, and most of them—the ones which survived—were in the shape of men.

Even the dreaming of a thousand thousand whales could not create a true facsimile of man. True, there were the same number of chromosomes, and they even interbred with Men. But some things they could not change.

Your perception of beauty. How many times has this been commented on by the other races? With you it is instinctive: the twisted tea-bowls, the joy in imperfection is a legacy from us; the wails of the hichiriki and shakuhachi am cries from the depths of your ancestral memories. Your joy in death, too—it is a remembrance of that leap into eternity, as when the whalt: in his transcendent revelation rushes with joy to meet the harpoon.

This child Ryoko is one who has inherited most strongly the ability to communicate with us. That is why she seems so Japanese to you, when many of your values, though revived, are obsolescent. But all of you are children of the whales.

She collapsed into her father's arms.

Ishida held his daughter tightly, shielding her from the wind. The old man rowed like a machine, drained by terror. The implications of the whale's revelation came to him gradually: the Japanese people had been guilty of mass patricide. For so heinous a transgression, there was almost no expiation.

Except the one thing that would transmute any guilt into beauty. No, there were no alternatives. He realized that there was no way of silencing them, and that another national wave of suicides was inevitable. The shore came nearer. Everything was gray, like an antique motion picture. His daughter's hair trailed lightly across her face, black on white. Her lips were parted, as though about to speak and she was cold.

Minister Ishida's memories reached back to a time before the Millennial War to a tutor and a schoolroom, to the lines of the; immortal Basho:

mono ieba
kuchibiru samushi
aki no kaze

when a thing is spoken
The lips become cold,
like the autumn wind.

Winter, 2022/2023

A vague elapsing of time in her awareness; little else. She! drifted out of her coma and she was in a cold bed, in an old room with steel-gray walls, and she felt her belly and knew that she had been drained. Her first thought was, *I'm sterile.*

"When can I leave the hospital?"') She saw the nurse: tired, hard-faced, like many workers a Caucasian. *An alien!* thought Ryoko. *After all, I am not human.*

Fragments, confused, distorted: in the cavern with the whale's mind. Spray-splashings, wind, the death-dance, the yearning for Ending.

The nurse picked up a swab with her chopsticks and dabbed deftly at Ryoko's arm.

"Sleep now. In a few hours they will come for you, the people from the Ministry."

Water rippling ...waves washing her face ...whispering ...

And sank, effortlessly, into unconsciousness.

Later——she could not be sure of the time of day—she was escorted past innumerable rooms with metal doors, down escalators. A masked orderly or two would shuffle deferentially by, their eyes averted. She became aware that she was known to them all.

Four of them hustled past, wheeling a trolley. She almost recoiled. It was loaded down with corpses, piled every which way. Arms and legs stuck stiffly out, and the faces were tea-green and twisted. They were so grotesque that she could not think of them as having ever been human.

She and her guides pressed against the cold wall to let them pass. They did not smell of death, but sweet, like incense.

" ... not suicide."

"No," replied her guide. "Plague, Miss Ishida."

So it had come to Tokyo now, and would soon be spreading into all of their homes. She wondered whether her father's project would have enough time. She had messages locked inside her mind, what to do when the whale's ova reached their new home. If it was not too late.

She watched the pile of corpses, and wondered if her mother was among them-she must by now be dead, but of course it was impossible to recognize a plague victim ...

The whale, the whale.

My forefathers killed them, their—our—very own ancestors. Ignorance was not an excuse. She shuddered with the shame of it. *And I'm sterile,* she thought, *just like the earth.*

REMEMBER YOUR ANCESTORS

blinked the neons that glittered along the Ginza. Shadowing the intersection, the Pavilion of Ending loomed above the crumbling Matsuzakaya department store.

"Yes, Ryochan, there have been thousands of suicides. Takahashi announced the whale's story all over the country, and when they understood what their forefathers had done, they lost face. Our whole nation, our whole race lost face. There was no self respect left for a Japanese to feel.

"The most popular death was leaping off a cliff into the sea. Lovers still do it together, fathers and sons, old business associates ...the immigrants are dumbfounded. They will have the country soon, I thing."

REMEMBER *YOUR* ANCESTORS
ONLY HONOR *ENDURES*

He's so old, Ryoko thought. She felt a new admiration for him, standing as he did for something as cowardly as survival, against the opinions of all. It made him a hero to her, for the first eime.

"Ryochan—"

"*Otosan?*"

"Will you go on the starship?"

"But who can—"

THE PAVILION OF ENDING

They were cut off by the hubbub as they stepped into the reception hall. A commotion of kimonos, stiff hairdos bobbing like buoys in the current, old tailcoats, dazzling lights from antique chandeliers. Little pieces of conversation crystallized out of the confusion:

" …of course, the integral serialism of the pseudo-occident al era was ultimately based on the sonorities of the Bali nese gamelan …"

" … read Mishima? Greatest prophet of the last century."

" … I've planned my suicide for the cherry blossom season, will be spectacularly beautiful, to lie dying among the petals …"

" …These Caucasian servants have no idea of the points of etiquette, my dear'"

Turning to her father: "Father … why is Takahashi giving party?"

"I don't know."

They handed in their shoes and changed into slippers for upper level where they would relax on floor cushions at the tables and be served. There was a pungent sake, perhaps not synthetic; elegant, machine-carved sashimi in the shapes petals and leaves. The porcelain seemed to be genuine arita with the character *fuku* in blue on white on each item. Ryoko did know here was so much antique porcelain left, after the war.

Her father was withdrawn, and she did not find herself participating much in the conversations. It all turned on Endings and plague deaths.

The long tables seemed to converge against the high far wall where the Minister of Ending sat, above the others, haughty in his gold-brocade regalia and mitre. He talked to nobody, she noticed. and seemed to be walled in by silence. On reflection, she realized that she had not observed him talk to anyone at all that evening.

A faint cry, like a gull's, cut in on her thoughts. Someone in the kitchens, she thought: a plague-death. But just then a civil servant asked her to relate-for the hundredth time since she had come out of the hospital—the story of her encounter with the whale, and they listened to her, those around her, with the stricken awe that she had come to expect from her listeners; and their eyes glittered with envy when she told of the beauty of the whales' death-dance and death-song, and she began herself to hear, in the cacophony of small talk, the rush and whisper of the sea.

But as she talked, she was thinking: Why did her father want her to go on the spaceship? Could he not see that she was coming to a crisis, perhaps to a decision to die?

Just then, Takahashi rose. The voices died down, the clinking of glasses thinned. He began to make a speech.

"Many of you have called me a coward—" There was a sensation at this. Clearly something unusual was about to happen. "I freely admit this. I have encouraged Ending; thus far, I have not had the strength to seek it out for myself.

"This is the message of the whale: it is the final revelation of Ending. It is now time for me to acknowledge the guilt of my ancestors, my own guilt. The time of Ending is here"—he was quoting his own writings now—"and we must make way, we must purify the world.

"And so I call upon all of you—when you have put your affairs in order, not rashly or unpremeditatedly-to follow the ancient path. Japan has ceased to be sacred. We are a nation of genocides, of patricides.

"Had you been observant, you might have noted the laser generators surrounding my table. Before the war, such holotapes as you are now watching were not uncommon, if you can remember that far back. I have already killed myself, in a traditional manner, discreetly and honorably."

He disappeared. There was an instant babble of discussion; a sudden silence; then, breathtakingly, applause.

***

She was serving him green tea in his private tea room. He smiled frostily at her, a trifle vacantly; she knew he could not hear her, because he had taken another silence tablet that morning. So she crouched on the *tatami,* in the background, while her father sipped, alone, in his private world of utter soundlessness.

After a while she slid open the shoji. The Rock Garden was flaked with snow, and the wind was whistling softly. She moved the *hibachi* nearer him, for the warmth.

He motioned to her. She could not help noticing how easily he tired now. If only he were not so addicted to the silence tablets! It was such an easy escape.

"Did you know?" he said, half to himself-for she would not have been heard if she had answered him—"There is a new *Kabuki* play. They are playing it all over the country; it is called *The Romance of the Young Girl and the Whale.*

"It's about a young girl who meets a whale. The spirit of the whale communicates with her, all very mystical, and in the final scene the girl leaps off a cliff and dies because there is no way to resolve the terrible love which she has grown to" feel for him … When they played it at Kyoto, there were busloads trundling down to Lake Hamamatsu, and they found bodies everywhere for weeks afterwards."

Ryoko had not left the house for a month; she had heard no news. But the story did not surprise her. She only thought: *Now they expect me to die.*

It was to her a fulfillment, the only possible ending for the story. Her determination strengthened. The vision was so satisfying. To plunge headlong into the wombwarmth, to drink deeply what she had only tasted before when the waves and the whale's mind had swallowed her up. She closed her eyes, reliving the ecstasy.

"Ryochan," her father said gently, "I don't want you to die. I want you to leave on the spaceship. Beyond the atmosphere,' among the stars, you may be able to begin again, without guilt."

"Oh, *otosan*," she sighed—had he heard her? Yes, he seemed to be reacting a little. There was no knowing when the silence tablets would wear off. "I have arranged for you to be sent to Aishima next month. They'll train you there, for the journey."

"Father—"

"You were mother to the whale children, after all, for a while you carried them in your body. You gave the instructions for caring for the ova. You have the right to leave."

"Father, I'm more guilty than the others. I brought them the news of their shame. Without an inkling of this, they would not have died."

He seemed to understand her—he had heard very dimly, or else was lip-reading a little.

"How old are you now, daughter?"

"Twenty."

"I dreamed of finding you a husband, grandchildren. I am old enough to remember a time when everyone dreamed those dreams, not dreams of expiation, not nightmares of hideous self-recrimination. You are a wise girl, but still you should obey your father."

She bowed to him, submissively, but denied his statements in her heart.

"I defied all my own ethics for this project, Ryochan. None of the volunteers are Japanese; they're all immigrants, and can't understand the peculiar agony of these decisions. And in the end, I only created this project so that I could enable you to escape the necessity of death."

It was the closest that he'd ever come to saying that he loved her. "But I'm empty inside, father. I'd be dead weight, useless for a multi-generation journey."

"I know little about these things. I only found the money, which was difficult because the people were starving and there was no one who would understand. I was very selfish about it, too. Maybe the trip won't last four thousand years, subjectively. There were so many things being discovered before the war, before we came to the Ending.

"And perhaps you won't be sterile, either; in all those years, with all the facilities and the brains that I have put on the ship, they might discover something. How to clone you, perhaps, from a piece of tissue, so that in the end—the beginning—some part of you—of me—will be there.

"Give up your right to die, Ryochan," he pleaded.

"No, father!" she cried out. She stopped short, realizing with a shock that she had been about to defy her own father. When he had revealed his need for her, his need to be a part of what he had helped to create …

She bowed again, but remained unconvinced. She had fallen in love with the image in the play, the virgin girl tumbling into the vastness of the sea. It was an almost sexual thing, an expression of her love for a being of total compassion, a terrible compassion beyond life. She saw herself as the playwright had seen her; an actor in a myth, a symbol. Without the death, perfection was marred.

"Father," she said, to avoid the subject, "recite me some haiku."

Her father did so. They sat beside the hibachi, in its puddle of warmth, and the snow in the Rock Garden became an eiderdown of white, and the wind sang sadly. He recited many poems, new and old, and mostly sad ones, about winter; but then he came to the most famous of Basho's poems. the one that all the world used to quote, even the gaijin, though usually in bafflement:

> *furu ike ya*
> *kawazu tobikomu*

"An old pool. A frog jumps; I can't think of the last line," her father said. Trying to keep her voice calm, she supplied the line:" Mizu no oto." But her cheeks were moist.

> *Mizu no oto—the sound of water!*

There was a roaring in her ears: the sound of wind and of conversations and of electric Toyotas in the empty streets and the pounding of her own blood in her head, all echoes of the endless ocean.

In the morning, in the snow, beside a great rock, he was dead. It was a beautiful death; despite his lack of experience, he had killed himself most artistically, so that he and the rocks and the snow were a tableau of the utmost elegance and restraint.

Spring, 2023

It was a very different voyage.

The boat was similar to the one she had first sailed in, perhaps the same one; there were the sails, the bare wooden decks, the nights silent and bleak. She would stand beside the railings as she had done before. More at night than in the daytime, though, and she was more alone than ever before, because she had turned her back on the concrete world and stepped forward into the cosmos of the about-to-die. A world rarefied and crystalline, untainted by the sublunary, untouched and still. The people and the boat and the sea and the sky blurred before the beckoning siren of release.

I am in love with death, she told herself. And thought of the death-dance of the hundred whales.

A night came when she felt herself ready. She rose and stood, naked to expose her shame, by the prow where the railings were knee-high. Wisps of fog caressed her nudity.

When the fog cleared the moon lit up her face so that it gleamed with an actor's powdery whiteness. She thought of her remote ancestors, shadow-dark and warm under the water.

For a while she half-expected the whale to come, to see her triumphant leap, to share her one moment of supreme beauty. He did not.

She whispered, "I do love you, father," to her own father and to countless fathers and back to the parents of Aaaaaiookekaia, the greatest dreamer of all.

She steadied herself to jump, a trifle self-consciously, and her eyes were caught by ... stars glittering on the black water, alien, but the dots in the water were so near that she could have touched them with wet hands ...

... and knew that she had lied to herself.

She had made herself play a role, a role written by a playwright she had never known. She realized she did not want to drown among the stars, but to walk among them. The new longing was an ache, without any joy at all. There was no ecstasy, but only terror and awesome desire. And it had come from finally understanding her father. She had not been in love with death, but only with herself.

And now she would still leap, but into an ocean more unknown, and truly endless.

Land was at the limit of her vision. Glimmering above the black needles that were trees, there were tiny sticks of silver that were the first stage in a journey to the unimaginable. And seagulls, circling the rocks.

For of course this was the voyage's purpose: to bring her

and the other volunteers to the island Aishima, where the rockets awaited them.

And for that one night, before the preparations and the strenuous training were to begin, with the unearthly music of the sea to lull her, she was free to sleep the sleep of the dead.

***

There was a night like this for several of those who thought they has succumbed to the enchantment of death. So Ryoko was not the only Japanese whose remote descendants reached the fourth planet of the star Tau Ceti.

One ought to describe endings, especially this one, as swift and beautiful, made sublime by their very transience; but the poisoning of the earth was a slow process, and there were still many more years when the whales daneed the death-dance on the death-giving oceans, and haunted the minds of dying men with their songs.

—Tokyo and Arlington. 1977 and 1979

The Thirteenth Utopia

He came to Shtoma in the cadent lightfall, his tachyon bubble breaching the gilt-fringed incandescent clouds like a dark meteor.

Some feelings are never unlearned. Some wonders never fade with experience. So he reflected, Ton Davaryush, master iconoclast, purger of planets, transformer of societies. Especially one—the thrill of power, of potentiality—of a virgin utopia, ripe for the unmasking of its purifying flaw.

Every utopia has its flaw. Ton Davaryush wished it were not so. He was sad—but only for a moment—that he must wreak havoc on this planet, even though it lay at the very limits of the Dispersal of Man; but he had learned not to compromise. With the destruction of twelve deceptive utopias, experience had at least banished misgivings. For Davaryush was two hundred and thirteen years old, and at the height of his analytic powers.

He closed his curiously heavy-lidded eyes to the shimmering of the cloud-banks and the extravagance of the alien landscape that grew constantly as he fell, with its strange sharp-angled trees like gigantic pink spiders, their photosynthesizing pigment having a ferric, not a magnesium base, and its whimsical spiral dwellings of transparent plastic, jutting up at irregular intervals from the blanket of dense vegetation, crimsons and vermilions. He ignored them, and the savage thrashings of the wind as his translucent sphere automatically adjusted to the gravity, softening his fall for landing on Shtoma.

And thought of the covenant: *for the breaking of joy is the beginning of wisdom.* And thought, pathetically: *I, Ton Davaryush, expelled from the mainstream of human society by time dilations and the gulfs of space, am too alone.*

He tried to bury himself—eyes still closed to the atmospheric turmoil—in analyses of what he had been told about this world. How they had fallen into a pattern, an ecological stasis, from which he must release them, whatever the cost. And this was no backward, back-to-nature primitivistic planet, exulting in its own self-conscious apartness and ignorance, but a world whose technical sophistication rivaled his own; exceeded it, in at least one respect, for Shtoma alone, in the entire Dispersal of Man, knew the secret of gravity control. For which they had no use, except for the manufacture of toys. And which they guarded with such miserliness and irrational fervor as to belie their much-vaunted saintliness, their notorious lack of greed, of any other human quality. And the rumor that Shtoma was a utopia was more than could be tolerated.

If it was a utopia it could be destroyed. This he knew. He understood every facet of the utopian heresy. He was a

master iconoclast, dedicated to the perpetuation of change. Every utopia has its *flaw*. He clutched this knowledge to him like a secret prayer.

I may be a savior.

He opened his eyes finally. And saw the incredible wildness, the intractable angularity of the landscape, the lurid carmines and scarlets of the trees that lurched toward him with their arachnoid arms outstretched. His bubble slowed itself, gradually, to bring him to the field of rust-colored grass. Alien buzzings and high-pitched song-snatches assailed his ears.

He deactivated his tachyon bubble with a flick of his mind—the keys were cybernetically brain-implanted —and was now at the mercy of the alien environment. At some indeterminate future, he would be rescue—when the thinkhive on the homeworld decided.

I may be a savior. This was more important to him than why they had jealously hidden their secret from a galaxy where knowledge was not for concealing, why they had not used their secret for conquest, as was their right. But this would come. *I am bringing them their human nature, he thought.* The thrill of it lived in his heart. (For this thrill he had joined the Inquest.)

He drew his shimmercloak over his shoulder. It absorbed the fresh air and began to radiate in the safe range, as he knew it would: he stroked it softly as it blushed, pink against the aquamarine fur; wishing, as always, that it was not a dumb semisentient. For he was alone.

Turning in the direction of the nearest habitation, he reviewed once more all he had been told about Shtoma.

A planet unaccountably close to its primary, a white dwarf, yet environmentally anomalous: Earth-sized, temperate, with the wrong atmosphere. With incredible potential for economic power, yet with no armed forces, which ignored the rest of the Dispersal of Man, the galactic authority—leading inexorably to the heretic suspicion of utopia! He began walking. It was not the Inquest's way to arrive conspicuously, gaudy with the trappings of salvation.

But then a stranger stood in his path, unmoving. An oldish man, clad severely in a brown tunic; clearly a peasant or slave. He was looking at the ground, and Davaryush had come quite close to him.; The stranger looked up at Davaryush and sang, in a clear tenor, the first alien words he had heard since his arrival, the words:

> *qithe qithembara*
> *udres a kilima shtoisti*

Davaryush signalled to his polyglot implant, then closed his eyes to see, as though inscribed on a white page before him, the words "soul, renounce suffering; you have danced on the face of the sun." It appeared to be a form of greeting. But the strange words, with their opaque and patently sinful meaning, strengthened his suspicions; and he approached the stranger diffidently. There was one other thing experience never banished: fear. Activating his implant so that it would intervene in his speech functions, he said: "I am from another world. Who may I address?"

The alien's gaze chilled him, though it contained no malice. "You are Inquestor Davaryush, of the Clan of Ton. Welcome." Abruptly the stranger beamed and stretched out his arms to embrace Davaryush. The Inquestor yielded ungracefully. He had misjudged; this was no peasant. "We were expecting you."

"Yes. I come to investigate Shtoma's utopian possibilities, so that it may be considered for the honor of being named a Human Sanctuary." Davaryush did not blush at the lie, for it came easily to him by now.

"So! How delightful." His eyes laughed themselves into a hatchwork of wrinkles. "I am your host, Ernad. You must be weary; come."

Who was this man, poorly dressed and without a single

attendant, who dared to address a Master Inquestor by name and who knew his mission? Again the alienness of the world unnerved him. The clouds had parted to reveal the white dwarf unnaturally close. The rough wind tousled the grass, blood-red and tall. He started to answer Ernad, but the old man had turned, expecting Davaryush to follow him.

A stony path, pebbled with shiny stones, led to the first recognizably human artifact: a displacement plate, metallic and . incongruous in the middle of the field. He was unprepared for it. He was forced to remind himself that this was no primitive world—in spite of the absence of war or, apparently, slavery.

"When can I begin my investigation? The Inquest must know on in time for the Grand Convocation," he said.

Ernad beckoned Davaryush onto the plate. "Frankly, we have so little involvement with the worlds outside—" he began, then stopped himself. "Well, as you wish; whenever you wish." Davaryush was suspicious of the warmth in his voice, but it appeared convincing. Clearly he was dealing with a master of ambiguity. But the impropriety and unashamedness of "little involvement" compounded his bewilderment.

They materialized in what appeared to be one of the structures he had glimpsed during the landing. He reeled with the vertigo of it—the crazy swirlings and spiralings of transparent walls, the cacophony of chimings and . chirpings that bombarded his senses. How could they live amid such a wilderness of sensual stimuli? Where was their discipline, their culture? A woman nearly ran into him, then trotted away, laughing; children and young people sauntered by, gaily calling out "qithe qithembara; udres a kilima shtoisti!" completely without respect. "You must forgive them," said Ernad, interrupting his dismay. "You are an off-worlder, and …well, it is especially exciting for them now. It is almost time for the festival of initiation, and anything can spark their enthusiasm." He said this matter-of-factly, with no trace of criticism in his voice, again pointing up his alienness.

"They are your attendants?" Surely someone important enough to be his host would have servants of a kind. "No; neighbors, relatives, friends. My house is theirs."

But Davaryush was thinking: what of the initiation ceremony? Perhaps that was the flaw. Perhaps there was some unspeakable rite, some trauma they were all forced to go through … perhaps this would be the handle he could use to save this misguided people.

"Ernad, I must rest," he said. "But after, I would see everything on your world: your games, your pleasures, your prisons, your criminals, your asylums, your places of execution."

"Ah. Yes, I have heard of madmen and criminals. I am not uneducated, Inquestor Ton," replied Ernad mysteriously. They turned down a corridor of glass that swerved upwards into the air, and Davaryush felt a sudden dislocation, as though he had changed weight or down had become sideways, and he found they were walking upside down, on the ceiling.

"What is happening?"

Ernad laughed mildly. "It is the same principle, you know, as the varigrav coasters. You must have seen them, our principal export—"

"Buy why fool around with gravity inside your dwellings?"

"Why not? Would you not be bored, if all directions remained constantly the same …?"

Up became *down* again. They reached a large chamber that seemed to be perched, precariously, on the point of a translucent pyramid in the sky. "Your resting place. It is my own chamber, Inquestor; I trust you will find it comfortable."

Davaryush's eye alighted on the only adornment of the room; apart from the resting-pad. It was a huge, capelike sheet of some sheer material that hung on one wall, like a rainbow sail, rippling: softly in the ventilating breeze. It was beautiful, he conceded, but bewilderingly complex, uncivilized.

"This cape? What is it for?"

"Oh. My wings," Ernad said.

Davaryush knew then how addicted they must be to the varigrav coasters, those toys they had inflicted on the rest of the galaxy. And he looked at the old man, who seemed utterly disingenuous, and wondered if it were possible that this sincerity were not, after all, the product of a trained deviousness, but merely a product of his lower mentality. For here was a toy, hanging on the wall as though it were a god.

"Leave me, Ernad," he said brusquely.

He was trying to establish authority, the distancing proper for an Inquestor. He needed to preserve his mask of sternness, for he was already sad. He was vulnerable, he realized, even after twelve successful missions.

For he was nothing if not compassionate.

You have compassion, Davaryush.

"Yes, Father." He was twelve years old, veteran of three wars, and now an initiate. And alone, in the small room, with the Inquestor, whose eyes glared fire and millennial wisdom. Now after more than two centuries, the scene returned, vivid.

When you came to kill the condemned criminal, you did not torture him or play with him. as was your right, an essential part of the initiation. You killed him cleanly. in a matter of seconds. slicing him into two congruent parts with your energizer. It was artistically done. But why?

"Father. it was necessary to show skill, not cruelty. I have already killed many people. He feigned an assurance that was far from his true feelings.

Very well. I name you to the Clan of Ton.

Davaryush started, gasped audibly despite his knowledge of roper conduct … he had come expecting to fail, to be returned to homeworld. The Clan of Ton …that would mean seminary, long lonely years on harsh, inhospitable planets, unwelcome, thankless labor for the sake of pure altruism. "Father—"

You are unworthy. I know. Nevertheless, the Inquest takes what it can get.

His first mission was the planet Gom, a hot planet of a blue-white star. The people lived in tall buildings, thousands to a building, fifteen billion to the planet. But they were happy. They were quite ignorant of their responsibilities as a fallen race; reliant on automata, they pursued their hedonistic existence without regard for their true natures. They suffered from the heresy of utopia.

He remembered how he found the flaw to that utopia. Every year, in a special ceremony marked by compulsive gratifications of the senses, all those over the age of fifty intoxicated themselves and then committed suicide, leaping by thousands into the volcanic lava lakes that boiled ubiquitously on every continent.

He had saved them. Whispering to only one or two: *And what* if you did *not* die? he had created civil wars, revolutions, unhappiness. People ran mad, setting fire to the machines that had succored them. Then the ships of the Inquest came, bringing comfort with them, comfort and truth.

But the happiness had tempted him. *Remember. man is a fallen creature. Davaryush. Utopias exist only in the mind. a state to which it is given us to aspire. But to imagine we have attained that state—that is to deny life. The breaking of joy is the beginning of wisdom.*

Now he was no longer tempted. For he had seen such as the planet Eldereldad, where the happy ones feasted on their own children, which they produced in great litters, by hormonal stimulation; and the planet Xurdeg, his most recent mission. where the people smiled constantly, irritatingly, showing no face except the face of rapt ecstasy, until he finally learned that the penalty for grief was dismemberment, to feed the hungry demands of the degenerating bodies of five-thousand-year-old patriarchs ... yet when he had asked one of these ancients, what he most desired, he had replied: To *feel* grief. But I am *afraid* to die for it.

Ton Alkamathdes, Grand Inquestor of his Sector, who had watched his initiation and had chosen him out for the Clan of Ton, had said to him that day when he was a young boy facin his new destiny: *Never forget the lie. This lie is the sacrifice tho, you must make, the little sin that you must commit, for the saki of saving countless millions. The lie is this: the Inquest is seeking a perfect utopia, a planet that will be designated a Humo Sanctuary, for the edification and glory of the Dispersal of Man.*

You will tell them that always, and always you will understand in your heart that there will exist one tragic flaw.

And always, the ships of the Inquest would follow him. An after, in a year or two, or perhaps a few decades, they would awake to their true natures, and they would fight wars and exhibit avarice and pitilessness, like all the other worlds. Man, is a fallen being.

Remember: you are a guardian of the human condition. He felt the eyes of Ton Alkamathdes on him, even two centuries away and countless parsecs, boring into his soul, purifying him;, and in their sternness he drew a kind of comfort. But then he awoke, long before dawn, and was on Shtoma and frighteningly; alone, exposed to the alien sky under the structures of glass and clear plastics. He found a young girl singing to him, "*qithe qithembara,* Lord Inquestor."

He sat up abruptly, reaching for a nonexistent weapon. "Who; are you?"

"I am Alk, daughter of Ernad." (The voice haunted his:! thoughts for many days, reminding him of the whispering sea on homeworld.) "Will you be pleased with me? Of all the children who saw you, I was most taken by you, Inquestor."

They were depraved, shockingly amoral! They sent their own children to sleep with strangers! "No!" he cried out, and the severity of his own emotion startled them both. "On our worlds we do not do things like this."

"But father said to show you our love, the love of udara." *Udara?* (Their name for the dwarf star, their sun, whispered his polyglot implant. Again he was puzzled.)

"Leave me, please." He tried to exclude the pain from his voice. Shame flooded him. In the starlight he saw disappointment on her face, and thought: they do not even hide their emotions! what savages, what innocents! And without a further word she rose and left him, noiseless as a breeze.

Quickly he ran through what he had learnt in those few hours. They dressed severely, denying all rank and pomp and self-importance; they made curious fetish of their wings, they were morally loose, they did not make any effort to conceal their feelings, but were like children, wholly innocent of the need for tact and diplomacy—and this last thing, the love of *udara.*

That could mean anything. Every perversion, every practIce of perversion was possible, because of the human condition.

And, under the strange constellations, knowing that he had no weapons and that he could not know when he would be rescued, he began to recite the first prayer he had ever learnt. Its meaning, for its language was no longer spoken, was a sublime mystery to the Inquest, but all who went through the seminary could repeat it, as a solace, in times of emotional turmoil. The nonsense words—perhaps little more than gibberish distorted by man's long history—were a kind of bond between the members of the Inquest, all solitary men: *"pater noster, qui es in inferno …"*

"But—what is in these black boxes? I have seen several during my stay here," Davaryush demanded of the heretic priest.

The white-bearded old man—a magnificent mottlement of wrinkles and discolorations, without the common decency of cosmetics—smiled beneficently at him. *"Udara,"* he said. *"Udara* is in them."

"Will you not touch it?" the priest said, beckoning to him. The temple's black box—it was perhaps a meter square—stood in the center of the transparent hall which could have held ten thousand people without any trouble. It was the only object in the chamber. "Come, touch; you will feel *udara."*

Hesitantly, Davaryush went up to it with his hand outstretched. He felt wobbly-kneed, as though his weight were constantly shifting, as though he were losing control of his limbs. Gingerly, he brushed the cool metal with his fingertips.

Overwhelming joy coursed through his thoughts for a moment. He saw homeworld fleetingly, and ached for it, heard the music of the sea, saw vividly the faces of his parents, whom his own time dilation had stranded in an unreachable past … they smiled at him, he was a child half their height, reaching up to touch their faces, laughing …

And snatched away his hand as though he had been burnt. This was dangerous, clearly some powerful hallucinogenic device. He stared at his hand in terror.

The happiness he had just felt echoed in his mind. He was tempted to reach out again, and he controlled himself with tremendous difficulty, and knew he had stumbled upon one of the key clues to what was wrong with Shtoma.

They were self-deluders, obviously, intoxicating themselves with false memories and artificially induced joys. "Did you not feel the love of *udara,* stranger?"

"No, priest. I felt—I remembered something I thought I'd lost forever."

He turned to leave. "You do not wish for more? Ah, but you have not danced on the face of the sun."

He turned again, saw the look of pity in the priest's face, the expression of *ah, but you are incapable of understanding.* So he walked hurriedly out, not bothering to acknowledge the priest hearty *"qithe qithembara."*

Ernad was waiting for him, and the girl Alk, who was— by daylight—a creature of striking beauty, not in her facial features but in the way she moved and spoke; and another of Ernad's children, Eshly, a little boy of about six, who prattled and asked questions as though he were much younger, and was quite devoid of discipline. They walked on to the next displacement plate, Ernad smiling, the girl and her brother running excitedly, then lagging behind, Davaryush moody.

Ernad told him more about the Shtoikitha, the people of the dance (and they called their planet Shtoma, Danceworld.)

"Yes, we're a very thinly populated planet, only half a million souls ... what do we eat? There is fruit in the forests, small animals too, crustacea of fantastical shapes in the rivers; we don't have agriculture here. The fruit of the gruyesh falls to the ground and ripens, and when it turns mauve we tap it for the *zul,* tha mildly fermented sweet juice that you drank this morning ..."

"Crime?"

"Why should anyone commit it?" Ernad laughed gently. "We have *udara*, you see, so it isn't necessary."

"I don't understand. My polyglot implant translates that word simply as "sun"; but I have heard it in at least a dozen, meanings since I came to Shtoma. I know that semantics aren't perfect, but could I be missing something? You can't tell me that your people, in all their evident complexity, attribute all your fortunes to some mythical property of your sun!"

Davaryush was exasperated now. It was becoming a strain to maintain his investigator's pose. Clearly the problem on this planet had to do with some fundamental misunderstanding of the workings of the universe.

They had come to a small clearing, having vanished and rematerialized several times: it was level, dotted with pink shrubs … the two children, or rather the young woman and the boy, had run forward, breathless, and had collapsed, exhausted, on the grass … *by now, they would both be warriors, in the real world,* he thought. How sad, that they were trapped in a permanent preadolescence.

The boy he felt compassion for: he was like a retarded child who is nevertheless extremely beautiful. But Ernad was talking again.

"Still you don't see, you don't comprehend the elegant simplicity of it. Relax! Feel the singing in the sky: one *cannot* comrnit evil here."

He tried to feel, sensing, in the absurdity of the old man's beliefs, some core of faith that he would never be able to alter …

The soft susurrant rustlings of the red forests sang to him, but in their singing was mingled, chillingly, an image of homeworld … he tensed, instinctively, knowing he was playing with fire.

"Have you ever ridden a varigrav coaster?"

"No!" The thought horrified him. Abandonment to the senses, to utter helplessness! Never would he …"It is a pity. What did you feel, when I asked you to listen to the music of *udara?*" (Again, some obscure semantic twist.) "I don't know. A memory. It doesn't matter."

"On the contrary; it probably does matter. But you will learn at the initiation ceremony, perhaps."

"I am to take part?" Nothing would induce him to take part in any barbarian rite! Why, he might be mutilated, he might have to watch some unspeakable evil … but Ernad smiled the smile that excluded him from those who understood, frustrating him even more. "*Udara* is the key to what you are searching for, you know. Without it, this world would surely not be the paradise it has become."

"Why, that's ridiculous."

The two children of his host had come up and were watching him intently. "Father," said the boy Eshly, "don't be hard on the poor man."

He was so naive, so tactless, so ignorant! But Alk only looked at him, knowing what had passed between them in the night. (He knew now that no stigma was attached to sexual promiscuity; an expression of affection, nothing more. Finally, he had had to concede that this in itself was no flaw.)

"I must show you—" Ernad began.

"Take him to the nearest varigrav coaster, *please,* Father," Eshly cried urgently. He clasped Davaryush's hand—such presumption in a stripling, such undeserved trust—and propelled him toward the nearest displacement plate.

And in an instant they were at the edge of a cliff, sheer and blindingly white, that stretched perhaps half a klomet down to a cleared and endless plain, without the pink of vegetation. The plate where they had arrived stood in the shadow of a tremendously tall column of the transparent building material they used.

It was slender—the width of a few men, and it reached up to vanish somewhere in the vague loftiness of the clouds that hid *udara* from view then. This was nothing like the varigrav coasters he had seen, children's pleasure things. This was overpoweringly stark, and huge, a quasi-religious luminousness emanated from it. Its vastness distorted the scale of everything so he felt a crazy disorientation, while the two children, in nonchalant irreverence, were pushing him to the other side shouting at him to hurry.

"Quick, come, Inquestor!" shouted Eshly. A lift platform was descending for them. Turning to watch the sky beyond the cliff Davaryush saw black dots and smudges, microscopic in the expanse of sky and white plain, and he knew what they were. An ancient fear petrified him, he was like a robot as they buckled him in to the elevator. Suddenly, with a wild jerk, they were aloft racing up to the starting point in the clouds, and the rushing blood in his brain crashed against the rushing of the mad winds. He was nauseated; he closed his eyes and muttered his ancient prayer' longing for an end.

At the top there was a sort of control room, diving platform of various sizes, racks where sets of wings were set out, not the rainbow-colored type that adorned his resting-room, but plaid ones, black or gray. Alk and Eshly each seized a set of wings and had run to the platforms and leapt off the edge while Davaryush, fought a wild impulse to go to their rescue.

He saw them in the air, falling, falling with dizzying speed; and soon they had vanished—and then he saw them again, flung violently upward by the interplay of differing gravity fields, screeching with delight as the varigravs hurled them into!, turbulent whirlpools, and the wind, which was pulled in so many different directions that it was a distended, distorted tornado blasting his ears. He found himself clutching the railings in terror,!he who had seen nine wars.

But the squeals of pleasure became fainter. The two became black dots, joining the rapidly shifting patterns of swirling: specks in the distance. It was more tolerable to look at, pretty patterns against the sky, but when he thought about what was happening to them (gravity fields wrenching them in different directions, stretching their bodies' tolerance to its very limits, how could anyone find it pleasurable?) he—"

"Please, take me out of this."

"As you wish."

They went into the control room. They shut out the roaring of the winds and the silence shocked him for a moment, before he gathered his analytic senses enough to look around him ...It was an empty room, like all the others he had seen on Shtoma, domed in the standard material, so that *udara* shone relentlessly inside, with a half-dozen of the black boxes predIctably scattered, haphazardly, across the floor.

"I'm impressed." Davaryush tried to sound sincere. "How does it all work, incidentally?" He labored a little over the casual tone of this question, since finding out the secret would make a great difference to the other civilized worlds.

"The scientific principle, or the technical aspects?" Davaryush was startled for a moment by the man's willingness to reveal.

"Both."

"Well, you know as well as I do that gravity control works by selective graviton exchange ...the coaster also manufactures antigravitons, which exist of course only with some difficulty under normal conditions."

"But how do you manufacture antigravitons?"

Davaryush was excited; uncautiously he let it slip through, was not devious enough in asking the question. Ernad seemed not to be aware of such things.

"I'm simply not a scientist," he said— he did not sound at all as if he was trying to put Davaryush off—" and in any case *udara* controls details like that." He pointed happily to the boxes.

Again the evasive tactics, the semantic deceptions! If the people of Shtoma were able to lie with such easy naturalness, perhaps Shtoma had never been a logical candidate for utopiahood. Perhaps his journey had been wasted.

But the Grand Inquestor had entrusted him, and the Inquest was wise.

He saw the children returning, swung upwards in a golden arc that transected *udara* through the shimmering cloud banks …

"Time to go home. It will be night." Ernad motioned to his guest. "I hope you will feel more comfortable this time, and not be so afraid of the height."

The black boxes glinted in the *udara*-light. They attributed everything to those boxes, Davaryush thought. Was there something in it? Of course not. They were lying to him, creating some enormous joke at his expense.

Walking home through the ruddy terrain, Ernad told him how everybody on Shtoma participated in the initiation ceremonies every five years, almost to a man, because those who been through it once could be renewed, purified.

"You'll understand everything, you know, once you have taken part … the black boxes, the *udara*-concepts. I know that you find us strange. He chuckled to himself, then added earnestly, "You will take part, won't you?"

Slowly, with the realization that he might well be falling a trap, a trap cleverly constructed upon his own curiosity and the necessities of his mission, he said: "I have no choice."

For mission was to understand, and after understanding to co Even now, compassion touched him, more than ever before.

The accident happened.

Eshly, the boy, had run on ahead to the next plate. He tripped and stumbled, face down, and the power surged. They were upon him, the resounding clang echoing in the woods The three of them knelt down by the plate.

He lay like a discarded toy. The displacement field aborted—it was an accident that practically never occurred, almost unthinkable—and had wrenched half his body away then slung it back in a nanosecond, so that he was in one but impossibly bent.

Davaryush waited for the tears, for the signs of grief. But only sighing was the breeze and the voices of the alien Lightfall was ending.

"Go on, Alk," Ernad whispered to his daughter, "the others will want to know." His voice was icy calm.

Davaryush stood to follow as he lifted up the corpse, seemed merely asleep until one saw the inhuman angle of arms, and carried it into the encroaching forest, and returned without it, with the red shadows darkening him. There seemed to be no sadness in his face. Indeed, he almost smiled. Was this some incredible fortitude, even in the face of an impossible tragedy? Davaryush devoured the man with his eyes, seeking some clue to his emotions. And he thought, I have found the *flaw.*

And now it was time to plant the doubt, because the lowest point in a man's being is also the beginning of his ascent. Davaryush thought bitterly: here is a people that blithely throws the bodies of its sons into the forests to rot, that has forgotten grief that does not value human life at all. Here was the flaw.

Davaryush tried to put a lot of anger into his voice, to

exclude compassion while not striving too much for an oracular effect: "You don't care about your child," he said. "Love is not part of your utopia, is it? Humanity is what you have abandoned, isn't it?" *Now you are going to break down. Now your repressed humanity will come rushing to the surface.* It had happened twelve times before, and countless other times with other Inquestors.

Ernad did not collapse. He stared at Davaryush with unmitigated pity.

"Of course I grieve for him. I am desolate, Davaryush. But you do not understand our perspectives, or our overview of life.

"With renewal my grief will be cleansed. And I grieve for him most, that he did not live to dance on the face of the sun."

And Davaryush knew that he had understood nothing at all, nothing. Never had he felt so palpably the alienness of this world, the total incommunicableness of it. His mind whirled in a wild kaleidoscope of images: strange winds, blood-crimson forests with spider arms, flagrantly immodest buildings open to the elements, a dead child unmourned, a dead child who had been playing games amidst the incomprehensible forces of black boxes that manipulated gravity fields … and this strange man's face, which should be racked with sorrow, yet insulted him with an unwanted pity. *I wish I could kill him.*

The death-impulse rose in him, a monster of the subconscious, and he suppressed it with a superhuman effort. *He is a product of his misguided culture, not to be blamed,* he reminded himself. *I have come to save him; I must never forget that; even if I cause his death, I come as a savior.*

He had miscalculated again. Thinking to elicit from the stranger his hidden guilt, his dormant human responses, he had instead forced his own desire to kill to the surface. This desire should long have been dead, since he had renounced it for the sake of the salvation of the Dispersal of Man; yet it haunted him still, a spectre from the buried past. Perhaps the will of the man was stronger than his …

At last he found he could feel a bond between himself and the alien, in this moment of deepest misunderstanding. For they were both men, both fallen beings.

"Ernad," said Davaryush, "I pity you." The two of them walked, through the miscolored landscape, up to the twisted house.

Asleep that night, he was nine years old, celebrating the end of his first war.

And they came to Alykh, the pleasure planet. He and Tymyon and Ayulla and Kyg and the other companions, losing themselves in the cacophony of the crowds.

"Wait till you see *this!*" Kyg shouted, and she leapt on to the plate like a cat. They disappeared—

And Davaryush saw it, a topless tower of brick and and concrete and plastic and sparkling amethysts, studding walls like jewelled knuckle-dusters …

"What is it?"

"Daavye, don't you know anything?" Tymyon cackled offensively.

Kyg said, with mock primness: "It's a …*varigrav coaster!*"

The tower glinted oddly, catching the sunset. "Look," Kyg impatiently, "you dive off the top, you see, and it sets action a series of random gravity-field interferences, and you plummet like a hawk and you float upward and you swing dangerously and you curve and then you land where you started, like a feather."

("It's beautiful" whispered Ayulla the silent.)

"Well, let's go!" Tymyon and Kyg raced each other to the tower, and the crowds were everywhere, aliens, child-warrior brandishing their weapons, pimps, crusader-flagellant Inquestors and their retinues, slave-hunters, veiled Whispershadows from the borders of the Dispersal, dirty children strumming on dreamharps, dissonant alien musics, and an itinerant space opera howling full-blast through amplification jewels, and Davaryush was spellbound, unmoving.

He had never …

The tower held him.

And the little specks that were people, dust-motes in violet sunset.

"Aren't you coming?" Ayulla's voice was almost lost in confusion.

"No." He was petrified.

"Come *on!* They're all the rage now, all the way from Shtoma you know, from the limits of the Dispersal …"

"No! No!" (It was said that the greatest thrill, when you fell, was the very certainty of death, suddenly averted by a twist the field. At the moment of inevitable doom, it was said, you felt so *alive.)*

Ayulla was laughing at him. "How many people have you killed, Daavye? How can you be so scared of *life?"*

(He was ashamed. He resolved, then, to change his circle of friends.)

Now wake up. Face the hostile planet.

He moved, murmuring "Homeworld." Shrill cries of children awakened him. And then Alk was at the entrance to his room: "Initiation, Inquestor; hurry."

He threw on his shimmercloak. It tightened around him, sensing his need for warmth, though it was not cold.

The wings on the walls had gone.

The whole family, a dozen or more of them, trooped without ceremony into his room, heady exhilaration in their faces. Quickly he followed them outside, struggling to keep up with them. His heart had sunk when he saw that the wings had vanished. For he had an inkling, now, of what this rite must involve, and it terrified him.

Many displacements later, they were on a mountaintop overlooking a vast plain that glittered silver-gray with a thousand spaceships. The ships littered the fields, end to end so that the red grass was quite covered, all the way to the horizon …he could not imagine what they were for. Shtoma had hardly any commerce with other worlds.

Isn't it breathtaking?" Alk grasped his arm, and he felt himself shivering …

"How many of them are there, Ernad?" he said, wonderingly. This ceremony involved a journey, it seemed; perhaps on some satellite, some other planet.

The children were dancing and tugging at him and hollering in circles round him, and Ernad did not seem disposed to answer his questions. "Come," he said, and after another displacement they were at the entrance to a ship. (It was much as he knew them; ships did not differ much, having been perfected many millennia ago, before the Dispersal.) But the number of them! And the mobs of people, their wings tucked under the arms, giggling, chattering away as they climbed into them!

In the mid-distance, some of them had already risen. They rose at even intervals, in perfect order, and he could see a long chain of them stretching into the sky, where they glittered like a jewelled necklace in the early lightfall. Quickly (almost shamefacedly) he stifled his wonder, for he knew he must analyze everything, if he was to solve the most taxing problem of his life, the enigma of Shtoma. So he climbed the steep steps into the belly of the ship.

It was only a small cruiser, built for perhaps five hundred; there must be a thousand of them, then, to hold the whole population of Shtoma. It was impersonal, gray-walled like every ship; and it appeared to be a short-hauler, so Davaryush knew they Were not going off-system. People were filing into their chambers, seeming to know exactly where they belonged, Davaryush stood stupidly for a few moments before Alk came for him, and took him to the family's cabin.

After a while, he felt the noiseless lifting of the ship.

Some time later Ernad led him to the viewroom, screens afforded an unobstructed three hundred and degree view of space; and he saw how the line of ships behind and before, each an exact distance from the other, links a metal serpent of space …he asked Ernad where they going.

"To *udara*, of course!"

The old man looked blankly at "Not seriously."

"Are there any other planets in this system? Any moons? are not a mendacious people, Davaryush; perhaps that has occurred to you yet." He spoke patiently, as though reproving favorite child, and the attitude stung Davaryush.

He turned to see, on the other side of the room, that *udara* had swollen and was a blindingly white flame ball against blackness. He knew by now that when the word *udara* came he would get nowhere; so he tried something else. The ubiquitous black boxes were everywhere; in the viewroom they were stacked neatly in the middle of the floor.

"Those *udara*-boxes: they power the ship perhaps?" he only half-skeptical.

Ernad laughed again, enjoying his guest's ignorance. (Again Davaryush felt a bitter hate, a death-lust, for his host). "Not all; they are quite empty, and our spaceships work in the. normal way."

After a moment, he said: "Now look, Inquestor: they are darkening the screen otherwise *udara* would become unbearable."

"How can you say we are going there?"

"Just look at the face of the sun. There, look."

Udara was growing rapidly, and Davaryush saw: "There's a black spot on the sun's surface!"

"*That's* where we are going."

The black dot was perfectly round. This was impossible. "It must be artificial!" he gasped. These people, far from being simple utopians, were capable of galaxy-dominating technological feats!

"Artificial? In a manner of speaking." Then he explained, "The dot of course is only black by comparison, obviously; when we get there it will appear white and incandescent."

The screen was cut in half! One side was completely black, the other painfully bright, and there were white flame-tongues that shot up, a hundred kilometers high. They were approaching the sun's atmosphere; in its heart, Davaryush knew, matter was packed into inconceivable density.

"And now …there are tablets you must take, since you will not be able to breathe for a few hours; they will release oxygen into your bloodstream."

"What do you mean?"

"You're going to jump into the sun."

Davaryush understood now. They had led him on, and all the time were preparing this elaborate fiery execution. "I'll vaporize instantly!" he said.

"You don't understand, do you?" Ernad countered with surprising vehemence. "Gravity is under control, heat is under control! This is no ordinary star, this is *udara*. Every five years, we all ride on the gravity-fields here, and become clean …"

Davaryush's mind reeled under the impact of this revelation. The sun filled the screen completely now, unbelievably white …"You mean that you *built* this star?

You built a varigrav coaster . on the surface of a sun?"

"If only we had the technology!" Ernad smiled a little. "Why, the mind boggles. You are so close to the answer, and yet so far, so incredibly far! Well, we are all bound by the limits of our experience. It is time to live; explanations will follow."

They were in the airlock, then; waves of nausea crashed in his head, and he stood stock-still like a martyr waiting for death (which he felt himself to be) while they put the wings on him and the tittering of the children pelted his brain like painful hail-pellets—

The airlock opened! There was whiteness, such whiteness. He shut his eyes and fell. Fell. Fell. His blood was burning. He was burning, he was falling into hell, plummeting helplessly into the scorch-swift firebreath of the sunwind. He screamed, he thrashed his body uselessly against emptiness, he opened his eyes and the whiteness shattered his vision, the featureless whiteness, so he screamed and screamed, until he was no longer aware of his screaming.

He heard voices out of the past *(Kill the criminal Daavye no I can't I can't you have compassion my son compassion man is a fallen being).*

He reached the limit of his falling. And soared! And was flung upwards, upwards, on an antigraviton tide! And swerved, and fell headlong again, and swooped in tandem with a tongue of flame, and his scream was a whisper in the thunder of the wind *(come on Daavye you fool it's the latest craze no! are you afraid of life or something Daavye Daavye?)* and fell and fell *(pater noster qui es in inferno)* and fell …

And soared! And caromed into the roaring flame! And fem And saw death, suddenly, and came face to face with himself, and knew death intimately … and fell *(Kill the criminal Daavye compassion compassion)* and fell …

Trust me.

Falling, the voice embraced him. The voice sang through him:, The voice made him tingle like a perfect harp-string, dispelling his terror in a moment. He was a nothing touched by love. (*Memories came like endless printouts but there was one memory on the verge of crystallizing, and he was waiting for it, waiting for it to come, clear as a presence—*)

The voice was like homeworld. The roaring was the whisper of the sea. He could almost see his parents again: and fell and fell …

… and was touched by love and fell and lost consciousness, becoming one with an ineffable serenity.

"Answers! I want answers!"

He woke, sweating, in the room in the twisted house. Ernad was there, and the whole family; he felt their concern, and then he broke down and sobbed violently," hopelessly.

"I think we deserve some answers too, Ton Davaryush," Ernad said softly; there was iron in his gentleness. (He heard the others whispering among themselves: "When he came back to the ship, he was in a trance, unconscious."

"He's been like this for weeks."

"Now understand this, Davaryush," said Ernad, "you are not the first Inquestor to visit our planet. And will not be the last either."

Davaryush did what he never dreamed he would do: between fits of weeping, he told them the whole story, how he had come to Shtoma to save the people from themselves, how he had been defeated, how he understood nothing now, nothing at all.

(They fed him with sweet *zul* and were so kind to him. This, too, evoked a strange wonder and respect in him; for he had wanted to betray them.)

"Well, you were promised an explanation. Listen, then:

Udara is no ordinary star. Of course we didn't build him: that's ridiculous. But—what do you know about the origins of sentience? Well, you know how life evolves: how certain arrangements of atoms, certain paradigms, created purely by chance interactions, you understand, becoming living beings, self-aware, sometimes … white dwarfs are created by incredible cataclysms, by a star going nova, dying … somehow, a spark of life was made, after the nova, and *udara* became self-aware. *Udara* is *alive*, Davaryush! and we have acquired a symbiotic relationship with him that permits us to exist in the scientifically anomalous state … do you follow? In the black boxes, Davaryush: pieces of the sun."

Davaryush lay back, stupefied, his thought fired by the incredible imagery of it. "Did you imagine that mere humans such as we could create and uncreate gravitons and anti-gravitons? How much power is available, without the resources of a star? Could we make and unmake gravitational fields? Could we dim the sunlight on one area of the sun, so as to be unharmed by its heat? *Udara* does this, by his own will; his knowledge of physical laws is several orders beyond our understanding. We think that he is aware of himself, not only in this four-dimensional continuum, but also in other continua."

"But with this power," Davaryush said, "with this sun to do your bidding, can't you conquer the galaxy, win wars?"

"You still don't understand! The sun does not do our bidding; the sun does all this because he *loves* us." (Davaryush remembered, suddenly, how love had touched him when he was plummeting towards death.) "You felt it in the sunlight. You would always have felt it, but you were so full of confusion and contradiction, and so many people had lied to you …but when you fell into the sun, when you danced on the sun's face, then you understood. You see, we can't commit evil, because in the act of dancing

—what the rest of humanity thinks of as our little children's game—we have partaken of a tiny fragment of his nature …

"But let me plant a doubt in your mind. That is what you came to do to us, isn't it? Well: what if the Inquest existed, not for salvation, but for destruction? What if its sole purpose were to perpetuate its leaders' desire for conquest, and its mouthpieces, the 'Inquestors,' were simply indoctrinated with pseudo-religiousness to make them more fanatical, more serviceable?"

And Davaryush knew that he had lost his faith. (He wondered what answer he would give them about Shtoma. It would probably be unsatisfactory; they would undoubtedly have to send another Inquestor. But he no longer cared what the Inquest thought.)

***

Finally there came a day when Alk came running in to him, breathlessly: "Your tachyon bubble, it's hovering above the house!" He stepped outside. The sun shone on him, bathing him with inexpressible joy. Suddenly the memory came to him, the memory that was just beginning to come to him, before he became unconscious—

He was six years old. The ship was waiting to take him to the war. He was standing there with his father, by the sea shore, and his father seized him, on impulse, and threw him into the air, an he screamed for help, half-laughing, and fell for an eternity, in{ the arms that were for him, for protecting him, for loving him:

At last he understood the love of *udara* .

…But the children of the house had come and were clustered around him, making much of him, and Ernad stood at the entrance, waving to him.

"*Qithe qithembara!*" he yelled frantically, forcing back his tears—

He took one more step towards the bubble.
You have danced on the face of the sun.

—Arlington, Virginia 1978

Aquila

Once, when I was very young, father took me in the motor-car to the Via Appia, to see a man being crucified. It was some slave, some minor offense that I don't recall; but it was the first time I had ever seen such a thing. All the way there—and the way from our estate is olive-tree country, beautiful in the height of summer—Father was lecturing me about the good old-fashioned values. It was as much for the benefit of Nikias my tutor as for myself.

As we approached the Via Appia we would run across peasants or slaves; I remember that their awe at seeing my father's gilded motor-car, with its steam chamber stoked by uniformed slaves, with its miniature Ionian columns supporting a canopy of Indish silk, was sometimes comical, sometimes touching. Only someone of at least the rank of tribune might possess such a vehicle—although they are much slower than horses—for their secret parts are manufactured, somewhere deep in the heart of the Temple of Capitoline Jove, by tongueless and footless slaves who can reveal little of the mysterious rites involved. Truly the Emperor Nero must favor my father, who had never plotted against him and always sent him curious and witty gifts, such as that funny glowing shroud from Asia Minor that had been used to wrap up the living corn-god, sacrificed each year only to be found reborn in some unfortunate young man.

It was stifling. My toga praextexta was drenched with sweat. When we got to the crucifixion, it was late in the day and hard to get a good view; and even my father was weary of lecturing me, and did so only intermittently as Briseis the pretty little cupbearer filled and refilled our goblets with snow-chilled Falernian. I was young then, as I have said, and remember little of the poor wretch's agonies; he put on a good show at first, shrieking hideously as the ropes were tightened and the cross raised, but presently he sank into lethargy, his eyes (which I only saw by virtue of being perched on the motor-car's driver's seat) glazed over, and flies stormed all over him. We gorged ourselves on melons and on a concoction of peacocks' brains and honey.

As we started home, my father, stimulated by the sight of bloodshed, harangued me all over again, standing proudly over the prow of the motor-car with his white mane and his senator's toga trailing in the evening breeze.

"Titus, old boy," he growled gruffly, dropping pointedly into Latin instead of using the Greek of casual conversations, "remember that you're a Roman. As a citizen you'll never be crucified, of course; but even so, a lesson well learnt and all that. The old ways are the best—I don't mean to espouse the Republic or anything foolish like that, Jove forbid, only to make sure you grow up straight and true and my son, eh, what! We should never have let those slimy Greeks come over and transform us into culture vultures... in the old days men were hard, fighting hard, playing hard, not like your mincing tutor over here." (Nikias and I were giggling in the back over some childish matter.)

"Listen, young man, when I talk to you! After all, the Divine Emperor Lucius Domitius (or Nero as he likes to be called) may do all this acting and singing, but he chose me, a sober and staunch man of courage and integrity, to receive the gift of this magical horseless chariot, of whose locomotive secrets only the gods Vulcan and Jove know."

"But Sire," said curly-haired, beardless Nikias of the gaudy tunic and scented hair, "it is said that this device was invented by a Greek scientist, Epaminondas of Alexandria, by enlarging on the theses of the ancients Aristotle and Archimedes; that this same Greek now holds an important, but secret, position in the Temple of Jove; that this mysterious engine, over which rites must be said and sacrificial blood spilt before it will run, is a simple mechanical device, the basis also of the equally mysterious ships which even now have returned from Terra Nova laden with curiosities—"

"Impudent scum! You can't buy a decent slave for a thousand gold pieces," my father said. "I suppose I'll have to beat you for impertinence." He pulled a little flail from a fold in his toga. "Damn these horseless monstrosities anyway! Nothing to whip, the thing just chugs along without any feel to it—" At that he began to lay into my poor tutor; but it was more of a gesture than anything, and he missed more often than not.

"Tell me about Terra Nova, Nikias!" I cried. It was the first interesting thing to happen that day. "Is it true they've found barbarians?"

"Yes, and giant chickens, too, that go gobble-gobble-gobble, and vast herds of aurochs, and the fiercest barbarians imaginable—thousands in number! Why, they decimated the Tenth Legion before General Gaius Pomponius Piso—"

"Insufferable!" my father said. "Everyone knows that the Roman army, in its discipline, its order, and its bravery, has not been beaten in a thousand years."

"Tell that to the Parthians," said Nikias, deftly dodging a blow.

"They must be really fierce, these Terra Novans," I said. I know I had stars in my eyes, because even then I knew I was going to be a general and have a legion all to myself. Father could

afford, after all, the kind of bribery that would get me some minor foothold in the establishment, and I'd go from there. "Are they as fierce as the Britons?"

"Fiercer. Wilder," said Nikias, and then added (keeping an eye out for my father) "but I'm not going to tell you a thing about them until after you've memorized all the aorist and second aorist forms of these contracted verbs. See, when alpha, epsilon or omicron stems come into conjunction with the conjugatory endings—"

"Bloody Greek grammar," my father grumbled as we pulled into the estate.

"He's just jealous," Nikias whispered in my ear, "and besides the Emperor only invites him to those parties so that wily Petronius can make fun of him when they have those

poetry-improvising sessions, and your blessed father, who can't tell a hexameter from a hole in the ground, has to get up and warble to the lyre—I hear Petronius is writing him into his new novel, and the in-group at the palace is just in stitches—"

Perhaps I've painted too genial a picture of those days But alas, they were all too short. My father lost favor with the Emperor, got accused by the Empress Poppaea of some tom foolery, and was permitted to commit suicide. Despite the law, which is quite firm on the fact that descendants of traitors who honorably run on their swords may inherit as though the escutcheon had never been blighted, the Emperor somehow managed to confiscate the estate.

It was Nikias, that slimy Greek as Father used to call him, who saved my hide. He had a cousin, a eunuch, who was high up in the palace bureaucracy, who had become a millionaire simply by accepting one out of every three bribes that came his way, regardless of whether he followed up on the request to which the bribe was attached; and so our truncated family came to live at

court.

Meanwhile I grew tall. Nero and a few other emperors expired in various unpleasant ways. Terra Nova was all the rage for a while, and several modern cities with all the amenities—baths, arenas, circuses—were built, mostly along the eastern shore of that huge land mass, and procurators sent to govern the thriving colonies of settlers and Romanized natives.

The legions pushed westward into what is now the province of Lacotia. Some of our horses escaped and began to breed in the wild; the Terra Novans, in only a few years, became by all accounts the most adept of horsemen.

Frankly, I changed a great deal after Father's death, which taught me a salutary lesson about the human condition. I determined to become a fine Roman; to become, in fact, the very man my father had thought himself to be. I boned up on my Caesar and on all those battles; I studied Xenophon and all the Greek military historians; went off with the legion and got myself a few border commands; saw action in Britain, when the Picts came down on Eburacum, and again against some recalcitrant barbarians on the Dacian border....

After a while I was noticed by the Divine Domitian; and it was on the very day that the Emperor granted Roman citizenship to all the barbarians of Terra Nova, and awarded himself the title of Pater Maximus Candidusque, or White and Greatest Father, that he also honored me with the command of the Thirty-fourth Legion.

***

"Titus, old chap," the Emperor said to me, "have I conquered anything lately?"

We were ensconced in the Imperial Box at the Circus; Domitian was choking on a pickled lark's tongue with laughter over some lions who were making mincemeat of a bunch of recalcitrant Judaeans. His favorite, a peculiar-looking dwarf with an enormous head and staring eyes, sat at his feet.

"Well," I said, feeling very silly to be out of uniform and having long since lost interest in the sight of gore, "there's not much of the world left, Your Magnificence. West of Lacotia, perhaps, in Terra Nova—"

"Boring, boring, boring, you silly general. Those savages are fierce, and they certainly put on a spectacle in the arena, though I suppose you haven't seen any of the new shows, being out in the backwaters quelling Visigoths and Picts."

"True, my lord, but—"

"I want spectacle, Titus!" The crowd was roaring now as the slaves with meathooks dragged the corpses out through the gates of death. A lone lion straggled. Domitian clapped his pudgy hands; a bow and arrow was handed him on a silver platter. He waved for silence, and it fell just like that, twenty thousand people gulping in mid-sentence. "I haven't had an interesting spectacle since... last year, when I had Amazons in motor-cars fighting pygmies on bicycles."

"Yes, where are the motor-cars these days, my Lord? I haven't seen a single one since I got back from the campaign."

"Shush, shush, old chap." He clambered up onto the seat of his throne and transfixed the lion in the neck with a single shot. The crowd burst out in carefully rehearsed spontaneous cheering.

He sat down as they began to flood the arena for a mock sea-battle. "Ah yes, the motor-cars—I used them all up in the one circus show, Titus, and the priests of Jove haven't deigned to

cough up another one."

"And how's Epaminondas of Alexandria?" I said pointedly. "Oh, we tortured him. Didn't get anything, though; it seems

that his 'visions from the future' have ceased. At least we got all the shipbuilding secrets from him before he passed on, or else we'd lose all contact with the New World. But you're changing the subject," he said warningly.

"Of course, my lord. The spectacle."

"Do you remember... Marcus Ulpius Trajanus?" "How could I forget? Brilliant strategist. Taught me

everything I know, Trajan did. Very clever of him to lead the Dacians up the wrong way on the Danube.   "

"A little too brilliant," said Domitian. "Oh, he had plans —big plans. Subjugate the Parthians. Blah blah blah. Well, we got Cappadocia out of it, but after that he went a bit far— wanted to march on up the Tigris and push the Parthians into India or some other such grandiose notion. Fortunately, I was able to send him off to subdue the Seminolii, an absolutely frightful tribe of Terra Novan savages. Maybe I should recall him, but you know how it is. These ships— even with Epaminondas's improvements—I mean the revelations of Jupiter Optimus Maximus—take a year to get here. And as it happens, the Parthians are attacking now."

"Which Parthians, Sire? I thought they were all wrangling over the throne since old Vologesus died."

"God knows. Some petty king of theirs, fancies himself Vologesus's successor, busy reuniting the place. Just a few thousand of them, Titus old chap, I'm sure they'll easily be defeated by one of our matchless legions, eh, what? I wouldn't even bother with it much, except that ...the point is, my precious aurochs herds are in danger."

"Excuse me, Sire, but... I've been on campaign so long..."

"The aurochs herds, you fool! You know, bison. I've been breeding them in Cappadocia for the arena. Good grazing, you know. You've no idea what trouble it is to capture the damned creatures, to send good legionaries up through Dacia and into the forests of Sarmatia north of the Black Sea... and every one of the soldiers itching to slaughter barbarians! And since the aurochs have been rendered virtually extinct by the demands of the games—you remember Vespasian and his hundred-day opening celebration of the Coliseum, don't you?—these Imperial aurochs are the only ones to be had on short notice. I understand that gigantic ones roam the Great Plains of Lacotia in Terra Nova, but shipping costs are prohibitive. I'd have to impose some capricious tax on adultery or theatergoers or pumpkins."

"I see."

"You'll do more than see! You'll lead the expeditionary force, that's what you'll do!"

"Yes, my Lord," I said, my heart sinking. At least I would miss the reign of terror which, rumor had it, Domitian was about to instigate. I had no desire to end up being devoured by lions—or crocodiles, I reflected grimly as I saw them being released into the flooded arena to mop up the survivors of the sea-battle.

"You'll take the Thirty-fourth," he said. "What a spectacle! I may even come and watch the carnage."

"But your subjects need you here in Rome, Caesar," I said. "Beware, beware, I've a purge coming. Your best bet is to be

far from here; and fighting is, after all, the only thing you do well."

That was true. I remembered the last major purge; for a moment, after twenty-odd years, I saw my father as he lay dying

on a couch, back on the estate with the olive groves. "Thank you, Caesar, for the signal honor," I said, going down on one knee; but Domitian was busy shooting the crocodiles, cackling with glee as the draining arena churned red.

We set sail shortly from Brundisium. We used traditional triremes because it wasn't too far; but to show our status as purveyors of the Imperial Wrath, we were preceded and followed by a full escort of the new fast little ships. They wove in and out among our old-fashioned ones, making a thorough nuisance of themselves.

The Thirty-fourth was garrisoned in Thrace at the time, fresh from its foray into the land of the Dacians. My tutor Nikias was there, wizened but waggish as ever. We marched eastward.

At first it was clear that we were in the land of the Pax Romana. Town after town followed the prefabricated Roman pattern: country estates of the rich, a temple to the local god and another to Jove or Augustus or someone, a circus for family entertainments, an enormous public baths, insular apartment complexes for the poor, markets, and so forth. The terrain would change from the hills of Bithynia to the plains of Galatia, but the towns all looked alike; it was one of the less agreeable aspects of the Empire.

Naturally I adhered to strict discipline throughout. I didn't hesitate to have men flogged or executed, and all down the good straight Roman roads I never once heard a sour rhythm in the thump, thump, thump of infantry, nor did the legion's eagles once waver as the aquiliferi held them high. In spite of himself, Father had made a man of me.

When I got to Cappadocia I found that Domitian had been grossly misinformed.

The Parthian host had pushed right through the mountains and into the western plain of Cappadocia, where lies a great salt

lake. We were outnumbered five to one, and they had already taken the border town of Domitianopolis, only a year old. The precious herds of aurochs and their grazing grounds were behind the enemy lines!

I did my dogged best. We set up castra about a mile from where they were, up the side of a hill, and engaged them in the traditional manner, to little avail. There were just too many of them. In the second battle I lost one of my eagles, the sacrificial ram had three livers and its heart on the wrong side, and I sat down to compose a letter to Caesar asking for help. I retired my legion to the next town, Trajanopolis (ah, human vanity) and prepared for reinforcements.

Some weeks later came the reply, as I was having my back rubbed in the local baths:

> To Titus Papinianus, Dux of the Thirty-fourth, greeting: Well, Titus old boy, got more than you bargained for, eh?
>
> Well, there's not too much I can do. Terra Nova's acting up—for some reason the Seminolii (who are a union of the southeastern savages, formed when we drove the Chrichii, the Chirochii, and the Choctavii southwards, and these barbarians interbred with certain of our runaway Nubian slaves) think there's

something wrong with our teaching them to take baths and go to the circus and so on. Trajan is busy quelling them—only the northern provinces, Iracuavia and Lacotia, are friendly.

So I'm afraid there's little I can do, unless I want to expose some other border elsewhere.

A curiosity, though, Titus. In his last shipment of entertainers for the arena, the impresario Lucretius Lupus, who is vacationing in Terra Nova, sent me a whole tribe of Lacotians. Their leader, Aquila (actually some barbaric tongue-twister, but it means eagle) was the very man who defeated Pomponius Piso

thirty-five years ago. They were supposed to do battle against Numidian archers in the Coliseum, but... why not?

I'm sending them on the next ship. Who knows, perhaps these Lacotians may know something—and they're screamingly funny besides. Fight well—come back with your shield or on it, as the saying goes.

Ave atque vale,

Titus Flavius Domitianus, Caesar, Augustus, Imperator, Pater Patriae, Pater Maximus Candidusque, and various other titles, your Emperor and God.

Apparently I was a victim of the purge, after all. But at least I would fulfill my childhood dream of meeting one of those legendary Terra Novan savages face to face, before I died gloriously in battle.

***

It had been an exhausting day. We had returned to the old castra, and I was studying the war histories, trying to work out a viable stratagem, and, for fear of keeping the legion too idle, had detailed two maniples of infantry to dig more trenches and build more ramparts. Alone in the shade of my praetorium with a flagon of Chian wine, I tried different ways of deploying our meager artillery, our scorpiones, ballistae, and catapultae, by arranging pebbles around a clay model of the terrain. About two thousand men, a third of the legion, were dead or wounded. It was depressing.

I'd fallen asleep at the table. A lamp burned still, causing the shadows to flit along the flaps of my praetorium. I was in my bare tunic; outside, guards watched, their pila crossed over the entrance. Suddenly I opened my eyes.

The shadow on the wall... was there someone in the room with me? I listened. Was it a breathing? Ah no, my own, but—

There. A shadow on the wall, dancing against the quivering lamplight... I reached for my dagger. It was jerked out of my hands. I whirled around. In the eerie flickering, an apparition leered at me.

"Jupiter defend me!" I cried, doing every avert-the-omen sign I could remember.

The ghost did not disappear. It didn't move either. I took a good cool look at it (I knew by now I must be dreaming, or else why would the guards not have noticed?) and Virgil's description of the hell-beings of Avernus, whom Aeneas saw on his descent into Hades, was nothing compared to this.

It was a weatherbeaten face with a hooked nose and hawklike brown eyes, and it was painted in garish reds and yellows and striped with black. Its hair was long and white; and, in a headband, a number of eagle feathers stuck out.

It was almost naked; it stooped with age, and its chest sagged like an old man's. A breechclout of some kind of leather hid its privates. It smelled of some strange oil; if it had bathed at all, it was no Roman bath it took.

It grinned at me.

"Who in Hades are you?" I gasped at last, when pinching myself several more times resulted only in an itchy arm. "And how did you get in here?"

It shrugged. "I've never yet met a Roman I couldn't creep up

on," it said genially. 'You mean you're—"

"Hechitu welo. I am Aquila the Barbarian." "Oh, but you do speak Latin, I see."

"What do you think? We've been taking your baths, reading your ghastly poets, and watching your indecently gory spectacles for the past thirty-five years."

So this was the famous tactician who had demolished the legions of Pomponius Piso! "I'm pleased," I said, "to have such a distinguished leader as yourself working under my command."

"Under your command!" The savage began to cackle. I was somewhat disgruntled; he said, "The White and

Greatest Father said nothing about working under anybody. We came of our own free will, in friendship, to make war with honor if we so choose. Do you have any wine?"

"Oh. Sorry." I picked up the flagon to pour some, but he relieved me of the whole thing and began to guzzle. "And your men? How many are there?"

"How should I know? Who can count the trees of the forest?" "Show me then." I lifted the tent flaps; outside, the two

guards lay bound and gagged. The moon was full, and a fire was roaring at the crossroads of the via principalis and the via praetoria. I saw them in the half-light, a comical procession such as you might see in one of Plautus's farces.

Some of the men were mounted; their horses were painted as bizarrely as they were themselves. Some wore their hair braided in the Gaulish manner, but unlike the

Gauls' it was well-oiled and sleek. Feathers adorned their heads. They had little armor, although a few had borrowed cuirasses and one or two sported

ill-fitting helmets. Some were bare-chested; others had bewildering neckpieces hung with beads, animal claws, seashells, and silver denarii. All the way down the via principals they came. It was amazing that they had made no noise. Their women followed, carrying burdens, or leading dogs with packs tied behind them.

"Are these," I asked Aquila, "my reinforcements? Can they take orders?"

"I don't know," Aquila said. "Is there good fighting to be had here?"

"Well, there are twenty thousand Parthians back there," I said, jerking my thumb eastward.

"And who might the Parthians be?"

"Parthians," I said (slowly, in the legionaries' pidgin Latin, so they'd understand every word) "are a race of extremely wicked people from the east, who revile the name of Rome and seek, in their overweening hubris, to rob us of our territory and set up a rival Empire of their own. They have already taken Domitianopolis and are about to ravage all Cappadocia."

"And what about the Cappadocians? Perhaps they would prefer the Parthian masters to the Romans?" he said with a nasty chuckle.

What ignorant idiots! I cursed Domitian for playing this terrible trick on me. "Obviously," I said with painstaking clarity, "it is the destiny of Rome to rule the world; the Emperor, who is a god and bloody well ought to know, is divinely charged with the right to conquer all inferior nations! Everyone knows that. I mean, you Lacotians have been Roman citizens for some time now, haven't you? What a ridiculous thing to be arguing about, with those beastly Parthians beating at the very gates of the Empire.   "

"You Romans never listen, do you? By what right, pray, are you in Cappadocia, as opposed to the Parthians or indeed, the Cappadocians?"

Casuistry has never been my strong point. Nikias could never get me to understand the simplest Platonic dialogue, so you can imagine my confusion as I faced this foul-stenched savage who was making me defend the obvious. I glared at these Terra Novans, getting very red in the face. "Damn it, we own this land here!" I said.

"What a strange philosophy! How can land be owned? You Romans came charging into Lacotia, you gave us horses and pushed us out of the forests into the plains. What we had we shared with you, but you wanted everything. And all you give us is those bloody spectacles. You don't have true wars, wars that hone a man's spirit and sharpen his senses; you have wasteful wars in which men are like the cogs of your motor-cars and ships. I do not come to fight in your war. The others, of course, may do exactly as they wish."

"You're not going to give them any orders?"

"Why should I? We are all equal; as their chief I shall certainly advise them, but public opinion may gainsay me."

What a way to run an army. "Are you sure you're the great Aquila who vanquished Pomponius Piso?"

"Ah, that funny little Roman who watched from afar and never once got a spot of blood on his toga! That was a wonderful war indeed. Some mercenaries of yours, from Hispania I believe, taught us the art of taking scalps, which we have adopted into our culture." For the first time I noticed the grisly assortment that dangled from his waistband. "But you Romans didn't play by the rules. After you lost the war, you didn't return to your own land.

Now that I have seen your land I can understand why, though."

What! This man dared to impugn the sacred name of Rome? I had a mind to have him flogged immediately, white-haired though he was. "How can you possibly say this?"

"Ugh! Your crowds, the noise of your thoroughfares, the ugly monstrosities you call palaces, the stone images that you dote on and pray to... I thought I was in hell itself, General. Where I live the land is green for a thousand miles, and the brooks are clear and men's hearts soar like hawks. Much like this Cappadocia which you are even now despoiling with aqueducts that change the flow of nature, with circuses that exterminate whole species of beasts—"

"That's enough," I said. "We'll fight this war without you! Go home!"

"How can we? We no longer have a home. Our sacred burial grounds were razed to make room for a public baths. An evil spirit has descended upon our tribe, don't you see, and there isn't much we can do about it. We went hungry; we ate even our own dogs, such was our shame. That is why we took Lucretius Lupus up on his offer to come to Rome. We look for an honorable war in which to redeem ourselves —we didn't know that Lucretius Lupus had signed us up to kill Numidian archers in the circus for the general amusement. But the Pater Maximus Candidusque heard our plea with compassion; that is why we're here.   "

"I see," I said without conviction. I was resigned to an ignominious defeat. I'd already lost one eagle after all, and in the days of the Republic I would probably already have committed suicide, but such was the decadence to which contemporary society had fallen that I did not even contemplate such a step. I decided to dismiss them for now and get back to serious work. "Go see the quaestor, Quintus Publius Cinna; he'll feed and pay you. You'll have to pitch castra outside, but in the morning I'll assign a detail to help you dig fossae and build vallae."

"Bah!" the old man snorted. "Are we women, that we must hide behind trenches and walls? We will put our tipis at the foot of this hill, in the very sight of the enemy—"

"But their catapultae—their ballistae—"

"What do a few machines matter? Since we have lost our burial grounds we do not care to live." So saying the old savage made a gesture of dismissal at me—me! and swept out; the weird parade followed him, silent as shadow. Even the dogs made no noise. When I returned to my tent it was as if the whole thing had been a dream.

***

At dawn, driven by curiosity, I drove out of the camp with Nikias and a couple of tribunes. I was hoping that the Terra Novans would miraculously have vanished, but far from it. An encampment lay at the foot of the hill, just as Aquila had promised. If the enemy wanted to storm our castra it would probably be over the Terra Novans' dead bodies.

What an undisciplined hodgepodge of a castra it was! Their tents, scattered without any pattern or thoroughfare, were shaped like inverted funnels of the type alchemists use for straining their filtrates. Infants squalled; horses were tethered at random; and the tents, which seemed to be of the hides of cows or aurochs stretched over a frame of poles, were decorated with crude likenesses of animals and men. No doubt Domitian found these savages comical; lacking his sense of humor, I found them rather pitiable.

And were they engaged in drill exercises, or marching up and down the hill to keep in shape for the coming conflict? Not a bit?

The men, all naked save for scant loincloths, beads, feathers, and soft leather caligae, were lazing about in clumps, muttering in their guttural tongue.

I saw Aquila among them.

"Ave, General," he said, looking up. "The Parthians have mobilized a wing of their army; I believe it's young Chosroes leading them. They're on their way."

"How in heaven could you know such a thing?" Aquila got up and pointed to the east.

"Whatever do you mean?" At the limit of my vision, a hillock much like our own seemed to be emitting little puffs of smoke.

"Ah, some of our braves are restless, General, you see. They decided to go for a closer look. Those are smoke signals."

"Secret codes in smoke? Good heavens, how sophisticated," I said; in truth I could hardly make it out at all, in the dazzling sunlight, and I was certain that Aquila was having me on. "From behind enemy lines, no less! How large was the party you sent out?" I asked sarcastically.

"What party? You know how young men are. I could not restrain them from this display of bravery.　　"

"Perhaps there is something in your savage tactics, Aquila," I said. "I shall look forward to your fighting by my side—"

"And whyever should I do that?" said the chieftain. His puzzlement seemed genuine.

I threw my hands up in despair. "Oh, Marcellus—"

The tribune by that name rode up to me. "Tell the signifer and the aquiliferi to ready their banners. Let the tubicines stand ready to sound my orders, and let the cornicines be not far behind, to relay the commands to the appropriate maniples."

"Yes, General. Any particular formation?"

I sighed. "Oh, acies triplex, I suppose." A doomed general might as well go out in good classical style.

"You haven't much time, General," Aquila said, chuckling. "They're due in about five minutes."

"How do you know?" I said, knowing that he would only come up with some outrageous boast of his men's prowess.

"Oh, I've been putting my ear to the ground—" Suddenly an earsplitting din rent the air. My horse reared up. I waved vaguely to the tribune. Somewhere a bucina wailed, and then I heard the shouts of thousands of men as they fell into the three lines of Julius Caesar's favorite formation. I heard the deep-voiced tuba bray and be echoed by the shrill screech of cornua.

"Have fun," Aquila shouted after me as I spurred my horse down the hill.

***

At sunset we straggled back to the castra, roundly beaten. I didn't even want to reckon the casualties. I found my way to the praetorium and summoned Nikias to me. We had run out of the good Chian wine and were down to cheap Italian wines, but I was past caring. I downed a whole pitcher of it before Nikias arrived.

"Sit at the table, Nikias. There, opposite me, like you used to when you taught me all those contracted verbs. Did you bring your pen and parchment?" He opened his toolbox.

"Letters to write?" he said.

"Yes, I want to dictate a letter to Caesar. But first... write me up a document of manumission."

"You wish to free a slave, Master Titus?" An expression of alarm crossed his face.

"Yes. You." The oil lamp sputtered briefly; the wick was low.

The tent dimmed; the shadows deepened. "You're not planning to—"

"Yes, as a matter of fact I am. You can hold the sword while I run on it. But I want you to be a free man first."

"That's absurd! We Greeks have always considered the Roman predilection for suicide to be wasteful and unaesthetic, and—" He was in tears suddenly.

We were both sobbing our guts out, recalling the happy days of the estate with the olive orchard and the motor-car, wallowing in paroxysms of grief, when—

Behind me, in the tent, someone cleared his throat. I nearly fell out of the chair. "Am I interrupting something?"

"Aquila!" I was almost incoherent. "How dare you interrupt this most private moment, you impudent savage —"

"There now, there now. I have no wish to see you suffer so. I come to offer help."

"Help?"

As I looked around my tent, other savages resolved out of the shadows. Far from having an intimate tête-a-tête with my tutor and friend of thirty-five years, I might as well have been a clown in a Plautus comedy, waving my leather phallus at the hooting masses.

"These are," said Aquila, "some of the young braves of my tribe. Here is Ursus Erectus... Nimbus Rufus..." The names were, of course, in his savage speech; I have translated them into a humanly comprehensible tongue. "... Alces Nigra... Lupus Solitarius.   "

"I am beyond your help," I said. "I'm weary. Domitian surely intends me to die here, and he shall be satisfied. I don't know what I've done to offend Caesar, but it appears to be the will of the gods—at least the will of one rather insistent one—"

"There now, don't kill yourself," Aquila said. "These four braves are bored. They've decided to invade the enemy camp, and they won't rest unless they penetrate to the tent of their very leader."

"What rubbish! Four people against ten, twenty thousand?

Your boasts have been plentiful, but this one—"

"The Lacota do not boast," the chief said matter-of-factly. "You may have noticed that we sneaked up to your tent and were able to watch your entire little scene with Nikias unobserved.

Rather maudlin, I may add."

I could not deny that. "Since you insist—"

"Oh, they certainly do. They haven't had a good raid since they crossed the Big Water."

"Very well then," I said, trying to gather up what shreds of dignity I yet possessed. "You shall each have a standard issue of weaponry: pilum, gladius, and scutum. Nikias, see to that. You will depart immediately."

"Thanks for the weapons, but our own will do very nicely," Aquila said. "As for leaving immediately, though—"

"Well?"

"They can't leave for at least two hours. A man's got to look his best for a sacred thing like war. It'll take them that long to get their warpaint on."

"What? What kind of fighting is this, where you stop to adjust your makeup and your hair? Is this a war or is it a Corinthian brothel?"

"Relax, General!" Aquila said jovially. "Honor and glory will soon be ours." I blinked and they were gone.

For the next five or six hours I sat twiddling my thumbs. Even if they didn't come back, I reflected, they might be able to slip into Chosroes's tent and assassinate him. A dirty trick, and hardly the Roman way to do business—my father would turn over in his grave!—but I could salvage my conscience by noting that savages could hardly be expected to know about the refinements of civilized warfare.

I pulled out my military texts and studied them. But I was too nervous to concentrate. I pulled out some light reading, a scroll of scientifictiones.

I was a little way into the epic poem Fundatio: Fundatio et Imperium: Fundatio Secunda—which predicts, amusingly, that Rome will collapse and we will enter an age of barbarity —when...

"What's that noise?" I shouted. Nikias was awake too, and hollering for the tribunes. "It's an ambush!" I staggered outside.

Coming up the via principals of the castra, the four Lacotians were dancing up a storm, screaming incantations in their language, and hitting their lances on shields. Alarums were sounding around the camp. Centurions rushed hither and thither, bumping into each other and tripping.

The Lacotians were cavorting around in a bacchanalian frenzy, and I saw that fresh scalps dangled from their spears and their face paint was streaked with blood.

When they saw me they calmed down a little. "What on earth—" I said. They began clamoring in their tongue all at once.

I finally saw Aquila, shuffling up the via principalis.

"Victory!" he said. The braves began to throw assorted spoils at my feet. Chests of precious metals. An aurochs hide.

Parchments written in the Parthian language. Aquila came forward and embraced me, beaming and smelling like a he-goat.

"They reached the tent of Chosroes?" I stared dumbly as one of the braves hurled what was unmistakably Chosroes's armor at my feet. I could hardly believe my luck. Surely the

Parthians (whose military organization was far less disciplined than ours, and who would be thrown into utter chaos by the death of a leader) would be confused enough to return whence they came.

"You have evidence of Chosroes's death?" I said excitedly. "His head, perhaps, or some other such trinket I can send to Domitian?"

A pause. Aquila spoke to his four savages while I stood nervously.

Finally he said, "I have the honor to report that all four of my braves have counted coup on the Parthian leader."

I smelled a rat. "Counted coup? What does that mean?" "Among my people it is considered the mark of highest

bravery to touch the enemy with one of these"—he held up a short, cudgel-like baton—"and return alive. Killing the man hardly seemed necessary."

"You took these spoils and you didn't... even... harm. "

"Oh, he was harmed all right. Nasty bruise on his forehead, given by Ursus Erectus, here. And Nimbus Rufus fetched him a smart one on the posterior—he won't be able to sit down for a week."

"I want him killed! I want him killed!"

There was a terse discussion amongst them; then Aquila turned gravely to me. "Alas, General, they've decided they don't want to kill him. Seems that he fought so gallantly that he's won their respect, or something."

"But I command it!"

"We've been through all this before."

I stalked into my tent. "Nikias! The sword!" I shouted. "It's now or never!" Nikias followed me, shaking all over; poor soul, I'd never dictated his certificate of manumission, and I was too distraught to think of it now.

Aquila—of all the impudence—followed me in. "Come now, General!" he said. "I'll never understand you palefaces. Here we come from over the Big Water to inspire you with noble deeds and courageous acts, and what do you do? You decide to kill yourself! It's cowardice pure and simple. All you Romans are cowards! When you fight you put up barriers of metal so you can jab safely at the enemy. You throw great balls of flame with your thunder-machines and watch from a distance. You are no true men, but a gaggle of women. Or if you are men then you are hawks whose wings Wakantanka, the Great Mystery, has clipped. You are devils who have taken paradise from us. It grieves me to see such cowardice, for it declares your subhumanity to all men." He paused for breath.

"Are you calling me a coward? Me, Titus Papinianus, son of Caius Papinianus, nicknamed The Stalwart, equestrian by birth, dux by the Emperor's decree, scourge of the Dacians, a coward?"

"The same."

I leaped for the man's throat. Deftly he stepped aside and, I went crashing into the wall, ripping a hole in the fabric. "You see what I mean?" he said calmly. "Only a coward would attack a man old enough to be his father."

I lunged again; this time I knocked my head on a tent pole. "I'll prove it to you," I said. "Send me your strongest brave and I'll—"

"Brute force won't show anything," Aquila said. "However, if you wish to convince me of your bravery.   "

I waited, glaring at him.

"Tomorrow," he said, "I have a mind to ride far to the east, behind the enemy lines; to see the limits of your Roman Empire. And while I have no enmity for your Parthians, yet I will ride into their very maw and taunt them, so you will see that Aquila is no woman. You see me here, a man past eighty; yet I will do this thing. Do you dare come with me?"

A general doesn't permit himself to indulge in personal challenges, I told myself brutally. My father had beaten good Roman ethics into me often enough. But when I looked at this old savage something in me cracked. Here they were, these people who had stolen straight into the enemy camp and yet had scorned the easy victory of dispatching the enemy leader. What was it about Aquila and the Lacotians? After all, they had defeated Pomponius Piso himself. Perhaps they were sorcerers; perhaps they had some cloak of invisibility or potion of invincibility. I had to know. I no longer cared about Domitian, or his purge, or his precious aurochs herds for which we had wasted the lives of thousands of good legionaries. All I wanted to do was teach this insolent, supercilious savage a lesson he would never forget.

***

The sun had not risen when when we set off downthe hill. There were four of us: Nikias and I came in simple tunicae, although it galled me to be so disguised; Ursus Erectus, the young brawny one I had met the previous evening; and Aquila himself, who came clothed in a painted aurochs hide and wearing a bundle around his neck which he called his fascis medicinae.

Exchanging not a word, we rode towards the east, the sky gray-purpled by impending dawn. At the horizon was a line of low hills, at the foot of which the Parthians lay encamped; beyond them, I knew, was Domitianopolis.

"To the north," said Aquila, bringing his roan abreast of me, "there is a way around the hill. My braves found it yesterday. The Parthians, being the invaders, are unfamiliar with the country, yet they have not the Lacotian knack for sizing up the terrain; this is to our advantage." His smugness was annoying me; and also the fact that he was easing himself into the position of leader. I thanked the gods that my cohorts were not here to see me made a fool of.

"Shall I believe this braggart?" I asked Nikias in Greek. "Watch it!" Aquila said in the same tongue. "There are

Greeks in every village in Lacotia, for we find the tales of their

Homer far nobler than your superficial love poems and the boasts of your historians."

"Is there no way we can speak privately?" I said, frustrated. Nikias and I lashed our mounts on ahead; but I confess I did not know which way to go next, and had to allow.the Lacotians to slip into the lead again.

Presently we tethered our horses in a copse at the foot of the hill and Aquila began picking his way through a rocky trail that led upwards. He moved swiftly, gracefully, like a wild animal.

Ha! I thought, remembering one of the popular theories about the Terra Novans, which averred that they were indeed part animal, thus lacking souls and being oblivious to pain.

"I see you've snooped around here before," I said.

"No," said Aquila, "I'm just following the signs left by last night's raiding party."

"What signs?"

Quickly he pointed around us. Here an arrangement of leaves and twigs, there a few rocks heaped in a natural-seeming pattern. These he claimed to be sophisticated messages that warned of pitfalls, unsteady footholds, and the like. For a moment, I almost believed him. Then I realized that reading the signs of nature was a special ability of such primitive sorcerers, and that he was just having a little fun with me. I laughed at myself for being so gullible.

In a few hours we were overlooking the Parthian host from behind.

It took my breath away. Their tents were gaudy—brash reds, vibrant oranges, vivid against the green. They stretched far into the hill's shadow. There were chariots, points of fire in the carpet of grass. There were alien standards. There were soldiers crawling like ants: I couldn't begin to recognize all the types of costumes. And in the center of it all, an oriental palace in fabric, was the tent of their leader. How unlike my sparse, classical praetorium, or the rough hides of the Lacotians' tipis!

"There are many," I whispered. It wasn't like the Dacians, who were, after all, barbarians not much more advanced than the Lacotians.

"Bah! Old women, the lot of them. They are river reeds that sway when a child blows on them. They are even less courageous than the Romans, whom I once subdued."

"Will you taunt them now?"

"No," Aquila said. "First I've a mind to see your precious

Cappadocia. Let's go east."

"Very well," I said grimly, ready for anything. Now that I had seen the extent of the Parthian host I knew that death would not be far. I felt a reckless exhilaration, as though I were a child again.

We scrambled down cautiously, fetched our horses, and rounded the hill. A little forest hugged the eastern slope of it; and then we were on a plain. Lush grass thinned in the distance as the hills rose.

Suddenly there was a burst of gibberish from the lips of Ursus Erectus, who had been silent all day. He was pointing wildly at the far hills. I squinted.

At first it seemed like a scar, a brown patch on the hillside; and then I saw it move.

"The pta! Our sacred pta!" Aquila cried. He sounded younger. "At last our tribe may be freed of its curse, may find new hunting grounds! Would that I were a young brave, to find such pta and pte.   "

Without waiting, reckless, the two Lacotians spurred their horses into a gallop. Nikias and I caught up with them, and soon I saw the brown patch resolve into little brown patches; my vision blurred from the horseback riding—

"The Imperial aurochs herd!" Nikias shouted.

I knew that such creatures existed in the new world, but I had not known that they would exert such power over the savages.

The Lacotians were laughing now, whooping with glee, throwing their lances and catching them as they raced forward.

They were grazing. Thousands of them. Majestic creatures, bearded and sleek-furred.

And then, as we passed a rock mound, Aquila's steed stopped and whinnied.

I slowed to a trot behind him. A sickening sight greeted me. They were lying in the grass, one or two of them, rotting.

Carrion birds had settled on them, and when I looked up I saw more vultures wheeling.

The bison had been completely flayed.

"Why?" Aquila screamed at the sky, raging. I saw him weep copiously, without shame, like a woman. We rode on, but now their demeanor was grim.

As we neared the herd we found more carcasses. Always the skin would be stripped from them and their flesh remain moldering in the heat. Aquila's weeping did not cease.

And then, peering from behind a boulder, we saw mounds of piled pelts. And armed guards watching over them.

"Poaching," I said, "on a grand scale. At this rate they'll have killed and skinned the entire herd by year's end."

Aquila said, "Can this be true? Can they really take the skins and leave the flesh to rot, disrupt man's balance with nature?"

"Probably they plan to trade them further east. To the people of India, or those folk with skins of gold who inhabit the lands beyond, these pelts may be worth more than silks and spices."

"We have rediscovered paradise," said Aquila, "only to lose it a second time."

The Lacotians exchanged words rapidly in their tongue. I caught the words pta and pte, which seemed to be the male and female aurochs. Then Aquila turned to me and said, his voice quavering with emotion, "My heart is like a stone, General. I can no longer even weep. When your people drove us into the great

plains and gave us horses, we hunted the aurochs and our bellies were full. We took no more than what would fill us, and the hide and the bones we made good use of. When we were full we made war: holy war, not a war of senseless killing, but war to strengthen a man's heart and give him honor. Now when I look upon this land I see what could be another paradise. We could be happy here, for when we hunt we are part of nature's harmony.

But these Parthians hunt wantonly, they take only the skins and discard the meat. They must truly be cursed. I cannot bear to look upon this—" He faltered. "I have seen too much. I am too old. It is a good day to die. I shall lie here on the grass until death comes for me."

I was moved by his words. The savage spoke of strange ways and customs; but when I thought more deeply I saw that we were kin. For my father had had much the same thought, the day he learned of the Emperor's disfavor and took it upon himself to execute sentence. But I didn't want Aquila to die. I said, "Old man, last night you forced me to live. You called me a coward.

Must I remind you?"

Aquila seemed puzzled for a moment. Then he chuckled and said, "Of course, you're right. That isn't the answer at all, is it?

Obviously we shouldn't take this lying down. Instead, we'll take on the whole bloody pack of them."

"You'll fight beside us?" "What do you think?"

"So finally I'll get to see the fabled Lacotian art warfare.. .the unorthodox tactics so elliptically alluded to by Pomponius Piso in his Memoir of the Lacotian Wars?

"Huka hey! Alea jacta est!"

***

Later I squatted uncomfortably in Aquila's tent. There were four or five of them, the quaestor, one or two of my tribunes, sweating in their full regalia, Nikias taking notes, and me. Aquila pulled out a pipe, filled it with herbs from his fascis medicinae, and lit it, whereupon a foul stench filled the tent and I could hardly see for the smoke; this he puffed on, and then insisted I do the same. On complying I seemed to fall into a shadow world; everything felt hazy, unreal. So this was one of their secrets... a magic drug that no doubt rendered them invulnerable.

"Does the nearby town have a public baths?" said Aquila. "Of course," I said hazily. "How could a Roman town not

have any?"

"I want exclusive use of them for my braves for a day." "Righty-ho." Perhaps they were getting civilized.

"I want some trees, felled in a ritual way which I shall prescribe, set up at the foot of this hill—"

"Aha! A Lacotian war machine!" I knew they'd have something up their sleeve; for magic, in itself, is rarely effective unless blended with careful planning, as I had myself learned in my dealings with the Dacians and Picts.

"You might call it that," Aquila said, and he started to giggle ferociously.

A few more puffs, and it was as if I was seeing the world from underwater. The Lacotians rippled. In the distance, Father drove up in his motorcar, scolding me, and off in a corner Domitian was shooting some chimera full of arrows, and I was

laughing helplessly...

There was a great deal of grumbling from the townspeople when I requisitioned the public baths. But eventually we barricaded them off and the Lacotians—perhaps two hundred strong—trooped inside. A maniple was dispatched to a nearby forest to fell the trees Aquila had requested, accompanied by one of their priests or homines medicinae who would perform the appropriate ritual.

After a while I wearied of pacing the colonade outside the baths; I decided that I might as well join them. It's good to get the kinks out of your body before a major battle, even one you've little chance of surviving.

I went inside. Signs led to the tepidarium, caldarium and frigidarium. The place was unusually quiet. Normally the buzz of social banter never ceases at a bath. I disrobed in the vestiarium, which was piled high with the animal skins and feathers the savages wore, and then tried the caldarium.

I rubbed my eyes. At first you couldn't see for the steam and then—

The pool proper had been drained, Lacotians squatted in ranks inside. Steam poured out from the heating vents; the slaves must be working overtime underneath. Steam tendrilled out then as they sat, unspeaking, each of them apparently lost in some private vision. Fetishes, the skulls of aurochs, ritual pipes littered the tile floor, which was a mosaic depicting the rape of the Sabine women. I made out Aquila, a shrunken man with age-blotched skin, kneeling in the center of the throng.

I descended into the empty pool, my feet smarting against the hot tiles.

"Ah, there you are, Aquila old chap!" I said. "Thought we ought to discuss a little strategy, eh, before tomorrow?"

Silence. The man's eyes stared ahead far away. He didn't move.

"Hello? Hello?" I said.

He snapped to. "Oh, General Titus. Sshhh"—his voice dropped—"wouldn't want to disturb these fellows, would you?"

"What's going on?"

"Lacotian custom. Sweat bath, you know. Some of the men are, oh, far away, on spirit journeys. Usually we have special tents for this purpose, but it seemed a good idea to take advantage of your modern Roman technology...." He fell into a trance again, and I couldn't rouse him.

I bathed alone in the tepidarium for a while and returned to the castra, where an even more incredible sight awaited me.

At the foot of the hill, some distance eastward from the camp, several circles had been marked off with stones, aurochs skulls, pipes, and fetishes. At their centers stood the tree trunks that my soldiers had felled, and from them radiated hundreds of strings.

"Ho, there!" I called out, dismounting. "What's the meaning of this?"

A tribune came puffing up. "General, these savages have gone out of their minds!"

"Is this some kind of war engine?"

Distant hoofbeats. The Lacotians were returning from the city. In a moment they had all split into groups and were lined up naked in the circles.

"I don't rightly know, General, just what the blighters are up to. It could be some kind of rapid-firing slingshot, I suppose."

"No," I said, "those strings are strips of hide; anything for firing ammunition would require tormenta, twisted ropes with a

spring action as in the catapultae. I can't see any possible use for them."

"Perhaps they mean to swing down on the strings, as apes with vines in Africa."

"Then surely they would camouflage the engines so that their swoopings might contain some element of surprise."

"Good heavens, sir, what are they doing now?"

One of the homines medicinae was solemnly mutilating the young men one after another, cutting slits under the skin of their chests, sliding in little sticks, and then attaching them to the poles by means of the strings. Another homo medicinae distributed rattles to them and placed little wooden flutes in their mouths.

The braves gave no show of pain at all, but walked out to the edge of the circle, facing the center, stretching the strings to their limits.

"It seems awfully gruesome," Nikias said, approaching from the castra with welcome bowls of Lesbian wine, just purchased in the town.

All at once came the pounding of drums and a most monstrous caterwauling from a group of old men, chanting a wavering, out-of-tune melody whose long notes were punctuated by peculiar rhythmic gurgling sounds. At this the braves began to dance and blow on their flutes, staring steadfastly at the sun, which was shining fiercely. As the men danced they tugged at the strings, trying it seemed to yank themselves free; blood spurted from their chests. The din was astonishing. Presently a crowd of legionaries had gathered, and were staring at this display, cheering and jeering with the typical Romans' love of spectacle; one might as well have been at the bloody circus. Even I, professional butcher as I am, felt queasy at this eerie exhibition.

I finally caught sight of Aquila, moving unconcernedly through the crowd.

"What the hell is going on?" I yelled above the cacophony. "Oh, nothing," he said. "They are merely offering up their

pain. It is the sundance, you know. You do want to win the battle, don't you?"

"Yes, but—"

"They must dance," he said, "until the skin tears and they break free. After that they will dress in all their finery and go to war."

Children were running amok, poking at the men with grass blades. Women sang, their voices blending with the grunting hey-hey-hey of the old men.

"Do you mean to say," I began indignantly, "that you have made me go to all this trouble, just so you could have some horrid rite?" Never had these people seemed more alien to me. I had been wrong even to attempt to gain their co-operation. We were doomed, and I had only been stalling for time. The best thing would be to fling ourselves on the Parthians and die with a good grace.

Well, as if in answer to my sentiments, bucinae and cornua began to bray above the din. I looked to the east. A line of glitter was rolling slowly across the plain, like a monstrous worm of gold.

"The Parthians!" I cried. Instantly the tribunes were by my side. "Aquila, enough of this rubbish!" I said. "We're in real trouble now, and we need all the men we've got! Let everyone grab a weapon!"

Aquila just laughed at me. "What?" he said. "This is a sacred thing the men do. We cannot interrupt it. When they are ready, they will come."

It was useless. I should have known better than to attempt to deal rationally with savages. Superstitious primitives. It was our job to civilize these people—with fire and sword if necessary—not reason with them. With a final shrug of exasperation, I mounted, barked some orders to the tribune, which were presently relayed by tubae all over the castra above. Legionaries rushed for their shields and weapons, and the audience for the Lacotians' curious ritual of self-mutilation wilted away in an instant.

***

I had barely two squadrons of cavalry, and all save one of my praefecti equitum had perished. These I held in reserve, placing them on the hillside under my own command. I had five cohorts of infantry and a scattering of auxiliaries: a few slingers, perhaps a hundred of the Cretan sagitarii, and so on. These, under the command of the quaestor Quintus Publius Cinna, I deployed, again in Julius Caesar's favorite acies triplex formation, in three lines directly facing the onslaught, the troops in front forming an iron barrier with their shields. The artillery I scattered at intervals throughout the lines.

As I shouted my commands and the tribunes hastened to obey, the Lacotians continued their frenzied dancing, jerking at the rawhide strings and wildly piping on their flutes, so that it was almost impossible to make myself heard. The tramp-tramp of the distant enemy was something you felt more than heard, like a heartbeat, an impalpable dread. It had oozed halfway across the plain now, that multicolored worm of an army, and there was no time to lose. I chose a little cliff from which to watch the fray, as far as possible from the distracting noise of the Lacotians' rite.

Nikias was there; this time I remembered the certificate of manumission, and he was at my side a freeman and my hired scribe. Behind me I concealed the cavalry as best I could.

I gazed over the plain.

It seemed infinitely slow, the crawling forward of the enemy, froom my lofty vantage point. But I knew there was little time. I saw Cinna ride back and forth behind the lines, haranguing the pedites.

The enemy stopped.

I looked them over. They were neat squares of color, each square perhaps a thousand men. We were strung out a long way, but not very deeply; it was only a matter of time before they broke through. I saw, in the distance, the range of foothills in which their camp nestled; behind them were the cursed aurochs herds which Domitian was about to make me die for.

I heard their trumpets sound. They charged in one chaotic melee: chariots, infantry, cavalry all jumbled together. It was their numbers that had been our bane, not their brilliant organization. The first wave crashed into our shield wall; the shields clanged open at a single command and a volley of

fire-arrows burst forth. Horses whinnied and perished. Chariots overturned and upset other chariots. But they kept coming.

And lo! Our wall of scuta was breached by a suicidal charioteer, and hundreds of the Parthians were streaming through the gap, swords waving! Even from on high I smelled the blood, and the dust clouds were dyed scarlet, obscuring the view. I averted my eyes; the sight of hacking and bloodletting was not new to me, and held no interest. It was now up to me to decide whether to condemn the cavalry too, or to sound the retreat and commit suicide. It had been hardly an hour, and the outcome was already clear.

"Nikias," I said, adopting a brusque tone to hide my sorrow, "bring the sword at once."

"Yes... master." His eyes were red. I did not weep—we had been through all that before, in the tent, when Aquila and his braves had so callously spied on us.

Suddenly—

An earsplitting screeching assailed my ears! Down below the fighting froze for a moment, the dust started to settle, everyone turned and stared to the east.

Demons on horseback were charging from behind the enemy lines, firing streams of fire-arrows into the dumbfounded Parthian ranks. The figures were painted in dazzling colors, the horses' legs were decorated with bright lightning streaks, and they wore bonnets of feathers that trailed behind, and they were uttering such piercing screams as would make the very mummies burst forth from their pyramids. In the hills, I saw pillars of flame and smoke, and my spirits lifted. I knew the enemy camp was on fire. The Lacotians must have ridden as fast as the wind, and as silently, to have been able to accomplish all this.

Now the Parthians were scattering randomly, and my infantry were having an easy time of it as they rushed, crazed with fear, into their arms. I gave the order to give chase. The Lacotians had formed a circle of horsemen that surrounded the enemy host, and were riding around and around and firing.

"Quite a spectacle, eh, general?" I started. It was Aquila. He was mounted on a white horse, decorated with crimson lightning-stripes; his face was painted in red and white, and on his wrinkled brow sat a crown of feathers; behind him more feathers streamed. In his right hand he held high a feathered lance. He was magnificent. Although he wore no golden cuirass, his horse carried no gilt caparison, no cloak of purple flapped behind him... yet he looked like a god, his demeanor stern and implacable. The

Parthians, who had never seen a Lacotian decked in his war regalia, must surely have thought them devils, for they are a superstitious folk, without the benefit of the Empire's enlightenment.

"Aquila!" I said. "You've saved us! I've a mind to make all the legionaries perform your sundance from now on—"

"You are far from saved," he said. "Quickly. Bring your cavalry. Your men on the plain will pursue them; my men there will lure them. Meanwhile your cavalry and what remains of mine will round the hills, swifter than thought itself. If we become one with the wind, and soar like eagles, we may be able to head them off at yonder pass." He pointed to a crack, far off behind the enemy camp, which I could barely distinguish. But I wasn't going to argue now. I sent the herald with the summons and we were off.

The war-fever was in me now. We hurtled over the other side of the hill, Lacotians and Romans together, following Aquila's white steed. When we reached the pass I saw that Aquila's men had been busy indeed. For, as the Parthians fought their way through the bottleneck, pushed by our men and terrified out of their wits by the screeching of the Lacotians, other Lacotians had been at work rousing the herds of aurochs. Hither and thither they galloped, in and out of the herd, prodding, poking, luring.

A few at a time, the Parthians broke through the pass— to run head-on into a stampeding herd of aurochs.

"Huka hey!" the Lacotians shouted in thunderous unison.

Then they broke into a babble of war cries and shrill ululations, and charged frantically into the fray. Aquila turned to me and winked; then he too charged.

"Huka hey!" I yelled madly, wondering what it meant, as it finally dawned on me that a handful of eccentric savages had rescued the honor of Rome.

***

In the evening, the women danced the scalps of the slain around a roaring fire, and the Lacotians feasted on fresh meat from the humps of aurochs. We Romans were all invited. In the midst of the festivities we had a surprise visitor—Domitian himself.

He came up the hill in a palanquin borne by eight burly slaves. Couches had been set up for the Romans, a little way off from the dancing; Aquila and I were quaffing Samian wine from the same goblet as though we'd known each other for ages. When Domitian stepped off the litter I gaped and dropped my goblet.

"No ceremony, Titus old boy," the emperor said. "I told you, didn't I, that I'd half a mind to come along and observe the spectacle? And you didn't disappoint me. Ah, if only I could recreate this battle on the Campus Martius outside Rome... set up bleachers for the populace, with vending stands for cold drinks and sausages ...how the people would love me! I imagine I could stave off assassination for quite a while with a show like that."

"Caesar—"

"Imagine it! This Sundance they've described to me— could it be done in the arena, do you think?"

"Certainly not," Aquila said. "It is a sacred thing."

"Oh, don't worry, old chap, I'm only joking. That's what I like about savages though—you dare to contradict me, unlike these spineless Romans." I started to say something, but checked myself."What's this you're eating, barbarian victuals? Let's try some." He stuffed a piece of roast aurochs haunch into his mouth. "You shall have a triumph, Titus! And a new title. And I shall make you a procurator."

"I'm deeply flattered, Caesar," I said, hoping I would not be packed off to some rebellious wasteland like Judaea.

"Though, frankly, things haven't gone according to plan. I was rather hoping you'd be out of my hair by now."

"Caesar is merciful."

"And as for you, Aquila—"

"O Pater Maximus Candidusque," Aquila said softly, "I have seen the land of my dreams. When I was a young brave I came to this land in a spirit journey. I knew that the old ways were dying in Lacotia, but still I hoped—"

"Very well, old man," said Domitian. "You and your people shall stay here in Cappadocia. I only ask that you defend my herds. Take what you need for sustenance, and cull the best each year for my games, but protect them and see that they multiply."

When Aquila had translated these words to the Lacotians, they cheered the Emperor loud and long. Domitian beamed. He was like a child, really, and liked to do the right thing, when it didn't involve too much work.

"As for you, Titus, what do you want?"

What did I want? I turned it over in my mind. I wanted to retire from fighting. I wanted a comfortable house in the country. Simple things. I didn't think the Emperor would understand, so I said, "I want whatever you want, my lord."

"Yes, yes, old chap. You're rather lucky in a way, you know, being an incompetent idiot and all that. No one of any competence has been permitted to rise in power ever since my father Vespasian became Emperor. Your well-meaning stupidity has served you well...and you're damned lucky besides! After your victories in Dacia you were on the short list for purging, you know... so what do you think of these barbarians, eh? Do you think you could whip them into shape, lead them down the golden path to Roman citizenship, and all that?"

"Well—er—" Frankly, I don't think I ever wanted to set eyes on another Lacotian again.

"How succinct of you. Well, you're leaving for Lacotia right after the triumph—as my new governor."

I looked wildly about me. Was I seeing things, or had Aquila and Domitian just exchanged a sly wink? Mustering all my confidence, I said, my face getting redder by the second, "You can rely on me, Caesar. By next year, these barbarians will bloody well enjoy taking baths and going to spectacles. They'll read Virgil every morning before breakfast, and they'll all wear togas and speak Latin and they'll worship Venus and Mars and Jupiter and Minerva instead of their heathen idols, even if it kills me!"

I turned and saw Aquila guffawing uproariously. Then I took another swig of wine and laughed myself into a stupor.

—Alexandria, 1983

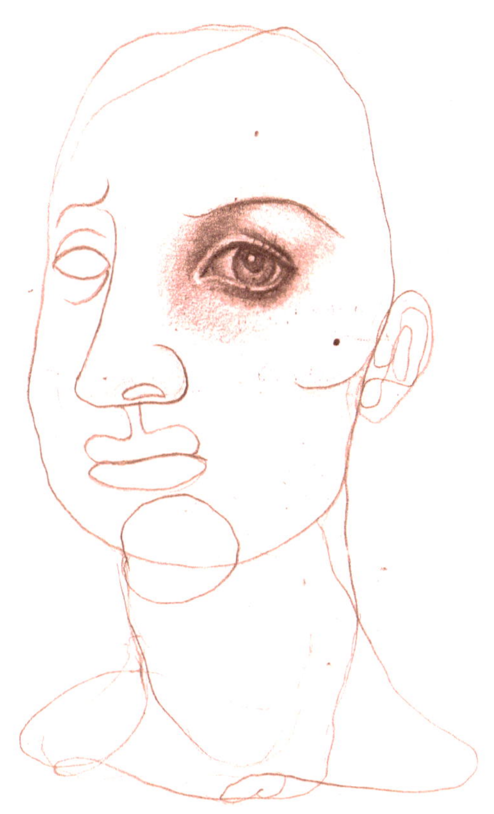

Absent Thee from Felicity Awhile

You remember silence, don't you?

There were many silences once: silence for a great speech, silence before an outburst of thunderous applause, silence after laughter.

Silence is gone forever, now.

When you listen to the places where the silence used to be, you hear the soft insidious buzzing, like a swarm of distant flies, that proclaims the end of man's solitude …

For me, it happened like this:

It was opening night, and Hamlet was just dying, and I was watching from the wings, being already dead, of course, as Guildenstern. I wanted to stay for curtain call anyway, even though I knew the audience wouldn't notice. It hadn't been too long since my first job, and I was new in New York. But here everything revolved around Sir Francis FitzHenry, brought over from England at ridiculous expense with his new title clinging to him like wrapping paper.

Everything else was as low-budget as possible, including me. They did a stark, empty staging, ostensibly as a sop to modernism, but really because the backers were penniless after paying FitzHenry's advance, and so Sir Francis was laid out on a barren proscenium with nothing but an old leather armchair for Claudius's throne and a garish green spot on him. Not that there was any of that Joseph Papp-type avant-garde rubbish. Everything was straight.

Me, I didn't know what people saw in Sir Francis FitzHenry till I saw him live—I'd only seen him in that ridiculous Fellini remake of Ben Hur—but he was dynamite, just the right thing for the old Jewish ladies. There he was, then, making his final scene so heartrending I could have drowned in an ocean of molasses; arranging himself into elaborate poses that could have been plucked from the Acropolis; and uttering each iambic pentameter as though he were the New York Philharmonic and the Mormon Tabernacle Choir all rolled into one.

And they were lapping it up, what with the swing away from the really modern interpretations. He was a triumph of the old school, there on that stage turning the other actors into ornamental papier-maché all around him. He had just gotten, you know, to that line:

Absent thee from felicity awhile …
To tell my story.

and was just about to fall, with consummate grace, into Horatio's arms. You could feel the collective catch of breath, the palpable silence, and I was thinking, What could ever top that, my God? … and I had that good feeling you get when you know you're going to be drawing your paycheck for at least another year or so. And maybe Gail would come back, even.

Then—

Buzz, buzz, buzz, buzz. "What's wrong?" I turned to the little stage manager, who was wildly pushing buttons.

The buzzing came, louder and louder. You couldn't hear a word Horatio was saying. The buzzing kept coming, from every direction now, hurting my ears.

Sir Francis sat up in mid-tumble and glared balefully at the wings, then the first scream could be heard above the racket, and I finally had the nerve to poke my head out and saw the tumult in the audience …

"For Chrissakes, why doesn't someone turn on the house lights?"

Claudius had risen from where he was sprawled dead and was stomping around the stage. The buzzing became more and more intense, and now there were scattered shrieks of terror and the thunder of an incipient stampede mixed into the buzzing, and I cursed loudly about the one dim spotlight.

The screaming came continuously. People were trooping all over the stage and were tripping on swords and shields, a lady-in-waiting hurtled into me and squished makeup onto my cloak, corpses were groping around in the dark, and finally I found the right switch where the stage manager had run away and all the lights came on and the leather armchair went whizzing into the flies. I caught one word amid all this commotion—

Aliens.

A few minutes later everybody knew everything. Messages were being piped into our minds somehow.

At first they just said *don't panic, don't panic* and were hypnotically soothing, but then it all became more bewildering as the enormity of it all sank in.

I noticed that the audience were sitting down again, and the buzzing had died down to an insistent whisper. Everything was returning to a surface normal, but stiff, somehow; artificial.

They were all sitting, a row of glassy-eyed mannequins in expensive clothes, under the glare of the house lights, and we knew we were all hearing the same thing in our minds.

They were bringing us the gift of immortality, they said. They were some kind of galactic federation. No, we wouldn't really be able to understand what they were, but they would not harm us. In return for their gift, they were exacting one small favor from us. They would try to explain it in our terms.

Apparently something like a sort of hyperspatial junior high school was doing a project on uncivilized planets, something like "one day in the life of a barbarian world." The solar system was now in some kind of time loop, and would we be kind enough to repeat the same day over and over again for a while, with two hours off from 6 to 8 every morning, while their kids came over and studied everything in detail.

We were very lucky, they added; it was an excellent deal. No, there wasn't anything we could do about it I wondered to myself, how long is "over and over again for a while"?

They answered it for me. "Oh, nothing much. About seven million of your years."

I felt rather short-changed, though I realized that it was nothing in comparison with immortality. And, standing there stock-still and not knowing what to think, I saw the most amazing sight.

We all saw the aliens as gossamer veils of light that drifted and danced across the field of vision, almost imperceptible, miniature auroras that sparkled and vanished …

I saw Sir Francis's face through a gauze of shimmering blue lights. I wanted to touch them so badly; I reached out and my hand passed right through one without feeling a thing.

Then they were gone.

 We turned off the house lights—we had until midnight—and went on with the play.

The buzzing subsided almost completely, but was very obviously there all the time, so everybody gabbled their lines and tried to cut in quickly between speeches to cover up the noise.

The applause was perfunctory, and Sir Francis seemed considerably distressed that he had been so easily upstaged.

I walked home at a few minutes to midnight. I saw peculiar poles with colored metallic knobs on them, all along Broadway every couple of blocks, like giant parking meters.

The streets were virtually empty, and there were a couple of overturned Yellow cabs and an old Chevy sticking out of a store window.

It had been too much for some, I supposed.

But I was so confused about what had happened, I tried to think about nothing but Gail and about the bad thing that had happened that morning. I climbed up the dirty staircase to my efficiency above an Indian grocery store and jumped into bed with all my clothes on, thinking about the bad thing between me and Gail, and at midnight I suddenly noticed I was in pyjamas and she was lying there beside me, and there was a sudden jerk of dislocation and I knew that it wasn't today anymore, it was yesterday, it was all true.

I squeezed my eyes tightly and wished I was dead.

2

I woke up around 11 o'clock. Gail stirred uneasily. We made love, like machines. I kept trying to pull myself away, knowing what was coming. Whatever the aliens had done, it had turned me into a needle in a groove, following the line of least resistance.

We got up and had breakfast.

She wore her ominous dishevelled look, strands of black hair fishnetting her startlingly blue eyes.

"John?" The dinette table seemed as wide as all space. She seemed incredibly unreachable, like the stars.

"Umm?" I found myself saying in a banal voice.

I knew what she was going to say; I knew what I was going to do.

But whatever it was dealt only with appearances. In my thoughts I was free, as though I were somehow outside the whole thing, experiencing my own past as a recording.

I wondered at my own detachment. "

John, I'm leaving you."

Anger rose in me. I got up, knocking over the coffee mug and shouting, "What for, who with?" like an idiot before going off into incoherent cursing.

"Francis FitzHenry has asked me to stay with him—in his suite at the Plaza!" The anger welled up again. Blindly, I slapped her face.

She went white, then red, and then she said quietly, dangerously: "You're too petty, John. That's why you're going to be a Guildenstern for the rest of your life."

That hurt.

Then she walked out of my life.

I shaved and walked slowly over to the theater. We played to a full house. The aliens came. Sir Francis seemed considerably distressed that he had been so easily upstaged.

I walked home, casually noting the two overturned Yellow cabs and the old Chevy stuck in a store window, past the overgrown parking meters, to my efficiency above an Indian grocery store, and threw myself fully clothed on the bed. I fell asleep.

I woke up around 11 o'clock, Gail stirred uneasily. We made love mechanically, and I knew that the two people who were lying there together had become totally divorced from themselves, and were going through preordained motions that bore no relationship whatsoever to what was in their minds. And there was no way of communicating.

We ate breakfast. She wore her ominous dishevelled look, and I desperately wanted to apologize to her, but when I tried to speak my facial muscles were frozen and the buzzing seemed to get louder, drowning my thoughts. Was the buzzing an external sound, or was it some mental monitor to enforce the status quo?

"I'm leaving you." Anger rose in me. I quenched it at once, but it made no difference either to my posture or to my words. "Francis FitzHenry has asked me to stay with him—in his suite at the Plaza!"

I slapped her face. Suddenly the veils of light came, caressing the musty stale air of my apartment, touching the dust and making it sparkle, like a golden snow between the two of us.

They faded. We had been watched; we were trapped in a galactic Peyton Place. "You're too petty, John. That's why you're going to be a Guildenstern for the rest of your life."

And walked out of my life.

It hurt me more every time. I was doomed to be a Guildenstern inthis play too, a Guildenstern for the old ladies and a Guildenstern for the veils of light. It was hell.

I shaved and walked slowly over to the theater. We played to a full house.

The aliens came; Sir Francis seemed considerably distressed that he had been so easily upstaged. I walked home, past the overturned cars and the gigantic parking meters that had materialized out of nowhere.

As I fell asleep, just before midnight, a thought surfaced: we were supposed to have two free hours every morning, weren't we? For months now, I had slept through those two hours.

I resolved to force myself to wake up at six.

3

I jerked myself awake at 6:30, snaked into unostentatious jeans and a T-shirt, and came down.

The brilliant summer morning hit me between the eyes. It had been autumn the previous night. Everything was to wonder at: the trash drifting down the sidewalk in the breeze, the briskness of the air, the clarity of the sunlight ...

Two tramps were leaning against the first of the alien poles. They had their eyes closed and were very peaceful, so I crept away.

Portholes exuded smoke, people jostled each other, and everything seemed astonishingly normal, except for the insistent buzzing.

Another of the poles had a man in a scruffy three-piece suit and blatantly orange tie, holding up a sign on which was scrawled VON DÄNIKEN LIVES! He had acquired a squalid-looking collection of onlookers, whom I joined for a moment.

" ... man, these critters built the Pyramids! They built the Empire State Building! They're the Gods! Alexander the Great was one! Richard M. Nixon was one! God was one! ... and you, too, can be saved, if only you'll just throw a quarter on the altar of repentance! Hallelujah! Thank you, ma'am ..."

I walked on.

At the next extraterrestrial parking meter a group of Hare Krishna types was dancing round and round like they had a missionary in the pot.

In the middle a scrawny, bespectacled shaven man was caressing the shaft, which was glowing a dull crimson. He seemed transfigured, almost beautiful, much more like the real thing than Sir Francis FitzHenry could ever be.

I watched for a long time, fascinated, my mind dulled by the hypnotic repetitiveness of their chanting. They ceased, jolting me from my reverie.

The lanky one came up to me and started to whisper confidentially, intensely.

"Did you know they're only a few microns thick? Did you know that they're called the T' tat? Did you know they have a shared consciousness that works over vast reaches of space-time? Did you know they've reached an incredibly high evolutionary phase, huh?"

"You don't talk like a Hare Krishna person."

"Hey! … oh, the clothes, you mean. Actually, I have a Ph.D. from M.I.T. I talk to them, you know."

"No kidding!"

"Hey, really! Listen, come here," he pulled me roughly over to the pole, which had stopped glowing.

"Just sit down here, relax now, touch the pole. Totem pole, divine antenna, whatever. Can't you hear anything … ?"

Hello.

I was shivering. The voice was so close; it was speaking inside me. I drew back quickly.

"Hey, did you know they have many doctors, that each color shows their status based on age? Did you know that, huh? Did you know they don't join up with the collective consciousness until they're almost half a billion years old, that they have these learning centers all over the galaxy, that they originally crossed over from the Great Nebula in Andromeda? No kidding, man!"

I didn't know what he was talking about. "Here, touch it again, it isn't so bad the second time."

He was twitching all over, a bundle of nerves. "Sorry I'm acting like this. It's my only chance to act normal, you see, the rest of the day I'm either stoned or asleep, according to the script I can't wait till we all wake up!"

I reached out.

Hello.

"Isn't there any way we can resist them?"

"What for? Don't you want to live forever? This is just a sort of Purgatory, isn't it? We all get to go to heaven."

"But suppose I wanted to, you know, contradict them, or something."

"Dunno. They can't control *everything*."

He paused for a moment, but then launched himself into a stream of information again, as though I'd fed him another quarter.

"I have the general equations worked out." He flashed a bit of paper in front of my face, then thrust it back into his pocket—"but you obviously have to be in control of unified field theory, and even then there's the power source to worry about. I have a couple of theories—f'rinstance, if they had sort of a portable mini-quasar, like, a miniature white hole worming through space-time into a transdimensional universe, they could tap the energy, you see, and—"

He had lost me. I touched the pole, and his voice faded into nothingness. The buzzing intensified.

Hello.

"We're just dirt to you, laboratory animals," I said bitterly. "I wish it was back to the way it was."

You can't help being a lower being, you know. There's nothing you or I can do about that.

"Well, will you tell me one thing?" It suddenly occurred to me that everyone had left.

The Hare Krishnas, hands linked, had gone dancing off. Sure.

"Is this thing really worth it, for us? Seven million years is a long, long, time; it's the same as eternity for all practical purposes."

Hah! Fat lot you know.

"You didn't answer my question."

All in good time. But it's almost 8 o'clock. Hold on, you'll be dislocated back to yesterday in a few seconds. You're pretty lucky, you know; in some parts of the world the two hours' grace comes at some ridiculous time and nobody ever gets up.

"Goodbye."

Goodbye.

I woke up around 11 o'clock. Gail stirred uneasily. We made love mechanically, like machines, with living sheets of light, only a few microns thick, darting between us, weaving delicately transient patterns in the air, and I felt hollow, transparent, empty.

4

I met Amy Schechter in Grand Central Station, coming out of the autumn night into a biting blizzard of a winter morning. We were both standing at a doughnut stand.

I looked at her, helpless, frail, as she stared into a cup of cold coffee. I had seen her before, but this morning there were just the two of us.

She suddenly looked up at me. Her eyes were brown and lost.

"Hi. Amy."

"John."

A pause, full of noisome buzzing, fell between us. For a while, I watched the breath-haze form and dissipate about her face, wanting to make conversation, but I couldn't think what to say.

"Will you talk to me? Nobody ever does, they always back off, as if they knew."

"Okay."

"I've been standing here for five years, waiting for my train. Sometimes I come an hour or so before 8 o'clock, you know, just to stand around. There's nothing for me at where I'm staying."

Her voice was really small, hard to hear against the buzzing.

"Where are you going?"

"Oh, Havertown, Pennsylvania. You've never heard of it." I hadn't. "It's sort of a suburb of Philadelphia," she added helpfully. "My folks live there."

"Buy you a doughnut?"

"You must be joking!" She laughed quickly and stopped herself, then cast her eyes down as though scrutinizing a hypothetical insect in her styrofoam cup.

Then she turned her back on me, hugging her shaggy old coat to her thin body, and crumpled the cup firmly and threw it into the garbage.

"Wait, come back! We've got an hour and a half, you know, before you have to leave—"

"Oh, so it's score and run? Nothing doing, friend."

"Well, I will buy you a doughnut then."

"Oh, all right. A romantic memory," she added cynically, "when I'll be dead by dinner anyway."

"Huh?"

She came closer.

We were almost touching, both leaning against the grubby counter.

"I'm one of the ghosts, you know," she said.

"I don't get it."

"What do you do every day?"

"My girlfriend walks out on me, then I play a poor third fiddle to a pretentious British actor in Hamlet."

"Lucky. In my script, the train crashes into an eighteen-wheeler 25 miles outside of Philadelphia. Smash! Everybody dead. And then every morning I find myself at the station again. I was pretty muddled at first, the aliens never made any announcements to me while I was lying in the wreckage. So I do it all over and over again. One day I may even enjoy it."

It didn't sink in.

"Chocolate covered?" I asked inanely.

"Yeah."

There was another pause. I realized how much I needed another person, not Gail, how much I needed someone real … "

We should get to know each other, maybe," I ventured. "After it's all over, maybe we could—"

"No, John. Nothing doing. I'm a ghost. I'm not immortal, don't you see! The whole deal ignores me completely! I'm dead already, dead, permanently dead! You don't get to be part of the deal if you die sometime during the day, you have to survive through till midnight, don't you see?"

" … oh God." I saw.

"They've just left me in the show to make everything as accurate as can be. I'm an echo. I'm nothing."

I didn't say a word. I just grabbed her and kissed her, right there in the middle of the doughnut stand. She was quite cold, like marble, like stone.

"Come on," she said.

We found a short-time hotel around the block; I paid the eight dollars and we clung together urgently, desperately, for a terribly brief time.

I woke up at around 11 o'clock. Gail stirred uneasily. As I went through the motions for the thousandth time I was thinking all the time, this isn't fair, this isn't fair.

Gail was alive, she was going to live forever, and she's just like a machine, she might just as well be dead.

Amy, now, she was dead, but so alive! Then I realized a terrible truth: Immortality kills!

I was very bitter and very angry. I felt cheated, and the buzzing sounded louder, like a warning, and I knew then that I was going to try and do something dreadful.

("They can't control everything," wasn't that what the

Krishna freak had said?) I struggled, trying to push myself out of the groove, trying to change a little bit of one little movement, but always falling back to the immutable past ...

We got up and had breakfast. She wore her ominous dishevelled look, strands of black hair fishnetting her startling blue eyes.

"John?"

"Umm?"

"John, I'm leaving you."

"What for, who with?"

"Francis FitzHenry has asked me to stay with him—in his suite at the Plaza!"

I lifted my hand, then willed with every ounce of strength I could dredge up from every hidden source.

I didn't slap her face.

A look of utter bewilderment crossed her face, just for one split second, and I looked at her and she looked at me, her emotions unfathomable; and then the whole thing swung grotesquely back to the original track, and she said quietly, dangerously, "You're too petty, John. That's why you're going to be a Guildenstern for the rest of your life."

As though nothing were different.

That hurt.

Then she walked out of my life.

But I had *changed* something! And we had communicated; for a split second something had passed between us!

The buzzing became a roar. I walked slowly to the theater, bathed in the glow of a hundred diaphanous wisps of light.

5

It was a couple of minutes before 8 when the phone rang in my apartment. I decided to make a run for it, so I made for the kitchenette in the nude. "Yeah?"

"This is Michael, John." Michael played Horatio. He was sobbing, all broken up.

I didn't know him very well, so I played it cool.

"John, I'm going to do something terrible! I can't stand it, you're the first person I could get through to this morning, I'm going to try and—"

I woke up around 11 o'clock. Gail stirred uneasily. We had breakfast, and I didn't slap her face.

It seemed too natural.

I realized that I had changed the pattern. This is the way it would always be from now on. I had never slapped her face.

A look of utter bewilderment ... but it was no longer a communication, it was just a reflex, part of the pattern, and then she said quietly, dangerously, "You're too petty, John. That's why you're going to be a Guildenstern for the rest of your life." That hurt.

Then she walked out of my life.

I went to the theater. There was Sir Francis, making his final scene so heartrending I could have drowned in a sea of molasses; arranging himself into elaborate poses that could have been plucked from the Acropolis; and uttering each iambic pentameter as though he were the New York Philharmonic and the Mormon Tabernacle Choir all rolled into one. He was dying, and he clutched at Horatio, and he said, measuring each phrase for the right mixture of honey and gall—

Absent thee from felicity awhile ...

To tell my story.

and was just about to fall, with consummate grace, into Horatio's arms, and you could feel the collective catch of breath, the palpable silence except for the quiet buzzing, when Horatio drew a revolver from his doublet and emptied it into Sir Francis's stomach.

After the aliens departed from the theater, the play went on, since Hamlet was dead anyway, and afterwards I walked home.

I saw peculiar poles with metallic knobs on them, all along Broadway every couple of blocks, and there were a couple of overturned Yellow cabs, but the old Chevy was gone from the store window.

Good for them.

In the morning I met Amy. I told her about what had happened.

"When you get to just before your accident, try to jump out of the car or something. Keep trying, Amy, just keep trying."

She chewed her doughnut, deliberating. "I don't know."

"Well, we've got another six million, nine hundred thousand, nine hundred and ninety-four years to try in. So keep at it, okay?"

She seemed unconvinced.

"Just for me, try." I kissed her quickly on the forehead and she disappeared into the crowd that was heading towards the platform.

6

The pole was glowing a pale crimson when I touched it.

Hello.

I couldn't contain my rage, "You bastards! Well, we're not powerless after all, we've got free will, we can change things. We can ruin your high school project completely, rats that we are!"

Oh. Well, that too is one of the things under study at the moment.

"Well, let me tell you something. I don't want your immortality! Because I'd have to give up being a person. Being a person means changing all the time, not being indifferent, and you're changing us into machines."

Oh? And do you deny that you've changed?

It was true. I had changed. I wasn't going to be a Guildenstern for the rest of my life anymore. I was going to fight them; I was going to learn everything I could about them so I could try and twist it against them; I was going to be a real human being.

There are things you can't do anything about. You're in a transitional stage, you see. With immortality will come a change in perspectives. You won't feel the same anymore about your barbarian ways, Earthling.

I had to laugh. "Where did you learn to talk like that?"

We monitored your science fiction TV broadcasts.

The picture of these alien schoolkids, clustering around a television set in some galactic suburbia somewhere in the sky … I laughed and laughed and laughed.

But then, seriously: "I'm still going to fight you, you know. For the sake of being human."

I had a new fuel to use, after all, against them. Love. Revenge. Heroism. I was thinking of Amy. The good old-fashioned stuff of drama.

Go ahead.

I woke up around 11 o'clock.

                                                        —Arlington, 1981

Comets and Kings

When you are a boy, all the trees of all the forests seem to stretch up forever, to merge into a leaf-dark zenith as far away as the sky. When you're older, I suppose you laugh at yourself. But there is one forest of my boyhood whose trees, I sometimes fantasize, have kept pace with my growing. Even now, when I stand at the edge of the universe, the shadows touch me, across Greece, across Persia, across India.

Do you believe in hubris?

But of course you do. Yet it is a far more complex issue than our ancients could possibly have imagined …Well, I shan't philosophize. This isn't even my story; and I am no visionary, as Alexander is.

There was a forest in Macedonia where we played at being men, in an autumn much like any other. He was a petty princeling with a crazy fire in him; and I had only just found out how terrible it is to love the great. "Hephaistion!" he called me, and flashed into the forest, his gray chiton crisscrossed by the evening sun. He ran ahead, I caught up, we walked arm in arm, we laughed together, senselessly; we wrestled, we sank, panting, onto the damp moss …Then he got up, without a word, and went off by himself in an unknown direction.

Already I knew better than to follow him unbidden.

"Hephaistion!" he cried out again. I could not fathom the emotion. I saw a strange man lurking in the shadows; Alexander had practically walked into him.

A sudden terror seized me. Did he only seem to be a man? "He's harmless," I said. "Just a peasant of these parts, I bet."

His body was blurred against the trees, shimmering. My eyes smarted. Alex was cautious, so I stayed frozen too. The glare forced my eyes away from the bearded face, from the bloodchilling eyes, down to the chiton, woven of some alien stuff, like the stuff of rainbow.

Perhaps he was one of the forgotten gods of Macedon, driven into oblivion when civilization came to the North. Alexander showed no fear, as always. He didn't flinch at all from the alien's gaze.

Past the old man's head, in a little gap between the trees, stood a structure of polished bronze, something like an inverted amphora. A field of metallic reeds protruded, waving delicately in the breeze. It was perhaps large enough to house the stranger. I thought it quaint, a prop in a satyr play, perhaps.

Alex spoke first. "Are you a god?"

"It might be expedient to think of me that way, yes," said the stranger. He laughed suddenly, but his eyes remained expressionless. "Call me Ectogeos … 'outside the earth.'"

He spoke Attic atrociously. His sibilants lisped, and he didn't contract his verbs, which gave his speech a peculiar, mock-Homeric quality. "You wonder why I come to you, Alexander?"

Nothing was being addressed to me. I was just an insignificant witness to some key event in his life. I tried not to be jealous.

"I am an observer," the ancient continued. "All my kind are … incessant observers. And here there is surely something to observe, even if he is only a boy as yet!"

Alex was drinking it in. I don't know how, but he seemed half to recognize the stranger …

Ectogeos said, "You stand out against your human background like a supernova against the stars. Observing you, one sees the whole world; influence you, and one could —well, it is forbidden of course. Even my visit here is a little risky."

Had he said too much? "Think of me as your guardian from above."

Alexander nodded.

"But," the old man said, "I wish to ask you some questions, in the name of research—or you might call it curiosity. What do you plan to do in your life?"

"Conquer the world." This without hesitation.

"The world?"

"When I was born a comet came."

I had to interrupt, then. "Why are you asking him questions?

Are you a god then, or is he? Is it your place to question him?"

Then I said, "Are you or are you not a god?"

"A god?" I saw he had no intention of answering me. Alexander said: "If you are a god of these woods, your kind is dying. Soon they will forget you, and you need worship to sustain you. Times are changing …"

It was true enough. The man laughed again. It was a throaty chuckle that seemed to grow out of the forest depths. "It's kind of you to worry about me." It was kind, I thought; he had always been concerned about the aged. Was he destined never to see age, then? "But I am more than capable of seeing to myself."

My eye was drawn again to the structure. Softly the silvery reeds rustled. I wanted to dare to go up to it and peer inside ….

"It is forbidden, Hephaistion!" he said sharply.

He *has* read my thoughts! Fear and guilt shot through me. I, withdrew my thoughts, shielding them. They were deep in conversation, those two; it was boyish stuff, about conquering the Persians and the rest of the world. Alexander had always, been extravagant; I found it charming, but Ectogeos looked very grave.

Finally the alien said, "Thank you for your information," and he made to return to his inverted amphora.

"Not yet!" It was a challenge. "You have not told me who *you* are."

Alexander … the forest sunlight mottled his face. My heart almost stopped beating.

"You tempt me, earthchild," said the stranger. "We cannot, as a rule, reveal our identity to the worlds we observe … but there is something special about you, and … no, no, I doubt you could accept what I am."

"If you don't tell me, I won't rest till I've found out. My father is King here." Alexander's eyes flashed, defiant.

"I know." The stranger spoke reluctantly. "But you could not imagine what I am. Perhaps, though, at the end of your Quest …when it no longer matters …"

"My Quest?"

"Well, it won't hurt to tell you what you know already. The world is yours."

"*All* the world?" asked Alex, wonder creeping into his voice.

"Why not?" And he had gone into the structure.

He seemed bewitched as we walked home; he moved ahead, striding rapidly, crunching twigs, not looking in front of him. It was hard to keep up with him. And now the twilight seemed to settle. Of a sudden we had stepped out of the forest; I picked the leaves from my cloak and wrapped it around his shoulders as he paused. It was chillier now. The breeze and the half light toyed with his long, untameable golden hair.

"Don't be so withdrawn, Alex," I said. "How can you hide so from me?"

"You saw. My dreams are coming true, faster than I can cope with them." He looked steadily at the dark earth. Only when he had said it aloud, I thought, did he know it was true.

I knew he would sulk tonight, and be surly to our tutor, Aristotle; that he would sit alone at the edge of his bed, dreaming dreams, excluding me—not by design, for he would not do that, but because the dreams transcended me.

"Who was the man?" I asked him. "What was the dream?" The name, 'outside the world,' does not ring true. Alex did not answer me; I do not think he knew.

"Alex," I said, breaking another silence, "was it a visitation from a god?"

I felt the shadows of trees, and was uneasy.

His eyes were on me. I wanted so much to give him everything, if I could reassure him just a little … To love the great is terrible.

But he turned to me on impulse. Without a word he embraced me in a desperate clinging, like a lost child.

Many images follow in the memory: the stench of blood, the sun eclipsed by black blankets of arrows …and Alexander and I growing tall together.

They have all merged for me, these images: all the forests and woods and taiga and sweltering jungles, the towers and pyramids, the ziggurats and obelisks, the empty tombs, the wide-trousered dancing boys, the kohl-eyes priestesses, the satraps with beards like terraces, the camp whores with bosoms spilling out of gaudy corsets, and the countless Kings, overdressed, like life-size dolls, dwarfed by their golden thrones.

But he conquered Persia and became Great King, and we sacrificed at the tomb of Achilles and Patroklos.

And after, flushed with wine and victory, he stormed into the tent. Our friends were posturing drunkenly at one another; and after a while they staggered home, and the Persian domestics vanished like a magician's coins, and we were alone.

"Aren't you ever going to turn back?" I asked him. I was not the first to ask; well, perhaps the first to ask to his face.

He flung down his empty wineskin. "What do you mean?" His speech unslurred abruptly; his eyes flashed clear in the half dark.

"I mean, consolidate your empire ..." I was always more practical than he, not a visionary, as I have said.

"I have no time for that!" He began to explain: "There's so much of the world left, and I have to have all of it! It's nothing personal, this conquest, it's just ... I *have* to. It's a destiny." He said the word with a funny self-consciousness.

"By now you ought to have seen reason."

His voice slurred again. "Don't you remember? In the woods, with the god ...?"

I struggled to place the memory. It was hazy at first: a shimmering old man, an autumn haze, dreary conversations in the half dark

... the forest sunlight mottling his face.

It was an image of fragile transience and cutting clarity. Like a magnet, it drew the memory to the surface. But I tried to laugh it off. "It was just a practical joke, or something ..."

"You don't believe that." Alexander was right. I turned

away from him, watching the fire and the dance of shadows against canvas. I heard him say, urgently, "He came to me. And he gave me the world."

"Maybe it wasn't his to give," I countered with involuntary sharpness, although I was trying to humor him. His confidence had always terrified me—and convinced me, by its sheer intensity.

So we argued, for the sake of form, a few minutes longer. *It's a mistake,* I thought, *to judge him by values which he has rendered meaningless. And we both know how such arguments usually end.*

In the flickering orange light he touched me, touched my hands, my face.

How can I refuse you, I thought, *what is yours by right of conquest?*

He yielded to me as marble to a sculptor; giving, he only became more and more himself.

The night he burned Persepolis ...

Towering, fantastical spires of flame were lapping. at the corners of the sky, and in our noses was the suffocating stench of incense and charred flesh.

We followed Alexander into the empty, endless throne room. As they cleared a path through the rubble, he wielded his torch like a fury, staggering toward the Great King's throne, clambering up the hundred giddy steps of solid gold. Across the vastness of the hall, I heard him shout for a footstool—he was too short—and then he became like the other Kings, countless Kings, deposed and dying, dwarfed in their own thrones. *They were living gods,* I thought, *and now he has cast them down.*

The wild laughter sounded small. Soldiers were hurling their firebrands into the splendor. A courtesan was screeching elegantly, quaffing from a looted wine cup. From the foot of the steps I watched him; the brightness of his eyes still cowed me, even at this distance.

I thought: *This fire rages so he can breathe life anew into the defenseless city.*

The fire evoked a sense of wonder, with columns snapping like lyre strings overtaut. For a moment we were all openmouthed. like children at our first funeral.

I heard him call me. so I went up to him. almost stumbling over a severed arm. Urgently I asked him. "Why are you burning Persepolis?"

But he sat impassively on the throne.

Then he said: "Because no God has visited me since I was a young boy. I make this fire so they can see me."

A great palace burning … a great man. burning with desire … a great man. desperately feeding on the love of so many. yet knowing they cannot touch his solitude … the brightness hurt my eyes. Then. after some hours. it flickered and smouldered and was spent. The morning came: gray, rainy.

Always I shall remember this night. not only because the brilliance of the flames made day where night should be. and usurped the functions of the Gods. but because there sprang to my mind unbidden the sound of a chuckling forest. and the sight of an alien personage in front of an unearthly structure of polished bronze.

Perhaps it was some kind of purging for him. I hoped it was a fire to drive out fire; inside. I hoped for an ending. though all our hopes would be transmuted by the catalyst of his personality. and we would become mere aspects of him.

And then. more merging images: white sand that blinded. pyramids that littered the sand like a child's building blocks. Nilos which runs backward. Strange gods. Strange rites. Soldiers digging up mummies from the sand, mummies whose faces glared stone-hardened across unimaginable time.

There was an oracle in the desert. in an oasis. We waited while Alexander went to consult the strange gods that had become his own.

It was an idyllic time. without bloodshed; soldier's children played at the desert's edge. and there was water and grain toward the river. It was a place of luxurious plenty. sprouting out of a devastated vastness.

One day a Bedouin scout, shouting frenziedly, whipping his camel, rode into camp.

The oracle has declared Alexander a God. the son of Zeus! Alexander would return, perhaps in a few days, perhaps a week, to receive the homage of his subjects.

The scout did not say that Alexander had met Ectogeos again …

We were alone together, and it was one of those times increasingly rare now—when he talked freely, almost as though we were still boys together. "Let them believe that they deified me!" he said. laughing. "The priests. muttering in their weird languages, the incense everywhere. At least it was cool there in that temple under the rocks. I listened to their god with great courtesy, but …there was another meeting, too."

I stared at him, already guessing. An oppressive tension fell out of a clear blue sky.

"I'll tell you a secret!" he said, half laughing like in the old days; but it was not the same. You'd think he had become an oriental, with all the bowing and scraping … I waited as I was supposed to, listening to the date palms rustling.

Finally, "Well, what?"

"Relax! I'll tell you!" His eyes sparkled.

After a sufficient pause, he told me. He had gone off by himself in the desert, after the fuss at the Siwa Oasis was over. The others must have been frantic trying to find him. And, just as he knew it would be, he was standing there, beside the comical structure.

"He says it's a flying machine, but won't elaborate."

"What," I said, "is he a Daedalus too, as well as a peasant and a guardian from above and a wood god?"

"After I spoke to him, he got into it and flew off," he said matter-of-factly. His eyes were distant. "Well, say something."

"I don't believe it." But I believed every word.

"Oh, nonsense, Heph. Do take me seriously. He said many things which tempt me to believe, you know, that oracle. We played questions and answers again. He was very ambiguous ...I think, you know, he tries to cover his tracks ..."

As *though* he *might* be *reprimanded if caught?* I thought.

"You know what the first thing he said to me was? Go on, guess."

"How should I know? 'How you've grown,' maybe."

"Exactly so! You see, you *can* read my mind."

We both burst out laughing. Almost at once, the tension returned.

"Actually, he said: 'How you've grown; you shortlivers always surprise me,' " said Alexander.

Shortlivers? And what had he called Alex before: *earthchild?* These were not the sorts of words gods used of mortals, exactly ... and then I thought, what if someone *had* invented a flying machine? Many of the wonders that had been asaulting our senses were no less implausible.

Alex said: "He said to me, 'I hear they have given you divinity now. How does your halo fit?' I said I wasn't at all sure. 'Ha!' he said. 'Isn't *sureness* a measure of one's divinity? Of course it is!'

"But I said, "If I'm to be a god, then I am one of you, but

you see, I can't fly."

"'What's bigger—flying, or conquering the world? I didn't invent this contraption, you know. Someone else— let's call him—Hephaestus, so as not to distort your world perception too much—makes all these things.'"

"So what came of it?" I asked him.

"I said to him, 'So you still maintain that I'll conquer the world—even though my army doesn't want to go on? They all miss home, don't you know that?'

"'I maintain nothing. Actually, they keep telling me not to interfere.'"

"'Who're *they?*' I was insistent. I don't like riddles." Alex was very serious. I tried to see the mystery of the story, but it was broad daylight, the breeze was blowing softly through the trees, children were playing "leap-the-steps" on a little step pyramid (they've looted it since) …Somehow it was not as terrifying to me as it might have been brooding by night on a battle's eve. He sensed, I think, that I was trying to hide something from him, not disbelief exactly, but … the delicate tension of our relationship had drifted away.

Looking at him, sitting on a rude bench, travel soiled, I saw he had battle scars but there were no lines under his eyes. He had shaken off the foreboding of warfare like a sea lion erupting from the water. His eyes reflected the sky.

Even when I looked away, his presence was something palpable. "Don't you want to know, then, what he said next?" he asked me.

"Of course." I did, really; I did not know why it came out so offhand, so blasé.

"Well then. He didn't answer. In fact, he just looked at me, the way Aristotle used to peer at a specimen.

A sandstorm was brewing, but I had to wait, even though it wasn't funny anymore. Abruptly he said to me, 'Define a god.'

"I was stuck for an answer. He chuckled, the way he had done in Macedonia long ago; you could hear it echoing in the wind and sand, and then he walked up to his structure and sort of faded into it. Fire leaped from under it.

Then he poked his head out, as though tempted to say one final thing: "'Go on! Be what they say you are! Isn't that what *being* is all about?'"

Alex assumed that distant look again. The conversation was not satisfying; it had all the logic of a dream, and all the essential reality of one.

I fell to thinking, under the scorching heat:

I have known him intimately, in the most profound sense that a man can know, ever since we were boys ...How old were we now? I had lost track, not yet thirty, though. And now that he was elevated to godhead by an oracle, I was left a poor relation, Polydeuces to Castor. How did they manage these questions after we were dead?

As I watched Alexander, locked in his terrible solitude, thought of death fell like a tree's shadow across my mind.

Does he still think of conquering the world, of absorbing the universe into his fiery corona? In the final analysis, the vision was alone. Even I could not see it.

Ectogeos had called himself an observer. I did not understand why he should observe. The gods see everything anyway; did not have to send someone down to gawk. Were the gods voyeurs? There are men and gods ... Was there a third category?

I wished he would come and talk to me.
***

More images, from the last days of the great conquering:
The world grew wider, wilder.

There were markets reeking with strangers' sweat, green jungles, serpents of myth coiled around nameless trees emerald …and everything growing, upward, outward, inward, downward, in a frenzy of growing as we neared the edge of the. earth. There were whirlwinds, assaults of rain; the horizon never moved any closer, and black Ganga coursed sluggishly beneath a lowering sky. There were faces so alien that I forgot *the alien's* face; there were the giant gardens of King Poros, once green, now dipped in the purple of bloodshed.

And the animals: elephants, rhinoceroses, dolphins, tigers, unicorns, and women with diamonds in their noses, women naked from the waist up, their breasts dangling like ripe mangoes that glistened in the sunshine, brown children leaping into rivers, widows leaping into funeral pyres—

Amid the amazing fertility, the armies came to rest, perhaps only eight hundred stades from the other shore of Oceanos, the boundary of the world—and were on the brink of mutiny.

"Pull down the tent flaps, shut out the noise!" Alexander screamed.

"Can't you see, Alexander, they want to turn back?" I was pleading with him.

He talked like a child, sure of his reward, but knowing he has to play a silly begging game first. "But I haven't *seen* yet!"

I was irritated. By then I knew exactly how much of this conquest was due to his charisma, and how much merely to his understanding of the mob.

"If you don't turn back, they'll mutiny and leave you here."

They were outside the tent, cursing, demanding, the old veterans, making threats in Macedonian. "Can't you hear them?"

"They would never leave me," he said. Then, with a quiet, terrible intensity, "I must see this through to the end! I must fulfill my destiny!"

"Destiny? *Hubris?*"

I had stung him. He turned to me and said, with a strained calmness, "I know he will be there to meet me."

"You mean you think you'll run into that man who claims to be your guardian from above? What a farce! In the desert, back in Egypt—I wasn't even there with you! Prove it!"

He flared up, then fell back, speechless. I pressed my advantage. "I'll send them back, with or without you!"

"You!" He was livid. "By what authority do you flout your supreme commander?" He reached for his weapon, then put his hand down, staring at it dully, not knowing where to put it. "Who do you think you are?"

I said, very softly, *"He, too, is Alexander."*

Those had been his words to the mother of Darius (they are history) when she had prostrated herself before me, the taller, by mistake.

He was about to speak, but his voice was drowned by the clamor from outside.

"Yes, Hephaistion," he said.

An admission.

"But I *must* see it, the limit of the world, the horizon extending until it merges with Ocean, the boundary of our cosmos. Send them home; it's only eight hundred stades from here and I can catch up …"

"But—why leave me out?" I said. I should live up to this blurring of our identities … He planted a single kiss upon my cheek, this boy with his face mottled by the forest sunlight.

In history, we turned back; and what is not in the records does not constitute history. Truth does not enter into it …
***

He was standing by the seashore in the twilight, beside

the shining structure. We tethered our horses to a tree. Hands touching, feet sinking in step in the warm wet sand, we approached the alien.

The wind at the world's end howled over the sea. There was no horizon; sea and sky merged into one gray. You could not tell where the end came, for the gods are masters of illusion.

I saw recognition burst out in Alexander's face. He left me running behind, in his eagerness to meet the ancient. "Rejoice," he greeted him, like a friend.

Ectogeos said nothing. His eyes were closed, his lips move soundlessly as though he were in communication with something far away.

He woke with a start and saw us, smiled broadly.

"Now that your destiny is accomplished," he said, "I have been liberated from observing; I am free to answer your questions."

I expected Alexander to ask the questions one asks of gods: questions like *when will I die?* or some such.

But all he asked was: "Is there not more?"

"Why? Does your Quest's ending disappoint you?"

I saw how perceptive the alien had been, though Alex would never admit it to himself.

For I understood him, how he was driven by the desire to push forever into the unknown.

We all followed him, of course, but our desires were limited: a little treasure, a little land, a kingdom, a satrapy even, a little sexual adventure …and we were content.

For him, ending was catastrophe.

Ectogeos turned to me. "Well, Hephaistion, are you not satisfied? I did not come to observe you. You could have asked me anything; I have been reading your mind always."

I didn't know what to reply.

He shrugged. His rainbow chiton shone brilliantly in the

dusk. A shaft of light from the structure fell on Alexander's face, and I saw for the first time that his eyes had become lined.

Alexander repeated his question.

"Come into my spaceship," said the alien. He had coined a strange word, full of power. We followed him in, and all the while the world's-end ocean sighed and heaved in the world's-end wind.

The interior of the structure—I cannot describe it; I have no referents in my experience of the world …a mirror curved into forever. Hazes that became solids. Lights without source, shifting like lights of a faceted crystal.

"This," said the ancient, "is a space-time scanner." There was a square mirror of highly polished silver. I was struggling with the name of the thing. "Don't bother to understand," he said to me, not unkindly.

Alex accepted without question the old man's assertion that the mirror could show all places in the cosmos, and all times. First we saw the world's end, but from a peculiar distance, as though suspended far above it.

We saw a round world spinning crazily like a top in the nothingness; and on that world countless nations springing up wildly, everywhere, in its most inacccessible corners, immense buildings crashing into the firmament on an undiscovered continent where Aztecs built pyramids to bloodstained Helios and starfarers leaped into the sky. The moon was full of people.

Alex clenched and unclenched his fist.

"So there's more. Our cosmology is wrong," he said tonelessly. "I haven't achieved anything yet! It isn't over yet!"

"My poor child! Your whole world doesn't begin to contain the totality of life!"

Rushing past our eyes at a continually accelerated rate—

the seven planets, and a few more besides, crowded with life forms, microscopic, macroscopic, insubstantial, massless, waveless, thought forms … I gave up trying to understand.

Alexander watched, engrossed. I felt his heart sinking.

The solar system shrank to a point.

We flew past thousands, then millions of stars, all full of life: green, purple, gold, black, ultraviolet, X-ray-colored life. The galaxy collapsed into a single point. Alexander looked up, relieved that it was over.

"So that is why it could never be mine," he said, almost reconciled.

The scanner was black for some moments; then another galaxy swam into view. The same process began again: a cluster of galaxies shrank into nothingness, a cluster of clusters, a cluster of clusters of clusters …the universe shrank into nothingness.

The mirror was empty for perhaps ten minutes. Then, to his horror, another universe began to form, and another, a cluster of of universes, a cluster of clusters, a cluster of clusters of clusters …

The alien said: "And now you have the truth. I wanted to spare you the pain of looking more."

It was midnight. The wind had never ceased to howl; we were outside the structure. A pale, cold light from the structure illuminated Alexander's face, and I saw the despair in his eyes, and the innocence.

"I may have mocked you," continued the stranger. "If so I apologize; there are so many rules governing scientific research. I wish I could have helped." His garment glowed faintly.

Alex was silent, so finally it was I who asked the question that I had wanted answered for so long:

"Who, in all truth, are you?"

"My name is Zethtep," he said; "in your language,

'Watcher.' My friends call me 'Meddler.'" Already he was going into the spaceship. Alex and I watched, alone together on the shore. The ship streaked into the blackness of the sky. In the distance, against the stars, it blazed like a comet; then slowly, like the dying of a plucked lyre string, it faded and melded with the night.

We found our horses. Alex was silent all the way to the camp. But I was not as shaken as he, for it was not, after all, my vision ...

We rode in a darkness further darkened by compound shadows of strange trees. Wind gusted, damp and warm.

I remembered the ship, splashed out across the sky like a living fire. *Are all comets born this way?* I thought. Alex was spurring on his horse, impatient. I could not see his face, and for once I was glad I couldn't.

I remembered how he had told the alien, that first time, in the forest in Macedonia: *When I was born a comet came.* I remembered the casual pride of that statement. But—

Had they come, even then, to observe him? Had they gathered round, like students round a specimen?

I sped up to a gallop. The wind streamed on either side of me; and I abandoned myself to it, hardly noticing which way we went.

I think it *has broken his heart.*

—*Tokyo and Alexandria, 1977 and 1981*

Coaster Time

My relationship with Trina had begun to settle…like a fly on the head of a cigar store Indian. I was restless and I could see what was coming. Dawn would find me half—heartedly humping her, when suddenly across the gulf of my closed eyes would come the warm and the chill, the darkness roaring, and I'd want to slough off my body as it clanked like a dead machine.

And I'd know it was summer, coaster time.

Twelve different suburbs of twelve different cities. Twelve women: white, black, blotchy, dumpy, willowy, brim-bursty…

Trina was the beautiful one. Three summers I'd resisted the urge.

Because I almost loved her.

Twelve tree-lined shady streets.

Twelve sets of prefabricated kids. Trina's I'd almost loved.

I sprang from the bed. She murmured something. "I'm going," I said softly.

She was wide awake now. Wind rippled the drapes behind her, dazzle-drenched beige. "I've been expecting it, Jack." No rancor at all; Trina alone of the twelve might have understood me. "Don't wake the kids." She was deathly calm.

"Her eyes were tight shut against the brightness. Black hair muzzled her and curlicued the floral bedspread, weaving like sunsmears to the shadow. I ached. Did she hear it too, in her own way? I tiptoed out, closing my eyes and hearing only the roaring darkness.

On the street stood the van, all I'd come with, waxed and cherry red. On the doors in back was painted a secret symbol that only coaster people know. As I pulled away the past melted from me, and as I hit the freeway I began to sing.

***

A ways past Woodbridge I picked up a girl hitching. But she wasn't one of us.

"Coaster time?" I said. She smiled pertly, vacuously. "Oh, you don't know what I mean. But I thought you gave the sign, over there."

"My nose was itching." She shot me an are-you-one-of-those maniacs look.

"No, I mean—" I took my hands off the wheel and did the recognition signal of the coaster people.

"Huh? Oh, saw a bunch of weirdoes doing that on 95 and the beltway. New fad?"

"Get out."

"You creep!"

I screeched onto the shoulder. "You're making fun of me, girl, mocking our secrets. I don't care to ride with you." I pushed her off and peeled out, my mind roaring with the roller coaster in King's Dominion, eighty miles down the pike.

***

I shouldn't have. But she'd scared me, a stranger flashing our greeting on the road. Maybe something had changed with the coaster people.

Shit, Jacko, I thought, you haven't hit the coaster trail in three years. Maybe there isn't even a coaster trail anymore. But I knew that couldn't be true. Come summer there will always be people who take the twisted circle across the country, living only for the big ones: Rebel Yell, Scream Machine, Python, King Corkscrew, Terror Tunnel. We're the people who hear the roaring darkness, whose winter dreams are of forever falling. I brushed off my unease and drove on recklessly; perhaps I could be the very first at the gate when it opened, the first to sprint to the head of the line for the front car, a perfect beginning to coaster time…

In about a half hour I got lucky. By an eviscerated McDonald's that sleazed out onto an exit ramp, I saw coaster folk. Real ones. I could tell by how they smiled. I pulled in; they were leaning neatly against the plexiglass wall under an arm of the golden arch. "Rrrowrrr!" I said, doing the gesture.

"Whoooooshhhh!" A unison ritual response.

"Need a ride down to Richmond? I'm Jack."

"Ernesto." A thin man, hooked like a shepherd's crook; only his eyes, twinkling, showed he was one of us.

"I'm Princess." A crone with a toothless smile. "We don't know who this is, though." And next to her, in the archway's shadow, was a willow-woman all in white, white-gloved, and veiled, I mean totally veiled, a temptress in purdah, from a Sin bad movie.

The veiled woman whispered; I couldn't catch what she said. The boy like man beside her said, in a lilty, almost unearthly voice, "She says her name is Shirenzheh. It means the Eternal Quiet." The woman made our secret sign—with such grace!—her gloved arm arcing against the arching shadow of the tacky big M. I knew then that I belonged here. "Oh, you joined the trail here?" I said. "We picked it up in New Jersey. We've already done the Super Dooper Looper in Hershey Park," said Ernesto. "It was—"

"Whooooshhhh!"

"Rrowrrr!" The familiar words ripped the memories from me. It was like I'd never left the trail.

"Anyone need a ride? We could hit the first big one by mid afternoon. The amusement park doesn't close till ten so we call do some by starlight, too…"

"We're six people squelched into a Honda," Ernesto said.

"I'll take someone—"

And Shirenzheh had already stepped forward. She touched my hand. A sharp chill seared me for a moment and then faded into the sunlight. Her gloved hand had felt gritty, abrasive, like shark's hide.

Virginia countryside; lush even green, picture-booky, unreal somehow. *King's Dominion, 49 miles!* Ernesto and I played car games, passing each other and speeding heedlessly. The veiled woman sat, saying nothing. I don't think I even heard her breathe. I thought nothing of her strangeness, though; coaster folk are always unusual, driven, often graceless; they are discarded people who have chanced upon the roaring darkness only by daring to take the obscure exits of the human highway. I set the cruise control and looked at my passenger. Shirenzheh…some Middle Eastern name doubtless, full of exotic music.

"How long have you heard the roaring?" A whispery voice, a little childlike; definitely foreign.

"Fifteen years now. Old-timer, you might call me." For a moment I thought of Trina and those three years, and I wondered if I should tell her I'd cheated in my reckoning. "And you, Shiren—"

"They call me Shirra sometimes." The r was rolled once. lightly, on the tongue-tip.

"Shirra...how long have you heard the roaring?"

"Oh, a million years. A million and five, to be exact."

"Bizarre." I laughed; we coaster folk lived in the present, we weren't supposed to pry. But she had made it sound almost reasonable. "Those gloves must be great for repelling muggers," I said, groping for a new subject.

"They are not gloves."

"You certainly have a sense of humor."

She laughed: a twitter of far-off cicadas.

After a while I told her about the first girl I'd picked up.

"Things aren't the way they used to be. Time was, we were few, we all knew each other even, and no wandering mundanes took *our* secret signs from us.

"Things will of necessity run riot now, in these final days."

"Huh? Oh, you mean those wars and famines and things..." But I was in no mood for apocalypses.

Silence. Then I said, "And what made you take the coaster trail?" Something about her nagged me; I had to talk, to fill the silence.

"I have come," she said, "to greet the Coaster King, the Enlightened One. It is time." Well, there were crazies aplenty among the coaster people, and we tolerated all of them, gave them their niche in our midst, because of our bond, the darkness roaring. I couldn't comment; she had a way of answering you that cut off all argument.

Soon we were there. Gaudy families were gushing into bottleneck ticket booths. We parked side by side, van and Honda, Laurel and Hardy; and we rushed for the gate like children, straining through the crowd and brandishing our plastic money. I didn't care about Shirenzheh or anyone else. A man pushing forty, but I ran dodgem through the throng like a kid, past the stunted Eiffel Tower and through the rainbow arch where Yogi Bear and Boo-Boo strutted about like presidential candidates. Then 1saw, up ahead, the King Cobra, slimy sick-green monster of a looping coaster, and in the distance, soaring pure as a sine wave, the Rebel Yell. Already came a whisper-roar icinged with children's shrieks. I couldn't wait now. I ran harder, thrusting through walls of warring muzaks. Waiting in line I tapped the railings like a scurrying rat. I edged ahead, casually it seemed, but really counting heads to insinuate myself into the front seat, a knack that I'd learned my first year on the trail.

It worked. I was sitting in the car, the belt locked in, when

I turned. She was there, beside me. "How'd you get here?"

She said nothing. I saw her eyes clearly for the first time, cornflower-blue through slits in the white veil, and I noticed that she never blinked. We exchanged one of the secret signals, and I smiled. With a jerk we were pulling out of the shelter into the sunlight; abreast of us the mirror-car moved too, for the Rebel Yell is a twin coaster, its curve-matched tracks haunching high into the sky.

Up now, with a ratchet … ratchet … ound, up, up … the people shrinking into ants. I threw my hands up, straining, waiting … up, up, then—

The roaring hit me! My lap shoved hard against the restrainers. My body twanged taut like a bowstring, gave into the curve of falling. For a moment there was no past, I was a timeless darkness. The kids were yelling, but I sat in proud silence, ecstatic. We hit bottom and soared; I opened my eyes, at peace at last. But…

Beside me Shirenzheh murmured in a foreign language. She was still, untouched by the coaster's violence. Under her robelike garment she seemed rock-solid; she didn't even seem to be breathing.

But we were falling again, and I gave into the joy, little joys now, none so all-embracing as the first and steepest. Then we raced for the end of the line like demons, we got the back this time, bumpiest but without the sheer bravura of the foremost.

After ten or eleven I was tired; I found Ernesto and Princess and the others by the skyride, ranked by height and licking ice cream cones in unison.

"Look," said Ernesto, "more of us!"

Quick introductions: "Here's Tweeny. Here's Polypheme." A woman bandanaed like a pirate, with a patch over one eye. "And Hieronymo." I saw a teenaged gangler with brushfire hair. "He's dangerous, they busted him for a pyro when he was navel-high. But he's found the darkness now. Smile, Hero."

We exchanged quick, sharp smiles.

"Where's the veiled woman?" Ernesto said. I pointed at the Rebel Yell. "Ah, she should be here. I've learned a little more about the Coaster King."

That name again…"Who's that?"

"The Enlightened One. You been off the trail a couple years?"

"Uh huh."

"Then you don't know. We—you, me, all of us, we're special.

The Coaster King is coming."

"His compassion will touch us all." It was the voice of Shirenzheh, who seemed to have materialized beside me. "I'm dreaming," I said. "No, Jacko, never a dream," said Shirenzheh. Ernesto said, 'Tve heard. On the grapevine. He's coming soon, tomorrow maybe. There are more of us here, waiting. Waiting."

"Oh, Jack," Shirenzheh said, "you do not see us yet. Let me tear the blinkers from your eyes—"

I was pinioned against the ice cream booth. A child with a balloon ran right by me, not seeing. A scream was frozen to my lips. I looked straight up at the sun, the light burned, then

Shirenzheh's gloved hands, clamping over my face. A roaring darkness like a coaster's falling, and then her hands raked slowly across me. I felt them sandpapering my eyes; I tried to squeeze them shut but my eyelids were torn, squirt-rheumy with blood—

"Open your eyes. It is only in the mind. This is no magic trick. You see no hallucinations. It is technology."

"Extraterrestrial," Princess croaked.

"Open them!" Ernesto said.

They were lidded again now, but crusty. I freed my arms and rubbed my eyes. Plates of dried mucus flaked away, tugging out eyelashes.

"You won't see them well at first. But I have exchanged your eyes for better ones." As the light burst on me I saw Shirenzheh slipping a clawed, knobbed tool into the eyeslit of her veil. She let go and it vacuumed down into where her face should be. "They are alien eyes. Soon you will truly be of the coaster folk. The true coaster folk, of which your little tribe has been but a shadow, a mirror-mimic..."

I looked around. The group was clustered around; I could see nothing but concern in their eyes. And then, ghosted against the garish crowds, leaning against the plastic Flintstones ... shadowshapes at first. Some like Shirenzheh, their white veils fluttering. Some...like scaly unicorns, pawing the sun. Some tentacled, some winged, some mere tendril-wisps of smoke.

I began to understand. "They're on the coaster trail too, then."

"Some of them. Others are camp-followers, the Enlightened One's disciples."

"And you come from—" I looked up at the sky, cloudless, serene, brilliant. "Well, what are we waiting for?" Princess screeched. "The coasters! The coasters!" And again we ran for the line.

And soared. And plummeted. And ran for the line. And

Towards evening I sat with Hieronymo. He always held his arms the highest. He crooned. Each time we came back he shook as if palsied. "Kid sick or something, mister?" An attendant was bent solicitously over us. "You been riding for hours."

"He is fine." Shirenzheh stood behind her. To me she said, "It was not because he was insane that he had so much trouble with the law, that he was in and out of the juvenile courts. It is because the darkness is always with him. Truly the Enlightened One's grace has fallen on him…"

As night fell I held him; he was drunk on diving and flying, sobbing, and still we flew and we dived. His arms rose straight as spears, when mine tottered and flailed emptiness.

The stars came out; we saw few, because of the amusemement park's glare.

And after, cleansed, stoned on the big darkness, we met at the gate. The lot was sieving out now; in the moonlight, Princess and Polypheme were dancing solemnly around our cars. "A convoy!"

Ernesto cried. "We must have a convoy!" There followed some debate as to whether we should stay on our go south, towards Williamsburg, where we could do the Loch Ness Monster.

"Loch Ness Monster," Hieronymo said at last. It was all I'd ever heard him say. His voice was a whisper, perhaps an echo of the dark roaring.

"You must obey him," Shirenzheh said at last. "Of all you humans, Hieronymo is closest to the Coaster King. He is closest to achieving his last journey…" So it was settled. And in my van came Shirra and the boy; and then we caravaned onto the highway, five or six cars hugging each other and the speed limit, a weird procession. Shirra and I were in the front seat, the boy behind. It was only an hour or two to Busch Gardens; we'd have to sack out in the van awhile before the park opened. In the rear view mirror I saw him, shivering, hugging himself in a far corner of the van.

"Why have you come here?" I demanded, angry. "What have you done to him? to us?"

"We have awakened you," she said.

"If you're from somewhere up there, somewhere so inconceivably superior … why ride our coasters, why run our lives?"

"They are not your coasters. Listen, human. Our people live a billion years. We are tired, human, tired … a million years or so ago, a teacher came to our worlds. He had found the great extinction at the root of all being; yet he was so filled with compassion for the myriad shapes of life that he remained behind to tell us of it. For every sentient being in the universe has a number. Mine is some six million, and I have only begun the journey to the dark … one has but to experience the great falling, over and over, that number of times, and he will come to know eternal peace."

"You take the coaster trail to heaven?"

"In a sense …"

"Why don't you stay on your own planets? We had fun once. More than fun. We washed our souls clean in the roaring darkness. But now…"

"We are exiles." Her sadness touched me, even across t1w barrier of species. "It is part of the testing, you see; to awaken backworlds to such a state that they may build roller coasters, to remain inconspicuous always—"

"You've tampered with us? Toyed with us?" I hated them then, because they claimed to have snatched our very wills from us. "Do you think we enjoy it here? On our worlds we can move continents with a thought. We can travel the silence between the stars on beams of tachyons. We can fashion cities from our dreams, and populate them as we please, with humanoids or chimaeras or with beings shaped from light itself...Here is Hell, Jacko, Hell itself. But you creatures of Hell, tormented, your noses in the planet's mud, are closer to truth than we are. So the Coaster King has taught us..."

"You're saying that all the human race's advancement stems from ... a religious fad?"

"You cannot call it that."

"But the monuments, the discoveries, the great human achievement—"

"Side issues. You learned quickly, in mere thousands of years; you branched out every which way. It usually happens with the worlds we touch. Call them fringe benefits, perhaps." I watched her; her tranquility terrified me. Behind, the boy moaned.

"You're driving him crazy."

"No. He is like us. He sees what lies behind the roaring darkness. He is frightened now, but later he will become one with eternity."

"You're crazy! Galactic lunatics, playing havoc with a backward race!"

"No! No!" I opened my eyes. In the darkling wayside I saw creatures gathering, inhuman creatures suffused with moonlight. I stepped harder on the gas.

"You too have had teachers. All life yearns for the great extinction. It is no myth. You call it nirvana, human." Seeing me accelerate, the convoy sped up too. The inner wind came rushing, sweeping me up, I didn't struggle.

We'd been at Busch Gardens for some days now; the others were impatient, fretting for the Coaster King. The park was tortuous, more artfully landscaped than King's Dominion; the Loch Ness Monster reared up from greenery and a man-made lake, its loops coiling one across the other, yellow and green. When we tired we would go stand on the bridge, between the remote-controlled boatlets and a souvenir stand, where the loops loomed overhead and the cars hurtled straight down at you, skimming three feet from water.

There was a thunderburst, and then the sun emerged more dazzling than ever. I'd been riding with Shirra and with Hero and with another guy, bulging from an old cheesecloth shirt. Hero hadn't eaten, hadn't slept. As we set off—he and I in the front for the fifth time that day—he was trembling more than ever. his cheeks were puckered in, yellowing, his eyes wild, the fimile soldered in place.

"I'll make him get off next time," I shouted. "Force some food down his throat—"

"No! He is full of grace now! He has almost reached his number of fulfilment!" Shirenzheh cried over the rattling, as We scaled the hill.

"Fucking numerologist aliens!" I sat back; a harness came over your neck so you couldn't raise your arms. The coaster dragged upwards, so slow, so-'

The top! A moment of stasis, frozen out of time, then—

Windroar! The world giving beneath me! My whole being stretching like elastic in a slingshot, then-

Up! Around! Gravity-wrench of the three sixty, fireworks in my guts, burning, soaring—

The tunnel. I caught my breath now, ready for the spiralling darkness. Sparks flew where the coaster flinted on the track. And then I felt my arm vised in a grip of terror. "Steady, Hero, steady..."

The clutch tightened. He was thrashing against the restraint. Did he want off? We burst out into the light. And then we were pulleying up again, agonizingly slow, and I saw his face, ashen in the bright sun; I saw his wide eyes glistening like crystal marbles, gazing on some horror...I strained to follow his line of vision, but we were falling again now, and as soon as we fell our stomachs reversed and we were in the upkick of the second loop and then back at the exit, getting off....

"Something's wrong!" I said, as we trotted around the back to find the end of the line again.

"I don't want to! I don't want to!" he screamed suddenly. It was only the second sentence I had ever heard him utter. Around us, kids burst out laughing, thinking him some chickens hit jerk.

"He must! He must!" Shirra was saying, but he broke loos!~ from the line and hurled himself into the crowd; a hail of popcorn hid him from us.

"The King is here," said Shirra. "Come, the coaster is waiting."

We rode. The joy came back to me, but it was a ghost-joy, ged with anger. And still we rode. Until nightfall.

And when I looked at the line that zigzagged back and forth to the log shelter where you got on the coaster, when I looked in a certain way—I can't describe it, it was something about my new eyes—I would see that there were others. I mean aliens. Peering over a child's shoulder, hunched against a post. I saw a fat man with twins in tow go right through one, a thing of tentacles and porcupine-spines. I thought I must be going mad. But when you have experienced the dark roaring the way I have, knowing as you do that most people get on the coasters and scream with terror and pleasure and get nothing more from them, that they come face to face with the big darkness and are too blind to see it…I was not insane. It was the simple truth that we had been made civilized, been dragged up from barbarity, in what must have seemed the twinkling of a eye to these beings, merely to be brief props in an alien drama of birth and extinction. But it was too huge to grasp, yet.

We had gone to a little snack stand across the lake. Hero was still missing. I turned to Ernesto to make some casual remark. He was coughing, spluttering. Then I saw smoke, I saw the Loch Ness Monster nesting on a bed of fire. People had begun to stampede, crushing onto the narrow bridge. "It's Hero!" Ernesto gasped. "He couldn't handle it, he's on his pyro trip again!" Shirra clutched me, saying, "There's nothing to be done, the King's here now," but I wrenched free and elbowed into the crowd. When I reached the coaster, I saw that the shelter was on fire. People were crunched together, speechless. And then I saw him lit up in a flicker of flame, straddling the loop-top overhead, doing a wild dance.

Cries of Jump! Get him down! "Hieronymo!" I screamed.

"You know him?" Some kind of uniformed man pulled me from the crowd. Hot air washed my face, dried up my throat. Suddenly Shirra was beside us. "Don't touch him," she said quietly, dangerously. He muttered something about questioning me. The gloved hand struck out. I knew now it was no glove but her natural exoskeleton, crusty and chitinous. In the glare the blood spurted luridly from his nose, his forehead, his eyes. "Now! Come now!" She threw a fold of the veil around my head. I shook from the sudden death-chill. When she released me we were in the parking lot, all of us. I whirled around. Behind me, past the veneer of forest. I saw the flames leap higher, I saw the coaster's steel circle rise above it and the shrunken figure. blackened in the moonlight and firelight. still grotesquely dancing…

I wrenched myself from the sight. And then I looked at the coaster folk. They were stock-still, serene, expectant.

"Forget now," said Shirra. Her voice was flutelike in the quiet. "He came close to eternity, but he was not ready. The cycle continues."

"Hush," said another veiled figure like her.

"He is here," said another. The unicorn-like creatures pawed the concrete noiselessly. A van much like mine was parked beside Ernesto's Civic. The coaster folk looked up at it in unison. "he is resting," said the third veiled woman. "He has counted his final number but one. He has waited an eon for this journey; for his compassion was such that he delayed his voyage into the void until he could pass on his teachings…"

"Are you asking me to believe—" I said.

"Your belief or disbelief is quite irrelevant," Shirenzheh said "Come, we're at his beck and call now."

"But the boy—"

"He's beyond us. The darkness has driven him mad." I peeled out like a maniac. The coaster trail was dreary after Williamsburg; in the Carolinas there were no coasters, not until Atlanta's Six Flags' Scream Machine. I drove alone, leading the convoy now grown to a dozen vehicles or more. But in the rear view mirror I could see that the van wasn't empty, that aliens had hitched with me. I saw them clearly now that I was used to the eyes. We did not speak to each other. Shirenzheh's species seemed to be the only one that could be bothered with human speech; and I knew by now that they were lowest in the visitors' hierarchy…

I was angry when we left. They'd been callous about Hieronymo, brushing his memory off now that their precious King was here. But as I drove farther, the roaring in my mind came ever louder, tempting me into surrender, and my dreams were all of leaping into the arms of darkness, dissolving into the darkness, loving the darkness.

***

The next amusement parks are all run together in my mind; the Scream Machine, the Cyclone and the Cyclotron, the Python and the Scorpion. We drove at night mostly, a stately parade of some dozen vans and cars; we camped in parking lots, humans and aliens wary of each other, keeping mostly to themselves; we rode the coasters, all of them, from dawn until far into the night, until the roaring rang ceaselessly and our dreams whirled, giddy and gaudy, blurring into wakefulness. At such times in the past I would have felt so much at peace. But now Hero haunted me.

I wrote *Dear Trina* and crumpled the postcard out the window as I drove. It was dark and we were well into Florida now, with Kissimee the next big stop. Disney World was there, with its Space Mountain and its Thunder-watchamacallit-Railroad, kiddie thrills livened with stunning graphics; not for the coaster people really, these rides, but sometimes worth a stop for the sake of the spectacle. From Orlando the coaster trail veers westward and inward.

I stared at the van of the Coaster King, in front of me, setting the slow pace. Its brights smeared the dark road. I didn't recognize the make of van; I think it was like Shirenzheh, a simulacrum, an alien thing camouflaged behind a familiar shape.

"Will he ever come out?"

"When he's ready. He know the moment of his passing."

"And then?"

"Be calm. Hear the roaring." We were on a dim road that threaded Tampa to Yeehaw Junction on the Florida Turnpike: bleak, unpopulated. The roaring sang in my mind's ear like an ocean.

"And us?" I persisted. "What will become of you and me and his other followers?"

"Perhaps, one day, we too will pursue the coaster trail to its end."

"You, perhaps. Living a billion years and all. But humans —"

"I have no answers, Jack. Perhaps the Coaster King knows...."

"No one's ever even seen him!" She didn't answer. I remembered the other parks; the veiled ones hastening to the King's van to find out if this was the designated time, being refused. I remembered the radio broadcast too, about the bizarre young flake who'd set fire to the Loch Ness Monster and tumbled to his death. I had once tried to ask whether they believed in reincarnation, whether they imagined it might take lifetimes for every soul to count the fallings until he reached his personal number. But Shirra had been vague, telling me only that life was a continuum, not a jigsaw of disparate entities.

We came to Orlando. It was night. We drove down Route 4; I expected the Coaster King's van to turn at Disney, the only place open past midnight. But no, we rode on, following the master. From this vantage one saw little of Disney World; it is a fantasy in plastic, shielded from reality by miles of landscaping. "He's starting with Circus World," I said. In a few moments we would see its tent-top cresting the highway and the moon-silvery serpent of a coaster. , . what was it called? Something tiger. The very names were running into onp. another, the litany of magic words that once I could recite in a rush, without taking a breath.

"Wait," Shirenzheh said. Other aliens, crouching in hack hunched closer. "I sense something."

"What?" And there it was. I could tell by the roar within me. *Whoosh!* one of the shadowshapes moaned. "The final day is here. The Coaster King has chosen this place for his final journey. It will be now."

The procession turned, climbed a ramp, made a left into the deserted lot. A big top flanked by little tops rose up behind wrought-iron fencing; the garish reds, oranges, blues muter! into shades of a single grayness.

We halted as one. It was the higher of the two parking spaces.

Two of the veiled women scuttled to the van. And then it opened.

We rushed to see, jostling, cramming into the little opening. And there was light, bursting, blinding, a river that rived the dark ness and streamed past the locked gates.

The van was a window over another world. It was sunlight that was pouring into our night world, alien sunlight. There were mountains like crystals of blue vitriol. Black telephone-pole trees, forests of them, topped with amethyst taffy and ivory spirals and giant sea anemones of shocking pink, bridged with inverted rainbows slung with quivering slinkies. And things I can't begin to describe.

The landscape shimmered for a moment. Then it dissolved into the back of a van. There was a glass bottle, shoulder high, linked to an apparatus that clanked and tittered; in it a wizened being squatted. Its blue fur was balding; it had no eyes. Shirenzheh and another creature, horned and coppery-eyed, climbed into the van; Shirra pulled a tool from her eyeslit, the same one I'd seen her use before on me, and did something that shattered the glass. Then they helped the Coaster King totter to his feet. We dwarfed him, all of us. They made for the gate.

The others had to scramble to keep up. I came up behind, shouted, "The place is closed now! What's he going to do?"

"Silence, human!" Shirenzheh's voice grated like chalk on a blackboard.And when I looked up the gate had dissolved, and the tents, guarded by plaster elephants and clowns, were gauzed in an alien light. I heard Ernesto muttering, "You're right, Princess, they can do anything..." There were shouts of glee now. We were dashing, all of us, as madly as that first day, splashing through the puddled porpoise pool, laughing in the darkness. And then the path forked, each fork leading to a different coaster. Til the right, soaring like a scimitar from a clutter of concession booths, was the big one, almost a mile of it; to the left the Daredevil dangling from the blackness like a titan's earring. Our laughter stilled itself; we waited, respectful, for the King.

I heard whispers ... "He can't breathe our air long. he's weakening. Dying. They broke his life-supporter."

The King lifted an arm, pointed, batwing hands of silverblue. It was the Daredevil. At the signal the veiled ones pulled out their instruments and the coasters clattered to life, eerie in the alien light. The troop went left. The coaster reared over us, a coil of roaring. They could not make the elevator work for some reason; we began up the stairs, zigzags of white steel encased in a flimsy scaffolding. I was directly behind the King. His expression—insofar as he seemed to have one—was utterly blank.

His creatures clutched him tightly. The steps rattled; in the gaps you could see down to the ground.

Higher, higher. I was out of breath now. The coaster car waited at the platform; they helped the King into the front car, and I stepped in behind him. Quickly, silently it filled. In the distance I could hear the other coaster, its roaring hollow because it was not topped with screams. I saw the great loop ahead, diving a hundred feet and more.

The slingshot clanged. And then we broke out of the shelter into the charging wind! Thunder in my ears, the blood surging, and—

Swooping! The night-circus spinning, the stars below, tiny leather paws shivering, my twisting guts—

Now we froze for one terrible instant on the far platform, perched over precarious nothing, and the catapult struck again and I was plummeting asswards into the loop. I squeezed my eyes tight, and when I opened them we were shooting onto the planform and-

The seat in front of me, empty.

I jumped out. Others were yelling with excitement, dying to get on. I ran downstairs, my knees buckling. I saw Shirenzheh and others, gathered, waiting.

"What have you done to him?" I screamed. A tiny sound in the big night.

They turned, all of them, on me. Their veils fell from them. With their strange tools they peeled the eyes from their faces and tossed them down. As the eyes touched concrete, they fumed, corroded. They pried away their ears and noses and lips, flinging them into fizz-smoking heaps. "What are you doing?" I cried. They weren't human-looking at all now; their faces were angled, armored with plates of chitin, and empty. They seemed soulless, dybbuklike.

"He has faced the darkness now. He has gone out, like the flame of a candle." Shirra's voice, still lovely. "The final days are here. We can go back now…"

"What final days? What about us? You brought us to this state, didn't you? will you just leave us, bombing ourselves to bits, fighting starvation and pestilence?"

"I don't know. Those are material things, and the Coaster King has taught us to cast them aside, to live only for the final journey. We will waken other worlds to a brief splendor. each world a flower in the desert universe, each visit like a drop of rain. Kings will come again, and the universe will turn till the end of time. Some of the worlds we have touched … survive, become great. Most of them do not; that is the way of things. But we will leave you alone, mostly; there will be tourists, exiles, lovers of curiosity, but no more interference…"

I left her then. The coaster folk had piled into the big one. They had jimmied it to run without stopping. I got on.

"Whooosh!" Polypheme yelled.

"Rrowrr!" A weight had fallen from us. We were drunk with coaster madness now. We would ride till dawn, till they came and found the gateways vanished and the machines mysteriously running. I saw how most of them were overcome by the big darkness, how they gave their hearts to it completely; but for me it was like … like clawing at a dying dream. Like clinging on to childhood, or to someone you've stopped loving.

In the morning I saw the past more clearly: the serenity of the King who passed beyond, Hieronymo driven mad by touching the darkness too close. There was no choice, really. For Hero had been a human, and the alien dream had broken him. And now we humans were alone with our crumbling societies. Now we could dream our own dreams. Our freedom was bitter and joyful both. I stole away while the others slept, and I drove north.

    ***

Summer was ending. Outside, the house seemed changed; the walls spattered with rustflake leaves, the chilling air scented by unswept foliage, heaped against shedding trees. But when I entered it seemed like I'd never left.

She was standing in the kitchen door, casually, as though she'd just come out to get something. But I knew she must have seen me pull in. Behind her the dishwasher hummed.

Suddenly the children's clatter shattered the tension. They ran by in a blur of dirt and color.

"Will you take us to King's Dominion, Jack, huh? before it closes, before Labor Day? Will you?"

"Maybe..." but I was answering an emptiness. Only their smell lingered, lemony detergent tangled with a tang of fresh sweat and old sneakers.

"Kids," she said, shrugging.

"They shoot up, summers. I never knew that."

"As if they thirsted for the sun itself." She had always been good at finishing my thoughts for me. "I'm back."

"That's fine, Jack, just fine. It's all right."

"But ... questions?" She smiled then. Not like the coaster people as they contemplated the big darkness, but an earthy smile wrinkled with a half-laugh. "No questions, Jack, my love." The dishwasher thunked, changing its tune from thrum to sloshing. We did not touch.

"But I want to answer you anyway."

"Go on," she said seriously.

And then a shadow crossed her face, an elastic unicorn of darkness. I knew what I would see if I looked behind me. For my eyes were alien eyes and would still see aliens, if I cared to look. "I've left the coaster trail, Trina. I've seen to the end of the roaring void. There was nothing there, and it isn't in me to love the emptiness." She pursed her lips; I don't think she really understood, she was just humoring me. "Now I don't need the big darkness any more." But I heard it still, calling me, haunting, chilling. It trilled like the syrinx of a cosmic vulture. I embraced her then, Trina the beautiful. the compassionate.

"One day you'll love me," she said. I knew now it was true. It was this that the aliens could not have. Hadn't Shirenzheh said it herself? *You creatures of Hell. tormented. your noses in the planet's mud. are closer to truth than we are.*

After all, they had come to *us*.

I turned and saw the aliens watching. But they were ghostly now, less real. In time they will fade.

—Alexandria, 1981

ResurrecTech™

Owen Gallenkamp suffered a peculiarly unpleasant mishap while mowing the postage-stamp-sized front lawn of his townhouse in a middle income Washington suburb. He had been cursing ferociously at the power mower, much to the amusement of the kids next door, who had, as usual, been playing hooky. At long last, the confounded device whirred into action; and Gallenkamp, returning to his labors, was forced to swerve suddenly to avoid an encounter with a monstrous turd that glistened on the unkempt grass like a baroque jewel.

He could not have known, alas, that this was no piece of squishy excrement, but a lump of painted and varnished plaster of Paris that the hooky-playing neighbors had planted there for the express purpose of arousing his ire. But so offensive was the spectacle to his refined sensibilities that Gallenkamp lost control of his mower.

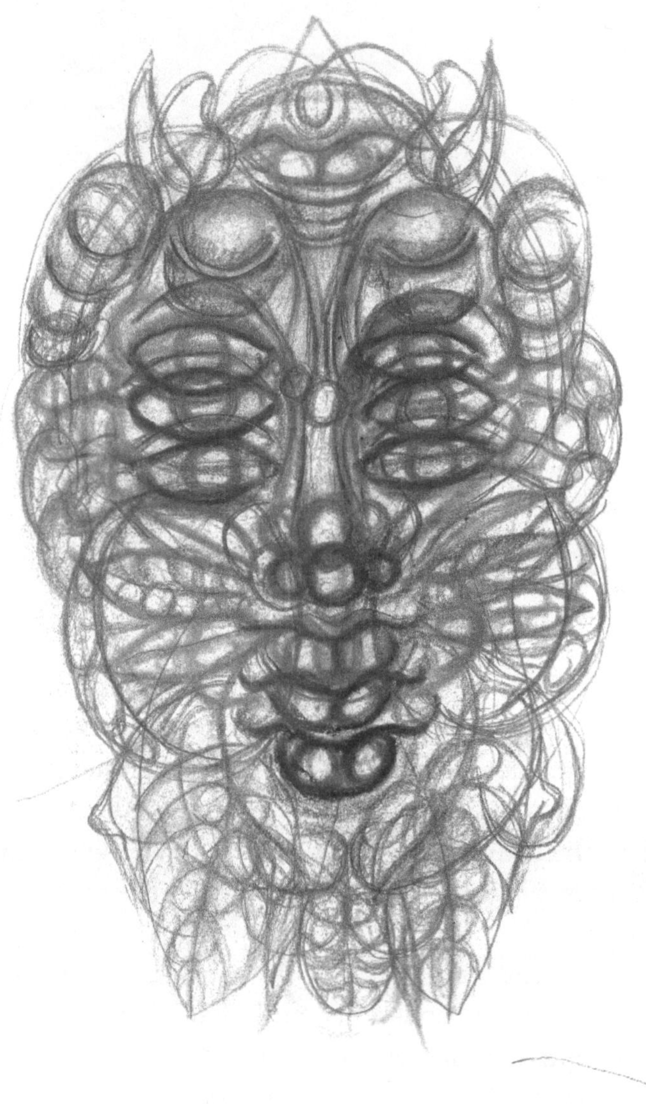

The coprous simulacrum caught in its mechanism. Pieces of plaster began to shrapnel the lawn, and one such shard was propelled through Gallenkamp's left eye with such force that it invaded his brain, killing him almost instantly.

He fell forward, arms outstretched, against the mower's handles, and it was in this position, a sort of hybrid of Christ and scarecrow, that his wife Elayne (having returned from the drugstore with a fresh supply of sanitary napkins) found him ten minutes later.

She sighed, went inside, and telephoned my office.

Although it took me only twenty minutes to arrive, the house was already swarming with sycophants and leeches when I stepped inside.

"Oh, there you are, Whitey," Elayne said, wringing her hands in a convincingly distraught manner. "Gentlemen, this is Whitey Jefferson, our attorney."

A row of earnest-looking, cadaverous men in dark suits was standing against the far wall, from which depended several tomahawks and painted Plains Indian shields. A veritable aviary of war bonnets graced the lid of the Steinway grand piano that blocked the stairway to the second floor. Another wall sported a futuristic poster with the legend *ResurrecTech*™ in embossed chrome letters. The significance of that poster was at that time known only to me. Apart from the undertakers, then, the room was precisely as I had last seen it. Except, of course, that Elayne had not been wearing that half-zippered black dress. She had been naked.

I said, "How could there be so many undertakers so soon?"

"Mr. Gallenkamp had a device that monitored his heartbeat," said one of the undertakers with his nose in the air, "designed by the Sargnagel Corporation. It outputted directly to the Morticians' Union headquarters."

Before I had time to gape, they all started talking in turn. "Mr. Jefferson," said another of the undertakers, "I represent the firm of Mortworth, Mortworth and

Mortworth, specializing in the expeditious beautification of the Loved One's remains and offering a choice of three easy payment plans —"

"Shut up, Mortworth!" a second interrupted. "I was here first. My dear, dear Mrs. Gallenkamp! Forgive my colleague's untimely and insensitive sales pitch. I am Mr. Ruddigore, president of Ruddigore's Rapturous Havens. Wouldn't your husband have loved to lie in gentle repose amongst others of his breeding, listening to the strains of Mozart on our twenty-four hour string quartet service? We also have easy listening."

"That's nothing!" crowed a third. "Surely, Mrs. Gallenkamp, a woman of your sensibilities must understand the importance of racial purity! I represent Sampson's Segregated Cemeteries. Our motto is, 'Paradise or bussed!' Get it? Har, har."

Elayne looked at me imploringly.

Suddenly the undertaker stopped gabbing. "Look! Outside!" another one screeched.

"It's him!" said Ruddigore.

They ran to the open front door. I and Elayne followed. We saw an elderly gentleman in a top hat and tails, busily directing two lackeys, who were about to lift Gallenkamp off the mower.

The other undertakers were clustered around the body, protesting their right of precedence. The one in the top hat, spying us, came over and pulled out a business card.

I took it and read, "Lord Texas-Chainsaw, President, Olde Worlde Funeral Services."

"That's _Tanshawe,_" he said stiffly.

"What are you talking about?"

"My name," he said, and I noticed the British accent, perhaps fake. "It's _spelt_ Texas-Chainsaw, pronounced _Tanshawe._ We are a very ancient family."

"I think I'm going to puke," Elayne said, as we both noticed the viscous rheum dripping from Gallenkamp's jellying eye socket.

"Go ahead, dear madam," said Texas-Chainsaw suavely. "A little regurgitation is nothing to be ashamed of in this hour of ultimate bereavement."

"I think I'm going to scream!"

"I suppose I'd better do something," I said. "I mean, to repel the invasion of the body snatchers."

"Get them out of here already!" Elayne screamed.

"Leave at once!" I said in my most majestic voice.

"Bu t—the body—" said Mortworth.

"As Mrs. Gallenkamp's attorney, I shall inform you of her final decision in the matter of the disposition of the body."

I waved grandly, in my most Perry Masonesque manner, and the morticians fled like a herd of kine down the gentle incline of the front yard into their waiting limousines. All but this Texas-Chainsaw, that is, who stood scrutinizing me for some moments (as a biologist might peruse a microbe) before he shambled off. As he left, I knew him—as though by a sudden prescience—for my mortal enemy.

Elayne followed me into the house. I slammed the door shut. Then I embraced her, and we kissed passionately.

"What a stroke of luck!" Elayne said when our ardor had abated somewhat, steering me toward the very couch where we had last made love.

"Yes," I said, "it seems that dear Owen will be out to lunch more frequently from now on."

"And dinner," Elayne panted.

"And breakfast!" I said, anticipating the wild abandon of the night to come.

"Though I rather regret," Elayne said, "that we won't have to murder him. That was so thrilling … the whispered plans over the lunch breaks … the debates over the most appropriate murder weapon… ."

"Darling!"

Just then, we heard voices squawking outside: "Totally awesome! Icky! Ooooh, gross! Daddy's dead!"

"C'mon, it's just a rubber corpse. Don't you remember, he brought one down from the studio when he was doing the novelization of *The Beast that Decapitated Nuns?*"

"Crap, you can tell from the stink, stupid. Like, he's totally dead."

I opened the door and saw two dirty identical ten-year-old girls with braces and freckles. "Oh, shit!" I said. "It's Heckle and Jeckle."

"Oh, Uncle Whitey! Is he really dead, I mean, <u>dead</u> dead?"

"Come in, kids," I said, "I suppose you'd better hear the will."

"Then I'll have to decide on which of those creeps to hire for the funeral," Elayne said.

"I don't think so," I said. "Not after you hear what's in the will."

The moment of truth had finally come, and it was with a heavy heart that I pulled the sealed document from an inner pocket of my gray three-piece suit.

***

"So," Elayne said at last. "It's worse than we ever imagined."

"I'm afraid so."

"Want a drink?"

"Scotch." One of the twins went into the kitchen to fix it, and Elayne and I sat down and pored over the document again.

"God! Look at that part!" she said.

I read: *I know you've been screwing that scumbag of a lawyer, Elayne darling. At first, I thought I would make the inheritance contingent on your never seeing him again, but I've thought of a worse plan.*

"Oh, God, the plan, the plan," Elayne moaned.

"Now, the Sioux used to leave their dead on platforms on the premises. I see no reason why you should not do so. If I die, I must insist that you leave my body precisely at the place of death undisturbed. Especially if I die at home. My grisly, rotting corpse will haunt you daily as you rut with that shyster, you tacky, disloyal slut. How wonderful the Sioux were! They were never tainted by your petit bourgeous sensibilities. As for those hideous children I sired, the continuous presence of a memento mori in their home will be a salutary exposure to the human condition. No one is to perform any embalming or anything else on my carcass except Dr. Sargnagel."

"Sargnagel ... who's he?" Elayne said.

"My, he's certainly kept his life a secret from you, hasn't he?   Owen owned 46% of the Sargnagel Corporation, a holding corporation which includes —— *ResurrecTech*™ —I glanced at the poster on the wall."

"I thought that was just a movie he was novelizing," Elayne said.

"It could almost be one. *Resurrectech*™ specializes in mad scientist sort of experiments... ."

"How are we going to get out of this?" Elayne wailed.

"I don't see how we can. I drew it up myself. I was humoring him, really. Didn't expect him to croak before I had a chance to monkey with it. Look at this part: *If my instructions are not obeyed to the letter, my entire estate will be bequeathed to the Sioux Nation. The corpse is not to be moved more than twelve feet from the scene of my death, and only for the purpose of cleaning or cosmetic decoration or effecting a more aesthetic arrangement."*

"What does he mean, the Sioux Nation?" Elayne said. "He's never even met an Indian in his life."

"Our mutual friend was even more eccentric than I thought."

"Can't we just let the Indians have it? How much can there have been, anyway?"

"About eight million."

"What!" The screeches came simultaneously from the woman and the two little girls.

"My dear, it appears that dear Owen, whose literary works were critical and commercial failures, who appeared to be just struggling along in this decidedly unsumptuous condominium, actually amassed a vast fortune by shrewd investment of the royalties from the novelizations of *The Beast that Decapitated Nuns* and *Gangbanged on Ganymede*. A computer error at Stupendous Publishing, you see, apportioned his share of the royalties to the studio, and the studio's to him. In fact, I've known this for some time; that's why I agreed to become executor of the estate."

"My God ... you've always known ... do you mean to say that you've inveigled yourself into my bed for purely materialistic purposes, that you've been —"

"Using you? I hardly think you're in a position to make that accusation, darling, considering you've been guilty of adultery for the past eleven years. By the way, who <u>is</u> the father of those hideous twins?"

"You parasite!"

"Elayne darling, I know what I am. You have yet to learn."

"How dare you —"

"Now, you wouldn't want to upset the executor of the estate, would you?"

"So what's the plan?"

We were interrupted by a scurrying sound outside. "Let's go and see," I said, anxious for any diversion, for I dreaded having to call Sargnagel's office. The sun was setting over the kiddie playground across the street. I got a whiff of Gallenkamp, and didn't terribly much care for the smell. Two figures were hulking over the corpse; a police car was parked on the curb, and farther up the service road was a limousine I recognized as belonging to Lord Texas-Chainsaw's body shop. The lord himself was there, attired in a sort of Dracula cape, and he was grimly orchestrating the theft of Owen's corpse.

"There, there," he was saying. "We don't want to take away the handle of the mower, would we? That would be stealing."

"And what do you think this is?" I said. "Trespassing. Stealing the personal effects of the owner, no less!"

"My dear fellow —"

"I, Whitey Jefferson of Jefferson, Shapiro and Tablecloth, happen to be the executor of this estate. Since no formal transfer has taken place, you are stealing the late lamented's property."

As though in agreement, Gallenkamp's head craned forward on its neck. Assorted fluids drooled from his nose and mouth. A dog ran by, sniffing longingly at the cadaver's brain-besmirched buttocks until I shooed it away.

"But I am leaving the mower intact!" Texas-Chainsaw said.

"The mower? Who cares about the mower? It's the body I'm concerned with. If a man doesn't own his own body, what *can* he call his own?"

"I see I shall have to call upon the law for assistance, Mr. Jefferson," Texas-Chainsaw said imperturbably. "I say, officer!"

From behind one of the parked police cars emerged a grotesquely blubbery policewoman brandishing a badge. "I'm officer Heartfelt," she said.

"Stay where you are!" I said. "The sidewalk may be public, but the grass isn't. Got a warrant?"

"Sir," the officer said, "It is illegal in this state of ours to leave a body lying around rotting for more than twenty-four hours without having it removed by a licensed undertaker."

"So what are you going to do?" I said. "Give it a ticket?"

"Well —" She pulled out a notebook, fished a pencil from her pocket, and began scribbling.

"Furthermore, I demand the immediate extradition of Lord Texas-Chainsaw from the premises."

"Oh, I say, I object, what. I was only doing my duty as a citizen. Why, if I didn't report your shameful neglect of the deceased, I'd be an accessory after the fact, wouldn't I?"

"Ah —" said the officer, patting her paunch thoughtfully while Elayne did a passable imitation of a grief-stricken widow.

"In any case," I said, "it isn't even twenty-four hours yet. Now will you get this idiot off the Gallenkamp turf before I call the police?"

"I am the police," said Officer Heartfelt. "I suppose you'd better come with me," she said to Texas-Chainsaw.

"Foiled again!" said the twins, who had come from the house and were nibbling between them a leviathan hunk of amaretto cheesecake. "Nyah, nyah, nyah! Gash me with a ginsu! Totally radical!"

"Go to bed!" said their mother.

"But it's not our bedtime yet," said Heckle. By the way,

these are not their real names. In my years of involvement with the Gallenkamps, I had yet to learn to tell them apart. Nor would I have wanted to.

"Uncle Whitey and I have important business matters to discuss."

"You mean," said Jeckle, "that you're getting rid of us so you can fuck."

"The things these children are saying nowadays!" Texas-Chainsaw said. "Simply appalling!"

"Get him out of here," I said, and there was a concerted exeunt that left me alone with Elayne on the front lawn in the suburban sunset, about to cuckold the corpse of my best friend.

I patted the old fellow on the head. A hank of hair, matted with brain tissue, clung to my fingers. "I can see, my dear," I said, "that we must be prepared to fight a legal battle of epic proportions. But never fear! Whitey Jefferson's never lost a case yet!"

Inexplicably, Elayne began to cry. I guess it was all too much to take in, having me all to herself and all that.
     ***

When I climbed into bed with Elayne I was anticipating a night of rapturous and continuous orgasm. Instead, I was surprised to find her rather frigid. I was expecting a long and tender lay-in in the morning; indeed, I'd even left word at the office that we would be working over the details of the will and that they were to start without me on *Hobson vs. Hobbes*. Instead, we were awakened at the crack of dawn by the shrieking of the children.

I started. She moaned. I said, "So this is what actually living with a woman is like."

"Go for it, baby."

"I think I'm starting to feel nostalgic about the lunch break arrangement," I said, casually stroking one of her breasts.

"Come quickly!" one of the kids screamed from somewhere outside the house. "The storm troopers are back!"

I heard sirens, crowd noises, and various *ughs* and *ooohs* and other ejaculations of repugnance, as I helped myself to one of Owen's shirts from the closet. I even wore his underwear. I felt particularly evil doing that. It was a superb sensation. Grabbing a sheaf of papers from the living room to make it look like I had been burning the midnight oil, I flung the front door open. Elayne followed in a floral nightgown.

The sight that assailed me can only be described as a spectacle of insensate and unmitigated horror, equal to if not exceeding the notorious crowd scene from Owen Gallenkamp's *The Beast that Decapitated Nuns*, a scene which, I hasten to add, was not in the movie.

***

It seemed as though the entire population of Rattlesnake Junior High had played hooky that morning. My hapless friend's corpse—whose head was swarming with ants and centipedes—was completely surrounded by jeering children. Officer Heartfelt was protecting the corpse with one arm and waving a nightstick with the other. Lord Texas-Chainsaw and a gang of henchmen, all dressed in dark suits and wearing dark glasses, were beating back the children as he tried to make his way through to the corpse. Heckle and Jeckle were bombarding them with spitballs. Old Mrs. Snodgrass from across the street was standing on the doorstep, obliviously telling me the latest gossip. A Hare Krishna was selling everyone flowers.

"All right, all right," I said.

"Twenty-four hours is up," Officer Heartfelt said imposingly. "I'm now empowered to authorize the removal of the corpse."

"Over my dead body!" I shouted, gesticulating wildly. My hand smashed into Gallenkamp's decomposing face. I snatched it back. Several gloppy maggots adhered to my hand. The grim comedy of the situation was coming home to me. "Bring me the phone!" I shouted at the twins. One of them rushed into the house and emerged with the patio cordless. I dialed furiously as the maggots crawled from my hand to the mouthpiece. "Give me Judge Strickland," I said. "Now, this minute." To Texas-Chainsaw and Heartfelt I said, "Your asses are about to be in deep, deep, deep, deep shit."

"The law —" the officer began.

"—is the handmaiden of the well-heeled," I said, as I heard Judge Strickland's phthisic voice wheezing away at the other end. "Courtney? It's Whitey. I want a court order." It would hard be to go much higher that Courtney Strickland, who was head of the president's judiciary advisory commission or something. The crowd of truants was hemming us in tight now, and I had to kick away one intrepid child who, mayonnaise jar in hand, had been trying to scrape off a memento of the dear departed. "It's the Gallenkamp case —"

"Oh, is the old bugger dead?" the judge rasped. "Wonderful news. I'll have a rehoboam of Moët Chandon shipped over right away."

"Hold the booze," I said. "There's trouble. The will. He picked the front lawn to die in... ." Of course, the judge had known all about Gallenkamp's will. It had been the talk of his chambers for some months now. "They're trying to take him away."

"The rotters!" the judge said. He probably hadn't had this much fun since his triple bypass. "But of course, the state law clearly states —"

"You want me to reveal"—I cupped my hands and whispered into the phone —" your part in the seminary brownie molestation coverup?"

"Oh, I, ah —"

"I knew you could be reasonable, your honor." I turned to Officer Heartfelt. "The court order should be here in a half hour. Get out."

She drew herself up. "Until it appears, Mr. Jefferson, I am still the law around here. We'll bring the body back when we see the document."

It was at that dramatic juncture that an enormous van pulled up in front of the townhouse.   It was a sleek, streamlined thing, all black and chrome, with a futuristic hood ornament. The sides were blazoned with the legend

ResurrechTech™

and beneath that, in tiny letters, the words "Sargnagel Enterprises." Help had arrived at last! I thought. For Sargnagel Enterprises was, of course, one of Owen's own little projects, and Dr. Sargnagel had been mentioned in the will as the only person authorized to tinker with the corpse.

"I believed that the morticians specified in the deceased's will have finally arrived," I said.

Officer Heartfelt gave them no more than a cursory examination. Relieved that she no longer had to duel with me, she and her squad car departed; and I thumbed my nose at the unsavory Texas-Chainsaw as he and his cohorts drove away. It was only then that I turned my attention to the labcoated technicians who were piling out of the car, all carrying some high-tech device, each one more outlandish-looking than the last.

A tiny man, with dark glasses, was directing them. Were he not bald, I would have pegged him as about fourteen years old. I recognized him from the photo in the dossier I had in my office—his was the thinnest file in the cabinet. In all my years as a dirt-digger I had uncovered almost no information about this fellow at all. He didn't even seem to have a birth certificate or a social security number— if he did, they were well hidden even from the prying computers at Jefferson, Shapiro and Tablecloth.

"Dr. Sargnagel," I said.

He ignored me. "No, stupid!" he barked at one of the assistants. "He'll need at least a hundred feet radius circumambulation field. Plant the ROM module"—he stalked out into the middle of the lawn and pointed at a patch of ground a couple of yards away from the rotting cadaver and the power mower —" right here."

The assistant started digging immediately, while another began attaching electrodes to the body.

"Totally radical!" the twins screeched. "Can we help?"

"Hold this," Dr. Sargnagel said, thrusting wires and switches into their hands. He then advanced toward the body of my late friend and began to drill a hole in his skull with some kind of laser device. Brains spattered his head, but he didn't seem to notice. Then he gave a signal, and one of his assistants poked a sort of computer cable into Owen's cranium.

Owen fluttered his eyelids.

"Ah, good," Sargnagel said.

"Just what the hell do you think you're doing?" I said.

"What the—oh, you must be that Jefferson dude," Sargnagel said. "Well, we have like this gigabyte ROM module, kind of a simulacrum of Gallenkamp's brain processes, and we're like installing this like interface that will like function as a digital-to-analog coprocessor. Thing is, like there's virtually no RAM, so the loved one can't learn anything new, and so like it guarantees that his character doesn't like change, and aborts the Jekyll-and-Hyde complex, you know?"

"Awesome!" Heckle crooned, while her sister placed her hand to her forehead and pretended to swoon. "You're turning daddy's body into a robot!"

I must admit that that was not at all how I had translated Sargnagel's sentiments to myself. But the young are always much more knowledgeable about scientific jargon. It was clear that my dear friend had, in effect, donated his body to some bizarre experiment. Perhaps the interests of science were being served; perhaps not. Well, I would not let it deter me from the embraces of Elayne. Or from the eight million.

I went back inside, leaving the twins to help the mad doctor. Elayne was still in bed, whinnying and heaving like a steam locomotive. Exhilarated by my victory over Officer Heartfelt and Lord Texas-Chainsaw, and by the ease with which I had blackmailed Judge Strickland, I leaped eagerly into the fray. Then we watched daytime soaps for a few hours, consumed TV dinners, and resumed our feverish fornication. By midnight I was exhausted. Flattered though I was by Elayne's continued ardor, I decided to sleep on the couch downstairs. My rest was fitful, for it was continually punctuated by sounds of hammering and by electronic beeps and buzzes from the high-tech crew on the lawn. Eventually I went back upstairs. Mercifully, Elayne had fallen asleep; I did so too. My last thoughts before I passed out were of millions upon millions of greenbacks raining down from the sky.

***

I was awakened by the fragrance of hot coffee. I rubbed my eyes. "You needn't have, darling," I said. Then I noticed that Elayne was snoring away beside me. Could Heckle and Jeckle undergone so dramatic a transformation as to bring us our morning coffee in bed? "Thank you, children," I murmured.

"You're welcome." A rasping, buzzing voice. I opened my eyes wide. A tray was being held out at me. "I thought you and my harlot wife would like a little something for breakfast."

There was an odor of putrescence behind the smell of coffee, and the tray was covered with slime.

The bearer of the tray was none other than the corpse of my old friend. He stood, quite still, stinking up the bedroom. An electronic cable led from an opening in his back (through which the spinal chord glistened with beads of coagulated blood) all the way out the bedroom door, from behind which came the diabolical giggling of the twins. Such was my astonishment that the horror of having my friend's zombie resurrection did not register at first.

"Enjoying my wife, are you?" Owen said. He gaped wide and I saw the glint of some metal device implanted in his throat. I was reminded of the prosthetics certain laryngectomy patients use to simulate speech. Owen leered. I noticed that there was a trail of slime leading to the door and presumably all the way downstairs and into the lawn.

At that moment, Elayne stirred. "Coffee? How thoughtful of you, darling," she said.

She opened her eyes and saw the rotting animated corpse of her late husband, who attempted a sheepish grin through lips stained with blood, pus, and decaying vomit.

Elayne screamed.

***

The television crews had been gathering since dawn. When Elayne had calmed down enough, I made her make herself up nicely and put on a moderately yuppie dress. Then I carefully waved a sliced onion in front of her face for a few minutes, so that the tears would streak the mascara so as to suggest a woman heroically struggling with her grief.

Meanwhile, the corpse puttered around the living room. It had a go at vacuuming, but the power cord became hopelessly entangled in Owen's own I/O cables, so that he tripped and made a gloppy mess out of that nice pseudo-Persian carpet Elayne had purchased from Bloomingdale's. The sight of her dead husband jerkily attempting to rise from the floor and to disentangle his entrails from the various wires and cables set off another screaming fit.

"Shut up!" I said. "They'll hear you outside. We've got to act as though this is all perfectly normal."

"I want that corpse out of my house!"

"That's a fine thing to say," the cadaver riposted. "The three of us should have a threesome sometime. I used to fantasize about that over my word-processor when I was alive." It managed to straighten itself out; it then proceeded to shamble to the sofa.

"Are we ready to meet the public?" I said.

Numbly Elayne nodded.

"Think of the money," I said.

We opened the door.

Sargnagel was already holding forth from the front steps. All the networks were there. "Well like none of the hardware is really new, but like there are whole areas in applications that we haven't had the imagination to like effectuate. I'd say the *ResurrecTech*™ process should be like totally available within like maybe a couple months. The subject's memory is downloaded from the brain like before death and cut down to fit the gigabyte ROM module and there's like this hierarchical memory banking file-management user-independent operating system. We're totally backed up with orders though."

"Are you saying that we'll soon be seeing a plethora of zombies, Dr. Sargnagel?" a reporter said, nervously eyeing Owen, who had come outside. The cables that controlled him emanated from a machine buried in the lawn; a spooling device kept them taut, sort of like fishing tackle.

"I wouldn't exactly call them zombies," Sargnagel continued, "I just think of them as computer-enhanced cadavers —CECs for short."

To my horror I saw that the Texas-Chainsaw limo had arrived. Moreover, this time Lord Texas-Chainsaw had brought with him about half a dozen Plains Indians in war-bonnets, and they were dancing up a storm on the sidewalk.

"This is the most awesome spectacle since the Philippine election!" one reporter rhapsodized, as the videocameras turned and the microphone booms swivelled, causing a hardware traffic jam above our heads.

"Why are they dancing?" Elayne said.

"These representatives of the Sioux Nation have been flown in to collect their ten-million dollar windfall," an earnest woman reporter was declaiming into one camera. "But will they get it or not? Will Elayne Gallenkamp and ace legal expert Whitey Jefferson be able to keep the body of Owen Gallenkamp in defiance of city ordinances about proper removal of the dead?"

Texas Chainsaw was waving a document. "I have here a court order from Judge Strickland —"

"Wait a minute!" I said. I ran back into the house and returned with my own court order. I brandished it, pushing Texas-Chainsaw out of camera range. He rearranged his Dracula cape and came bouncing back. The cameras reshuffled themselves as Owen's computer-enhanced cadaver came back into view. It was socializing with the Indians, joining in the dance. I took the opportunity to look at Texas-Chainsaw's paper. *Expeditious removal of the deceased ...* Astonished, I said, "How did you manage to get Judge Strickland —"

"My dear Mr. Jefferson! How could you be so naïve as to suppose that you have a monopoly on Judge Strickland's little, ah, foibles? I don't know which one you used on him, but one teeny dropped hint of his involvement in the Boy Scout heroin scandal was enough to render him *most* cooperative."

Even I hadn't known about that.

"Well," I said, "we do seem to have two conflicting court orders —"

Texas-Chainsaw stepped in front of the nearest camera and began to speak in doleful, dulcet tones: "What we have here, ladies and gentlemen of the media, is a clear case of environmental pollution ... corrupt lawyers ... poor, deprived Native Americans being cheated of their inheritance to satisfy the craven lusts of —"

He went on in this vein for sometime. If there's anything I hate, it's one of these bleeding heart appeals, whether it's whales or Indians or anything else. I was getting steadily angrier. Elayne, who stood beside me, was weakening, though. I could see that she was not relishing the prospect of sharing life with her husband's corpse. "Please, let's just give up the whole thing," she whispered.

"We'll go away somewhere ... at least we have each other...."

That was precisely what I was afraid of. I saw a vision of ten million smackers swirling down the toilet bowl ... and only a supply of mediocre free pussy to show for it. "Are you kidding?" I said. "This means war!"

"Totally rad!" said the twins. "Get 'em, Rambo!"

Texas-Chainsaw was saying, "... the sad state of contemporary culture ... when a man is deprived of a decent burial and made into a monster ..."

Suddenly I had an inspiration. I shoved him onto the lawn. "This is a constitutional issue," I said. "The man wants to be able to rot on his own private turf, and these henchmen of the state would deprive him of that right! I say just because a man is dead doesn't abrogate his civil rights—let alone his human rights! You, Lord Texas-Chainsaw, and you, Officer Heartfelt, are Big Brother personified! Communists! Fascist pigs!"

Texas-Chainsaw's face was becoming steadily more livid in hue. "I fail to see how you can accuse me of being both," he said.

"We've passed laws to stop discrimination against blacks and women and homosexuals," I said. "Well, I say there's one more barrier of prejudice to be overcome—our discriminatory practices against the deceased! We'll get another restraining order"—I was going to play my trump card, the fact that Judge Strickland had been getting kickbacks from the mafia —" and we'll resist this un-American living/dead apartheid all the way to the Supreme Court ... all the way to the President of the United States!"

I paused to take a breath. That was when the applause began. How sweet that applause was! As a lawyer I well knew that the content of a speech doesn't matter, only its rhetoric, its tone, its fervor. I had delivered a classic speech, on national television; my words were going to echo through the land.

***

That evening, Sargnagel's crew were making adjustments to Owen: spraying him with a fixative that hardened into sort of a Saran Wrap around him, so he would ooze and leak all over the place; fine-tuning his interfaces and cables; and—so help me—brushing and flossing his teeth.

The phone rang. It was the Reverend Obadiah Crackerjack, a popular TV evangelist. Oh, no, I thought. He's going to berate me for not allowing people their proper Christian burial. I sat down on the sofa, carefully wiping off Owen's slime, and tried to decide on the least actionable brushoff.

"Mister Jefferson, sir, I'm a-telling you, the Lord has touched you, sir, he has chosen you to bear his word."

"What?" I said, not quite believing my ears.

"I mean, I heard you on the news today, sir, and it is my belief that you have been singled out to bear a divine revelation. I got to thinking about all you said—about discriminating against the souls and wishes of the dear departed—and I think this whole sick thing is just another example of the sin and degradation that's tainting this Christian country of ours. One moment they're telling us that the right to life is only applicable after the wee, pathetic embryo has been delivered ... and now these sodomitic sinners are saying that the right to life stops at the moment of death!"

"That's very interesting," I said noncommitally, wishing I could hand this lunatic over to my secretary. "Quite a paradox you've—ah—uncovered, reverend."

"—when everyone knows that the soul is immortal and the death of the flesh is but the beginning of life eternal—of the glories of hell or the fires of damnation! That's why I'm a-fixing to hold a special telethon for your cause —"

Horrified, I realized that I had been sucked into an unholy alliance with the forces of excruciating moral rectitude.

The reverend continued (obviously rehearsing his sermon for later that night), "I'm a-galvanizing my congregation for a march on Washington. They'll come, believe me! Dead or alive, they'll come! Should the earthly forms of some members of my church have succumbed to the corruption of the body, I intend to be raising enough capital to purchase CEC units for all! Sargagel's *ResurrecTech*™ process is the Lord's plan to prepare us for the more perfect resurrection of the life to come! Now, won't you say a few rousing words to my flock?"

"You're on TV again!" squealed Heckle or Jeckle from upstairs. "On some religious voodoo nut show! You're gonna be totally famous!"

So the reverend wasn't rehearsing. This was live. I had better make it good. But I didn't believe in any of this bullshit! And yet … ten million dollars … the computer-enhanced cadaver of my ex-best-friend hunkered in the hallway. He didn't smell bad anymore; they'd installed a couple of time-release fragrance ampoules in his armpits. Surely having him around couldn't be that bad. I mean, he might walk and talk, but he *was* dead. Dead and harmless. It was all psychological.   Just your typical Owen Gallenkampian emotional blackmail.

"Well, Mister Jefferson? Do you believe?" Jeckle had come in and turned on the living room TV, so I saw the Lord's ambassador in all his porcine splendor.

"Ahem," I said. I had to say something fast. "Ah—the constitution of the United States—the—ah—habeas corpus —human rights—can't descend to the level of the Soviet Union —" I knew that one would get them. I went on in that vein for a while, being careful to mention apple pie at least once per paragraph.

"That," Obadiah Crackerjack, "has got to be the most moving speech we've ever heard on Heavenly Hour. And now, a word from our sponsor —"

Their sponsor! It was the Sargnagel Corporation ... with an ad for a bible quotation PROM module, implantable in the computer-enhanced cadaver of your favorite atheist! *Why allow your beloved friends and relatives to die unsaved? Technology comes to the service of His word ... give your dead friends a second chance to accept Him into their hearts... .* It was sickening. PROMS—EPROMS would be next, whatever they were. The twins would know.

But it *was* pouring money into the coffers of Elayne and me ... as long as that talking corpse remained with us. If they took it away ... there'd be a new string of condos on the reservation.

"Hi, Owen," I said, smiling as he shambled in and sat down beside me. "Make yourself at home. Have a drink?"

"Don't be ridiculous. I'm dead."

***

At night, during our desultory lovemaking, I became conscious of someone else lying in bed with me and Elayne. Someone thrusting wildly and hapharzardly away at the sheets. In the half dark I saw who it was.

"Jesus Christ," I said.

Elayne, eyes closed and transported by ecstacy, had failed to notice that she was participating in a particularly unusual act.

"You were never like this when you were alive," I muttered. "If you had been, Elayne would never have turned to me."

"Being a cyborg does have its advantages," he said, as Elayne heaved and panted passionately and obliviously.

Owen neither panted nor heaved. He didn't even breathe. Maybe that was the secret of his newfound sexual prowess—he didn't have to worry about his heart, his cholesterol, or his ulcers.

At last, he rolled away. There wasn't much slime; the plastic sheath was holding up quite well. Elayne cried, "Oh, not yet, not yet, darling."

"Want to finish her off?" he said.

Sighing, I returned to the ramparts of love. But somehow it wasn't the same with Owen sitting there, rotting away. I just couldn't ... well, I just couldn't. I had to let old Roy Rogers back into the saddle. I had never felt more stupid in my life.

"That was wonderful, darling," Elayne whispered, as the zombie slunk back into the shadows.

To be honest, I was not displeased at this turn of events. Without the element of furtiveness, my relationship with Elayne had been reduced to the level of bourgeois adultery. Let him have her, I thought. After all, what else does he have to live for?

***

Contributions from Obadiah Crackerjack's church started to arrive the very next morning. I began to realize that we could never pull out now. The ten million was nothing compared to this new racket. Elayne bought several fur coats. I didn't go into the office for the fourth day running. I considered quitting the law firm altogether in order to give my full attention to this great constitutional issue. Yes, I still had qualms about aligning myself with the Crackerjack Morality Squad; but how could I resist the checks that were flooding in through the mailbox?

One day later, a group of raving religious fanatics exhumed the entire contents of a local cemetery and loaded the coffins onto Sargnagel trucks.

Three days later, zombies were spotted in nearby Springfield Mall. Their leashes were attached to mobile processor units. The zombies purchased some new wave clothing at J.C.Penneys. There were some problems with expired credit cards, and the police were called in. A battle ensued between right-to-computer-enhanced-lifers and members of the morticians' solidarity group.

That evening, Lord Texas-Chainsaw and I were guests on CNN's *Crossfire*. He called me a environmental polluter; I called him a communist. It degenerated into a fistfight. Luckily, I had learned kung fu; in my line of work it's always good to be able to fend off some angry client. I climbed atop the heap of debaters' bodies and—to the nation at large—I announced that we were going to march on the White House. "Zombies out of the closet!" I screamed at the top of my lungs. "Corpses of the world unite!"

A whirlwind talk-show tour followed. Mornings I spoke to studio audiences of earnest housewives. Evenings I had spots on news hours. Late nights I did the call-in circuit ... "Mr. Jefferson, my mother has been dead for ten years and I was wondering whether computer-enhancement would be feasible." ... "Sure. Get a good plastics engineer to reconstruct the body on the old frame. But if you haven't had the ROM-dump done, you probably can't be helped—although you might consider redesigning her personality entirely and creating a character-simulacrum for the frame." "Great show! Whitey, my uncle was cremated last week, and —" … "Forget it! They might be able to build a plastic body, though. Did you do the dump?" … "Do you think I could get my kids embalmed *before* they die?" … "Most experts consider it inadvisable, but I'd make sure they sign a release first. If they're minors, you can of course do it on their behalf." … "What happens to my IRA if I try to draw on it and I'm already dead?" … "Call your local tax advisor." Etcetera, etcetera. I found a ready answer for almost any question they could throw at me.

Excitement grew. My best friend's right to rot had become a *cause célèbre,* and all the sickos were coming out of the woodwork … I mean, all the Norman Bates types with their stuffed mothers in their fruit cellars … you'd be surprised how many of them there were … every one of them fighting mad and militant as hell.

I finally did quit the job. Actually, they fired me after the firm was retained by the morticians' solidarity caucus. I didn't even notice.

Owen started filling in for me every night now; the task of servicing Elayne had become onerous to me. Elayne had found a man—or whatever—who could match her tireless passion thrust for thrust. At first she found it rather distasteful; but with the lights off, and with the perfume ampoule set on high, she hardly seemed to notice after a while.

And me? Only the good fight mattered now. I was a man possessed. I had a vision. I had a dream. I also had millions of dollars.

***

The day of the great march on the White House finally dawned. It was a fine summer's day. The stench of putrescence filled the street as Elayne and I emerged from the house. We were followed by Heckle and Jeckle, who carried between them a stripped-down version of the CPU that animated Owen's corpse.

Sargnagel and Crackerjack were there to greet us. The former was surrounded by a crowd of techie nerds; the latter was at the head of a motley assortment of people and corpses. The corpses were what had been stinking up the street. There were hundreds of them. Many of them had not been as smoothly animated as that of my friend Owen; for several fly-by-night CEC outfits had appeared in the past few weeks, each one seeking to bypass Sargnagel's patented microchips with bug-filled Taiwanese imitations. The corpses jerked, flailed and gibbered.

"My God," Elayne whispered, tripping over a human hand that had fallen by the wayside.

Then a fervent chanting arose from the gathered throng: "I'd rather be dead than dead! I'd rather be dead than dead!"

"What a singularly inspired slogan," I said. "It doesn't mean anything."

"Ah, Jefferson, my son," Crackerjack said expansively, "that's because you haven't yet come to a complete understanding of the mysterious ways of the Lord. It don't matter *what* they're chanting. The important thing is that they're chanting. The second coming is at hand ... the dead shall be raised incorruptible!"

"I don't know," I said, wrinkling my nose at a maggot-ridden liver that had landed at my feet. "Looks pretty corruptible to me."

"Believe."

"Yeah." I was in too deep now. It was my face on all those talk shows. I was the one most prominently identified with this latest extension of the right-to-life concept. I tried to keep a straight face as our contingent began to lead the marchers down the street toward the highway. After a while I got into the rhythm of it, and it seemed like no time at all before the gathering—now grown to perhaps a hundred thousand people, and a thousand or so dead bodies—reached Pennsylvania Avenue.

The corpses were a big hit. Two teenage corpse breakdanced frantically out front; one of them actually removed his own head and begun juggling with it. Not to be undone, the other unzipped his legs from his torso and executed some bizarre manoeuvres, such as doing a handstand ten yards away from his tapping feet, for example. As a consequence of the fine summer's day, however, the crowd was becoming increasingly rank, some of Sargnagel's shock troops moved in with hoses that sprayed embalming fluid over the celebrants.

Wellwishers lined the sidewalks, many of them waving frayed copies of *The Beast that Decapitated Nuns*. My heart swelled with pride. Here I was—I, Whitey Jefferson, a shyster from a second-rate law firm—elevated to a champion of the constitution— possibly even sainthood, at the rate the Reverend Crackerjack was carrying on!

The crowd marched on. Already we had reached Fifteenth Street; just ahead was the White House, splendid in the sunlight. The corpses began to sing, their raspy, electronic voices drowning out the sounds of traffic and police sirens.

We paused in front of the gates. The Reverend Obadiah Crackerjack gave a rousing sermon, although I had to admit that the biblical references went right over my head. I suppose that finding the right biblical quote is sort of like looking up obscure legal precedents in order to flummox the opposing attorney. As Crackerjack got into his stride, I admired him more and more. His ability to prove that black is white was equalled only by my own. I wish I'd had him with me on Hobson vs. Hobbes.

Then it was my turn. Crackerjack had just been warming up the crowd.

Nervously, I got up in front of the cameras and the throng. I cleared my throat a couple of times. What was I supposed to say? "Friends, Romans and countrymen"? Before I could begin the shouting began. Cheers, whistles, slogans, and above it all the song of the corpses bursting forth from thousands of computer-enhanced throats... .

At that moment—

Cries of "Sabotage! What an outrage!" I turned to see that fighting had broken out. Hundreds upon hundreds of Sioux Indians were leaping from Seventeenth Street office buildings, and, with bloodcurdling screams of "Hoka hey!", were hurling themselves upon the chanting dead.

"Like, I think there's trouble," Sargnagel said, and the Reverend Crackerjack made a dive for the public address system to try to restore order.

I knew who was behind it. I just knew. And there he was, his limousine thrusting through the throng and mowing down corpses like bowling pins. The street resounded with the crack of bone and hardware. There was a whole fleet of Texas-Chainsaw hearses. More Indians, in all all the feathered finery of war, were squatting on the hoods, tomahawks upraised. Others were dancing on the roofs and leaping from hearse to hearse, shooting rifles and fire arrows at the mob. Flaming zombies ran amok, sending up a stink of formaldehyde-marinated steak. Texas-Chainsaw's limo made a swath through the carnage and screeched to a halt in front of my podium. No sooner had the lord leapt out than he and Sargnagel were at each other's throats.

"You sold out!" Texas-Chainsaw was screaming. "The

world was supposed to be divided into three parts—and you and Crackerjack want it all to yourselves!"

I stood there, feeling helpless, as I realized that mine was by no means the first unholy triumvirate that Owen Gallenkamp caused to come into existence … that the entire edifice of my newfound wealth had been built upon the ruins of some previous entrepreneurial disaster.… .

"The money," I heard Elayne whimpering. "We'll lose it all unless you do something!"

I seized the microphone from the reverend and began to speak. It wasn't a good, logical speech, one point after another. It was a direct appeal to apple pie, motherhood, and the American flag. But no one heard me, because as I started, there came the whirring thunder of overhead gunships.… .

In a few moments it was all in shambles. Texas-Chainsaw, bleeding, a microphone stand draped around his neck, was shambling off into his limousine, whose windscreen was completely covered with flailing corpses. What kind of power had Gallenkamp held over him? What bargain had he made with Sargnagel? I struggled to make sense of it all as the Reverend Crackerjack blessed the throng.

Amid the chaos, the gates of the presidential mansion opened.

Silence fell.

"The president will see you now." A man in a black suit had come to escort me inside.

The crowd was hushed. Slowly I followed him inside.

***

"First I'd like to thank you, Mr. Jefferson. You've done a lot of the dirty work for us. You've established the right … ah … atmosphere, you see."

The familiar face, so full of sincerity and concern, watched me from the other side of the great desk. I noticed that Dr. Sargnagel had come in and was standing by the door. Some of Sargnagel's laboratory technicians were wheeling in a familiar looking apparatus.

"Thank you, Mr. President," I said. "But why —"

Suddenly I saw it. A cable that emerged from the back of the president's head and wound its way into an outlet in the wall. The presidential desk was covered with bloodstains and slime—sights familiar from the Gallenkamp living room.

"Jesus!" I said. "You're dead."

"An astute observation," he said. "But one which the rest of the populace has, as yet, failed to make—thanks to good makeup and tasteful camera angles."

I am, of course, well trained to adjust instantly to, for instance, startling new pieces of evidence in the courtroom, surprise witnesses, what have you. I looked around me and saw that I wouldn't get anywhere by agreeing ... after all, I was supposed to be here to espouse the rights of dead people, wasn't I? ... so I switched to my most ingratiating voice. "I must say, Mr. President, you've really kept in shape ... I've seen people alive who looked more moribund than you, sir. How long has this—ah—state of affairs been going on?"

"Thanks a lot for your compliments," said the president. "I don't recall my death that well—I think they edited out of the ROM—it was a while back. But enough small talk. The reason I brought you here is simple. You, miserable worm that you are, are the chosen instrument of God, I don't know why. The dead have clearly arisen, and the second coming is evidently at had, although not quite the way we'd imagined it. It took a rare man of God—the Reverend Crackerjack—to see the full implications of all this. But you're not … a believer, you see. That's the trouble."

"Oh, I believe, I believe," I said, looking around anxiously.

"Maybe. But we must be quite certain of it."

"I'll do anything."

"Anything?"

Too late! Secret servicemen had rushed in and pinned my arms behind my back. More machinery was being carted into the office.

"We need a good man to fill the post just vacated by Judge Strickland," he said. "Oh, you didn't know? He's dead."

"Can't you just … bring him back?"

"Shot himself in the head. Like, no time to do a brain dump beforehand," Sargnagel said as he fiddled with various knobs and levers on his equipment. An oscilloscope started to beep. It was just like a scene from *Gangbanged on Ganymede*.

"Poor Strickland," I said, shaking my head.

"Well, the media were threatening to reveal his AIDS test results," the president said. "That, coupled with his part in the brownie molestation coverup and the Boy Scout cocaine ring and the SPCA's pending investigation of his animal pornography business… ."

"I guess it's better this way," I said. "Oh, and … the morticians and the Indians, sir? What is their place in the new order?"

"My dear Jefferson, surely you have heard of manifest destiny?"

"Well, yes, but —"

"Che sera, sera," the president said. "Anyway, welcome to the government of the dead."

"I'm honored, sir," I said. But I didn't see why the

guards were holding on to me so tightly.

"As well you should be! We stand on the threshold of utopia!   In a CEC-controlled nation, no one need suffer again. Poverty will be abolished. By carefully monitoring brain dumps, we can ascertain that only desirable emotions and truths are transmitted to the people. Sargnagel is a genius … and Owen Gallenkamp, whose sleazy novelizations funded his research, is the greatest humanitarian benefactor of all time. Isn't it wonderful?" The president said, trembling at the vastness of his concept. "Wonderful … wonderful!"

He shook his finger at an imaginary TV camera—preparing a speech, obviously. The finger flew into the air and hit me in the face. My hands bound, I could not wipe off the smear of putrescent bodily fluids that were now oozing down my cheek into the corner of my mouth. "I'm terribly sorry," he said. "Now if I'd been alive, that would have hurt like hell. Now … one can always get another finger glued on. Finger, schminger!"

"Of course, sir," I said uneasily.   The stench was flooding my nostrils, but I couldn't show my anxiety.

"You see," the president continued, "the genius of Dr. Sargnagel is that he has made life itself obsolete. Life is no longer necessary … life is … a liability!"

"I couldn't agree more, Mr. President," I said, nodding enthusiastically.

Someone opened the window. The singing of corpses wafted into the room. Choral hallelujahs filled the air. Dr. Sargnagel and his assistants assumed a beatific expression. The president fumbled around in a drawer and pulled out a revolver.

"I'm so glad you feel that way, Mr. Jefferson," he said, pointing it at my chest. "I'm sure that you are going to be a stalwart ally in our fight to bring about the kingdom of heaven. And now, Dr. Sargnagel, if you could initialize the brain dumping hardware….."

I froze, terrified. I felt something cold at the base of my skull.

The president paused. "Oh, darn! I've lost that trigger finger again! Sargnagel, next time try glue. Er—would someone else care to do the honors?"

I don't remember dying. The brain dump was over seconds before the guard killed me. It's just as well. I wouldn't want any unpleasant memories to taint the new age.

Elayne and I were married the other day. She's thinking of having it done herself. Heckle and Jeckle want to wait for puberty. Owen and Elayne and I have a lot of fun together, although I don't really have that much time for sex and other light entertainments.

For one thing, there's this counterrevolution going on somewhere in Latin America. Rumor has it that the leader is none other than Lord Texas-Chainsaw, who fled there with a group of angry Indians after the collapse of the morticians' solidarity caucus. He has vowed to return, so they say, and "run every last zombie back into the grave."

I don't care. I'm too busy dealing with the present and preparing for our shining future. After all, I'm an important man now … the official prophet of the millenium.

As long as they don't turn the power off on me.

—Alexandria, Los Angeles, 1985

The Last Time I Died in Venice

He beckoned to me in the dying sun.

Venice? What a joke. The Venice of the East. Some antediluvian travel brochures still call it that, but the canals were filled in before I was born, and now a skein of highways and overpasses covers the city like a threadworn yarmulke. Instead of the *vaporetto*, there's fleets of neon-colored taxis; if you fancy a gondola, hop on the back of a brimstone-belching motorcycle taxi and weave like a maniac through harrowing streets; here you don't sit sipping a capuccino on the Lido, gazing at the hazy sea, but instead, nursing that selfsame capuccino, perched on the eighth level of an endless shopping mall, staring, glazed, at the consuming throng.

The name of that coffee nook is, ironically, The Rialto …

The second day of my thirty-ninth trip to Bangkok. A computer conference, this time, coupled with an Interpol sting of a RISC-chip pirating consortium; not even time for a

...massage yet. But I had to make time for my old friend Bob Halliday, who is to me as Virgil was to Dante. Bob knows

everything, from the arcane declensions of Finnish irregular nouns to the dialectic nuances of Malaysian shadow puppets. He is very humble about it all, though one does detect a certain smugness.

The Rialto, situated as it was in one of the four catty-corner shopping malls that loom over the infamous Brahma shrine in the busiest intersection of Bangkok, was as good a place as any to watch the chaos go by. It had a Venetian motif; there was a mural of the Piazza San Marco, in front of which a toothless crone pounded green papaya and chili right next to the espresso machines.

I was born within a stone's throw of here, but I try not to think about it when I'm debugging search-and-replace algorithms in Jacuzzi County, California. I belong here, in the embrace of a beautiful, dying woman.

"We can't stay too long, Chai," Bob said. "If you sit here for more than 15 minutes, you're bound to run into someone you want to avoid." In a city of seven million, there are only a few players, and each has his own turf. "Look: there's Khunying Ingsuwan, the gossip columnist for *Siam Daily Times*—she's got her notebook out and peering at us like an interrupted mink." We both laughed. "And over there, for example—don't turn your head—is Dr. Phetch. 'Phetch 'n' Carry', we call him at the *Post*. He owns the virtual whorehouse concession; pays a pretty penny for it in protection, I understand."

"Protection?" I said. "From what?"

"Prostitution is still illegal here in the sex capital of the world ..."

"But surely it's different, fucking a computer ... victimless crime and all that ..."

Bob laughed. "Bangkok," he said, "is not like other cities. The part is the whole. The illusion is the reality. Look around and you'll see all the trappings of the twenty-first century— the buildings shaped like giant robots, the shopping malls with built-in roller coasters, and the cellular faxes spitting out onto the upholstery of every chauffeur-driven Mercedes that's jammed into the alley—but just below the surface there's—well, a kind of churning emptiness."

"You mean, the diseased blood beneath the skin of a beautiful woman ... all that crap," I said.

Bob merely laughed, and said, "There's a sleazy dive across the river I've gotta take you to—they make a *khao man gai* that'll have you coming in your Calvins."

From the stereo section of a department store came the continuous cussing of Snoop Doggy Dog; the endless fucks and bitches sounded curiously innocent here; they had no power to shock; it was just background music. Bob knows many things, though his ostensible job description is as food critic for the *Bangkok Post*. His girth betrays his occupation. His Thai friends call him Elephant, a nickname he bears proudly.

I took a good look at the cadaverous Dr. Phetch. He was sipping a capuccino, working on a green papaya salad and a laptop. He turned to me and smiled. That, in Thailand, can be the kiss of death.

"Shit!" said Bob. "He's noticed you."

Dr. Phetch was slowly working his way through the maze of little tables. At every marble-topped table, he was accosted by someone: an overripe matron in diamonds and silk, a man in a yellow suit with a cellular phone in each hand, a Japanese businessman with a Louis Vuitton briefcase. He paused at each table, long enough to show his attentiveness, briefly enough to show his arrogance; but he was clearly coming our way, and there was no way to extricate ourselves without making tomorrow's gossip column.

"Khun Chai, isn't it?" he said, or rather growled, that tiger-on-the-prowl sort of growl. "You're one of those LA Thais," he said, long-haired, denim-clad, disrespectful. And," he added, "you're investigating me."

"No he isn't," Bob said, but the protestations of a food critic were of no interest to him; it wouldn't have done for him even to notice Bob's existence.

"We are small potatoes, Khun Chai. You should leave us alone."

"My company just wants to get a sense of who's copying our look and feel," I said. "If you really are small potatoes, they won't do anything. But we never expected our code to be used for something so depraved as … you know." That was a barefaced lie. Sex was the one use we were counting on to keep expanding our user base.

"Have you ever desired something, Khun Chai … something that tantalizes you … something that never quite seems to arrive within your grasp … that drives you insane with unfulfillment?

"No," I said.

He raised an eyebrow. "Nothing at all? I am a little surprised. You see, we are not without our own investigators. It should not surprise you that the observer is himself observed. There is something you yearn for. That's why you keep coming back. And once we find out what it is —"

"No," I said again, but couldn't look at him, because I had just seen, with my peripheral vision, just what he was talking about. A shadow, a glance, a blurry movement, a creature from a half-forgotten dream. She beckoned to me in the dying sun, only there was no sun, only the flickering neon of a malfunctioning McDonalds sign.

"Then why," he said, "are you in Bangkok?" And thrust a business card into my half-drained capuccino.

***

"Something," said Bob, "is haunting you, Chai."

We had fled the shopping mall. We were in a *tuk-tuk*, weaving through the pollution at breakneck speed—the traffic, unaccountably, had abated. Bob lent me only half an ear; mostly he was typing furiously on his laptop, which he'd plugged into his cellular modem; now and then he paused, nodded, typed again.

"That's true," I said, "but I don't really know what it is … a sense of rootlessness, maybe."

The business card read:

Misled by morality? Limited by laws?
All you desire can be virtually yours.

There was a phone number.

"Lend me your phone," I said.

Dying, she beckoned to me in the sun –

I blinked again. The *tuk-tuk* rounded a corner, wheezing and farting, and we were somewhere in Silom. She beckoned to me, her arms outstretched, a jasmine garland in one hand, the oily sunlight glancing off her nut-brown flesh, and—

"Can't," said Bob.

"And then when I come here I always see things," I said. "Things that I know aren't really there. Shroom flashbacks maybe. I keep thinking there's someone, you know, calling out to me. A woman. A dying woman."

"How Freudian. Is it your mother? I know a good exorcist."

"Fuck you," I said. I don't have a mother. I'm an R&R brat. But I was brought up by many Thai women, interchangeable; my dad had very predictable tastes. "Give me that phone."

"Wait," said Bob. "I'm deeply ensconced in this *Finnegans Wake* IRC. It's amazing. There's this monk in Hungary who has compiled eight thousand glosses on the first chapter, and he's going to upload it all to his web page."

I glanced over at his laptop screen. It was scrolling insanely—not a word of English, or Thai for that matter. "Bob—"

He tapped a few more keystrokes and told the driver to let us off. "The *khao man gai* place," he said, "is down that alley a ways."

Silom was still an oven, even though the sun was setting. The vendors of fake Rolexes, fake software, and fake designer clothes were all erecting their stands, and the barkers were already shuffling about, looking to entice tourists into live shows; I took Bob's phone in one hand and followed him as he skillfully infiltrated the throng. Bangkok doesn't smell like any other city—there's not that heady melange of exhaust fumes and jasmine, vomit and mangoes, incense and stale fish. The neon was starting to come on. Bankers, hustlers, shamans, and lottery ticket vendors conferred under the garish teal, electric green, bubble-gum pink.

"It can't hurt to call them," I said. "It's virtual. It's fictional. None of it is true."

"And what," he said, "is truth?"

"Don't crucify me," I said.

"I wash my hands of the whole thing," He paused as though he expected a laughtrack to click on.

"A Pilate for a new sitcom," I said.

"*Touché*. But you'll regret it. Dr. Phetch, I am sure, has your number. Don't let him hack your soul."

Soon we were wolfing down chicken and rice in a shithole perched above an, open sewer, and I was reading my Visa card number to an operator at the virtual whorehouse.

***

Dying, she beckons to me in the setting sun—

I've sampled most of the unsavory delights Bangkok has to offer: safely of course, ever so safely, always with my American-made condoms. Didn't really set foot here until I was full grown—well, maybe when I was little—but I thought I knew Thai women—all those stepmothers. They cook a lot. They're very smothering. They drive you to school and they drive to the supermarket and they go to the temple in North Hollywood on Sundays and eat barbecued pork, and they refuse to speak English and they lie in bed watching television until your Dad comes home to fuck them.

My real mother's dead, I've heard. When she got sick, Dad shipped her back to the brothel. Maybe Bob was right. Maybe the woman who haunted me was part of some kind of sick Oedipal fantasy.

I think of her, in the sunset, dying, beckoning to me. She used to wear a Brahma amulet around her neck. Brahma is good for business. I played with it when I suckled. Thai women will breast-feed long after Dr. Spock tells you to stop.

"I'm going to be thirty soon," I told Bob, "and even though I've had a shitload of sexual encounters, I've still never loved anyone."

"That's the Thai in you," Bob said. "Christians have love. Love thy neighbor, love this, love that. Buddhists have compassion. It puts a completely different spin on existence. Of course, Buddhists don't really believe in existence, either."

We ate in silence. For a moment, the waitress reminded me of someone. I considered tipping her, but of course I didn't. Mustn't give them ideas.

***

The first thing they do at the virtual whorehouse is ask you a lot of questions. You say the first thing that comes into your head. They ply you with stiff drinks and there's a masseuse working over your feet the whole time; that's so you'll relax and spit out your true nature. Another woman in an Armani suit, very butch, keys your answers into a mega-profile that supposedly helps the computer to select the right, ah, scenario.

They didn't tell me any of this. But I recognized the questions. I recognized the program. It was sort of a second-generation Minsky AI thing. I wrote part of the code myself.

I also had to look at images that flashed by on a monitor while a potentiometer measured my penile tension. Shades of scientology. The girl who took down the figures giggled now and then, and sucked on the juice of a coconut. Bob had run off to interview some big director passing through town —I don't know who, maybe Polanski.

The whole thing was transpiring in the basement of a nudie bar. The room was quite Spartan; its only decoration was a 'Thailand, the Golden Paradise' poster. In a wall niche was a statue of Nang Kwak, the goddess that draws in customers, one hand beckoning, the other daintily pressed against her hip.

Respond to the following words:
leather
jockstrap
breasts
big
mother
death.
***

"Have you visited us before, Khun Chai?" said the young woman who was zipping me into the suit. The clothes went back on over the second skin. Zippers are good. In classical Thai dance, they sew you into the clothes; one of my stepmothers told me that. The bodily fluids stay in.

"Why do you ask?"

"It seems, your sexual odyssey is on the house. You know important people, big people maybe, yes?"

So they were going to entertain me into ignoring their intellectual property peccadilloes. "Tell Dr. Phetch," I said, "that this better be good."

"It will be."

There was no huge contraption to strap on … no glorified dentist's chair. They just laid me down on a couch. The goggles went on. I was blind.

"Any special request? People from your country usually go for one of the pedo fantasies."

"No. Just play back what the computer says to play back."

I flexed my fingers. Hardly felt a thing. This dermoplast was good shit. Like a full body condom with a million nerve-endings sewn into its lining. I hadn't realized it was quite this snug. Like nothing at all.

"Time for your tailor-made trip," said the hostess.

Everything went black for a moment.

***

So I come to, and I'm in the same room, with the same vile disco music jangling upstairs. Something's changed. Is it the lighting? It's got to be video, it can't be reality. The colors are too vibrant, the audio too perfectly EQ'd. And then there's the fact that the walls are shimmering, that the geckoes are running too swiftly along the gray concrete. I blink again and the walls dissolve.

I'm moving slowly down a corridor. Not a corridor but a narrow alley … one of the tiny *sois* that interlace the city. Crowded. They've done that Bangkok smell just right, but sharpened it with a tinge of … I don't know, some sexual pheromone maybe. I'm drifting down the alley. I can't tell if the drifting sensation is from something that was in my drink or if it's part of the virtual reality experience. The alley narrows and until finally there's only room for one … my footsteps echo … I hear voices whispering … there's a lot of mist … and I see the open doorways … I pause outside each one for the merest moment, sensing that the proffered diversions are not for me … here a naked dwarf, twisting her own nipples with two pairs of pliers … here a Rapunzel draped in her own hair … a choirboy with a see-through surplice … I'm curious about these delights, but not aroused. The corridor narrows some more. The pheromonal odor is more powerful now. It seems to be sweating out of the very stucco. Go ahead. Look in every doorway. Sirens entice me. A three-hundred-pound ebony woman with a slave collar and strange tribal scars. Go on, try it. It's safe in here. You can do anything. Anything at all because it's not real.

Deeper, deeper into the labyrinth.

She beckons to me in the dying sun—

How? It's the last doorway. It's the woman who has haunted my dreams. She's not beautiful; not at first. Her cheeks are hollow, her eyes listless, her jaundice-colored skin sags against a tattered sarong that's held up by a chain of silver links; she too stretches her arms out to me, calls me by name: Chai, Chai, Chai.

"Who are you?" I say softly.

"You don't have to ask," she says in Thai—Thai with a lilting provincial quality to it; she's a peasant woman; perhaps she's not as old as she looks; they wear out quickly, these upcountry girls. "I been standing here, waiting for you, all your life long." She is beautiful after all. She wears a Brahma amulet around her neck.

"You're my mother?" I blurt out.

"Mother, sister, maiden, crone, it no matter; I'm the thing inside you long long time; your mind make me flesh."

In the back of my mind I'm thinking, Jesus, this is convincing, they've spiked the program somehow, done a shitload of fancy crunching, maybe called in the Taiwanese. How it managed to pluck this image from my one-word answers to a questionnaire ... then reconstitute it out of the stored characteristics of a thousand women ... the verisimilitude of it's bowling me over, but I've got to keep my cool.

"I can't make love to you," I say. "Not if you're—"

She smiles. "Who else you make love to," she says, "if not me?"

"But you're dying—" The contagion is inside her. Didn't they ship her back to the whorehouse to die? Isn't she long gone, burned to a crisp in a funeral pyre, her ashes in an urn somewhere? Is that what my secret desire really is ... to die from the embrace of a dying woman?

Sadly, she shakes her head. "Inside you, I never die. Come home to me now, my son."

I guess it's a little too real for me. I stumble back. Go into one of the other rooms ... not even sure which one now ... I think it's that black earth goddess, who envelops me in her folds and wiggles me to sleep.

***

Had breakfast with Bob—he actually came to my hotel—because he was on his way to the *Post* to deliver his review of the *khao man gai*. Couldn't upload it because his hard drive crashed. The hotel has a great river view, Temple of Dawn and everything, from one side of the top story dining room, but the other side overlooks a slum. To the left, you can imagine Somerset Maugham on a rattan chair, checking out the waiters' butts; to the right, it's *Sally Struthers* saving the children. They're building a big wall around the eyesore, having it painted, actually, with murals that give a sort of history of European art: there's Michelangelo's *Adam and Eve* being driven from paradise, for instance, and, oh, a colorized *Guernica.*

"Bangkok is just a big old movie set," Bob said, gazing glumly at the construction work. "They move the walls around, hey, presto, it's somewhere else. It's a chameleon of a city; it can imitate any other city. It's a virus of a city, copying other cities' DNA, insinuating itself into their genes."

"So you think I should have fucked her," I asked Bob, who was carefully lining up the dried shrimp, shortest to tallest, before dunking them in his rice soup.

"You said it, not me," Bob said.

I mean, you're saying that because it's all an illusion anyway, I might as well play out the Oedipal scenario, because that way, who knows, I might work through the trauma of my deprived childhood?"

"Sigmund couldn't have put it better," said Bob, "but I really don't know why you're asking me these things ... you seem to have decided already."

"Dr. Phetch is actually addressing the delegates today," I said. "He's going to offer some kind of rationale for his intellectual piracy."

Far below, I thought I saw the phantom woman by the river's edge. She was less dreamlike than she'd ever been before. I watched her for a while; it seemed to me that she was catching the water bus to Chinatown. Almost too mundane to be a figment of my tortured inner life.

"She won't get out of my waking life," I said, "so maybe you're right, maybe I should, you know, get it over with."

"The hero slays the dragon-earth-mother and sets himself free so he can love the princess," Bob said.

"That's Jung, not Freud."

"Don't I know it!"

I fixed Bob's hard drive over a capuccino, and used it to send an email to the virtual whorehouse.

***

The landscape is more twisted than before. I'm moving more swiftly, too; I know the doors I don't want to look into. Not the pouting beauties with their heaving breasts. Not the dainty little half women with their chocolate smiles. I move further and further into the labyrinth. She's always just out of reach, in the shadow of a coconut tree, hidden behind the awning-flap of a souvenir stall. Children run underfoot, touting their lottery tickets and their souls. The smells are so intense I can hardly breathe. Sweat hangs in the air. The perfume of a decaying jasmine garland rises from a heap of garbage. I think I see a severed human hand.

Finally. the dingy room, the sunset, the window with the blood-red light striped noirishly by the Venetian blinds …

"Come home to me, my son, my son."

She bares her breast to me. She is obviously dying. Her dugs process no milk. She touches my head—that most profane of touchings and pulls me forward until my lips touch her bosom.

I fumble in my pants for a condom.

"Why you want be safe?" she whispers. "This not real, this fantasy, this a dream."

I can't help myself. I start to unwrap it anyway. Old habits die hard and all that. It's not a satisfactory coupling. I can feel the contagion boiling inside her, but I cannot bring myself to let it touch me.

But the contagion is the core of my unfulfilled longing …

***

"Maybe that's what you really want," Bob said. This

time, the eatery was the basement of a department store; you could trade in your little coupons for everything from pig's feet to a frankfurter.

Dr. Phetch was seriously under investigation now, and my own little observations about pilfered pieces of code were minor compared to what Interpol had on him; the Thai papers were full of his leering mug, but I couldn't read Thai well enough to know how far up shit creek he'd paddled.

"That's my forbidden fantasy? To have sex with my mother, catch AIDS, and die?"

I couldn't believe I'd actually said it. I hadn't said it to my therapist. I hadn't said it to my minister, in the year that I flirted with fundamentalism. I hadn't said it in confession, the year I converted to Catholicism.

"What other dime store analyses have you got to offer me?" I said. I was furious. I was shaking. Beads of sweat were dripping off my face into my bowl of blood-red, pungent *yentafo*. "Maybe you think I'm all guilted up because you think I think I somehow caused my mom to go away and I think I ought to pay for it?"

"I'm not the dime store analyst," Bob said calmly. "You're doing a pretty good job of it all by yourself."

***

That night, I actually do it. A mere 3,000 baht a pop on the old company credit card, why not? The labyrinth seems more and more endless … the alleys branch off, twist, turn, like dividing viruses. There's an improvised quality about the streets, the buildings, the noodle stands; they're taking them up, putting them down, shuffling them, shifting them. Only the neon-tinged smog never changes. Only the fact that it's all too real, too clear, convinces me that this is a cybernetic simulacrum of the truth, illusion idealized.

And suddenly I come upon her, in a doorway, in a

tattered sarong, in a shaft of teal-pink light that strobes over her tarnished features. Her eyes are my eyes and her lips my lips. She says to me, in a quiet voice that carries above the screeching of broken mufflers, "You're coming home to me at last, my son."

"But you're dead," I say.

"Not until you make me dead," she says. "Do you love me?"

She's not just my earthly mother, but she's the city that mothered me and spat me out. She's the darkness past forgetting, "I don't want to love you," I say softly, "But—"

"Then I will love you," she says, "the way only the dead can love,"

I toy with the Brahma amulet around her neck. I have a desperate need to suckle. She is beautiful after all, though her breasts are speckled with tiny lesions. She enfolds me, and the world goes dark.

   ***

When I woke up, the tourist police were everywhere. Smashed computers all over the floors. Women in handcuffs. One of them—

This had to still be part of the illusion.

She stood between two policemen, haggard, the torn sarong tightly bound over her sagging breasts. She looked at me, stony-eyed. I said, "But you're not real."

She said, "What is reality?"

"But you told me lies ... you called me your son ... you let me indulge the darkest longings in myself ..."

She smiled sadly. Then she said to me in Thai, "You people think you're better than us because you left all this shit behind, you sit around in your American castles and look down on us like we're peasants."

"No I don't," I said.

"You wouldn't come back here if you didn't know you can still buy what you can't buy anywhere else. You can still buy love here, and you can still buy death."

They took her away. Later, I toured the labyrinth. The fog machines. The artificial alleyways that twisted and turned on casters, turning a few hundred square meters into a subterranean city, the odor generators, the cubicles where sat the women of our fantasies. The virtual world was a sham. The only computer output was the user profile, generated from those one-word answers by a program almost as antiquated as *Eliza*.

Why not? I thought bitterly. If you can fake a Rolex, a Super Nintendo cartridge, a Polo tennis shirt to perfection, why not go a step further and fake fakeness itself? Why bother with software when the cost of labor is so much lower? Dr. Phetch, I thought, is going to walk the plank for this.

I thought of the dying woman, and I began to wonder ...
***

She beckons to me, dying, in the setting sun ...

Today Bob comes to visit me in the hospital. My insurance cut me off, so I shipped myself to Bangkok to die. Dr. Phetch has become a cabinet minister, and nobody talks about the virtual whorehouse anymore, only about the possibilities of this technology for pilot training.

Bob brings me a new delicacy he has uncovered in the Northeast—a special kind of *laab* made with duck's heads and ground locusts. "I hope it's kept," he says. "I threw it in the fridge as soon as I got home, but you know, that five-hour traffic jam on the way back from the airport ..." He pauses. Looks at the display of orchids elegantly filling my window, masking my view of the pile-drivers as they put up another fifty-story condo. Reads the card. "Dr. Phetch sent you flowers?"

"Least he can do," I gasp, "considering he killed me."

"I brought you someone else, too," he says. A strange little woman totters in behind Bob. "She's a shamaness. She gets possessed by the god Brahma sometimes. Maybe she can help you ..."

"It's gotta be better for me than this AZT" I say.

The shamaness sits herself at the edge of my bed, in the lotus position, closes her eyes, and methodically begins putting herself in a trance. She wears a Brahma amulet around her neck, but otherwise there is no similarity.

"I should have known better," I say to Bob. "This is my own fucking fault. It was all too real to be virtual. I should have known better."

Bob smiles sadly in between mouthfuls. Crunching a duck's head in your teeth and spitting out the debris is an art form that still dazzles me. He lets me ramble on.

"Jesus," I say, "I'm actually gonna die."

He pats my hand.

"I should have known better. You were telling me all along, weren't you? You're the one who's always been saying, in this town, there's no distinction between the real world and the world of illusion. It's the only place in the world where all truths are true at the same time."

"Yeah," Bob says, "Bangkok is the north pole of existence; no matter which way you turn, it's all south."

Suddenly, the old woman begins to speak, in an eerie parody of a familiar voice: "Finally, you come home to me now, my son, my son."

And it's the truth.

—Bangkok, Los Angeles, 1995

Dear Caressa
or, This Towering Torment

I'd thought that moving to suburbia would save my marriage … save me from Dusty, my daughter of the Brooklyn Bridge braces … and the Nosferatu-ish smile. From my son Boogie, torn-teeshirted prepube of serpentine precociousness with the chocolatechip-cookie face and those kestrel eyes. And especially from my wife Rebecca, an immaculate, pre-feminist woman who worked for the household like a dog—and was about equal to one in I.Q.

I had no idea my life would turn into a science fiction story.

That, I suppose, lowed to Hermie Tebaldi.

You're surprised I know him, aren't you? Nobel laureate and all, author of "An Application of Irrelevance Theory to Synchronicity and Quantum Mechanics," the paper that crossed Einstein with Jung and spawned a monstrous hybrid that people are still arguing about to this day? Well, to me he was the boy next door. Got into scrapes together—somehow, though, only I got the spankings—went to Princeton together, ended up teaching at U. of Penn. together (although

naturally he was head of his department). I won the Rothman Fellowship and he got the Nobel prize, all in the same day.

He died. Or rather, he disappeared mysteriously while doing research on transfinite transdimensional interfaces. (If

this were science fiction, they'd dream up some

pseudoscientific nonsense to call it, "alternate-reality-paradigms" or "parallel universes" or something.) And left me the house in his will. My family and I thought we'd been saved.

But nothing changed. I was still a man who had married too early in life—one of Hermie's cast-offs, at that—with a couple of unsavory kids, an unfinished paper on archaeopteryxes, and a stupid wife.

That summer, the stupid wife discovered the romances of Caressa Byrd.

***

I turned over in bed and my nose hit an open paperback. I fumbled for the light. Becky must have gotten up, but the sheets smelled faintly of Givenchy and pepperoni. (Some days it was salami and Shalimar.) I elbowed the paperback off the bed: it was *This Towering Torment* by Caressa Byrd.

I groped for the curtains—

Midmorning light fell through the blinds, zebra-striping the primrose-studded sheets. I arose, tripped over a copy of *Chastity's Chastisement*, and made for the bathroom, cursing all dull Saturdays. I degrunged myself. Shaving was like brushing the dust from archaeopteryx bones. Better to be a character in one of Caressa Byrd's romances! That woman had written two hundred or more, all in the first person; many of the fans thought that they had all really happened to her. Coming out in a bathrobe, I felt paper prickle my feet and knelt down for a look. A trail of paper had dribbled from an old rattan wastebasket. I like all my things in the right place and this was on the wrong side of the bed. I picked up the papers and tossed them back in, thinking: *Funny, I haven't written anything lately, and Becky's too illiterate ...* I uncrumpled a piece and began to read:

Dear Caressa [it began, in spiky, awkward script]
This is my twentieth letter to you. I have read every one of your books and know that you are very experienced in matters of men. It's Arthur. I love him so much, but he doesn't love me any more. Maybe he doesn't want me. I wish I could be like in your Love's Ravening Ravishment when the old woman said to you "But do you love him enough to give him up?" and you cried for days afterward. He is a great scientist and I am only a high school sweetheart that he knocked up I mean had an indiscretion with, I know I am too dumb for him. Is it right for me to punish him like this? I know you arc very busy but I wd. appreciate a response at your convenience.
    Sincerely yours
    Rebecca Kurtz

I couldn't believe it. I unscrunched more paper (heavily Chanel No. 19-doused, I noticed) and found more uncompleted drafts.

That's it, I thought grimly. She's *over* the edge. I marched downstairs in a rage, brandishing the letter.

"Damn it," I shouted half-way into the kitchen,"do you have to use so much perfume?" The smell of baked ham and Nina Ricci filled the room.

She turned round from her cooking. She wasn't ugly; she had a mop of red hair over a face three shades too pale, liberally splotched with freckles. "I want to smell nice for you," she said. "Isn't that all that matters?" She looked very vulnerable; her eyes were watering and I felt both furious and guilty.

"Look!" I yelled, waving the letter. "You've gone crazy!"

"I need all the help I can get—"

"Damn it, I want a divorce!" I screamed, She started to

cry—went on and on as though it were some eye exercise—and said, "All right dear, if that's what you want. I knew it would come to this … here, eat your breakfast, it's your favorite …" Then she buried herself in *Passion's Fiery Dart* and the conversation was over. I hadn't even gotten her mad, damn it!

I stomped into the back yard, and—

The basement window! I found myself staring at it. It had been broken into! Damn raccoons! I started to panic. There wasn't any real reason for us to have kept the basement boarded up, even if it *had* housed the esoteric devices Hermie Tebaldi had been working on towards the end of his life. And yet …

Damn raccoons, I thought, cursing. Dog must *have* broken in after them.

I'd never thought of trying to get into the basement before.

But now—

Glass-shards lay on the grass, dazzling my eyes in the summer sunlight. The window was shattered; a man could easily squeeze through—

It wasn't snooping, damn it, it was my own house. And I'd had too many problems that day. My family. My unfinished paper and the pressure of publish-or-perish. No better way to deal with pressure than go and do something completely different.

I snaked over to the opening and lowered myself gingerly onto the—

There wasn't any floor!

I was falling, falling, falling—like Alice down the rabbit hole. Only I didn't have time to make inane comments like "Do bats eat cats?" or to calculate the distance to the center of the earth. I was too busy screaming.

First it was soft soft soft and dark dark dark, like being

on the couch at my analyst's and listening to the drone of her hypnotic voice. I was falling but there wasn't really any down; was screaming as hard as I could, but the sounds were lost; there wasn't any echo; this wasn't a mine-shaft or something that had somehow been grafted onto my basement, it was something far ~huger, and I knew I'd hit bottom sometime and it wouldn't be pleasant, but the thought was somehow so distant, so insignificant. I seemed to be shedding all my worries, my anxiety over the impending divorce, my anger, my self-frustration ...

Forget everything, I thought, *until this dream is over ...* Gradually I made out a sourceless red glow around me. I couldn't see very far. My feet were being sucked into something half solid, and then I hit some kind of ground and was running—

A wild *Wuthering Heights* landscape, gray helter-skelter heather, knee-high, cresting and ebbing in a singing wind. Black cloth flapping in my face, and I knew I wasn't wearing the same clothes I set out with. A starched, uncomfortable high collar hugged my neck, and it was a black cloak lined with crimson that I was wearing, streaming in the wind, and I was running. I tried to brake myself but I couldn't halt the momentum. I remember thinking all the time that the dog must be loose in the metamorphosed basement, with a raccoon backed into a corner somewhere-

The wind was warm. There was an enticing odor of French perfume, spiked unaccountably with pepperoni. Becky! I thought. She's at *the bottom* of this! I knew I wasn't making any sense at all, but neither was this whole experience.

After a while I managed to slow down. The moor stretched to the horizon all around me. There was no way to judge distance, except. ..yes, the horizon seemed strangely near. It was a distorted world. Two moons careened in the sky, blood-red and huge; they were the source of the strange red glow; and then ahead I saw a silvery glint among the … oh yes, weird, rocky outcroppings, I hadn't caught sight of them before …it was as if the whole landscape was coming more into focus and I was seeing more details all the time. I slowed down to a walk, panting heavily—I'm not that young anymore—and began to make for the silvery point of light that flickered between black fantastical monoliths. It was a demon force that pushed me forward. I stumbled onward, never quite coming to a full stop.

Arthur, oh Arthur …

Everyone dreams of a voice like that. It sang to me in the wind. It was a girl's voice, a child's voice almost. The wind blew on my cheek like a soft hand. I struggled to loosen my collar, my chafing Victorian clothes—

Then I saw the tower.

I couldn't tell how far it was. The scale was all wrong here, wherever "here" was. Both moons had moved behind it. The light had come from a window in its topmost turret.

But what a tower! It was like a rocket ship and it was like a tree. It was like a Corinthian column plated with silver and torn from a Greek temple and overgrown with chromium Vines.

Glitter-rich flying buttresses sprouted from the naked rock. It was a bewildering madness. *And it was singing my name.*

Arthur, oh Arthur, it sang to me in its achingly beautiful voice, I've waited for so long, Arthur, please come to me now, enter me, possess me, be one with me—

The wind was streaming against me. I was being drawn towards the tower, being sucked into a lorelei whirlwind …"No!" I screamed. "No! No!" I tried to think of Becky and the kids but they were so far away. I felt like a little genie battering away helplessly at the walls of his glass bottle.

A swath of light, tinseled like fairy light in a Disney cartoon, fell on me from the window. But somehow it wasn't kitsch. I felt like a kid again, wanting so hard to be someone, identifying with the prince on the horse, and my cloak was flapping behind me and billowing around me and it was like the time I pulled little Sharon out of the tree—

But Hermie Tebaldi was the one who made it with her, damn it! I remembered, coming down to earth. I remembered Hermie and I snapped. *I'm getting out of this nightmare,* I told myself. "Let go of me," I screamed. "Whatever you are, understand, let go, let go—"

In a flash, I saw two archaeopteryxes soar across the swath of light, noting how closely they conformed in gliding patterns to my hypothesis—

I came to on the hard damp concrete.

I looked around me.

Machines, dusty, an old typewriter. Nothing that seemed to make much sense. This was the basement, all right, though; ahead, the narrow stairs had to lead to the kitchen closet. I rubbed my eyes a couple of times. *Getting flaky,* I thought. *Must call Dr. Webern in the morning.*

I heaved myself off the concrete and shambled around. How weird, I thought, *I've been on the wagon for over six months now, I shouldn't have been seeing things …*

That voice came back to me, so enticing, so erotic. I colde! almost have stepped back into that moor under the red moons again, but—

No! I told myself quickly. *With all your problems, schizophrenia is something you can do without.* It was very dark in the basement, except where light fell in spider-strands, pinholing through chinks in the boards. And there was a big stripe of dazzling sunshine through the broken window, stippled with dancing dust-motes.

I glanced at the machines. I couldn't tell what they were,

of course. The theory of transdimensional interfaces wasn't exactly my field—and frankly I never had the math to follow even the simplest of Hermie's theories.

Everything was in obvious disarray. I hate messes, and it had always irked me that Hermie could dream up such elegant theories when he couldn't even tie his shoelaces or file a carbon. I looked around, getting angrier and angrier.

The light from the window fell on some kind of lab bench. A piece of paper, a page from a looseleaf notebook, weighted down by a book caught my eye. There was a message on it, in huge, childish capitals—

ARTIE MY FRIEND

HELP ME HELP ME—SHE'S GONNA KILL ME

HELP ME

HELP ME

I rubbed my eyes. The red ink glowed in the glare. What the hell was this? Who was she? How old was this message, anyway?

There was only one *she* I could think of right now—

The voice! The singing wind from the tower that sparkled silver in the blood-red moonlight! *Arthur, oh Arthur* —So sensual. so seductive. And me in my chafing collar and black cape, breasting the wind like a prince from a soppy novel or a childhood myth …haunting. Haunting. Haunting.

And, suddenly, somehow, I knew that the voice could be mine—I mean, the creature behind the voice—for instinct told me that inside the tower there must be a princess, a golden-haired Rapunzel who would sweep me away from Rebecca and Dusty and Boogie and the whole suburban schtick, and—

Get a grip on yourself. damn it! Dr. Sharon Webern will bring your back to earth.

I stood staring at the message. Unquestionably it was Hermie's handwriting and ... the ink was still wet! On second thought, it wasn't ink at all.

It was blood.

***

"I see you've put Dr. Webern on the calendar," Boogie said, sauntering into the kitchen Sunday morning just as I'd misflipped my eggs. "Want to talk about it?"

"Not to you."

"Don't be silly, Dad!" he said, coming closer. He seemed tense. It's devastating when one's child is so much smarter than oneself.

Without really meaning to, I started to tell him everything. "Sheesh, Dad," he said, "it sounds heavy as hell to me. Maybe you do need a shrink ...but then again, maybe not."

"What do you mean?" r said, plunking myself by the kitchen table and addressing my Jackson Pollocked eggs. (One thing about Rebecca—she did know how to fix food; and when she went to church of all places, which she did every Sunday morning, I had to eat my own glop.)

"Well, you just told me that the letter from Uncle Hermie was real, didn't you? Now, when you have eliminated the impossible ..."

"Oh, give me a break, Boogie!"

"Hold it, Dad. I've *read* Uncle Hermie's paper. It's all about parallel universes ...he starts off with the assumption, you know, that every time a subatomic particle must make a statistical decision within the limits of the uncertainty principle, a parallel universe splits off—"

"Huh?"

"Dad, that theory was way back in the seventies!"

"Yeah, like all of two years ago." I gulped down some of

the egg concoction. Sunlight played on the table, lightly leaf-dappled, too bright for my depression. Knowing you're on the verge of a nervous breakdown can be a pretty unnerving feeling—and I had been through *that* before.   ·

"You don't get jt!" Boogie cried, exasperated. I tried not to listen, but became marginally interested in spite of myself. "He was working on transdimensional interfaces when he died; That means channelling into parts of spacetime where universes overlap! He was talking about this new kind of particle, see, he was trying to generate them before he died, but he was running up against the law of conservation of strangeness ... but I guess you wouldn't know anything about quark theory either," he added disdainfully. "Hey!" Perhaps he succeeded in doing what he was working on, and perhaps there's a transdimensional interface right in our basement! Sheesh!" He paused for a breath. Then he went to the refrigerator to get a glass of milk.

"You're going to be just like Hermie when you grow up, you little bastard," I muttered, not quite concealing my bitterness.

"I knew it!" He whipped around, brandishing his milk. "You do suspect me of being *his* son ..."

I was shaking. He'd seen right through me, right to my innermost fears.

I tried to change the subject and go back to his theory, or whatever it was. "Okay, suppose it is another universe out there?" I said. "How would you account for the smell of Becky's cooking and Becky's perfume? And what about the Caressa Byrdlike gothic ambience?"

"Oh, *that*," Boogie said. But he was already leaving the kitchen. I'd hurt his feelings. Strange how Hermie still haunted this family ..."Well, I don't know everything, you know. Even if I am smarter than you are." He vanished into the hall. What a hateful shrimp. The obnoxiousness of his intelligence more than made up for the obnoxiousness of Rebecca's stupidity.

I closed my eyes and remembered the archaeopteryxes, crossing the faces of the bloody moons. Why had they been so close to the description in my unwritten paper? Didn't that prove that I was going insane? I piled up my dishes and went to the sink. Through the window, I saw Dusty and Boogie and their friends were trampling the hedges, but I was too tired for even a token yell.

Beside the sink, in a neat pile, and exuding a soft odor of Dior and spaghetti sauce, were some paperbacks: Love's Hideous Strength, Dark Touch of Desire, all vintage Caressa Byrds. I leafed through some of them. There were notes scrawled in the margins, things like "Apply to Arthur," and "Yes, yes, oh yes," and so on. Sickening.

I was just squeezing some soapsuds when a wild impulse took hold of me. I walked over to the kitchen closet. Behind the stacks of raisin bran was the door, boarded up now, that led to …

In my head I heard the song of the tower, high and breathy, passionate. I reached for the toolbox on the top shelf, hardly knowing what I was doing.

An hour later I was standing at the top of the steps. *At least there's a light switch here,* I thought, *when you come in the proper entrance.* I reached for it and I couldn't believe it. It was like a set for a mad scientist's lab in Hollywood. Nothing could have looked more thoroughly unscientific. Banks of equipment rose from an undergrowth of wires, leads, cables, with an occasional jack or plug sprouting like a jungle flower. There was the table with the scrawled not found the previous day. I walked down to it and scrutinized it again. The blood had caked now, rust on the yellow paper.

I laughed out loud. This stuff was supposed to create a transdimensional interface? Boogie was a bright kid, but he did read too much of that sci-fi nonsense. With light flooding the worn, it didn't seem nearly so daunting. I remembered suddenly, with astonishing clarity, the Christmas when Hermie and I had both been four years old and had both gotten Lego sets and I had built a car, following the instructions to the letter, and he had built a ramshackle madness so weird even he couldn't think up an explanation for what it was! That's all this basement mess was! High and mighty Nobel laureates had feet of clay after all. They still needed their Lego sets.

Just then I tripped over a wire and

No! Not again!

The familiar feeling. Falling into the soft darkness. This lime it didn't take nearly so long; it was as it there were less resistance, as though my previous journey had bored a wormhole through the dimensions ...no! I was starting to believe my son's pseudoscientific babblings!

And then—

I was running in the soft gray heather on the moor under the light of the crimson moons. The wind swept me along. I leapt into it, exhilarated. And ahead, past black tarns that loomed like I rolls over the landscape, I saw the tower. From its highest turret, a flock of archaeopteryxes glided, soared, their shadows shying against rock outcroppings ...it was amazing. Their flight patterns ... my theory was vindicated. And then I saw that the tower had grown a little. You couldn't put your finger on it. Around her chrome-shiny buttress, another row of sharktooth crenelations, perhaps ...I ran towards it. The singing had already begun.

Arthur. oh Arthur, come to me, enter me, be mine ...

I didn't resist. Anything had to be better than the life I was leading now. Even schizophrenia. I ran hard, and the wind helped me so I felt no strain, only a giddy exaltation. The perfume in the wind had transmuted now so that I couldn't recognize the smell. It wasn't one of Rebecca's. I stopped thinking. I ran towards the voice. hearing nothing but the voice.

Time and space—they were somehow all distorted here —

I couldn't have reached the tower yet, but it loomed above me, eclipsing the two moons, whose scarlet radiated from behind the silver glitter like distant fire, like light from a far flaming city. The buttresses soared like frozen rainbows. Turrets sprang from the sides, veined with metal moss. It was so huge I could get no sense of proportion out of it at all. And all the time it thrummed in the wind. And when I craned I caught sight of a window from which a light shone —like a searchlight, like the cover of a cheap romance. Then the wind ebbed a little.

Enter me. the voice sighed.

I stepped forward. A door irised in the metal wall. A delicate fragrance came from it, and I moved closer, took a step inside ...

A rich hallway. Velvet tapestries. Oak chairs around a banquet table. French windows, a glimpse of a sculpted garden. And a huge, curving staircase that spiralled, up and up and up until it vanished into a vague silvery height. It was all impossible!

Come up the stairs, oh Arthur, Arthur—

For the moment, I resisted. I went up to the table and banged my fist on it. Solid. As real as my nineteenth century clothes had been real ...

I shed my cloak. I tried to ignore the voice for a moment. In the walls of this antique salon, between the stuffed rhinoceros heads, were heavy, carved oak doors. I stepped across the hall, my steps on the polished wood resounding and echoing through the vast space above me. Gingerly I tried one of the doors.

Arthur, oh Arthur, why do you ignore me? I love you so much, I need you, I adore you, enter me, love me —

l stepped through. Nothing Victorian about this room. It was a thin corridor that stretched straight ahead until the walls seemed to converge in the distance. The walls were metal as the outside of the tower; and there was a faint acrid smell, vaguely discomforting.

Lining the corridor—A chill took hold of me. I forced myself to look at them, frozen creatures standing statue-still, staring—For sure, they weren't people. Their skins were green or blue or purple and they had scales, some of them, and tentacles … but all of them had eyes.

The eyes were all alive. The not-people had been transfixed in a hideous living death. I walked on, not daring to look too hard. Some would have been monsters by any standards, some of them were strange, delicate creatures with pale pink fur and lemur eyes …I couldn't look at the eyes. I was sure they were alive.

I hurried on, and then on my left—

I found myself looking at Hermie.

"My God!" I whispered. "What's happened?" For he was the last of them, and beyond him there were rows of low podia, stretching on as far as I could see—

And obviously all waiting for occupants.

Hermie was breathing. I shook him. He was soft, still alive. "Wake up, man, talk to me, explain all this!"

He began panting. Then he said, "Artie … hoped you'd. come …help …"

"How? How?"

"You wouldn't understand the math anyway, Artie … but we're in another universe, and …"

"What the hell is this tower doing here? Why is it trying to seduce me, for God's sake? How can we get out of here?"

"Look, it's an alien. I know you don't believe in science

fiction, but take my word for it, it's an alien, and this isn't Earth either.

"Look, it feeds on emotions! It *loves* people and not-people to death!

It's a parasite, and it's already devoured every sentient being on this planet ..."

"What?"

"Got to get back," he gasped. "Or else I'll never be able to turn off the field, and the two universes are going to go on leaking into each other ... the last time you came it was so busy trying to snare you that it weakened and I was able to escape for a few seconds; no blasted pen in that whole basement though, had to cut myself to leave the message and now it's wise to me and I can't get free ..."

"This has got to be a dream!" I said, squeezing my eyes tight shut and desperately hoping. Then I kept repeating, over and over, "Aliens don't read Caressa Byrd romances. Aliens don't know about archaeopteryxes. That's why I'm going crazy, dnd none of this is happening."

"Will you listen to me, numbskull! It's semi-telepathic, dnd it's got a range of about fifty meters beyond the transdimensional interface! It's been trying to lure you here for months ... and all it's got to go on is the thoughts of you and of all the people who love you who come into range! And Becky loves you. She loves you so much it's choking her own life, damn you. And I bet all she does in the kitchen is think thoughts of you and thoughts of Caressa Byrd's romances. And of course the archaeopteryxes conform to your theory ..."

His voice was weakening. I didn't know whether to be convinced or not. Insanity seemed a far saner hypothesis.

"You've got to get me out of here!"

"How?" I screamed. "How can I fight a thing that's eaten a whole planet?"

"You've got to find it, and face it, and convince it, somehow. You can't come in here with a Colt .45 and riddle it with bullets. But maybe you can talk to it—"

"No way! I'm getting out of here!"

"Look," he rasped. "If I don't go back and pull the plug on this interface, the interface-leakage will begin to spread. Understand? I'm not going to spout the formulae at you, idiot, but you're my best friend so you might try just believing me. If you resist it now, while you're free, it won't be able to hold on to you, but … if the leakage spreads—The alien's range will get bigger and bigger. It's slow, but it's practically immortal. It'll get you in the end. It'll get Becky and Dusty and Boogie and the Langbarts and everybody else on Bevan Street and everyone in Ardmore and everyone in Pennsylvania …there's no limit to its hunger! Look, I hate to sound melodramatic, but the fate of the universe is in your hands!"

"Hermie, be serious, cut the sci-fi crap—"

"Don't say sci-fi!" he snapped, and then fainted. I turned and ran. My shoes clanked on the metal floor. The frozen aliens stared at me. I ran and ran-—

Through the drawing room with the stuffed rhinos and the velvet drapes—

Arthur! Why are you leaving me? The voice whispered in my head, so soft and desirable, I almost turned back—

Resist, resist, I was thinking, *get yourself out of this nightmare and fix yourself a stiff drink—*

Oh, Arthur!

I didn't care about the fate of the universe. I just wanted to get out of there.

I burst through the iris-door and began running like crazy, against the singing wind that caressed me like soft hands of a young girl, against the voice, so pure and so knowing, across the waves of heather.

The voice sang more insistently and I started to scream to try and drown it out. And still it sang, so that I wanted to turn back and dive into the ocean of the tower's overpowering love.

Resist, imbecile, resist! I chanted over and over—

and staggered up the steps and burst out of the kitchen closet, screeching, sending a volley of raisin bran cascading across the linoleum tiles—

Dusty and Boogie looked up from their chess game.

"Oh, hi, Dad," Dusty said, smiling her undead smile. "Supper's in the oven."

"I've just seen your Uncle Hermie!" I gasped.

Boogie said, "Mom's upstairs packing." He smiled, a supercilious grin. "Says you're getting a divorce."

***

"Well, there it is." I couldn't believe what I'd done. The family was gathered around the kitchen table and I was laying my sanity on the line. Here we were, in the heart of suburbia, a mile from the Conshohocken State Highway, with the warm light of a summer evening streaming in through the window and the chatter of children and dogs from distant backyards and birds singing dnd the Sunday roast waiting in the oven …and I was trying to talk about the fate of the universe.

Dusty spoke up first. "I don't want to hear any more lJil his rubbish, Dad!" she said. "You've gone bananas. Fix an appointment with Dr Webern or something. I'm going upstairs to call Tommy and make him take me out to a movie or something…"

"Not until you've done your homework," Becky said thorugh her tears. But Dusty had run off.

"All I want to say," I said, trying to sound calm, "it that this is something I've got to try …for old Hermie's sake. I probably won't come back, so I want you to be a good family and try to make a go of it—"

"Stuff and nonsense, Daddy!" said Boogie.

He looked at me earnestly from across the table, more serious than he'd even been before. "I believe you, but … there's no point in making a big show of things and making a melodramatic stand just because you feel inadequate."

I started to argue but he went on. "Don't argue, I know why you're into this trip. I also know something about Uncle Hermie's theory, too—namely that the rate of interface leakage isn't going to be quick enough to get us. Especially if we move away from here. I vote we all split. Sure, it'll get the whole Earth and the solar system and galaxy and everything else. But not, for God's sake, in our lifetime. Dad! Not if we move, say, to California …"

"That's not responsible," I said. I knew he was at least half right about my motives. But there was something else too. "If *I* don't go out there and confront the thing, nobody will! I've got to do it!"

"*Sheesh,* Dad, I don't want to lose you!" he cried out, and then he rushed out of the kitchen. I heard him crying. He'd never said that before. I'd had no idea he cared. Suddenly I felt very strange inside.

I got up and started for the kitchen closet.

"Wait, Arthur," said Rebecca. She had stopped crying.

I waited.

"Listen. I know that if you come back we'll probably go our separate ways. I'm sorry it didn't work." She was struggling to keep her voice steady. "But …you say this thing creates illusions that …come from our minds, that it's been picking my mind for months and all it's come up with has been Caressa Byrd books. It must know how much I love you if it's read my mind, its whole set of illusions must be based on my illusions …"

"What are you saying?"

"Maybe I can do something. I'm the one who knows all Caressa Byrd's books by heart … and even if I don't understand any of your science, I love you and that's enough. I'm coming with you …"

"Don't be silly. Who's going to take care of the children?" Was she going to obstruct me even now, here when I finally had gotten a chance to do something important in my life? And yet …she was willing to risk her life. For the first time I felt a funny kind of warmth for her.

"Come on, then." We held hands. I kicked aside some cereal boxes and we started down the steps. Almost at once —

***

The singing came. My cloak flapped gently in the breeze. The heather was in bloom, a bleakly beautiful landscape. I saw that Becky was now dressed in a white gown that rippled softly. We ran towards the tower, in slow motion it seemed, like a gushy scene in a romantic movie. Ahead the tower rose up. It had grown a little more. A flock of archaeopteryxes crossed the faces of the moons, and the tower called to me, called my name over and over …

I saw where here another silver casement sprouted from its walls, there a vine of metal hugged the tower's trunk, new buds that had sprouted since the last visit. I knew then that it had been preying on Hermie's emotions. But when the tower sang I couldn't resist it. It was … like all the things my marriage had never given me.

Arthur! Arthur! Enter me, love me …

We reached the foot of the tower. I walked into the irising door and Becky followed. Now we were in the drawing room, a sombre, baroque chamber of velvet hangings and wood-panelling and varnished oil paintings of busty Venuses and flutter-winged Adonises …the room, too, had grown, it seemed.

And then the voice—

Arthur! Why have you brought this woman? I will deal with her in due course. But now, come, come, come to me—

And I saw the silvery staircase that stretched up to merge into the sky-high roof. spiral upon spiral, and in my mind there burned the image of a golden Rapunzel, fair and soft and sensual and I could hardly restrain myself from rushing up the stairs and throwing myself into her arms …

Come. come, why do you resist me? Do I not love you as no one else can?

I had to go up the staircase. I had to confront the very soul of the alien. Heart thumping. I mounted the stairs. with Becky close behind me.

Then we were caught up in a wind. it seemed. The stairs had been illusions. Now we were drifting upward in the wake of some kind of force. some kind of tractor beam. the science fiction people would call it.

Now we were in another room. a womblike room with a single window. high up in the tower I supposed. The walls glowed, the air itself glowed. It was blinding. The walls were festooned with starlike sparkle-points. as though they had been papered with Christmas trees.

I knew what this room was; it was the room with the lighted window that I had glimpsed before. the room in the topmost turret of the tower.

And then out of the glitter stepped the most beautiful woman I had ever seen. Becky gasped. I knew than that the image had been shaped out of Becky's fantasies. Perhaps this was how she dreamed she should look for me …

She resembled Becky. But idealized. The red hair liberated from its hairpins and sprays and billowing behind her. The same white gown. the same features. but somehow purified. The same eyes. but on this woman they glowed like emerald cabochons.

It was a woman I could love. And involuntarily I was stepping towards her. towards this creature I had come to destroy. She spoke to me.

Arthur. It was the same voice that had called me from the beginning. that had beckoned to me from beyond the dimensions. *You're here* at *last. Please stay with me. please don't leave* me. *I'll give* you *any illusion* you *want* to *sustain* you. *Just let me love you. here, forever....*

"No!" I managed to whisper. "No. you've got to release me and Hermie and all the other beings you've caught. that you've frozen into that terrible living death." But I hardly cared. I wanted to finish saying my piece and then just leap into her arms.

What are you saying, Arthur my dearest? Listen ...I come from an ancient race that needs to love, that needs to give ... we were millions once. We flew where we willed, from world to world, giving of ourselves and growing ... then came hunger and desolation. I think I may be the last of my kind, and even I lay dormant for millennia upon millennia, too weak to fly away even, a weak to love. But now I am strong. Please, Arthur. I have to love! I have to give of myself, completely and utterly! It's my nature. I can't help it if I destroy the things I love—and yet who would not willingly choose death in exchange for a brief time of my love?

She stepped towards me. Her scent, so enticing, wafted toward me, and I was shaking with desire. So much for my brave defiant act to save the universe! I had lost. I walked towards her, arms outstretched, my body resounding with the beauty of her—

Becky interposed herself between us.

"No!" she cried out. "This isn't love at all! You don't know the meaning of love, you interstellar hussy, if you think this is it—"

But I am love! I am the perfect giving—

"Nonsense," Becky said. "You know nothing about love. If you'd read a single Caressa Byrd book …but no. Let me tell you something! My husband asked me for a divorce and I didn't utter one word of complaint. Because I knew he would be better off without me. I'm only a stupid woman with no repartee whom he can't show off in front of his friends at the University. But I really love him. For all your words and your beauty and your gorgeous illusions—you don't love him as much as I do! *Because you don't love him enough to give him up!*"

And then the dream-princess uttered a bloodcurdling scream that rang through the tower and chilled me to the core.

"Quick," said Becky, "while she's still confused—" She clasped my hand and we burst through the wall of lights which hadn't really been there at all, and the staircase opened up and we ran down it, stumbling and holding onto each other for dear life, while the scream echoed and re-echoed, a monster's deathscream, the stairs trembled as a tremor shook the tower-

We were running outside now. The scream went on behind us. It was no heather-strewn moor now, but a rocky desert, brown and craggy and burning, gridded with ragged sulphur clefts that smoked foul fumes. A dead world. Dead for millions of years perhaps—

Hermie was running alongside us. "You released me!" he shouted, panting. And when I glanced back I saw the unlikeliest crowd of marathoners you could possible imagine: claw-waving, tentacle-shuffling, grunting, squeaking, hooting as they streamed out of the screaming tower. "Thank Becky, not me," I said. We jogged on. "Guess they'll rebuild their world now," Hermie said.

And then we stopped for a breath and turned around

and, saw-~

Flames spurting from the tower's roots, silvery debris flying in a whirlwind around its base, the ground shaking, and then … the whole tower lifting itself into the sky, streaking up past the dancing moons, an eye-smarting daytime comet that left behind only an echo of a terrible scream, that melded with the sky and vanished …

"Here," Hermie said. "Step through the interface." We trooped into Hermie's Lego land.

For some reason Hermie didn't want his old house back —in fact, he never set foot in it again after pulling the plug on the transdimensional interface—and he took an apartment in West Philly, on Larchwood, I think.

A day or two after that, Becky got a letter in the mail. It was from Caressa Byrd.

> *Dear Mrs Kurtz,* [it ran]
> *Thank you so much for your twenty-one letters. I was deeply moved. Ah, we women, what frail creatures we are! You are a real woman and I know you will suffer anguish, yea the fires of Hell itself, for the man you love. Why I myself, when I was captured by the evil Marquis von RingdahL .. but of course you've read that one, my dear. Continue to sacrifice yourself! One day he may come to understand …*
> Your true friend,
> *Caressa Byrd*

I was in town and I dropped in on Hermie. I wanted to show off the letter to him—it isn't every day that a real author writes to you.

After only a week, his apartment was a jungle. We sat on the floor and talked over a beer. It was like old times.

"I've learned a lot," I said. "I thought that everything

and everyone was my enemy before, and now I know that I haven't been exactly that perceptive myself. We're working things out, Rebecca and I. And the kids. Somehow it's not a war—anymore."

It was true. I was happier. I didn't feel inadequate anymore. I d a wife who was willing to die for me. And we *had* saved the universe—although somehow it didn't feel like that much of an achievement.

Anyhow, I pulled out the letter. Hermie scrutinzed it for a long time. Then he walked over to a big cardboard box and pulled out a pile of what looked like manuscripts of scientific papers. Only they weren't, They all had titles like *Love's Raging Fury* and *Passion's Ravishing Flame* and *Desire's Diaphanous Dart*…

"Caressa Byrd original manuscripts?" I gasped. "I've never seen *those* novels before …what is this?"

"Artie, my dear friend …I've a terrible confession to make. You see, when I was a starving high school student and needed money, the fastest way was to knock off one of these, and—"

"My God! *You're* Caressa Byrd!"

"I've never told a soul."

"And when you were away—"

"I had a backlog at my publishers. It only takes a week to write one of these things …"

"No wonder the alien was convinced! She'd read Becky's mind and was feeding off yours … she must have believed that the love of gothic romances was genuine, human emotion."

"You mean it isn't?" And Hermie smiled an enigmatic smile. Hermie was the most frustrating person I ever knew. You simply couldn't get the better of him. He always had an extra ace or three up his sleeve. I couldn't do anything without him being there first.

Hell, even the alien tower affair had been on the rebound.

—Arlington, 1980

Avoiding Close Encounters

"I think they're back, Ma," said Jason, bursting in on her dream of a warm blue sea. Helen had thought the wine would help, but her son's urgent tone was enough to break through any reverie.

The room was windowless. And chilly, of course; it took all of the village's resources to render the place even tolerably above freezing. The wine still sat there, half-drunk, gone bad by now; pity, thought Helen, since it's the last of this year's.

Jason pulled his mother up from her pallet. He was a thin little thing. "You shouldn't run around so much up there," said Helen. "Look, I'm going to have to mend your tunic—"

"And there aren't any more where that came from," he said, knowing her only too well. "You'd better hurry. I think there's even less time than usual."

"Do you know for a fact?" she asked him. "How do you know. Did you get Cassandra to double-check?"

"Yes, yes, Ma," Jason said. Kept tugging at her while she took out her frayed himation from the ancient chest. Laughed. It was only his second time, that was why. If only he knew how deadly serious it all was. If only he knew how much was at stake.

She decided to drink the wine, soured as it was. Every year the crop was thinner, stranger. It was becoming more and more a product of this place. As she left the room, she began buckling herself in. They walked past the vineyards, kept in bloom by an artificial sun, hurried down the corridor where the machines thrummed as they manufactured air from rock, reached the first of many flights of steps, stopped at the first of many landings to sip at the trickle from the water-maker.

At the last level before the outside, Helen found several elders already sitting in their niches, fretting. Especially Cassandra, true to her name, who was always ready to predict the worst.

"Don't worry, people," Helen said, trying to stay as matter-of-fact as she could. "We'll handle it; we always have."

"It's worse this time," said Cassandra. "I think it's an actual person this time. Not a machine."

"We'll deal with it." She sent Jason to fetch the watchman so we could have a real report, not rumors. "They were bound to send a person sooner or later."

"But why now?" It was Clement who spoke. "Now, when we're so helpless, so undefended?"

"I don't know," Helen said. "I'll have to think about it." These were the times when she sometimes wished we were back home. When her kind of people stayed in the back of the house, and had no say at all, let alone being a hereditary leader.

When Jason came back, he had Marcus with him. "It's bad," the watchman said. "We've got a day, maybe half a day. And their trajectory puts them within two miles of the entrance."

"Well, we'll clear everything, of course, as usual," Helen said. "Call everyone in. Do a head count. Make sure there aren't any stragglers. Or people like my son here, kids who don't understand the danger, who are liable to walk right into one of them."

"Ma," Jason began, "if I hadn't been on the surface, you wouldn't have gotten this warning for another hour. No one knows where you go away to dream, 'cept me."

"All right. I'll decide your fate after the crisis is over." She wasn't inclined to punish him, really; theirs was not a community of harshness, after all.

"Why do we always have to make the decisions?" Cassandra wailed. "Why can't they come down and help us? They brought us here—they ought at least to look in on us from time to time—"

"They're not gonna," Jason said.

Helen said, "Let's be practical, Cassandra. The last angel to come was in our grandparents' time."

"My god, my god," Clement murmured, "why hast thou forsaken me?"

***

Three of them went up to take a look—three was all that could squeeze into the ground chariot. It was a vehicle enclosed completely in a thick, clear glass, a gift from an angel naturally, powered by the same machines that made the air. Helen took the rudder; Marcus read the coordinates in the frosty screen that showed word and images; Jason should not have been there, but Helen knew that he would torment her about it for weeks afterward.

By Jesus, she thought, the world is beautiful. The blue-gray sky, the brooding crags, the whorls of rust-red dust … the mountains that bisected the horizon, anguished, angular; the lakes of ruddy sand, the ancient craters, craters within craters … so beautiful, and all I've ever known, she thought … so why do I always dream of oceans?

"Look," cried Jason. "There's the first one—"

Yes. Like a spider, on its back, its metal legs curled around its stomach. That one had been easy enough to sabotage, years ago. Not much of a brain, and it ran aground against the first big rock, and never budged again; the later ones were harder to deal with, since they could see in all directions; they had gotten more and more cunning; Helen knew they were determined to come.

"Two stades north of Parnassus," Marcus said. "That's what the sensors tell us. They mean to land here."

It was a nice-sized plain without too many craters. Along its perimeter ran the bed of long-dead river. Behind that, mountains. wine-red at ground level, easing into a muddy, dried-blood color at the tips. Here and there, a spear of rock cast a mile-long shadow.

"Any of us been out this way lately?" Helen asked him.

"Not to my knowledge. Except … I think … Paulina. The gravid one. Some children were playing, but I made sure they gathered all their toys."

"Looks clean to me," Helen said. "And sunset is in an hour."

"Wait," Jason said. "Over there."

He had sharp eyes, that one. A glint of bronze. Marcus brought the chariot closer. We slid into our pressure skins … no need for a cumbersome air maker, we'd only be a few moments … and ran out there, Jason leading the way.

Breathless, he held up his prize. You can't hear much up

here, the air is so thin, but the pressure skins have a way of projecting voices; she heard him right in her ear. "It's a rattle," he said. "That won't do at all, will it?"

His mother took it from him. Why would someone leave a thing like that out in the open, knowing the danger? She shook it. No amplifier on it, of course; she heard only a dry distant whisper, like sand in an hourglass ... it was a beautiful thing, with a horse's head with one ear broken off, a priceless bauble from back home, a piece of an unreachable past.

"Better stow it," she told her son.

He ran back to the chariot. Meanwhile, Marcus was finding an inconspicuous place to plant the seeing-stone. Murmuring a brief prayer to the Savior, he placed the stone among a thousand other stones, and it blended perfectly.

Helen didn't have to worry long about the rattle. The baby lay only a few paces away. She could have kicked herself for not realizing it early. "Marcus, Jason," she called out, "there's been an exposing."

Jason ran back. "Look at that thing!"

It was stiff. Helen couldn't feel the cold outside her pressure skin, but she saw it in the baby's eyes. They shone like polar ice beneath the winter starlight. Everything else had ruptured, of course; the veins had crystallized outside the burst skin.

"Thought Paulina was planning to keep this one," Marcus said. "Well, I hope she remembered to baptize it first."

Exposing was a time-honored custom, of course; without it there'd be no village at all; life beneath this world's dead skin was a perpetual war against the most unforgiving of elements. The machines could only do so much. And angels had not come down in a generation. She must have loved it, Helen thought. To leave the rattle, there's undying love. She held the shattered little corpse in her arms, and rocked it a little, crying to herself. And night fell. In this place, night fell in an instant; even though she'd never known the lingering sunsets of legend, she knew that this sudden night was an alien thing, that this home was not her home.

***

She didn't mention it to Paulina that night, as they sat in the vineyard, watching the images from the seeing-stone projected against one cavern wall. They huddled, the villagers, after their nightly love-feast, trying to get as close to the warming-stone as they could.

"Back it up again," Clement said. Now that there were pictures, he seemed less fearful, Helen thought. "No, no," he said at last, watching the figures lope across the plain, utterly encased in shielding suits. "Angels would not need such cumbersome pressure skins. They would breathe the empty air as easily as we breathe the air down here." He was something of an eschatologist. "This doesn't fulfill any of the known prophecies."

Helen watched. Her pulse pounded. They were getting close to the place where … she wondered if Paulina knew that her child had already returned to the resurrection tank, that the village had already consumed her flesh and her blood, baked into the bread of the love-feast; Paulina had not eaten with them that evening. Exposing a child is something that always gnaws at you, that never leaves you alone; Helen's first-born tormented her even now, twenty years later.

***

Where was Paulina anyway? She shouldn't be alone, Helen thought. They were replaying it again and again, the ungainly men shambling across the sand, their features stark in the moons' harsh light. Ugly creatures. Ugly and damned. Yet they too came from God. Didn't they? Had the kingdom come after all, and left this distant village in the cold? Was this place hell, after all, and not some waystation on the road to paradise.

"Jesus, but they're ugly," Cassandra said.

That, in truth, they were. After the twentieth repetition Helen could not take any more; she left to find Paulina, stopping off at the storeroom to pick up the rattle. She was in the spinning-room, where the cave walls were of a fibrous mineral that could be coerced into a kind of homespun. Paulina was spinning and weeping, and weeping and spinning, and now and then she would prick herself, and dye the thread red. Helen put her arm around the younger woman. Paulina pushed her away. "I've had enough," she said. "I want to give myself up."

"Give up?" said Helen.

"I watched her die!" said Paulina. "She exploded."

"I've killed seven of them myself," said Helen. "You have to have faith."

"Faith? It's been two thousand years since our ancestors put on their winding-sheets and sipped the laurel wine and lay down in the catacombs with silver obols in their mouths to pay the angel who bore them away in a fiery chariot … what a rescue it proved to be … I would rather have burned up like a torch at a banquet … I would rather have perished in the fire that engulfed the world."

"Faith," Helen said, and softly, calmly, she stroked the young woman's hair. "You can't give up now. Be strong. Why, my own grandmother saw the angel who came to warn us, who gave us the seeing-stones so we could stay hidden. And who told us that one would come in our generation, to show us the next stage. And who told us to keep the faith and be strong."

"You don't know how hard it is," Paulina said, sucking at her bloodstained finger.

"Oh yes," said Helen, "oh yes, oh yes." How could Paulina really understand. It's worse for me, she thought. I'm always bottling it up, hiding from my own despair, because I've got all these others who look to me … I always have to think of them, of shoring up up their faith … but what about mine?

Helen pulled the rattle from the bosom of her tunic and set it down beside the spinning wheel. "Look," she said. "I brought this back for you. You shouldn't be abandoning bits of the past up there; the past belongs to all of us."

Paulina took the rattle and clasped it to her chest and went into a paroxysm of grief. Now, at last, she allowed Helen to embrace her. Helen held her and let her cry. But suddenly Paulina stiffened and let out a shriek. "It's missing an ear," she said.

"It's two thousand years old," Helen said.

"No. You don't understand. The bronze was cracked there, the ear was coming off … it's still up there … Oh, God, I've put the whole village in mortal danger… ."

No time for tears now. The two women ran down the corridor to the vineyard, where many of the villagers had gone to sleep; only Marcus, and Jason, rubbing his eyes, and Clement the eschatologist were still staring at the images from the seeing-stone.

"Run it back," Helen said, "to where we found the rattle."

The blur of the rewind. The ugly demons in their monstrous suits, striding backwards over the sand. The movements of the seeing-stone, jittery and jarring in the high-speed mode. Now there was something she had missed … a giant glowing bubble next to their landing chariot … living quarters! How long were they going to stay? Were they going to remain there until they had rooted out all the humans in the world, capture them, send them all back to the slaughter? Could they really be so vindictive? Yet Helen's grandmother had been absolutely clear: the angel had told them to protect the village's secrecy at all costs ... even if it meant shedding blood ... what did a few lives matter when the kingdom of heaven was at risk?

And Helen, just a girl then, had asked her grandmother, in the very same chamber where she often went to dream her private dreams, "Is this the kingdom of heaven then, Grandma, these rooms, these machines, the vineyard, the great red world above?"

And her grandmother said, "Just a waystation, Helen. A wilderness where we must wait, and pray, and have faith."

She remembered then: Lowering her grandparents into the resurrection tank. The love-feast. The sharing of the bread and wine. The image was fleeting, quickly pushed back into the ocean of memory. Now she concentrated on the seeing-stone's recording.   The life-sized image on the wall shifted, back and forth, back and forth.

"Again," she said. "Slower."

Back again. Forth again. I should stop worrying, Helen thought. Paulina's distracted, imagining things ... the loss of a newborn child makes a woman go crazy, she knew that. And yet—

Bloated from the love-feast, her companions had all drifted off. The visitors, too, had retired into their bubble-dwelling; like other men, they had a cycle of sleep and wakefulness. That was why they were clearly not angels.

The vineyard was the warmest room; the grapes needed all the heat the machines could generate. She too was getting tired. This was needlessly obsessive, wasn't it? And yet—

No. There it was all right. She had rewound the record all the way past it four or five times. How could she have missed it? There was the bronze ear, sandwiched between two jagged rocks, as clear to the seeing-stone as it must be to the instruments of the visitors.

I mustn't panic the whole village, Helen thought. I'll deal with it now, alone, while they're all asleep.

She left the room and walked briskly toward the stairwell that led to the surface of the world.

***

"I'm coming," Jason said.

There were many passageways to the staging level. She was surprised, though, that he'd gotten there so quickly, that he'd managed to do it so quietly. He was already taking one of the child-sized pressure skins off the rack.

Helen said, "You'll be a lot safer here," but she already knew that he would get his own way. He was that kind of child. How could she deny him this taste of adventure, when the whole world comprised but a few corridors and a vast inhospitable desert?

At the last minute, Helen decided to take a thunderbolt. A weapon had not been fired here in a thousand years, but she was scared. The exploded baby … the fact that the visitors kept coming, kept sending their seeing-creatures, had kept the whole village on edge for a generation …

The thunderbolt fit in the palm of her hand. Just a squeeze could send death, seeking out the victim's heartbeat, ripping him apart. She had only seen it in the records of a seeing-stone. She shuddered, stuck it in the belt of the pressure skin.

Then they slipped on their skins and took the chariot up through the trapdoors, camouflaged by boulders. It was normally an hour's drive to Parnassus; this time it would take longer, because the chariot needed to take long detours and send out jamming-specters to confuse the visitors.

Helen leaned back in the seat. Jason rapped his fingers against the clear walls. "Ma," he said, "me and the other kids talk about giving ourselves up."

Helen said, "But the angels—the commandments—"

"No one living's seen an angel. Maybe it's all wrong. Maybe they've forgiven us and they've come to fetch us home."

"Home is the Kingdom of Heaven, Jason, not some Roman catacomb."

"Yeah. Ever think about oceans, Ma?"

Helen looked. The plain, frozen, stretched to the far horizon. What if it were all in motion? What if the very sand were to liquefy, and the hard rock become a sea of blood? The eschatologists always spoke of such things … but the ocean of her dream was a different thing … a warm and living thing … full of comfort … an end to pain.

"Yes, son," she said softly. "In dreams. But this world is not a dream."

"Sometimes I think it is a dream," said her boy, "and we'll wake up to a green world, a watery world. Sometimes I think the visitors will lead me there."

"That's Satan speaking, son," she said softly. "You must always tell him to get behind you."

"Don't believe in that crap," he said.

That disturbed her profoundly, and she began telling him the story of the Exodus all over again—as much for herself as him, for she was sure that repeating the familiar incidents would soothe her, lessen her apprehension. It was what her mother had told her, and her mother's mother.

They were persecuting us. Burning us alive. Feeding us to lions. Slashing, sawing, slicing, and impaling us. And still we kept the faith. They took us from our houses. They took us from the catacombs. They burned us out of the forests and the caves. And still we kept the faith. Death did not matter; it was the gateway to paradise.

It was whispered that, just before dying, we would be caught up in a great white light, and taken in golden chariots through the clouds, to the bosom of the Anointed One… .

One group of the Christianoi was specially favored of God. It was a terrible night. They were taking us to be dipped in pitch and set ablaze to illuminate the Emperor's midnight banquet. We were waiting, chained up, in an anteroom of the palace. We knew we would die soon … that the very world would end in fire. We tried not to be afraid. We remembered what we had been told; that we would be caught up, transfigured, enveloped in the eternal warmth of God's love. The screaming was terrible to hear, and many turned their backs on God and agreed to worship Caesar. But to those that remained in that terrible chamber, there came an angel of the lord… .

Clothed in light he was, and his face shone like the sun. He said, "O Christianoi, I have heard your cries. Have faith. This very night, a ship is prepared that will carry you into the sky."

"Will we be with Jesus?" said the first Helen, in whose honor the firstborn girl of our line has always been named Helen.

"Not in the flesh," said the angel. "I go to prepare a place for you … you are not yet ready for union with the ultimate. You shall live there forty generations, and then, perhaps, your people will be ready to join God's other chosen peoples."

The angel's lips never moved when he spoke; the voice came from a speaking-stone that he held in an outstretched hand. His shape also shimmered against the light; at times we could see right through him to the bloodstained walls of the holding cell. He lifted the stone to his lips and uttered words from his mouth for the first time, words in a guttural, primal language that must have been the very language of creation, for the room began to shake and one by one the Christianoi's chains shattered, and we were gathered up into a ship that sailed the sky, and passed through the night like a comet, straight upward to the star that astrologers call Ares, or, in the Roman tongue, Mars.

And so we lived, in the place prepared for us, carefully conserving our resources, carefully controlling our population so that we did not soil the pristine splendor of this Ares, which was a world, not a star, and a world that mortals are not equipped to live in without the aid of the angels' gifts: the machines that make air, the seeing-stones, the chariots that move by themselves.

But there was young Jason, bright-eyed, sullen, and all he could say was "Don't believe in that crap." He said it several times, and then added, "Besides, it was a long time ago. And we can't stay here forever. I have dreams, too, Ma. I want to touch the visitors. I want to speak to them."

"Not so long ago," Helen said. "Your great-grandmother saw an angel. I took his commandments from her: secrecy at all costs, even unto the shedding of blood. You think my grandmother would have lied to me?"

"I can't keep the faith. Maybe you should have had a daughter, another Helen, to carry on. Maybe you should have exposed me."

"Don't carry on so," Helen said. "I love you."

They had reached the vicinity of Parnassus now, and they needed to find the horse's ear quickly, and eradicate all traces of their coming, before the visitors broke their cycle of sleep.

Finding it was not hard. The seeing-stones were all connected to one another, and each could track the seeings of all the others. A huge outcropping concealed the chariot in its shadow. Mother and son went out, Jason carrying a pair of tongs to gather up the ear with, Helen a brush to smooth the sand back down. They walked in a patterned sequence, covering the tracks from one foot with dust thrown by the other; an angel had taught them that generations before. Knowing where to go, they discovered the horse's ear quickly enough; Jason picked it up, and Helen got on her hands and knees to eradicate their traces.

Tall, pointy boulders surrounded them. Carefully, she worked the dust back over the little gully that the ear had dug. It took her a moment to realize that she was no longer in Jason's shadow. She could still hear his shallow breathing through her pressure skin, but—

She looked up through the a V-shaped gap in the boulders. Her heart almost stopped beating. A man had emerged from the bubble. He was coming their way, slowly, bending over frequently to collect samples of the dust. And there was Jason, still in the boulders' shadow.

"Get back," she said. "He'll see you."

"I don't care," he said. There was a desperation in him she'd never heard before. The same feeling she'd seen in Paulina. The hopelessness.

"Despair is the devil's doing," she said. "Don't be tempted, son."

"I have to, Ma!" he said.

He began to walk toward the visitor. The visitor was still far away, had not seen him, doubtless was expecting nothing.

She heard him whisper the ancient words of greeting: "Rejoice, stranger. Our home is your home." But he was only talking to himself, practicing, perhaps, for the encounter.

But then her son began to shout. "Take me home!" he screamed. "I want to see the ocean!" The visitor did not hear it. She hoped he could not hear it. They did not have

the voice-sending pressure skins, did they? And yet ...
though the air was thin ... there was some air here. A shout
might become a pale thin cry—

"Forgive me," she whispered. She drew her thunderbolt
and shot him. He crumpled. The visitor had turned in
another direction, hadn't even seen. She ran to her dead boy.
Death from a thunderbolt is instantaneous. The puncture
was clean and the skin had already sealed back up by the
time she got to him, but inside that skin was death.

"In the name of the Father, the Son, and the Sacred
Paraclete," she said, and pushed down on the filmy fabric of
the pressure skin to close his eyes.

***

Only later, in the resurrection room, waiting for the tank
to fill up so that she could lower the body into it and cycle
the flesh and blood back into bread and wine, only then did
Helen weep. Only then did she feel that ultimate despair she
now knew the others had felt. Her son lay on a stone slab.
Death hadn't marred him; thunderbolts killed invisibly, and
the pressure skin had seared shut before the boy could
explode.

Thirty years of faith and prayer, and now she was left
with a gaping why, a chasm in her heart ... a chasm she had
never confronted, only dimly knew about. She had nurtured
a doubter in her own bosom, and in the end she, the one
whose duty was never to doubt, had been unable to allay his
doubts.

He was dead.

As Helen sat weeping, there came to her an angel… .

He had been in the room a long time, perhaps; the light
and warmth had come gradually. Warmth was a rare
commodity in this place. At first it was only a tingling. Then
it began to penetrate beneath her skin. She thought it must

be some interior heat generated by her grief … but no, there was a kind of joy in it. And finally she looked up to see the angel standing next to the corpse of her son.

He was just as her grandmother had described. Winged, shimmery, wreathed in light. She could see the ocean in his eyes. "Helen," said the angel, "don't be afraid. I've come to tell you the experiment is being dismantled."

"What does that mean?" Helen said. "Are we entering the Kingdom of Heaven?"

"I'm not here to tell you about that, Helen. Just to say that the tests have all been done, and you are free to make contact."

"Make contact? … with the Romans?"

"There are no more Romans."

"Then the world has ended."

"In a sense. You are the last people to think, to feel, to dream like the people of that ancient world; soon you will have to learn the ways of another world."

"No Romans?" Helen said again. But the world was Rome.

"Helen," said the angel, "there have been some changes in oversight. There was a fear in certain quarters that the revelation of our … meddling might be too inflammatory to the delicate balance of your home world, and so a last-minute effort was made to conceal the evidence; but there's been … well, a change of government. I won't bore you with details, but … well, we won't be coming back."

"A change of government! Then Armageddon has been fought—and lost?" It was going to be hard to adapt to a universe where Satan was king. Her dead child was proof of that.

"There's so little I can tell you. We are not supposed to reveal anything. But alas, no experiment is flawless when the subject is sentient. That's why we shall not return."

"And God? And the resurrection of the body? And the flaming chariots that are to carry us into the sky? And the redemption?"

"You are human," the angel said. "When faith goes, there first comes a terrible despair. Yet after such despair, you still persist. I can't answer you questions. In my own way—from the vantage of a vastly superior science, I suppose—I am still trying to ask them."

"But, but—" Helen cried, anguished, "I killed my son!"

"That, at least, I can remedy."

The angel gazed solemnly at Jason's pitiful body. He waved his hand—a casual thing, dismissive almost. And all at once Jason opened his eyes. The sourceless light in the chamber was so painful that Helen had to squint, and tears spurted from her eyes.

He sat up, and, seeing he was not alone, coyly covered his nakedness with one hand. "Ma, Ma," he said. "I think I died."

Helen went to embrace him. "Baby," she said, "you did, you did."

She wanted to ask the angel so much more—wanted to spit out that noisome why that was now stuck in her craw and would perhaps never be dislodged—but as she turned from kissing her warm son, the angel vanished.

No time for more despair. She knew she would never hurt her son again. No truth was worth killing one's child for. Abraham had been wrong to agree to kill Isaac. This discovery—and this second chance—was a greater miracle than anything in the ancient tales of Jesus' life. No time to lose. "Get your clothes back on. We're going back to Parnassus," she told him.

He looked at her. Questioning at first. But then—with the sureness of one who has harrowed hell, and returned to the living world—he said, "And when we've greeted them, they'll take us to the ocean, won't they?"

Helen wept. She could almost hear the crash of the waves. "Yes," she said She closed her eyes and savored the remembrance of her dream of the warm blue sea. "Yes, Jason, yes, they will."

—Bangkok, 2007

Fiddling for Waterbuffaloes

When my brother Lek and I were children we were only allowed to go to Prasongburi once a week. That was the day our mothers went to the marketplace and to make merit at the temple. Our grandmother, our mothers' mother, spent the days chewing betelnut and fashioning intricate mobiles out of dried palm leaves; not just the usual fish-shapes, dozens of tiny baby fish swinging from a big mother fish lacquered in bright red or orange, but also more elaborate shapes: spaceship and tigers and mythical beasts, nagas that swallowed their own tails. It was our job to sell them to the *thaokae* who owned the only souvenir shop in the town ... the only store with one of those aluminum gratings that you pull shut to lock up at night, just like the ones in Bangkok.

It was always difficult to get him to take the ones that weren't fish. Once we took in a mobile made hentirely of spaceships, which our grandmother had copied from one of the American TV shows. (In view of our later experiences, this proved particularly prophetic.) "Everyone knows," the *thaokae* said (that was the time he admitted us to his inner sanctum, where he would smoke opium from an impressive *bong* and puff it in our faces) "that a *plataphien* mobile has fish in it. Everyone wants sweet little fishies to hang over their baby's cradle. I mean, those spaceships are a tribute of your grandmother's skill at weaving dried palm leaves, but as far as the tourists are concerned, it's just fiddling for waterbuffaloes." He meant there was no point in doing such fine work because it would be wasted on his customers.

We ended up with maybe ten baht apiece for my grandmother's labors, and we'd carefully tuck away two of the little blue banknotes (this was in the year 2504 B.E., long before they debased the baht into a mere coin) so that we could go to the movies. The American ones were funniest—especially the James Bond ones—because the dubbers had the most outrageous adlibs. I remember that in "Goldfinger" the dubbers kept putting in jokes about the fairy tale of Jao Ngo, which is about a hideous monster who falls into a tank of gold paint and becomes very handsome. The audience became so wild with laughter that they actually stormed the dubbers' booth and started improvising their own puns. I particularly remember that day because we were waiting for the monsoon to burst, and the heat had been making everyone crazy.

Seconds after we left the theater it came all at once, and the way home was so impassable we had to stay at the village before our village, and then we had to go home by boat, rowing frantically by the side of the drowned road. The fish were so thick you could pull them from the water in handfulls.

That was when my brother Lek said to me, "You know, Noi, I think it would be grand to be a movie dubber."

"That's silly, Phii Lek," I said. "Someone has to herd the waterbuffaloes and sell the mobiles and —"

"That's what we both should do. So we don't have to

work on the farm anymore." Our mothers, who were rowing the boat, pricked up their ears at that. Something to report back to our father, perhaps. "We could live in the town. I love that town."

"It's not so great," my mother said.

My senior mother (Phii Lek's mother) agreed. "We went to Chiangmai once, for the beauty contest. Now there was a town. Streets that wind on and on ... and airconditioning in almost every public building!"

"We didn't win the beauty contest, though," my mother said sadly. She didn't say it, but she implied that that was how they'd both ended up marrying my father. "Our stars were bad. Maybe in my next life —"

"I'm not waiting till my next life," my brother said. "When I'm grown up they'll have airconditioning in Prasongburi, and I'll be dubbing movies every night."

The sun was beating down, blinding, sizzling. We threw off our clothes and dived from the boat. The water was cool, mudflecked; we pushed our way through the reeds.

The storm had blown the village's TV antenna out into the paddyfield. We watched <u>Star Trek</u> at the headsman's house, our arms clutching the railings on his porch, our feet dangling, slipping against the stilts that were still soaked with rain. It was fuzzy and the sound was off, so Phii Lek put on a magnificent performance, putting discreet obscenities into the mouths of Kirk and Spock while the old men laughed and the coils of mosquito incense smoked through the humid evening. At night, when we were both tucked in under our mosquito netting, I dreamed about going into space and finding my grandmother's palm-leaf mobiles hanging from the points of the stars.

***

Ten years later they built a highway from Bangkok to

Chiangmai, and there were no more casual tourists in Prasongburi. Some American archaeologists started digging at the site of an old Khmer city nearby. The movie theater never did get airconditioning, but my grandmother did get into faking antiques; it turned out to be infinitely more lucrative than fish mobiles, and when the *thaokae* died, she and my two mothers were actually able to buy the place from his intransigent nephew. The three of them turned it into an "antique" place (fakes in the front, the few genuine pieces carefully hoarded in the airconditioned back room) and our father set about looking for a third wife as befit his improved station in life.

My family were also able to buy a half-interest in the movie theater, and that was how my brother and I ended up in the dubbing booth after all. Now, the fact of the matter was, sound projection systems in theaters had become prevalent all over the country by then, and Lek and I both knew that live movie dubbing was a dying art. Only the fact that the highway didn't come anywhere near Prasongburi prevented its citizens from positively demanding talkies. But we were young and, relatively speaking, wealthy; we wanted to have a bit of fun before having the drudgery of marriage and earning a real living thrust upon us. Lek did most of the dubbing—he was astonishingly convincing at female voices as well as male—while I contributed the sound effects and played background music from the library of scratched records we'd inherited from the previous régime.

Since we two were the only purveyors of, well, foreign culture in the town, you'd think we would be the ones best equipped to deal with an alien invasion.

Apparently the aliens thought so too.

Aliens were farthest from my mind the day it happened, though. I was putting in some time at the shop and trying to pacify my three honored parents, who were going at it like cats and dogs in the back.

"If you dare bring that bitch into our house," Elder Mother was saying, fanning herself feverishly with a plastic fan—for our airconditioning had broken down, as usual —" I'll leave."

"Well," Younger Mother (my own) said, "I don't mind as long as you make sure she's a servant. But if you marry her —"

"Well, I mind, I'm telling you!" my other mother shouted. "If the two of us aren't enough for you, I've three more cousins up north, decent, hardworking girls who'll bring in money, not use it up."

"Anyway, if you simply <u>have</u> to spend money," Younger Mother said, "what's wrong with a new pick-up truck?"

"I'm not dealing with that usurious *thaokae* in Ban Kraduk," my father said, taking another swig of his Mekong whiskey, and "and there's no other way of coming up with a down payment … and besides, I happen to be a very horny man."

"All of you shut up," my grandmother said from somewhere out back, where she had been meticulously ageing some pots into a semblance of twelfth-century Sawankhalok ware. "All this chatter disturbs my work."

"Yes, *khun mae,*" the three of them chorused back respectfully.

My Elder Mother hissed, "But watch out, my dear husband. I read a story in *Siam Rath* about a woman who castrated her unfaithful husband and fed his eggs to the ducks!"

My father sucked in his breath and took a comforting gulp of whiskey as I went to the front to answer a customer.

She was one of those archaeologists or anthropologists or something. She was tall and smelly, as all *farangs* are (they have very active sweat glands); she wore a sort of safari outfit, and she had long hair, stringy from her digging and the humidity. She was scrutinizing the spaceship mobile my grandmother had made ten years ago—it still had not sold, and we had kept it as a memento of hard times—and muttering to herself words that sounded like, "Warp factor five!"

My brother and I know some English, and I was preparing to embarrass myself by exercising that ungrategul, toneless tongue, when she addressed me in Thai.

"Greetings to you, honored sir," she said, and brought her palms together in a clumsy but heartfelt *wai.* I couldn't suppress a laugh. "Why, didn't I do that right?" she demanded.

"You did it remarkably well," I said. "But you shouldn't go to such lengths. I'm only a shopkeeper, and you're not supposed to *wai* first. But I suppose I should give you 'E for effort,'" (I said this phrase in her language, having learned it from another archaeologist the previous year) "since few would even try as hard as you."

"Oh, but I'm doing my Ph.D. in Southeast Asian aesthetics at UCLA," she said. "By all means, correct me." She started to pull out a notebook.

I had never, as we say, "arrived" in America, though my sexual adventures had recently included an ageing, overwhelmingly odoriferous Frenchwoman and the daughter of the Indian *babu* who sold cloth in the next town, and the prospect suddenly seemed rather inviting. Emboldened, I said, "But to really study our culture, you might consider —" and eyed her with undisguised interest.

She laughed. *Farang* women are exceptional, in that one need not make overtures to them subtly, but may approach the matter in a non-nonsense, fashion, as a plumber might regard a sewage pipe. "Jesus," she said in English, "I think he's asking me for a date!"

"I understood that," I said.

"Where will we go?" she said in Thai, giggling. "I've got the day off. And the night, I might add. Oh, that's not correct, is it? You should send a go-between to my father, or something."

"Only if the liaison is intended to be permanent," I said quickly, lest anthropology get the better of lust. "Well, we could go to a movie."

"What's showing?" she said. "Why, this is just like back home, and me a teenager again." She bent down, anxious to please, and started to deliver a sloppy kiss to my forehead. I recoiled. "Oh, I forgot," she said. "You people frown on public displays."

"*Star Wars*," I said.

"Oh, but I've seen that twenty times."

"Ah, but have you seen it—dubbed *live,* in a provincial Thai theater without airconditioning? Think of the glorious field notes you could write."

"You Thai men are all alike," she said, intimating that she had had a vast experience of them. "Very well. What time? By the way, my name is Mary, Mary Mason."

***

We were an hour late getting the show started, which was pretty normal, and the audience was getting so restless that some of them had started an impromptu bawdy-rhyming contest in the front rows. My brother and I had manned the booth and were studying the script. He would do all the main characters, and I would do such meaty rôles as the Second Stormtrooper.

"Let's begin," Phii Lek said. "She won't come anyway."

Mary turned up just as we were lowering the house lights. She had bathed (my brother sniffed appreciatively as she entered the dubbing booth) and wore a clean <u>sarong,</u> which did not look too bad on her.

"Can I do Princess Leia?" she said, <u>wai</u>-ing to Phii Lek as though she were already his younger sibling by virtue of her as-yet-unconsummated association with me.

"You can <u>read</u> Thai?" Phii Lek said in astonishment.

"I have my Masters' in Siamese from Michigan U," she said huffily, "and studied under Bill Gedney." We shrugged.

"Yes, but you can't improvise," my brother said.

She agreed, pulled out her notebook, and sat down in a corner. My brother started to put on a wild performance, while I ran hither and thither putting on records and creating sound effects out of my box of props. We began the opening chase scene with Tchaikovsky's Piano Concerto, which kept skipping; at last the needle got stuck and I turned the volume down hastily just as my brother (in the tones of the heroic Princess Leia) was supposed to murmur, "Help me, Obiwan Kenobi. You're my only hope." Instead, he began to moan like a harlot in heat, screeching out, "Oh, I need a man, I do, I do! These robots are no good in bed!"

At that point Mary became hysterical with laughter. She fell out of her chair and collided with the shoe rack. I hastened to rescue her from the indignity of having her face next to a stack of filthy flipflops, and could not prevent myself from grabbing her. She put her arms around my waist and indecorously refused to let go, while my brother, warming to the audience reaction, began to ad lib ever more outrageously.

It was only after the movie, when I had put on the 45 of the Royal Anthem and everyone had stood up to pay homage to the Sacred Majesty of the King, that I noticed something wrong with my brother. For one thing, he did not rise in respect, even though he was ordinarily the most devout of people. He sat bunched up in a corner of the dubbing booth, with his eyes darting from side to side like window wipers.

I watched him anxiously but dared not move until the Royal Anthem had finished playing.

Then, tentatively, I tapped him on the shoulder. "Phii Lek," I said, "it's time we went home."

He turned on me and snarled … then he fell on the floor and began dragging himself forward in a very strange manner, propelling himself with his chin and elbows along the woven-rush matting at our feet.

Mary said, "Is <u>that</u> something worth reporting on?" and began scribbling wildly in her notebook.

"Phii Lek," I said to my brother in terms of utmost respect, for I thought he might be punishing me for some imagined grievance, "are you ill?" Suddenly I thought I had it figured out. "If you're playing 'putting on the anthropologists,' Elder Sibling, I don't think this one's going to be taken in."

"You are part of a rebel alliance, and a traitor!" my brother intoned—in English—in a harsh, unearthly voice. "Take her away!"

"That's … my God, that's James Earl Jones' voice," Mary said, forgetting in her confusion to speak Thai. "That's from the movie we just saw."

"What are we going to do?" I said, panicking. My older brother was crawling around at my feet, making me feel distinctly uncomfortable because of the elevation of my head over the head of a person of higher status, so I dropped down on my hands and knees so as to maintain my head at the properly respectful level. Meanwhile, he was wriggling around on his belly.

Amid all this, Mary's notebook and pens clattered to the floor and she began to scream.

At that moment, my grandmother entered the booth and stared about wildly. I attempted, from my prone position, to perform the appropriate *wai,* but Phii Lek was rolling around and making peculiar hissing noises. Mary started to stutter, *"Khun yaai,* I don't what happened, they just suddenly started acting this way —"

"Don't you *khun yaai* me," grandmother snapped. "I'm no kin to any foreigners, thank you!" She surveyed the spectacle before her with mounting horror. "Oh, my terrible karma!" she cried. "Demons have transformed my grandsons into dogs!"

***

On the street, there were crowds everywhere. I could hear people babbling about mysterious lights in the sky … portents and celestial signs. Someone said something about the spectacle outside being more impressive than the *Star Wars* effects inside the theater. Apparently the main pagoda of the temple had seemed on fire for a few minutes and they'd called in a fire-fighting squad from the next town. "Who'd have thought of it?" my grandmother was complaining. "A demon visits Prasongburi—and makes straight for my own grandson!"

When we got to the shop—Mary still tagging behind and furiously taking notes on our social customs—the situation was even worse. The skirmish between my father and mothers had crescendoed to an all-out war.

"That's why I came to fetch you, children," my grandmother said. "Maybe you can referee this boxing match." A hefty celadon pot came whistling through the air and shattered on the overhead electric fan. We scurried for cover … all except my brother, who obliviously crawled about on his hands and knees, occasionally spouting lines from *Star Wars.*

Shrieking, Mary ran after the potshards. "My god, that's thing's eight hundred years old —"

"Bah! I faked it last week," my grandmother said, forcing the *farang* woman to gape in mingled horror and admiration.

"All right, all right," my father said, fleeing from the back room with my mothers in hot pursuit. "I won't marry her … but I want a little more kindness out of the two of you … oh, my terrible karma."

He tripped over my brother and went sprawling to the floor. "What's wrong with him?"

"You fool!" my grandmother said. "Your own son has become possessed by demons … and it's all because of your sexual excesses."

My father stopped and stared at my brother. Then, murmuring a brief prayer to the Lord Buddha, he retired cowering behind the shop counter. "What must I do?"

His wives came marching out behind him. Elder Mother hastened to succor Phi Lek. Younger Mother took in the situation and said, "I haven't seen anyone this possessed since my cousin Phii Daeng spent the night in a graveyard trying to get a vision of a winning lottery ticket number."

"It's all your fault," Phi Lek's mother said, turning wrathfully on my father. "You're all too eager to douse your staff of passion, and now my son has been turned into a monster!" The logic of this accusation escaped me, but my father seemed convinced.

"I'll go and *buat phra* for three months," he said, affecting a tone of deep piety. "I'll cut my hair off tomorrow and enter the nearest monastery. That ought to do the trick. Oh, my son, my son, what have I done?"

"Well," my grandmother said, "a little abstinence should do you good. I always thought you were unwise not to enter the monkhood at twenty like an obedient son should … cursing me to be reborn on earth instead of spending my next life in heaven as I ought, considering how I've worked my fingers to the bone for you! It's about time, that's what I say. A twenty-year-old belongs in a temple, not in the village scouts killing communists. Time for that when you've done your filial duty … well, twenty-five years late is better than nothing."

Seeing himself trapped between several painful alternatives, my father bowed his hand, raised his palms in a gesture of respect, and said, "All right, *khun mae yaai,* if that's what you want."

***

When my father and the elder females of the family had left to pack his things, I was left with my older brother and with the bizarre American woman, in the antique shop in the middle of the night. They had taken the truck back to the village (which now boasted a good half-dozen motor vehicles, one of them ours) and we were stranded. In the heat of their argument and my father's repentance, they seemed to have forgotten all about us.

It was at that moment that my brother chose to snap out of whatever it was that possessed him.

Calmly he rose from the floor, wiped a few foam flecks from his mouth with his sleeve, and sat down on the stool behind the counter. It took him a minute or two to recognize us, and then he said, "Well, well, Ai Noi! I gave the family quite a scare, didn't I?"

I was even more frightened now than I had been before. I knew very well that night is the time of spirits, and I was completely convinced that some spirit or another had taken hold of Phii Lek, though I was unsure about the part about my father being punished for his roving eyes and hands. I said, "Yes, *Khun Phii,* it was the most astonishing performance I've ever seen. Indeed, a bit too astonishing, if you don't mind your Humble Younger Sibling saying so. I mean, do you think they really appreciated it? If you ask me, you were just fiddling for waterbuffaloes."

"The most amazing thing is this … they weren't even after me!" He pointed at Mary. "They're in the wrong brain! It was her they wanted. But we all look alike to them. And I was imitating a woman's voice when they were trying to get a fix on the psychic transference. So they made an error of a few decimal places, and—poof!—here I am!"

"Pen baa pai laew!" I whispered to Mary Mason.

"I heard that!" my brother riposted. "But I am not mad. I am quite, quite sane, and I have been taken over by a *manus tang dao.*"

"What's that?" Mary asked me. "A foreigner?"

"No, no, not *tang dào* with a falling tone. That would mean a foreigner. I mean *tang dao* with a level tone. That means a being from another star."

"Far frigging out! An extraterrestrial!" she said in English. I didn't understand a word of it; I thought it must be some kind of anthropology jargon.

"Look, I can't talk long, but … you see, they're after Mary. One of them is trying to send a message to America … something to do with the Khmer ruins … some kind of artifact … to another of these creatures who is walking around in the body of a professor at UCLA. This *farang* woman seemed ideal; she could journey back without causing any suspicion. But, you see, we all look alike to them, and —"

"Well, can't you tell whatever it is to stop inhabiting your body and transfer itself to—?"

"Hell, no!" Mary said, and started to back away. "Native customs are all very well, but this is a bit more than I bargained for."

"Psychic transference too difficult … additional expenditure of energy impractical at present stage … but message must get through … " Suddenly he clawed at his throat for a few moments, and then fell writhing to the floor in another fit. "Can't get used to this gravity," he moaned. "Legs instead of pseudopods— and the contents of the stomach make me sick—there's at least fifty whole undigested chilies down here—oh, I'm going to puke —"

"By Buddha, Dharma and Sangkha!" I cried. "Quick, Mary, help me with. Give me something to catch his vomit."

"Will this do?" she said, pulling down something from the shelf. Distractedly I motioned her to put it up to his mouth.

Only when he had begun regurgitating into the bowl did I realize what she's done. "You imbecile!" I said. "That's a genuine Ming spittoon!"

"I thought they were all fakes," she said, holding up my brother as he slowly turned green.

"We do have some *genuine* items here," I said disdainfully, "for those who can tell the difference."

"You mean, for *Thai* collectors," she said, hurt.

"Well, what can you expect?" I said, becoming furious. "You come here, you dig up all our ancient treasures, violate the chastity of our women —"

"Look who's talking!" Mary said gently. "Male chauvinist pig," she added in English.

"Let's not fight," I said. "He seems better now … what are we going to do with him?"

"Here. Help me drag him to the back room."

We lifted him up and laid him down on the couch.

We looked at each other in the close, humid, mosquito-infested room. Suddenly, providentially almost, the airconditioning kicked on. "I've been trying to get it to work all day," I whispered.

"Does this mean —"

"Yes! Soon it will cool enough to —"

She kissed me on the lips. By morning I had "arrived" in America several delicious times, and Mary was telephoning the hotel in Ban Kraduk so she could get her things moved into my father's house.

***

The next morning, over dinner, I tried to explain it all to my elders. On the one hand there was this *farang* woman sitting on the floor, clumsily rolling rice balls with one hand and attempting to address my mothers as *khun mae,* much to their discomfiture; on the other there was the mystery of my brother, who was now confined to his room and refused to eat anything with any chilies in it.

"It's your weird western ways," my grandmother said, eyeing my latest conquest critically. "No chilies indeed! He'll be demanding hamburgers next."

"It's nothing to do with western ways," I said.

"It's a *manus tang dao,*" Mary said, proudly displaying her latest lexical gem, "and it's trying to get a message to America, and there's some kind of artifact in the ruins that they need, and they travel by some kind of psychic transference —"

"You Americans are crazy!" my grandmother said, spitting out her betelnut so she could take a few mouthfuls of curried fish. "Any fool can see the boy's possessed. I remember my great-uncle had fits like this when he promised a donation of five hundred baht to the Sacred Pillar of the City and then reneged on his offer. My parents had to pay off the Brahmins—with interest!—before the curse was lifted. Oh, my karma, my karma!"

"Shouldn't we call in some scientists, or something? A psychiatrist?" Mary said.

"Nothing of the sort!" said my grandmother. "If we can't take care of this in the home, we'll not take care of it at all. No one's going to say my grandson is crazy. Possessed, maybe ... everyone can sympathize with that ... but crazy, never! The family honor is at stake."

"Well, what should we do?" I said helplessly. As the junior member of the family, I had no say in the matter at all. I was annoyed at Mary for mentioning psychiatrists, but I reminded myself that she was, after all, a barbarian, even though she could speak a human tongue after a fashion.

"We'll wait," grandmother said, "and see whether your father's penance will do the trick. If not … well, our stars are bad, that's all."

***

During the weeks to come, my brother became increasingly odd. He would enter the house without even removing his sandals, let alone washing his feet. When my Uncle Eed came to dinner one night, my brother actually pointed his left foot at our honored uncle's head. I would be most surprised if Uncle Eed ever came to dinner again after such unforgivable rudeness. I was forced to go into town every evening to dub the movies, which I did in so lackluster a manner that our usual audience began walking the two hours to Ban Kraduk for their entertainment. My heart sank when a passing visitor to the shop told me that the Ban Kraduk cinema had actually installed a projection sound system and could show talkies … not only the foreign films, with sound and subtitles, but the new domestic talkies … so you could actually find out what great actors like Mitr and Petchara sounded like! I knew we'd never compete with that. I knew the days of live movie dubbing were numbered. Maybe I could go to Bangkok and get a job with Channel 7, dubbing *Leave it to Beaver* and *Charlie's Angels.* But Bangkok was just about as distant as another galaxy, and I could imagine the fun those city people would have with my hick northern accent.

One night about two weeks later, Mary and I were

awakened by my brother, moaning from the mosquito net next to ours. I went across.

"Oh, there you are," Phii Lek said. "I've been trying to attract your attention for hours."

"I was busy," I said, and my brother leered knowingly. "Are you all right? Are you recovered?"

"Not exactly," he said. "But I'm, well, off-duty. The alien'll come back any minute, though, so I can't talk long." He paused. "Maybe that girlfriend of yours should hear this," he said. At that moment Mary crept in beside us, and we crouched together under the netting. The electric fan made the nets billow like ghosts.

"You have to take me to that archaeological dig of yours," he said. "There's an artifact ... it's got some kind of encoded information ... you have to take it back to Professor Übermuth at UCLA —"

"I've heard of him!" Mary whispered. "He's in a loony bin. Apparently he became convinced he was an extraterre— oh, Jesus!" she said in English.

"He *is* one," Phii Lek said. "So am I. There are hundreds us on this planet. But my controlling alien's resting right now. Look, Ai Noi, I want you to go down to the kitchen and get me as many chili peppers as you can find. On the *manus tang dao*'s home planet the food is about as bland as rice soup."

I hurried to obey. When I got back, he wolfed down the peppers until he started weeping from the influx of spiciness. Suspiciously I said, "If you're really an alien, what about spaceships?"

"Spaceships ... we do have them, but they are drones, taking millennia to reach the center of the galaxy. We ourselves travel by tachyon psychic transference. But the device is being sent by drone."

"Device?"

"From the excavation! Haven't you been listening? It's got to be dug up and secretly taken to America and ... I'm not sure what or why, but I get the feeling there's danger if we don't make our rendezvous. Something to do with upsetting the tachyon fields."

"I see," I said, humoring him.

"You know what I look like on the home planet, up there? I look like a giant *mangdaa*."

"What's that?" said Mary.

"It's sort of a giant cockroach," I said. "We use its wings to flavor some kinds of curry."

"Yech!" she squealed. "Eating insects. Gross!"

"What do you mean? You've been enjoying it all week, and you've never complained about eating insects," I said. She started to turn slightly bluish. A *farang's* complexion, when he or she is about to be sick, is one of the few truly indescribable hues on the face of this earth.

"Help me ..." Phii Lek said. "The sooner this artifact is unearthed and loaded onto the drone, the sooner I'll be released from this—oh, no, it's coming back!" Frantically he gobbled down several more chilies. But it was too late. They came right back up again, and he was scampering around the room on all fours and emitting pigeonlike cooing noises.

"Come to think of it," I said, "he <u>is</u> acting rather like a cockroach, isn't he?"

***

A week later I our home was invaded by nine monks. My mothers had been cooking all the previous day, and when I came into the main living room they had already been chanting for about an hour, their bass voices droning from behind huge prayer fans. The house was fragrant with jasmine and incense.

I prostrated myself along with the other members of the

family. My brother was there too, wriggling around on his belly; his hands were tied up with a sacred rope which ran all the way around the house and through the folded palms of each of the monks. Among them was my father, who looked rather self conscious and didn't seem to know all the words of the chants yet ... now and then he seemed to be opening his mouth at random, like a goldfish.

"This isn't going to work," I whispered to my grandmother, who was kneeling in the *pab phieb* position with her palms folded, her face frozen in an expression of beatific piety. "Mary and I have found out what the problem is, and it's not possession."

"*Buddhang sarnang gacchami,*" the monks intoned in unison.

"What are they talking about?" Mary said. She was properly prostrate, but seemed distracted. She was probably uncomfortable without her trusty notebook.

"I haven't the faintest idea. It's all in Pali or Sanskrit or something," I said.

"*Namodasa phrakhavato arahato —*" the monks continued inexorably.

At length they laid their prayer fans down and the chief *luangphoh* began doused a spray of twigs in a silver dipper of lustral water and began to sprinkle Phii Lek liberally.

"It's got to be over soon," I said to Mary. "It's getting toward noon, and you know monks are not allowed to eat after twelve o'clock."

As the odor of incense wafted over me and the chanting continued, I fell into a sort of trance. These were familiar feelings, sacred feelings. Maybe my brother <u>was</u> in the grip of some supernatural force that could be driven out by the proper application of Buddha, Dharma and Sangkha. However, as the *luangphoh* became ever more frantic, waving the twigs energetically over my writhing brother to no avail,

I began to lose hope.

Presently the monks took a break for their one meal of the day, and we took turns presenting them with trays of delicacies. After securing my brother carefully to the wall with the sacred twine, I went to the kitchen, where my grandmother was grinding fresh betelnut with a mortar and pestle. To my surprise, my father was there too. It was rather a shock to see him wearing a saffron robe and bald, when I was so used to seeing him barechested with a *phakhoma* loosely wrapped about his loins, and with a whiskey bottle rather than a begging bowl in his arms. I did not know whether to treat him as father or monk. To be on the safe side, I fell on my knees and placed my folded palms reverently at his feet.

My father was complaining animatedly to my grandmother in a weird mixture of normal talk and priestly talk. Sometimes he'd remember to refer to himself as *atma*, but at other times he'd speak like anyone off the street. He was saying, "But mother, *atma* is miserable, they only feed you once a day, and I'm hornier than ever! It's obviously not going to work, so why don't I just come home?"

My grandmother continued to pound vigorously at her betelnut.

"Anyway, *atma* thinks that it's time for more serious measures. I mean, calling in a professional exorcist."

At this, my grandmother looked up. "Perhaps you're right, holy one," she said. I could see that it galled her to have to address her wayward son-in-law in terms of such respect. "But can we afford it?"

"Phra Boddhisatphalo, *atma's* guru, is an astrologer on the side, and he's says that the stars for the movie theater are exceptionally bad. Well, *atma* was thinking, why not perform an act of merit while simultaneously ridding ourselves of a potential financial liability? I say sell out the half-share of the cinema and use the proceeds to hire a really competent exorcist. Besides," he added slyly, "with the rest of the cash I could probably obtain me one of those nieces of yours, the ones whose beauty your daughters are always bragging about."

"You despicable cad," my grandmother began, and then added, "holy one," to be on the safe side of the karmic balance.

"Honored father and grandmother," I ventured, "have you not considered the notion that Phii Lek's body might indeed be inhabited by an extraterrestrial being?"

"I fail to see the difference," my father said, "between a being from another planet and one from another spiritual plane. It is purely a matter of attitude. You and your brother, whose wits have been addled by exposure to too many American movies, think in terms of visitations from the stars; your grandmother and I, being older and wiser, know that 'alien' is merely another word for spirit. Earthly or unearthly, we are all spokes in the wheel of karma, no? Exorcism ought to work on both."

I didn't like my father's new approach at all; I thought his drunkenness far more palatable than his piety. But of course this would have been an unconscionably disrespectful thing to say, so I merely *wai*-ed in obeisance and waited for the ordeal to end.

My grandmother said, "Well, son-in-law, I can see a certain progress in you after all." My father turned around and winked at me. "Very well," she said, sighing heavily, "perhaps your mentor can find us a decent exorcist. But none of those foreigners, mind you," she added pointedly as Mary entered the kitchen to fetch another tray of comestibles for the monks' feast.

    ***

The interview with the spirit doctor was set for the following week. By that time the wonder of my brother's possession had attracted tourists from a radius of some ten kilometers; his performances were so spectacular as to outdraw even the talking cinema in Ban Kraduk.

It turned out to be a Brahmin, tall, dark, white-robed, with a long white beard that trailed all the way down to the floor. He wore a necklace of bones—they looked suspiciously human—and several flower wreaths over his uncut, wispy hair; moreover he had an elaborate third eye painted in the middle of his forehead.

"Narayana, Narayana," he said, with the portentousness of a paunchy deva in one of those Indian historical movies. This, I realized, was a sham to impress the credulous populace, who were swarming around the stilts of our house. One or two children were peering from behind the horns of waterbuffaloes, and one was even peeping from a huge rainwater jar. The Brahmin had an acolyte just for the purpose of removing his sandals and splashing his feet from the foot-washing trough, an occupation of such ignominy that I was surprised even a boy would stoop to it. He surveyed my family (which had been suddenly expanded by visiting cousins, aunts, uncles, and several other grandmothers junior to my own) and inquired haughtily, "And which of you is the possessed one?"

"He can't even tell?" my grandmother whispered to me. Then she pointed at Phii Lek, who was crawling around the front porch moaning "tachyon, tachyon."

"Ah," said the exorcist. "A classic case of possession by a *phii krasue*. Dire measures are indicated, I'm afraid."

At the mention of the dreaded *phii krasue*, the entire family recoiled as a single entity. For the *phii krasue* is, as everyone knows, a spirit who looks like a normal enough creature in the daytime, but at night detaches its head from its body and, dragging its entrails behind it, propels itself forward by its tongue. It also lives on human excrement. It is, in short, one of the most loathsome and feared of spirits. The idea that we might have been harboring one in our very house sent chills of terror through me.

Presently I heard dissenting voices. "But a *phii krasue* can't act this way in the daytime!" one said. "Anyway, where's the trail of guts?" said another. "This fellow's obviously a quack ... never trust a Brahmin exorcist, I tell you." "Well, let's give him the benefit. See if he comes up with anything."

The Brahmin spirit doctor took a good look at us, clearly appraising our finances. "Can he be cured?" my Elder Mother asked him.

"Given your very secure monetary standing," the Brahmin said, "I see no reason why not. You can take him inside now; I shall discuss the—ah, your merit-making donation—with the head of the household."

My grandmother came forward, her palms uplifted in supplication. "Fetch him a drink," she muttered to my mothers.

My mother said, "Does the *than mo phii* want a glass of water? Or would he prefer Coca-Cola?"

"A glass of Mekong whiskey," said the spirit doctor firmly. "Better yet, bring the whole bottle. We'll probably be haggling all night."

***

Since Phii Lek was no longer the center of attention, Mary and I obeyed the spirit doctor and brought him inside. He chose that moment to snap back into a state of relative sanity. We knew he had come to because he immediately began demanding chili peppers.

"All right," he said at last. "I've been authorized to tell

you a few more things, since it seems to be the only hope."

"What about that monstrous charlatan out there?" Mary said. "He's only going to delay your plans, isn't he?"

"Not necessarily. I want you to insist that he perform the exorcism *at* the archaelogical dig. Once there, I'll be able to home in on the device and get rid of the giant cockroach at the same time. You know, that exorcist wasn't far wrong when he said I'd been possessed by a *phii krasue*. Would you be interested in knowing what my alien overlords like for dinner?"

"I take it they're scavengers?" Mary said.

"Exactly," said my brother. "But no more of this excremental subject. You have to convince that exorcist of yours. Unless the device is returned, there will be awful consequences. You see, the aliens were here once before, about eight hundred years ago. They planted a number of these devices as ... well, tachyon calibration beacons. Well, this one is going dangerously out of synch, and some of the aliens aren't ending up in the bodies they're were destined for. I mean, this psychic transference business is expensive, and the military ruler of nine star systems doesn't want to get thrust into the body of a leprous janitor from Milwaukee. That is precisely what happened last week, and the diplomatic consequences happen to be rippling through the entire galaxy at this very minute. Anyway, if the beacon is sent back post-haste for deactivation, guess who gets it?"

"You?" I said.

"Worse. They call it a preventative measure. They randomize the solar system."

"I think that's a euphemism for —" Mary began.

"That's right, Beloved Younger Siblings! No more planet earth."

"Can they really do that?" I said.

"They do it all the time." My brother reverted for a

moment to cockroachlike behavior, then jerked back into a human pose with great effort. "They might not, though. All the xenobiologists, primitive cult fetishists, and so on are up in arms. So it might happen today ... it might happen in a couple of years ... it might never happen. Who knows? But galactic central things that no world, no matter how puny or insignificant, should be randomized without due process. But ... I don't think we should risk it, do you?"

"Maybe not," I said. The theory that my brother had contracted one of those American mental diseases, like schizophrenia, was becoming more and more attractive to me. But I had to do what he said. To be on the safe side.

Mary and I left Phii Lek and went out to the porch, where the spirit doctor had consumed half the whiskey and they had lit the anti-mosquito tapers, whose smoke perfumed the dense night air.

"Excuse me, honored grandmother," I said, trying to sound as unassuming as I could, "but Phii Lek says he wants the exorcism done at Mary's archaeological dig."

"Ha!" the exorcist said. "One must always do the opposite of what a possessed person said, for the evil spirit in him strives always to delude us!" His sentiments were expressed with such resounding ferocity that there was a burst of applause from crowd downstairs. "Besides," he added, "there's probably a whole arm of *phii krasue* out there, just waiting to swallow us up. It's a trap, I tell you! This possession is merely the vanguard of a wholesale demonic invasion!"

I looked despairingly at Mary. "Now what'll we do?" I said. "Sit around waiting for the earth to disappear?"

It was Mary who came to the rescue ... and I realized how much she had absorbed by quietly observing us and taking all those notes. She said, speaking in a Thai far more heavily accented than she normally used, "But please, honored spirit doctor, the field study group would be most interested in seeing a real live exorcism!"

The spirit doctor looked decidedly uncertain at being addressed in Thai by a *farang.* I could tell the questions racing through his mind: what status should the woman be accorded? She wasn't related to any of these people, nor was her social position immediately obvious. How could he respond without accidentally using the wrong pronoun, and giving her too much or little status—and perhaps rendering himself the laughingstock of these potential clients?

Taking advantage of his confusion, Mary pursued relentlessly. "Or does the honored spirit doctor perhaps *klua phii?"*

"Of course I'm not afraid of spirits!" the exorcist said.

"Then why would a few extra ones bother the honored spirit doctor?" Mary contrived to speak in so unprepossessing an accent that it was impossible to tell whether her polite words were ingenuous or insulting.

"Bah!" said the spirit doctor. "A few *phii krasue* are nothing. It's just a matter of convenience, that's all... ."

"I'm sure that the foundation that's sponsoring our field research here would be more than happy to make a small donation toward ameliorating the inconvenience... ."

"Since you put it that way... ." the exorcist said, defeated.

"Hmpf!" my grandmother said, triumphantly yanking the half-bottle of whiskey away and sending my mother back to the kitchen with it. "These *farangs* might be some use after all. They're as ugly as elephants, of course—and albino elephants at that—but who knows? One day their race may yet amount to something."

***

The whole street opera of an exorcism was in full swing by the time my brother, Mary and I pulled parked her official

Landrover about a half hour's walk away from the site. It had taken a week to make the preparations, with my brother's moments of lucidity getting briefer and his eschatological claims wilder each time.

By the time we had trudged through fields of young rice, squishing kneedeep in mud, several hundred people had gathered to watch. A good hundred or so were relatives of mine. Mary introduced me to some colleagues of hers, professors and suchlike, and they eyed me with curiosity as I fumbled around in their intractable language.

Four broken pagodas were silhouetted in the sunset. A waterbuffalo nuzzled at the pediment of an enormous stone Buddha, to whom I instinctively raised my palms in respect. Here and there, erupting from the brilliant green of the fields of young rice, were fragments of fortifications and walls topped with complex friezes that depicted grim, barbaric gods and garlanded, singing *apsaras*. A row of trunkless stucco elephants guarded a gateway to another paddy field.

Every part of the ruined city had been girded round with a *saisin*, a sacred rope that had been strung up along the walls and along the stumps of the elephant trunks and through the stone portals and finally into the folded palms of the spirit doctor himself, who sat, in the lotus position, on a woven rush mat, surrounded by a cloud of incense.

"You're late," he said angrily as we hastened to seat ourselves within the protected circle. "Get inside, inside. Or do you want to be swallowed up by spirits?"

If I had thought Phii Lek's actions bizarre before, his performance now shifted into an even more hyperbolic gear. He groaned. He danced about, his body coiling and coiling like a serpent.

I heard my grandmother cry out, *"Ui ta then!* Nuns dropping into the basement!" It was the strongest language I'd ever heard her use.

Mary clutched my hand. Some of my relatives stared disapprovingly at the impropriety, but I decided that they were just jealous.

"And now we'll see which it is to be," Mary said. "Science fiction or fantasy."

"He's mumbling himself into a trance now," I said, pointing to the exorcist, who had closed his eyes and from whose lips a strange buzzing issued.

"Are you sure he's not snoring?" one of my mothers said maliciously.

"What tranquillity! What perfect *samadhi!*" my other mother said admiringly, for the spirit doctor hadn't moved a muscle in some ten minutes.

Phii Lek's contortions became positively unnerving. He darted about the sacred circle, now and then flapping his arms as though to fly. Suddenly a bellow—like the cry of an angry waterbuffalo—burst from his lips. He flapped again and again—and then rose into the air!

"Be still, I command thee!" the exorcist's voice thundered, and he waved a rattle at my levitating brother and made mysterious passes. "I tell thee, be still!"

A ray of light shot upward from the earth, dazzlingly bright. The pagodas were lit up eerily. The ground opened up under Phii Lek as he hovered. There he was, brilliantly lit up in the pillar of radiance, with an iridiscent aura around him whose outlines vaguely resembled an enormous cockroach… .

The crowd was going wild now. They clamored, they cheered; some of the children were disobeying the sacred cord and having to be restrained by their elders. My brother was sitting, in lotus position, in the middle of the air with his palms folded, looking just like a postcard of the Emerald Buddha in Bangkok.

The flaming apparition that had been my brother

descended into the pit. We all rushed to the edge. The light from the abyss burned our eyes; we were blinded. Mary took advantage of the confusion to embrace me tightly; I was too overwhelmed to castigate her.

We waited.

The earth rumbled.

At last a figure crawled out. He was covered in mud and filth. He was clutching something under his arm ... something very much like a Ming spittoon.

"Phii Lek!" I cried out, overcome with relief that he was still alive.

"The tachyon calibrator —" he gasped, holding aloft the spittoon and waving it dramatically in the air. "You must get it to... ."

He fainted, still clasping the alien device firmly to his bosom.

The light shifted ... the ghostly, rainbow-fringed giant cockroach seemed to drift slowly across the field, toward the unmoving figure of the exorcist ... it danced grotesquely above his head, and he began to twitch and foam at the mouth... .

"I'll be dead!" my grandmother shouted. "The spirit is transferring itself into the body of the exorcist!"

In a moment the exorcist too fainted, and the sacred cord fell from his hands. The circle was broken. Whatever was done was done.

I rushed to the side of my brother, still lying prone by the side of the abyss.

"Wake up!" I said, shaking him. "Please wake up!"

He got up and grinned. Applause broke out. The exorcist, too, seemed to be recovering from his ordeal.

"And now," my brother said, holding out the alien artifact, "I can return this thing to the person who was sent to fetch it."

A small, white, palpitating hand was stretched forward to receive it. I turned to see who it was. "Oh, no," I said softly.

For it was Mary who had taken the artifact … and Mary who was now gyrating about the paddy field in a most unfeminine, most cockroachlike manner.

***

Later that night, Phii Lek and I sat on the floor of our room, waiting for Mary to snap out of her extraterrestrial seizure so we could find out what had happened.

Toward dawn the alien gave her her first break. "I can talk now," she said, suddenly, calmly.

"Do you need chilies?" I said.

"I think a good hamburger would be more my style," she said.

"We can probably fake it," my brother said, "if you don't mind having it on rice instead of a bun."

"Well," she said, when my brother had finished clattering about the kitchen fixing this unorthodox meal, and she was sitting cross-legged on my bedding munching furiously, "I suppose I should tell you what I'm allowed to tell you."

"Take your time," I said, not meaning it.

"Okay. Well, as you know, the exorcist is a total fake, a charlatan, a mountebank. But he does enter a passable state of *samadhi,* and apparently this was close enough to the psychic null state necessary for psychic transference to enable a mindswap to occur over a short distance. His blank mind was a sort of catalyst, if you will, through which, under the influence of the tachyon calibrator, I could leave Phii Lek's mind and enter Mary's."

"So you'll be taking the spittoon back to America?" I said.

"Right on schedule. And it's not a spittoon. That happens to be a very clever disguise."

"So… ." It suddenly occurred to me that she would soon

be leaving. I was irritated at that. I didn't know why. I should have been pleased, because, after all, I had essentially traded her for my brother, and family always comes first.

"Look," she said, noticing my unease, "do you think … maybe … one last time?" She caressed my arm.

"But you're a giant cockroach!" I said.

She kissed me.

"You've been bragging to your friends all month about 'arriving' in America," she said. "How'd you like to 'arrive' on another planet?"

***

In the middle of the act I became aware that someone else was there with us. I mean, I was used to the way Mary moved, the delicious abandon with which she made her whole body shudder. I thought, "The alien's here too! Well, I'm really going to show it how a Thai can drive. Here we go!"

The next morning, I said, "How was it?"

She said, "It was a fascinating activity, but frankly I prefer mitosis."

Fiddling for waterbuffaloes.

***

In a day or so I saw her off; I went back to the antique store; I found my grandmother hard at work in her antique faking studio. A perfect Ming spittoon lay beside her where she squatted. She saw me, spat out her betelnut, and motioned me to sit.

"Why, grandmother," I said, "That's a perfect copy of whatever it was the alien took to America."

"Look again, my grandson," she said, and chuckled to herself as she rocked back and forth kneading clay.

I picked it up. The morning light shone on it through the

window. I had an inkling that … no. Surely not. "You didn't!" I said.

She didn't answer.

"Grandmother… ."

No answer.

"But the solar system is at stake!" I blurted out. "If they find out that they've got the wrong tachyon callibrator… ."

"Maybe, maybe not," said my grandmother. "The way I think is this: it's obviously very important to someone, and anything that valuable is worth faking. You say these interstellar diplomats will be arguing the question for years, perhaps. Well, as the years go by, the price will undoubtedly go up."

"But *khun yaai,* how can you possibly play games with the destiny of the entire human race like this?"

"Oh, come, come. I'm just an old woman looking out for her family. The movie house has been sold, and we've lost maybe 50,000 baht on the exorcism and the feast. Besides, your father will insist on another wife, I'm afraid, and after all this brouhaha I can't blame him. We'll be out 100,000 baht by the time we're through. I have a perfect right to some kind of recompense. Hopefully, by the time they come looking for this thing, we'll be able to get enough for it to open a whole antique factory … who knows, move to Bangkok … buy up Channel Seven so your brother can dub movies to his heart's content."

"But couldn't the alien tell?" I said.

"Of course not. How many experts on disguised tachyon callibrators do you think there are, anyway?" My grandmother paused to turn the electric fan so that it blew exclusively on herself. The airconditioning, as usual, was off. "Anyway, *manus tang dao* are only another kind of foreigner, and anyone can tell you that all foreigners are suckers."

I heard the bell ring in the front.

"Go on!" she said. "There's a customer!"

"But what if —"   I got up with some trepidation. At the partition I hesitated.

"Courage!" she whispered. "Be a *luk phuchai!*"

I remembered that I had the family honor to think of. Boldly, I marched out to meet the next customer.

Tagging The Moon

I was there the night they shot Bobby Donahue. I saw him cartwheel through the air from the top edge of the overpass down toward the screaming traffic. But I never saw him hit the pavement. Nobody did. Not me, not the police, not even the dudes in the Fox 11 news chopper. I never saw him die.

And that's how I know that everything Bobby told me, and I saw, is true … the visions … the revelations … the aliens from another world.

It's hard to be a has-been at twenty-four, but that's what I was back in the summer of '92. I lived under an overpass with a half dozen homies. On the first Tuesday of the month I sold my blood; Saturdays I sold my sister. My sister was sullen and pockmarked and usually fetched less than what Dr. Sayeed paid for a pint of my extra rare blood type. But hey, I was doing her a favor compared to the shit they made her do at the home.

I wasn't a basehead no more, but I could still put away a fifth of Jim Beam all by myself, and that's what I liked to do Sundays. That, or sit leaning against the monuments at

Forest Lawn, far from the roar over the freeway, or kicking it in the old hood, up toward Sylmar, where I had like family, which I never spoke to, and friends, which I did.

And then there were the kids—the ones that looked up to me—the ones who had heard the stories. Half the stories were bullshit but they had enough truth in them that I had a hard time denying them. I'd known Bobby Donahue since he was five years old, which was when they moved to the trailer park off of Hubbard, maybe ten years ago. But he was like maybe fourteen when he started to hang with the other kids on the corner of Jackman. He was a dreamy kid who always read books and always understood what people were talking about on television. I don't know why he got into tagging. Maybe it was because his father blew off to Arizona and his mom became the neighborhood slut. Maybe it was because he stopped going to school, said it bored him. Maybe it was because his brother shot himself in the head with a .38. Shit, I don't know, but I ended up father, mother, and brother to him, even though I only saw him maybe once every two or three weekends ... whenever they weren't detaining him overnight or switching his social worker on him.

Bobby was obsessed with tagging. You'd be walking down the street together past that waist-high picket fence, just kicking it and talking about some dope bitch you saw last night, and then, glancing back, you see that every one of them pickets had a name, and that name was *NOVA,* which means an exploding star, with a rainbow-colored starburst over the *O.* And you'd be thinking, how the fuck'd *that* get there? Bobby was quick. Anything with a white surface wide enough to fit him seem to call out to him. He tagged with Mean Streaks, markers, spray cans, acrylics, pastels, crayons, finger paint, and at least once with his own blood.

Which is why I don't go back to the old hood that much no more.

Bobby's favorite saying was, "One day, I'm a tag the fucking *moon*. You'll fucking see then, everyone's gonna see me up."

I can still see him now, that last week. He was kind of small for his age. He had squinty dark green eyes and a mass of dirty brown hair, and he dressed like a cholo, in them oversize pants. He smelled of leather and tobacco. He was going to be sixteen soon, the magic age when driving becomes legal and crime stops paying, but he still had the look that gets you into movies for half price. He totally hated the idea of turning sixteen, and he was hanging out with me a lot, riding the RTD over the Hill and meeting me, as though by accident, next to my favorite dumpster or somewhere in Forest Lawn, gazing at the tombs of the rich and famous.

Or just in Hollywood somewhere, browsing at the Cahuenga newsstand. "Yo, buy my ass a burger, dude ... I ain't eaten in like days."

"Why not?" I'm putting down this copy of *Fat Leather Chicks* that I've been leafing through, wondering if they'll throw him out for loitering by the porn. "Don't you have a home to go to no more?"

"Shit no. Dad's in detox and Mom's at some big old battered women's shelter. Come on, just one burger, I'll totally pay you back."

"Yeah, right." I'm still all flush from selling blood to Dr. Sayeed. So we walk down to the McDonalds on Hollywood Boulevard and he eats more than just one burger: he gets three Big Macs plus two orders of fries, and I'm all watching him, wondering where it can all go.

"Tag the moon yet?" I ask him in the interval between a Big Mac and a gulp of Coke.

"Working on it," he says. And he sounds like he means it.

He usually has something on his mind when he comes all the way into Hollywood to find me, but I know that he's going to take his own sweet time getting to the point. So I wait. He tells me he's been tagging all over. "In one night," he says, "I hit up Van Nuys, Pacoima, Sun Valley, Studio City, and Reseda. You know that ten story building with the big Marilyn Monroe all the way down one side? I'm up on Marilyn's left tit, dude, I hid in the bathroom of some law office until after the closed and then I like climbed out along the ledge and I hung there with my legs wrapped around a flagpole, fucking *hung* there, and I wrote *Nova* all the way around her nipple. Wore out three Mean Streaks doing it, too," he adds. "I'll have to punk the stationery store for some more."

"Let me buy them for you, dude. It's a shame for you to get busted stealing markers." I knew what jail was like; Bobby didn't.

"You'd do that for me? Thanks, Todd." He looked at me with the kind of hero-worship I was getting less and less of these days.

"We didn't even have Mean Streaks in my day," I said. "Just spray cans and shit. No high technology."

"I love it when you old guys talk about them Stone Age times." The thing about that is, he was only half joking. To be twenty-four years old, in the minds of the kids Bobby Donahue hung out with, was to be a relic of an ancient civilization. "But you're the best," he said. "Last night I saw you still up on the 'F' on the roof of the Wells Fargo bank on Victory. That's been there almost all my life. None of my friends know how you did it. And nobody's fucking been able to wipe it off. And all them freeway signs. The piece you threw on the back of *Van Nuys Bvd—3/4 mile* ... you must of fucking had wings to get up there without getting caught."

He wolfed down another burger.

"Maybe we all had wings in them Stone Age days," I said, laughing.

Then Bobby's all, "You're probably wondering why I came looking for you all the way down in Hollywood. Dude, I been looking for you half the night. It's important."

"Okay." Out of the corner of my eye, up at the corner, I could see two kids stealing a car. They were too new at this to know that the seedy man with the WILL WORK FOR FOOD sign around his neck was a undercover cop. Life's a bitch. "What's your point?" I said.

"It's the aliens, dude. I been seeing them again. And like, now they want to meet you."

***

Okay, so maybe Bobby wasn't, like, all there. He had visions. He didn't need shrooming … his whole life was one long acid trip flashback. Once, he was maybe eight or nine, he was running for his life with four truant officers on his back, ready to slap the plastic ties around his wrists, and I saw him from the apartment window—I still had parents back then—and he was sprinting through traffic with his eyes closed, dodging the cars as they snarled and rammed one another to avoid him … but with the chaos raging around him he's all calm … concentrated … compacted into himself. He darted, he danced, he spun, beautiful as a pinball.

I ran down the stairs to let him into my building and he ran past me and I stopped the police at the door, I'm all, "Yeah, he's my brother, he's on C track, he ain't supposed to be in school until February …" Lying comes easy to me.

Then like, I turn around and see him and he asks me, "The aliens. Are they gone yet?"

"Police, Bobby. They were police."

"No, not *them,* Todd ... the *others!* They were in the boys' restroom when I was trying to pee. That's why I ditched."

***

Years later, I'm telling the story of this to Dr. Margaret Yao, who's some kind of therapist and who's writing a book about taggers. She's my friend, she thinks, though it's fucking transparent the way she tries to pump me for anecdotes she can use in her book.

"And what was Bobby Donahue doing when he had this ... ah ... extraterrestrial visitation?" she says, lighting her second joint from the butt end of her first.

"He was throwing a piece. On the bathroom wall."

"You mean putting up graffiti?" She notes my choice of words in the section of her notebook marked "special jargon".

"Well," I tell her, "piecing ain't the same as tagging. It's more complicated. It's when you do like, a whole picture ... kind of like *art.*"

She scribbles in her notebook. "But what I'm getting at," she says, "is this. The visitations from aliens ... they are associated with the graffiti somehow ... aren't they? So maybe it's his alienation speaking." She becomes all excited now. She pours me some of her special brew, Tsing Dao she calls it, some kind of Chinese beer. I love the way the Chinese characters curve around the beer can, the way the brushstrokes swell up and die away, like miniature waves. I wish I could write Chinese. Chinese is a tagger's dopeass dream language. I'm all watching the drops of condensation on the beer can and the way they distort the strokes of the calligraphy. I don't really hear Margaret when she launches into them theories of hers. She weaves them twenty-syllable words around each other like the way I used to write *Pricer* on the freeway signs, with the letters winding in and out of each other like snakes making love.

"Are you listening to me?" Margaret says. "Aliens and alienation. I mean, here's this kid, grows up on a diet of sci-fi, neglected, has a desperate need to throw up his ego-symbol all over town … the UFO angle's a natural. In the middle ages, he would've been seeing saints and angels. Like Joan of Arc did."

"Yeah," I say. "Can you lend me five bucks?"

She stops and looks at me like I'm a sort of a thing in a museum, which I guess, to her, I am. Every night she goes home to a one-bedroom in Tarzana, pool, jacuzzi, New Age music piped into the lobby. Shit.

She's all, "Are you a little short?"

"I'd love to buy like, a blanket. November's coming. There ain't no central heating in the overpass hotel. I saw a blanket in the dumpster Saturday, but it was on some Mexican dude's turf."

She goes on staring at me and I think she's getting, you know, *wet* over what I'm saying. I'm so horny I could fuck a hole in a toilet stall wall. She takes a five-dollar bill out of her purse and folds it and purses her lips, and she's all, "But tell me more about Bobby Donahue. He seems such a *character*, I mean, so full of the energy and rage of the streets."

"He's gone now," I said.

"Dead?" She tsk-tsked with the earnest sympathy they all seem to have, those Chinese women who went to Berkeley who live in Tarzana who are writing books about us who think they love us but who never ever know us.

"I didn't say *dead,* I said *gone.*"

"So you're into denial," she said. I tried to grab for the five bucks but it was just out of reach. Then she flicked it onto my lap.

***

So I'm all, "They want to meet me," as we deposit the trash and walk out onto Hollywood Boulevard, me in my year-old unwashed jeans and him in his cholo pants, ten sizes too big and freshly jacked from the swap meet. "You shrooming or something?"

Bobby skips from star to star alongside the street to the hip-hop beat of a sidewalk ghettoblaster. I walk as quick as I can but I don't know, I feel weak and old; maybe it's because I've been sapped of all that blood, maybe it's just I'm over the hill for being a street kid, just not up to it no more. I barely catch up to his ass when he's off again and yeah, when I glance over my shoulder there's the *Nova*-starburst up on the window of a B. Dalton, blocking the Rush Limbaugh dump display.

We turned down a side alley, a dead end, behind Cherokee. Where the alley met the boulevard there wasn't that much, just the usual gang initials, and, here and there, a name crossed out. But further in, here and there became a jumble, then a jungle ... letters and logos crisscrossing one another, melding into one great abstract swath of colors ... and full-scale pieces too ... there was a bad ass picture of the Rodney King beating, with Darrell Gates hovering over it in black robes and leathery wings and the eyes of a demon ... there was a dance of death, the old man with the sickle leading a capering procession of skaters, surfers, taggers, and gangbangers across a lurid cityscape silhouetted against vermilion flames ... there was a life-size Elvis in a *Hamlet* costume, with a guitar in one hand and a skull in the other ... there was a '57 Chevy pointing ass up from a sand dune circled by cactus … we saw all these things in the light from distant neon signs. And the names were everywhere, a whole history of tagging … names like, *Squirt, Tryer, Phaks, Silem, Carne,* kind of like the Vietnam Memorial, because like, half the taggers who were up were like, dead now, or maybe worse than dead, drowning in their own addictions, like me.

I saw myself up, real high, in the hardest to reach ass corner of the whole wall. *Pricer,* it still read, in the curlicue lettering style I invented which is now one of the most popular styles. Smog and acid rain had dulled the colors, but I still felt the tug of my own past self, and I wondered if I'd ever be free again.

I barely looked away and when I looked back up in the corner I saw *Nova* too, scrawled above me, and I saw the shadow of Bobby Donahue skittering down the wall … and I heard him laugh. Then he was right by me, smiling. "Jesus," I said, "you make me nervous, how you do that shit."

Bobby said, "It's like the story of the eagle and the robin; the eagle said he could fly the highest, but the robin rode on his back and like, when the eagle was so high he could barely flap his wings no more, the robin soared up a inch or two and won the bet."

"Where'd you hear that?" I knew his parents would never have told him a story, let alone his social worker or someone like that.

"The aliens told me," he said. And he pointed to the wall at the end of the blind alley, where there's a dope ass piece, maybe eight feet square, showing the L.A. riots, like, a view from a news chopper … and like, I see this black Porsche parked against the dead end, flush against the dumpster, with a homeless dude asleep against the wheel. The windows are all black and the license plate is black and it don't have no letters or numbers on it. It's a scary thing, because no way could this car have been driven into this position, stretched across the alley with each bumper a half inch or less from the walls; it was like the car had dropped into place out of the night sky. Still, there wasn't nothing *alien* about it. It was just a car.

I'm all, "Yeah. It's a car."

The door opens and there are two men: Laurel and Hardy—a tall man and a fat man. The fat man's all wearing surfer pants and a neon tank top and pink oversized shades. The tall man's dressed like an undertaker. But they look human to me, even if they aren't a matched set.

Bobby motions and I follow him. He's all eager; he doesn't have that I-don't-give-a-shit look that he usually does. He says, "Hey, I want you to meet my homie, Todd. He writes *Pricer*. You've heard of him."

"We certainly have," says the fat one, folding away his shades to reveal a second pair of eyeglasses underneath. "You're something of a legend, I understand."

"A *legend?* Hardly. I guess old Bobby been exaggerating, as usual."

"It's not through Bobby that we've learned of you," says the undertaker dude, who even *talks* like an undertaker, with a low-pitched, raspy, nervous-making voice. "It was through, ah, *other* channels."

"Fuck, Todd, they been watching us! All the time we thought we were alone, streaking our way from wall to wall, hanging from ledges, clinging to ducts, they were there too … watching … like, you know, guardian angels or something. Or like the dads we never had."

"So, they're undercovers?"

"No. Like I told you. They're aliens. They're fucking from another world. They came here in a fucking spaceship. And they're here to visit *us*. No 'take me to your leader' bullshit. They came here for *us* … because they're taggers too."

I glance from one to the other. The fat one's jowls are quivering. The undertaker one says, "He expresses himself forcefully, although he somewhat oversimplifies the situation. My companion and I have been traveling for some time now; eons, to be precise. Your friend calls us taggers, which is true only in the sense that it pleases us to leave behind us, on those worlds as yet unsullied by the presence of life, on those dead surfaces which cry out for the tumult of living souls … small traces of our being … signatures, if you will … tiny pieces of DNA that will, after eons to come, evolve to self-awareness and proclaim to those who follow us that we were here first."

There's a long silence. Bobby's all smiling, happy, expecting me to totally accept at face value the idea that these two geeks in a fancy car are not two geeks at all but like, the Creator, God. I don't know about Bobby but I've been on the street long enough to know what a rat smells like, and I'm real surprised at Bobby. I'm all wondering what drugs they've given him. Or worse, telling him they're God, maybe they've given him religion. And I'm thinking, Bobby, Bobby, what have they done to you? Ain't it enough that your parents didn't love you, that you didn't have no money and were born on the wrong side of town, so now the one thing that you really own, the thing inside of you that's you and no one else, has got to get sucked into some shitass cult that brainwashes taggers? I guess he realizes that I'm angry with him, with all of them. And so he cranks into his motormouth mode, which is what happens when he gets nervous, and he's all talking about me, about the legend I supposedly am … the tall tales the young taggers tell themselves when they're overnighting at juvenile detention waiting for parents who don't want to come pick them up.

"Let me tell you what Todd done one time," he says, and the so-called aliens both relax a little, smile, even, "the night before his sixteenth birthday … there's a wall that runs along the edge of California, next to a road called Oceanside, and on the street side it's a low wall you can lean against, but on the beach side it like falls straight down, a sheer drop, all the way down … sand in some parts, rock in others, concrete where they've built a concession stand or a shithouse. So it's like midnight, and it's a full moon, and Todd takes off there in this truck he stole, and he climbs over the wall and then … clinging to the wall like Spiderman … high above the sea … he writes on the bricks in white spray paint, over and over and over, brick by brick by brick, until you can see *Pricer* slowly forming on that wall, see it from way over on the pier, and it's all glimmering in the moonlight, and he's there, like Spidey, breaking all the fucking laws of gravity, for the longest time, scurrying up and down and fucking *breaking* that name out of the brick, and it's the most beautiful thing I ever saw—"

"You never saw it," I said, "and anyways, you were probably like five years old at the time—"

***

"—and anyways," I'm all telling this to Dr. Yao so she can toss me a miserable few bucks so I can buy myself some smokes, "it wasn't true. I had a rope ladder. It's just a myth."

But she writes it all down religiously, adding, "Myth, Todd, is perhaps the most profound truth of them all."

She can say that all she wants, because she makes more money by asking an hour's worth of dumb questions than I've ever made in a week, except when I was running drugs, of course, but that don't fucking count.

***

—"and anyways it *is* true, and I saw it and it is a true memory, cuz that was the first time I ever run away from home, and I took the RTD all the way to Santa Monica because I heard they have better child protection agents there." Five years old and running away from home, I thought. But the aliens just kind of tsk-tsked and went along with his bullshit. "I know," Bobby said, "because of that full moon … and looking up at it … and down the wall at the name that was materializing out of the dark brick wall … and thinking … the wall is cool, but one day I'm a write on the fucking *moon*."

The fat alien was all moaning and almost like having an orgasm right there in the alley over what Bobby was telling them. I had him pegged for a pervert. Hey, maybe the night wouldn't be wasted after all. Maybe I could sell him on a date with my sister, half now, half on delivery.

***

—"Plus," I tell Dr. Yao, "he didn't say that, at one minute past midnight, my birthday, they came to the wall and hauled my ass in and threw the book at me … not just the vandalism but the GTA, with that stolen truck … that's the reason I stopped tagging and became the, uh, legend."

"You were imprisoned?" Her upper lip trembles. I'd go at her right then if I could, but I know she'd only push that button underneath her desk and then that'd be the end of my probation.

"Yeah," I said, and then, because I know it titillates them and gets them all wet, "and well … you know how it is in prison … when you're young and …like, maybe kind of, uh, slender … not butt-ugly like some of the other dudes…."

"Oh, my God," she said, a tear forming in one eye. "They didn't … *rape* you?"

I knew she'd be good for more than five bucks this time.

***

So, I'm all, "Well, Bobby, you are a genius when it comes to tagging, but about life, dude, you're fucking dumb." I can say all this because our friends aren't really paying attention to us; they're roaming up and down the alley and making notes on the different pieces, taking pictures even. "A fat dude and a thin dude and a Porsche, that don't make E.T. in a starship."

"You're wrong, Todd," says Bobby. "Look at what it says on the rear of the car. Will you just look?"

"It says 'Porsche.'"

"Bitch!" he whispers. "Porsche, right. *P-r-o-s-c-h-e* don't spell Porsche."

"So I'm dyslexic." I'm getting ready to punch him one because I don't like to be reminded that I don't read too good. "Ain't my fault. What's your point?"

"It's a fake, you fool. They're trying to blend in, but they copy us damn near perfect, but little things slip by … they're careless. They don't dot their i's and cross their t's. Hey like, when the fat one comes back, take a good look at his hands. You won't need to read for that."

The fat one waddled back into view at that moment. He was stuffing his camera back into a jacket pocket. He had six fingers on his right hand. *That* scared me.

The sixth finger, the one beyond the pinky, wasn't even a real finger at all, but a kind of claw. I thought I saw scales. "Don't be afraid," said the fat alien. I wondered if he'd read my mind. "We're not going to do anything to you. We're only going to watch. If you please us … and I know you will … there could be rewards … wealth … journeys beyond your wildest imaginings … sexual fulfilment. Our fingers are in many pies."

"I only got two things in life I really have a hardon for," Bobby said. "And one of them's only like, a fantasy."

"And they are?" said the undertaker alien.

"I want to tag the moon. And I want to die."

***

I still remember the first time Bobby tried to commit suicide; he's about twelve and there's a drive-by on his his street and four people get killed; one of them's Smiley, who never smiled. After Smiley's funeral, Bobby's at his house and he's all trying to hold his breath until he turns blue, but his stepdad beats him, so he has to breathe so he can cry.

Dr. Yao tells me about the value of human life, the tragedy of throwing it away; and I'm all, "Fuck you, Margaret, how can you talk about value and shit, you're the ones who put a price tag on everything," and she says, "I'm not talking money, I'm talking intangible values … *higher values* …" and I'm all, "When you're like me and Bobby, there *ain't* no value higher than money. A kid'll rape you cause his dick needs a quenching. He'll fucking *kill* you for a pack of smokes. They don't teach you that in Tarzana, but you'd learn it on the street pretty damn fast. To be worth something you have to be worth something *to* somebody."

Dr. Yao mutters something about nihilism, and I tell her, "But when you're up on that wall, and the whole world knows you exist and you have a name and your name cries out over the chaos of the city … that's when, at least, you're somebody. For a while. Before they drag you away and bury your ass forever behind some prison wall."

She likes that. I think she's finally gonna let me do her.

***

What the two aliens have in mind is more than just sitting back and watching, though. They sort of want to participate. They want Bobby to go on the wildest tagging spree of his life, and they want to record all of it. And like, they want me along too, although maybe it's because Bobby's insisting on it. I'm like the crusty old commentator who's seen it all a million times ... they want my ancient wisdom. After all, I have a lofty vantage point. I'm twenty-four years old and I've done time. I can't decide if the aliens are making a documentary of some kind or whether they're just whacking off on our adrenalin.

Bobby'll be sixteen soon and then it better all be over. Or else they'll catch him and try him as an adult and send him to a *real* jail where they'll buttfuck all the dreaming out of him forever.

So like, we all pile into the Porsche that's not a Porsche. Inside it's all different ... a lot bigger, for one thing, because, the fat one tells me, space is all spindled up and twisting across itself like the strands of the writing we do; there's rooms within rooms and chambers within chambers. There's a room that turns into any place in the universe. There's a room with creatures preserved in columns of clear bubbly fluid. There's control panels and whirling lights and all that sci-fi stuff you see in movies. But you get the feeling that it's not what's really there at all, that it's like a virtual reality projection or something, because sometimes the images are weirdly superimposed or blur at the edges ... and you feel it's all there only to prove to me and Bobby that these dudes are from another world ... and that to them the place looks a whole lot different, or maybe doesn't *look* at all.

And sometimes it's just a little sports car jamming down the road, too small for four people. "Where to?" says the fat dude, and Bobby's all, I don't know, testing them, I guess, "Maybe like, the top of the Capitol Records tower."

And in a moment the Porsche's lifting off and we're up above Hollywood, and I look down and I can see it all: the lights, the filth, the pimps, the tourists, the burger wrappers fluttering in the Santa Ana wind like sagebrush in the desert … the stars above, where the aliens come from, you can barely make out through the layers of smog, but the stars in the sidewalk are bright enough to substitute for them … we rise up and no one sees us, or if they do they don't think there's any wizardry to it; after all, this is Hollywood, where all cars fly. We thread down Hollywood and sometimes we duck into side streets. A homeless man peers at us from inside a dumpster. Maybe, living closer to the hard real world, he can still see the wonder in a car that flies and has aliens in it.

We soar up to the Capitol needle and Bobby hangs from the window by a bungee cord and writes, *Nova Nova Nova Nova Nova,* in a frieze around the topmost edges of the building. We veer up toward the Griffith Observatory and Bobby tags the dome with a thousand-colored starburst. We zoom down to the Hollywood sign and now it has *Nova Nova Nova* painted along the side of each massive letter. We skim along Mulholland drive and Bobby hits up the side of the Santa Monica mountains, burning *Nova* into the brush with some kind of disintegrator beam. We head south and Bobby's up on every one of those towering jap banks that own our city. We go toward the sea and Bobby tags the beach from high overhead with a kind of laser gun pencil device that fuses the sand into a hundred glassy repetitions of *Nova Nova Nova Nova* and a hundred starbursts. The aliens love it. They've stuck a transmitter in Bobby's brain and they're getting off on his joy, and even I can feel it because I know what it's like to shout your name in man-tall letters from the tops of buildings and the heights of overpasses … I know what it's like to make the whole city that never fucking listens and never fucking cares sit up and stare me in the face and pay attention and know that I exist.

Tonight, they're *all* sitting up all right. The undertaker alien flicks a switch and we see a TV screen image hovering in the air. The airwaves are full of us. It's a gang, they're saying. A mega-gang that's decided to hit up every part of the city all at once. There's an expert on tagging on CBS now, explaining that NOVA is the initials of the New Order of Victorious Armies, some kind of neo-Nazi group ... yeah, right, that really cracks us up ... NBC says that as many as five hundred taggers are on the move ... a phone hot line is flashing on the screen ... they've preempted *Murphy Brown*. That's how fucking important we've become, two worthless street kids from beside the San Fernando railway tracks.

They give us anything we want, these aliens. Me and Bobby, we've both downed a couple of forty-ouncers by about three in the morning, and we're pissing out of the window onto the deserted streets. The experts on the TV are all explaining the different gang initials now, and there's like this psychiatrist who's all talking about alienated youth and street violence and all those other things they don't know shit about.

There's cop cars out patrolling now. They're looking for us. But the aliens cloak the flying Porsche in a cloud of pseudo-smog, and we don't show up on radar either, and anyway we're just too fast for them.

But by four in the morning Bobby's all sick of this shit. He's all, "This ain't tagging, there ain't no excitement to it, it's just high technology, there ain't no *mystery* ... no *danger*. We just go someplace, I hit it up, we push buttons, and then we escape. Fuck this, I'm a go home now."

The aliens look at each other. The fat dude says to me, "I don't understand. I thought we were giving him ... you know, the maximum adrenalin high. What can we do?" The undertaker takes a handful of pills out of the glove compartment, I don't know, some kind of uppers I guess. Bobby just stares at them.

"You don't get it," I tell the aliens. "You tell me that you do this kind of thing yourselves, that you write your names all over like *planets* and shit, you write your names in little strings of amino acids and *we're* nothing but your signature crawling over what would have been a dead world … but you don't seem to see that writing *big* isn't what makes it important. You've let Bobby write all over L.A. and you've let him stir up the city and upset a lot of people and there's black and whites all over town chasing us, but that ain't what it's about at all."

Right now, understand, we are parked on top of the Beverly Center, right next to the big Hard Rock Café sign, which flashes on and off and alternately makes Bobby's face white as a ghost and shadowy as death. The aliens confer with each other in whispers, in some foreign language … sounds kind of like Japanese … and then the tall one says to me, not at all jokingly, "So illuminate us, wise one."

So I knew something about these two aliens: they looked up to me, like the kids who used to cluster around me on the corner of Jackman and Hubbard all them years, repeating the stories about me until even I couldn't recognize them any more. At twenty-four, I was a has-been. I had passed through the fire and been burned alive and lived, kind of, even though it was only a kind of half-living. So maybe like, these aliens *were* a couple billion years old. They still hadn't gotten to the has-been stage. They couldn't see beyond themselves yet. And so I had something to teach them.

And that, to me, is a wonder in itself, and it's a fact that starts to bring me out of the death I'm in, the death I've sentenced myself to. And like, this is what I say to them:

"The sociologists, the analysts, they all think the kids do this because their world's a terrible place ... their daddies beat them and their homies kill them and they're stoned out of their minds and hanging themselves every five minutes ... but that's not true. They don't do it *because* of those things ... they do it *in spite of* them. They're like the corpse that thrusts its undead arm out through the soil and grabs you by the leg as you're walking through the graveyard. They're dead, all the way dead, dead inside, and still they can't let go of life."

"So what are we to do?" says the undertaker, while Bobby twitches his bony fingers, waiting.

"You let him go, dude," I say. "You follow him at a distance, but you don't chauffeur him to where he wants to write, and you don't pluck him away when he's done."

"But," says the fat one, "what about the authorities? The LAPD's out in force by now. They think there's an army out there, a *Nova* gang. What if they catch Bobby?"

"He's already thought of that," I say.
***

Sometimes my sister comes back from a trick, and she don't give me all the money. She buys flowers and she lays them on a grave at Forest Lawn. It ain't Bobby's grave, but she says it's the thought that counts.

She don't talk to me that much anymore; I guess she thinks I killed him.
***

It's 4:30 in the morning and the jet-black Porsche lands on a knoll in Forest Lawn lightly, like a baseball cap in the wind. Bobby slips out. He knows his way around here; we've spent more than enough time among the dead people, getting stoned together, thinking about our friends who've been shot and can't afford a resting place like this, considering our own deaths too, wondering how soon they'll be. The moon is full and the grass is silver-black, and there's monument after monument ... it's a peaceful place, the stones all clean and orderly, nothing like the hood.

There's like, this humungous Grecian temple thing that looms up out of the grass, I think it's a memorial to some movie mogul. As me and the aliens watch, Bobby shimmies up an Ionian column and puts up *Nova* with a Mean Streak and a few deft flicks of his bony wrist. We see him on a dozen TV screens inside the Porsche that's a spaceship, and we even hear him breathing, amplified, Dolby surround-sound, muttering to himself like, "Fuck you for being dead, fuck you," and now, suddenly, we hear the chopper way overhead and see the search beams criss-crossing in the dark, and there's Bobby, hung on a cross of light ... and we hear sirens. An alarms. Black and whites around here somewhere. We don't see them yet. They're just around the bend of the hill probably.

"Come on, dudes," I say, "pull up, grab him," and the Porsche peels out through the grass but Bobby doesn't get in the car, instead he starts sprinting downhill, in the direction of the freeway.

We follow, and the cop cars follow but they don't go on the grass because like, this is Forest Lawn ... this is a place for *rich* dead people ... no tire tracks on *these* people's grass or it's lawsuit city ... we see Bobby run ... a tiny stick-figure now, leaping over gravemarkers, pausing to tag on the brow of a marble angel with outstretched arms, then running again ... closeup of his face hanging in the air in front of me and his face is so composed, so serene, it scares me.

"The indexes are way up," says the fat alien. "This is going to be a fabulous recording after all."

"I told you," I said. "Just leave him be and you'll get everything you want."

We follow him. He hops a wall and hits the pavement running. We follow. The cop cars follow. They're on Glendale, diverting traffic. The chopper's not police, it's fucking news. Bobby dodges the search beams. And suddenly he's gone.

"Where the—" says the undertaker alien.

"The overpass," I say.

***

There's no traffic at all on this stretch of the freeway because they've diverted everything to the 5 or the 101. There's one particular overpass where they all jumble into the 134. There's like fourteen lanes converging and diverging and above them is a row of bright green signs with big white names and numbers on them … my guess is that we'll see Bobby there. We hurdle the blockade and we blend into the convoy of police cars that surrounds the overpass. Bobby's on his hands and knees, hugging the signs, and he has a can of green paint in one hand and a can of white in the other and he's writing, over and over, *Nova, Nova, Nova,* and the starburst, two-handed, covering the old legends with the green while writing his tagger name with the white.

They're shouting to him over the PA system. They say give yourself up, throw down your weapons, all that bullshit. There's reporters with video cameras. The Santa Ana's howling and through it there's the thrum of the helicopter. There's snipers with rifles trained on Bobby. An ambulance is pulling up. Me and the aliens, we get out of the Porsche. No one sees us because we are still cloaked in smog. We look up at where Bobby's writing.

On the signs, there's no more route numbers, no more *Burbank,* no more *Pasadena,* no more *Ventura, Los Angeles, Golden State Freeway* … no, all the signs read *Nova, Nova, Nova* … all roads lead to Nova. And he's all standing on top of the sign that once said *Pasadena Freeway*, balanced on the thin edge of the sign, his arms raised toward the moon … and even that spells *Nova*, the *N* a twisted ribbon of steel, the *O* the moon, the *V* himself with his arms up, the *A* scrawled across the concrete in black paint … he's made the whole city part of his name … even the moon itself … he's made himself bigger than the world.

"What's he trying to say?" the fat alien says.

And I'm all, "He's telling us who he is. The only way he knows how. Living in spite of himself. Like I told you."

I guess they gave up trying to divert the traffic because somehow it's started up again, there's eighteen-wheelers and buses and a few passenger cars now, filling the freeway except for the island of cop cars right beneath where Bobby's standing.

In the moonlight, Bobby Donahue smiles. His thin pale body's all wrapped in the moon's radiance and even from down here I see that his eyes are shining. He's all standing there, poised in the moment of childhood's end, between innocence and disillusion, and he has a grace and a beauty that no one but another tagger can understand; he's fulfilled, he's in balance. For the first time since he burst out screaming into the world of pain, he loves himself. He is free.

And then they shoot him down.

***

Today Margaret Yao actually has a copy of the *National Inquirer.* I don't know how she's managed to pay for it at the checkout without dying of embarrassment. Maybe she went in disguise.

The headline reads: *NEW EVIDENCE OF LIFE ON MOON.*

The photo, computer-enhanced and obviously retouched, shows what looks like a word, scratched in letters a hundred miles long in the lunar dust ... *Nova.*

***

Bobby Donahue never hits the ground. My sister says I killed him and doesn't talk to me. She always liked him, even in junior high.

***

... "But," Dr. Yao says, "you're telling me that ... when people finally get to the moon to investigate ... they might even find, I don't know, fragmentary DNA segments ... something that could one day evolve into...."

I tell her I don't want to sleep under the overpass anymore. I ask her if her bed in Tarzana's big enough for two. She smiles wryly. She is in love, I think; I just don't know if it's me, or merely what I stand for.

***

I sat scrunched up in the back seat as the aliens' car sped over the sleeping city. I said, "Where is he? What have you done to him?"

And they said, "Given him every honor due to him."

I watched the comet streaking, only it wasn't a comet because it burned a swath through the smog itself on its way up toward the moon.

And I said, "I don't get it. If you guys are such galactic big shots, why do you even bother to come here?"

And they said, "You might call it something like, revisiting the scene of the crime ... now and then we like to observe our handiwork."

"But ... if you really are these badass aliens from another world ... why don't you just swoop down out of the sky in your true forms, do the whole 'take me to your leader' thing? Why do you hang out with white trash like us? Why do you try to look like humans, even down to our cars? Don't you have anything better to do than to imitate us?"

The fat alien laughed for the first time. I felt they were making fun of me, treating me like a little kid. That was strange, since only an hour before they'd acted like I was the dope ass OG motherfucking guru grand master and like I knew all the secrets of the universe.

The tall alien patted me on the back and said, "You have it all backwards, Todd; we're not imitating you at all. *Au contraire.* It's just that—"

The fat alien said, "We made you in our image."

They they left me on the hillside, freezing my butt off in the Santa Ana wind, and soared way way up in the direction of the sunrise.

—Los Angeles, 1993

An Alien Heresy

I am not a heretic. I am a being from another world. I am lost. Send me home, I beg you.
***

You may say I am young to be an inquisitor, but in my brief existence in this world I have not remained unexposed to evil. For, in the Fourteen Hundred and Fortieth Year of Our Lord, I was a novice in the service of the Bishop of Nantes, and because I could scribe a fair round cursive hand, I was often called upon to set down confessions of such horror that it is hard to think of them even years later without a shudder; I mean revelations of deviltry, sorcery and heresy as would awaken doubt in the stoutest believer, and drive the purest of souls into the abyss of despair.

Thanks to that legible hand, I was appointed one of the scriveners at the trial of Gilles de Rais, called Bluebeard, and I was compelled to write down, dispassionately and accurately, descriptions of the mutilation of small children, onanistic rituals, and perversions I had never previously imagined. And when at last the Marshall of France came to be burned at the stake, I was asked to expunge some of the more lurid details from the record, for fear that the truth might give too much distress to future generations; and so my much-vaunted penmanship proved to be mere *vanitas*. What was torn from the pages, however, could not be expunged from our souls. We were scarred by it, and it still gives us nightmares.

Yet even that infamous trial would not prepare me for my encounter with the lost soul who claimed to have come from another world. It was only through my training and the sternest self-discipline that I would manage to survive the interrogation with my soul, to all appearances, intact.

The Gilles de Rais case was a dozen years ago, and now I was returning to Tiffauges, that cursed place where Bluebeard perpetrated his crimes. I was to investigate a new incident. It was a simple, open-and-shut case, just the kind of thing a junior inquisitor can handle in a week's work. His Grace the Bishop of Nantes used to favor me and often assigned me such routine cases, which help one to rise in the bureaucracy of the church and are not intellectually taxing.

These were the details: a fire from the sky. A strange man, mud-soaked, naked, seen by the river's edge. A strange man with strange eyes. Perhaps a demon; more likely a natural man, or a village idiot who had wandered back to the wrong village. I was either to quell their superstitions or, if necessary, act as the proper representative of the Church Militant.

Routine indeed. But of course no one wanted to travel to Tiffauges. I could feel the gloom long before I came in sight of the castle. Only three days by oxcart it might have been, but it felt as though I had left the world of men and entered a kingdom of ghosts. Beyond the hamlet of St.

Hilaire de Clisson, it seemed that the sky became perpetually gray. Though it was already March, much snow still lay on the ground. The River Crûme was still part frozen, and, where it joined the Sèvre Nantaise, which is where the castle stands, ice clanged against ice.

When we arrived in the village, the sun was already going down. We were well stocked with provender, and we had brought all the instruments for the Question with us, in case nothing could be found locally. Ahead of me rode two knights, or rather a knight and his squire. I had not bothered to find out their names. In the cart with me sat Brother Paolo, a Roman musician and general note-taker, the dour-faced Brother Pierre, and the ever-smiling Jean of Nantes, a genial fellow, by avocation a barber, by trade a torturer. And I, of course, another Jean of Nantes—how many are there, I wonder?—who am called Lenclud.

A few hours' behind us marched the secular arm, a small detail of a dozen foot soldiers and a captain on horse; they would reach the village by midnight, perhaps, and would camp in the field.

My traveling companions had been garrulous all through the journey. Now, in the sunset, they could all feel the oppression in this village. No children played in the one muddy path that ran through the center, where stood a well. The huts were hushed. One, a little larger, seemed to pass for an inn. A bit of light came from within and there was had been noise, although the sound of our horses and oxen seemed to still it.

"We should press on," I called out to the knights, our escort. "It's barely one league to the castle."

The chateau had been abandoned since the trial, but it must at least have walls, and a fireplace, and a room in which to conduct interrogations.

"We'll put up in the inn," said the elder of the two.

I had certain reasons for avoiding that, but they were not reasons I could admit. I said, "Sir chevalier, another hour's riding at best will bring us to a place with stone walls; we'll have a roaring fire and we'll be able to sleep in real beds. And not have to pay," I added, for the execution of Gilles de Rais had made his lands temporarily forfeit to the church, until such time as all the rights and papers were sorted out.

"All very well for you to say, mon père," said the knight. "But think of us. And my squire's frightened; he's heard the stories."

The younger one turned around and I saw that he was, indeed, younger than I had thought from just seeing the back of his head for three days; but I had to hold to my word, lest authority be lost. It is in our training.

"We're not here to disrupt the village," I said. "The inquisition is not a circus. Let's get to the castle as quickly as possible, set up, and have the case brought to us properly."

"As you wish," said the knight.

But at that moment the inn door flew open. There were faces I knew; the innkeeper, even more grizzled than when last I saw him, some villagers who had given evidence in the matter of the Marshall of France; but I did not yet see the face I most dread to see, and so I breathed a sigh of relief. My traveling companions must have mistaken it for relief at seeing that this was not, after all, a village of ghosts.

"Father Lenclud," the innkeeper said, "it's best you came in."

I started to protest, "We are bound for Tiffauges," but he interrupted me. "What you want," he said, "is all in here."

The door opened wider. We saw tables inside, and we could smell a rabbit stew on the pot. There was a smoky light and the air heated up just a little; I could see the others were tired, and perhaps, perhaps the person I wished to avoid was no longer there. After all, it had been ten years;

no, twelve. Perhaps I was safe after all. Perhaps she had gone away.

And in the grand scheme of things, it was, perhaps, a smallish sin, for which I had suffered seven painful penances already.

We piled inside, leaving our cart and our belongings unguarded; for who would steal from God? and we were offered benches inside; there were villagers there, and children, too, scurrying in the shadows; the walls were sooty and greasy; but the fire blazed, and the stew was filling.

The innkeeper said nothing while we ate, except to remind me of his name, which was Henri. I learned at supper that our knight was another Jean of Nantes; but this one we called Johan, because he had a Flemish mother.

It was only when we had eaten our fill that Henri was ready to tell us why the villagers had sent a letter to His Grace in Nantes.

"We've got him locked in the cellar," he said.

"And he is well rested, and has eaten?" It is true that we torture people, but we do love them; I never want to begin an investigation with threats and violence; that comes all too soon.

"Yes, he's eaten all right."

"Twelve fish," said a woman from the back. "I counted them myself. Raw. And all the bones. You've never heard such a crunching sound, mon père! Frightened out of our wits, we was."

"Bid her come out of the shadows," I said, "she seems to have a lot to say." And I regretted it as soon as I said it, because when she stepped into the light I recognized her, as I should have from the voice.

She knew me too. But she had the courtesy to lower her gaze, and gave no sign of it. In the firelight, in her grubby peasant shift, she was still beautiful, though. I looked longer than I ought to have. I was glad I had remembered to pack the flagellum.

"Your name?" I asked her, already knowing the answer.

"I am Alice, mon père. I am the innkeeper's wife."

So she had married. How much did the innkeeper know?

"Alice," I said softly, "tell me about the man in the cellar. If it is indeed a man; I have read the letter to the bishop, but we tend to view reports of devils in the flesh with a degree of cynicism."

The villagers looked at each other. Alice looked at me. Was there a hint of reproach? She did not reveal much. In the void in the conversations, all we could hear was the sizzle from the fireplace.

"Children, come out now," the innkeeper said at last, speaking at the shadows and at the space under the stairs. "The inquistor won't hurt you."

I realized then what it was that had subdued the noise. It was fear.

'You have to forgive us," Henri said, "they haven't trusted many people since … you know."

Three children emerged. One was a little girl with stringy hair, perhaps seven; an older girl, on the cusp of womanhood, her shapeless smock belying an incipient voluptuousness. The two girls curtsied. Then there was the boy. He was perhaps eleven; he had long blonde hair, a dirty face, and clear blue eyes. He seemed so familiar … I could not place him … he did not look at me at all. But Alice did. At me and him. And in that awkward moment I understood everything, and I knew that her marriage must have been loveless, born from desperation.

"They saw him," the innkeeper said. "They'll tell you."

"We're not to tell him anything," said the boy, defiant. "They're going to burn him at the stake. He's our friend."

"Let the church be the judge of that now, Guillaume," Alice said. Was her voice not edged with cynicism?

"Guillaume, sit by me," I said, with all the gentleness I could muster. "Tell me of your friend." I reached out to touch his cheek. He flinched quite visibly, but overcame it, and sat on the bench. Meanwhile, the musician, the knight, and the torturer were already heavily into their ale. I called for Brother Pierre to take notes.

Guillaume kept his distance from me. I did not yet dare think the unthinkable: that I should acknowledge him, that he should have my name, that I could, in this peasant village, live on; that I had a son.

He said, "I'm sorry about the mud, mon père; that was my idea. Not any of the others'."

I remembered that the strange man was reportedly coated in mud. I waited for him to go on.

"It was a week ago. I wouldn't have seen the fire, but there was this noise, first. It was a rustling sound. I thought it might be a wolf, and we've only the one cow. I took a knife. When I stepped out of our hut it was almost as bright as day. When I looked up it was like the sun was in the sky, only bigger and more blue."

"Our Guillaume is prone to fancifying," the innkeeper said. "You tell mon père the truth now, you hear, don't exaggerate." To me he grumbled, "The boy should have been whelped in a castle, not a hut, the way he carries on."

"Go on, Guillaume."

"I'm not making it up," he said. "I can show you where the fire fell."

"An accursed spot!" said Henri. "No one has gone there save the boy since it happened. A whole circle of forest seared into a blackened clearing. If it isn't the devil's work, I don't know what is."

"Me and my sisters," said Guillaume, "we wanted to

keep him as a pet. But someone saw him and denounced us to the inquisition. Are you going to torture him, mon père? Are you going to torture *me?"*

I would have embraced him then and there. But I knew that the pleasure of having him in my arms, the warmth of human love, was not for me; I am married only to Christ. And so I only said, "Guillaume, take me to that place."

"By the all the saints!" said the innkeeper. "Can you not burn the demon and be done with it?"

"I'll say this only once," I said. "Please listen. The men of the village could have handled this matter by themselves. They could have clubbed the stranger to death, hacked him up, buried him in an unmarked grave; without a feudal lord nearby, with the village's legal status still under negotiation, such a crime would almost certainly not have been noticed by anyone. But you chose to involve the Church. That was the right and honorable thing to do. But the Church is here now, and things will be done according to procedure. If a trial is necessary it will be a fair trial. If torture is demanded it will be strictly in accordance with the Papal Bull *Ad Exstirpanda,* which set appropriate guidelines over a century ago. If execution is required, it will be carried out by the secular arm in Nantes. We are not barbarians, Henri, and we shall not fall prey to peasant superstitions."

And that, it was to be hoped, was that.
***

And so I went out again into the cold, not yet having had a moment in private with Alice—for I dreaded that possibility—accompanied by Guillaume, by Brother Paolo, who fears nothing, and by Chevalier Johan and his squire, who held aloft a burning torch.

We entered the woods. Guillaume walked swiftly, knowing the location of every tree. We reached the clearing in only an hour, and when I stood there, with the bright moon shining down on every charred stalk, and the wind howling, I saw many hallmarks of the devil's work.

For example, the clearing was completely and perfectly circular. No random falling object, no hand of man could have made it so. The snow had melted and refrozen into a glassy shield, from whose center there projected a strange metal artifact. I say metal, but it had a purplish sheen unlike any steel or bronze I had ever looked upon.

Guillaume took me by the hand. "I'll show you the spaceship," he said. "Come, mon père. There's nothing living; it's just twisted metal."

"Spaceship?" said Johan the knight.

"That's the word *he* used," Guillaume said.

He tugged at my hand again, and, all in innocence, he tugged at my heart, too. I followed him, bold as he was, for he knew nothing of the dark powers, and I could not afford to show fear. The artfact was mostly concealed under the ice; we were seeing only the tip of it. It was a thing of delicate needles, of twists and twirls of metal, of gossamer webs no mortal hand could have woven. When I saw it my heart sank, for I knew that whatever was in the cellar of the inn was no lost village idiot. I prayed in my heart to the Blessed Virgin, and there sprang unbidden into my mind the image of Alice, Alice with unbound hair in the spring breeze, Alice of the ample breasts; and I trembled, knowing that the Dark One must have sent me that vision to divert me from my contemplation of all that is immaculate. I knew that tonight I was in for a long session with the knout, and that my hairshirt would be blooded come morning.

Now, I was truly afraid. But the boy was not. These infernal shards were just a new kind of toy for him, and the demon, perhaps, a new kind of pet. That is what is must be like, I thought, to grow up in the shadow of Tiffauges, in a world where evil, hanged and burned at the stake, still would not loose its grip. He bent down, stared at the metal with a natural curiosity, tried to pry the pieces from the ice, but they would not budge.

I looked at the boy, and past him, into the barren trees; beyond them I could see where the two rivers met, and I could see the castle as well; that is how bright the moon was, and how glistening the ice. The wind whistled. The chateau was a black and shapeless mass; one tower had already crumbled. Evil can rot even stone, rot it from within.

"We will turn back," I said curtly. The squire with the torch turned immediately. He sensed it too. Brother Paolo had been taking notes, even sketching the diabolical device on a scrap of vellum.

'Come, mon père," Guillaume said, "I'll take you to him now."

And on the way back to the village, the boy sang, in a hearty voice, the war-song *L'homme armé*, and because we were all afraid of the gathering dark, we followed his lead, and it was a raucous chorus; but as soon as we reentered the village something dampened our spirit and the singing petered out.

But Brother Paolo whispered in my ear, "That boy has a sweet voice, though untrained; he could really be something. I'll have him for the morning mass; he will brighten the gloom."

***

And so, with the others all fast asleep, or turning in, Guillaume led me down to the cellar. Always, our dour chevalier followed, his hand never leaving his sword-hilt. Brother Paolo had joined our friend the torturer in a room for six. I was to sleep alone.

He unlocked the door, lit a few more candles, and

showed me what manner of creature had arrived at Tiffauges in a ball of flame.

Completely covered from head to toe in mud, as they said he would be. He was naked, a state permitted only before the Fall. Hunched over, chained to the wall by his ankles. Perhaps this room had served as a holding pen for Gilles de Rais' victims; for they were slender chains, such as might be used to subjugate a child.

Guillaume lit yet more candles, and now I could see the face clearly. The eyes were large and round, haunting, oddly beautiful.

"Len … clud," he said. A sweet, small voice. It chilled me.

"Have you ever told it my name?" I said to Guillaume.

"No, mon père. He just knows things. He plucks them from people's heads, I think."

The eyes peered at me. Yes. I could feel something invading my thoughts. An alien presence. I tried to block it by thinking the words of the rosary over and over.

"Are you a demon?" I asked the stranger. When properly bound to answer by an emissary of the Church, a demon must speak the truth; for hell is ever subject to the will of heaven.

Suddenly, images filled my thoughts. I tried reciting the rosary aloud as though to drown them out. There were creatures with goats' horns, forked tails, hideous leering faces. He was answering me after all, in pictures if not in words.

"Stay back, Guillaume! Thiis creature has just shown me … terrifying things."

"Mon père," Guillaume said, "he is only showing you what's in your own heart."

"It's a monster!" I cried, and I leaped to shield the child from its gaze.

And it said, "I not a monster."

Tears rolled down its cheeks. They dug great chasms in the mud. And now I could see what lay beneath all that mire. It was something green. The squamous, reptilian skin that was a certain mark of the dark powers.

"My son," I said, "you tried to hide his skin from us?"

"They would have killed him," said Guillaume.

"There are worse things than death," I said, and more images sprang into my head … flames and bright red devil eyes, and I could almost smell the brimstone. "Tomorrow you will douse him with water, and we will see the extent of his monstrosity."

"I am not a monster."

His speech was much clearer than before. Before, he seemed to speak like the village idiot I had once thought him to be; now he had the more sophisticated accent of the city.

Guillaume said, "Mon père, he first learned to talk from us, but now he's getting it from you."

I stared into the monster's eyes and saw within them such a great despair that I knew he must be among those, once blessed by divine light, who were now eternally deprived of the presence of God.

"Perditus es," I said, for I knew that the devil must speak Latin.

"Per – di – tus." *Lost.* I did not know whether he understood, or if he was merely aping me; but then he continued: "Do – mum." He wanted to return home. He had even used the correct accusative of motion towards, so he could not have been simply copying my words.

"Ubi est domus tua?" I asked him where his home might be.

In response, he looked up at the dank ceiling. The candlelight flicked on old grime.

"In caelo," he said softly.

My home is in the sky.

Like Lucifer himself, he dared to claim heaven as his patrimony!

The cellar was cold, but the chill I felt was not from natural causes. I called for Chevalier Johan. "Sir Knight," I said, "the secular arm must have arrived by now. You must ride out quickly and tell them not to pitch their tents, but to ride straight to the chateau. They must clean out a few rooms and they must prepare a dungeon, and tell Brother Paolo to asperge the rooms with holy water, and celebrate mass in the chapel at dawn so as to purge the taint that hangs over it and over this village. Tell them to tie the accused up firmly and admit him there as the Church's ward. Ask them to clean the mud from the accused and to clothe him so that we do not have to be shamed in the sight of God with his nakedness."

The boy looked at me with alarm. "You'll burn him!" he said. "Our friend. He played with us."

"He is not your friend, my child. Go now."

I dismissed them all and told them to make fast the door of the cellar behind us.

And the stranger said, so quietly that indeed I was not sure whether he spoke aloud at all, or whether the words did not simply sound within the confines of my mind, "I am not a monster. I am from another world. I am lost. I beg of you, send me home."

#

I hoped for a few hours' peace before going to the chateau to say mass, but it was not to be. In the little cell they gave me, which was behind the kitchen, I scoured, by candlelight, the books I had brought with me, trying to glean some knowledge of just what this creature might be. Was he a denizen of hell who had somehow escaped the confines of the Dark One, and by saying "Send me home" was he actually begging for some kind of salvation, some reconciliation with God? Was there a village idiot underneath this skin, who had been possessed by a devil, who could yet be cured, if the devil could only be driven from the flesh? Was it a devious impostor, come to tempt me?

These were all possibilities. That was why a fair trial was essential.

In the brief hour of twilight, before the sunrise, I knelt down to pray. Before I did so, I stripped off my habit and my hair shirt, took the bloodstained knout from my satchel, and vigorously flagellated myself. To no avail. I had barely begun the paternoster when Alice, unbidden, entered the room. It was almost as though my penance had conjured up a further test.

"Mon père," she said. And then, again, "Oh Jean, my love."

I shook. My back was still bloody and it was perhaps the pain that convulsed me, though I should have been used to it by now; but no, it was the spiritual turmoil. "That was years ago. That was weakness. We can never think of it."

"That's easy for you to say, mon père," Alice said. "I've paid for it every day since then. I haven't come to reprove you. I know you scourge yourself. But there are other kinds of pain, too. Guillaume should not be growing up here, in this dreadful, desolate place. He's part of you. Can you not acknowledge that?"

"It's a lot to take in in a single day. Does he know?"

"Perhaps. I don't know.   I've seen you look at each other. He must have guessed. And he has your eyes. I love him most for that."

"Alice," I said, "there are cardinals who have sired children, and popes who have made their bastards cardinals. But the Bishop of Nantes doesn't have a very modern mind.

And I'm a Dominican. A *teacher*. How if it is seen that I do not follow my own preachings? Shall I give up even my vows to God?"

"Did you not do so already, Jean?"

And there she had me. But I had done penance. God forgives, even if the Bishop of Nantes would not. "What do you want me to do?"

"Take your son with you. You don't have to acknowledge him. Make him your servant. He could learn to read and write. He has a beautiful voice. He could have a future life as a singer."

"But they would have to cut him for that," I said. "And some boys do die under the barber's knife."

She has never seen what they do, I can tell. Oh, I have seen fine chanteurs with the voices of angels. The timeless melancholy of their songs comes, I think, from the wound to their manhood, which even when it has healed leaves a longing that can never be fulfilled.

"I don't understand those things. All know is that you have resources. You sleep in castles. You can call soldiers to throw people into dungeons. Your son has a grudging stepfather who doesn't want to spare the food to fill his belly, and he is the most powerless person in a village that men say is already damned. You must take him. Whipping yourself is all very well, but can't you see that you're also punishing *him?*"

I had come to Tiffauges to investigate a crime against God. But was I myself also to be subjected to the Question?

Alice kissed me. My flesh hardened, but I could not harden my heart. I turned away. I needed a pure heart for tomorrow.

"I'm sorry, mon père." She curtsied and left the room. Her scent remained. And so did the wound.

Why the wound, what wound? There was no wound.

Should I not have followed the example of almost-martyred Origen and made myself a eunuch for the sake of the Kingdom of Heaven? Obviously a vow to God was an empty promise. Only the slice of a knife held truth.

#

Both Brother Paolo and Alice had told me Guillaume could sing; I only knew how well that morning, when I said mass in the chapel. Brother Paolo had found an old psaltery, and he had badgered the boy into coming up to the chateau and had taught him, neume by neume, a short chanson by Dufay, the Burgundian; and during the offertorium they contrived to perform it, with the brother playing the tenor on the psaltery and essaying the contratenor himself, while Guillaume took the upper part, with the high notes that seem to hover in the air... .

I should say first that, at breakfast, over a loaf of black bread and a beaker of wine, the Chevalier Johan told me that all had been done as I had asked. They had requisitioned some of the peasants to dust and mop some of the rooms in the chateau; for they feared the soldiers more than they feared the curse of Bluebeard.

The chapel, wherein the Marshall of France had permitted the most repulsive abominations, had been scoured of dirt by dawn. The peasants who had been commanded to do the work stayed for mass, but several from the village came, too. Perhaps they thought that the touch of the host upon their tongues could take away the lingering taste of terror.

It was during the offertorium that Brother Paolo's ad hoc consort performed. The peasants had, of course, little to offer but a few loaves and cheeses; yet our torturer went among them, gracefully taking the gifts with a smile. They could never have guessed his normal profession.

The music was a setting of a holy sonnet by Francesco

Petrarca; I knew this must be Brother Paolo's doing, for though the composer was Flemish, he had been in service in Italy, and the chanson had an Italian lilt to it, for the Italians have the fashion of giving a soaring melody to the highest voice, reducing the others to little more than accompaniment.

When I heard the words, I ached; for Petrarca speaks of the beautiful virgin cloaked in the sun and the stars, and then the poem goes on to say, "I want to offer you my prayers, but I cannot even begin to pray without your help... ."

And it was the issue of my loins who sang those words, and he made the notes linger in the chill air as they climbed, note piling upon note, like a stairway to the sky—

In caelo.

That pitiful creature claimed to reside in the sky! And now he had put a curse on me, and I could not see the face of the Blessed Virgin with the raiment of starlight, but instead, a more earthly woman, a woman whose earthy scent and moist lips cried out for me to sin, whose every gesture was derived from the temptation of Eve and the wiles of the Serpent. I stood there, sweat pouring down my face even though the chapel was cold.

And my son's voice rose above the turmoil ... and there came dawn. A ray of light burst through the east window and illuminated the altar. And my son's voice was in that light. It lifted me out of darkness. In that melody was the voice of God himself.

And I saw the beauty in his eyes, my eyes... .

I knew now how I had to redeem my sinful past. I had to rescue my son. Woman though she was, Alice had been a messenger. Those sweet sounds must not perish. He must be cut; surely the Lord would guide the knife Hmself, for the saving of so perfect a voice. My son was not to know the sins of the flesh. He could not fall as I had fallen. I knew then why God had sent me back to Tiffauges.

But for now, I kept this knowledge in my heart.

\#

The papal regulations allow for only two sessions of Question; it is therefore the custom never to declare a session ended, so that the prescribed methods of ferreting out the truth may be applied until the truth is actually obtained.

The first session, which is intended to proceed without torture, I always like to stage in a well-lit room, without a threatening atmosphere. So we used the largest room in the chateau. Apart from a minimal chaining of the ankles, the prisoner was given free rein to stand or sit as he chose, and given a stool. I myself occupied what must have once been the Marshall's magisterial chair; flanking me were Brother Paolo, with his quill, ink, and parchment, and Jean the Barber; that, and our Chevalier and a few of the soldiers, were all that the huge council chamber held.

Now that I saw him in broad daylight, I knew why the children had covered him with mud. He was green. Oh, not *obviously* green, like grass or an emerald, but he had a gray-green cast to him. With a tunic, belt, and shoes, it was less noticeable, because the eyes were what held you most about him. But I did not fail to notice what I did not see in the dim light of the innkeeper's cellar; his hands were webbed, like the feet of a duck.

Once in a while, one hears of a child with webbed feet and hands being born in some remote village, and the peasants do not hesitate to kill it, for to dispose of a monster is not deemed murder. I had never heard of one surviving to adulthood.

Still, save for the odd coloration, the scales, the webbed hands, the creature did not exude an aura of evil. Not in this light, at least. I thought him more pitiful than terrifying.

Although I knew that he could speak Latin, I decided to begin the interrogation in the vulgar tongue.

"What is your name?" I asked.

"We have no names," he said. "We are all fragments of an All. Names are bad. They fracture us from the One." It was nonsense.

"But you must have a name," I said. It was a bureaucrat's nightmare; you have the papers, and you cannot even begin, because such things are filed away by name, and there is no name, how can one begin?

"We shall give you a name," I said. I turned to Brother Paolo. "Pick any name. We shall not fumble this case over some trickery."

"Call me Guillaume," said the creature.

Like Jean, Guillaume is one of the commonest names in France. But I could not help thinking that he took that name to taunt me with my sin. I was about to stop Brother Paolo, but he had already written it down.

"No, you are wrong," said Guillaume the Monster. "I honor him, he my first friend in this world." His French comes and goes; sometimes it is perfect; sometimes it is disjointed, as though he were stringing the sentences together from a heap of words.

"Why do you say this world? Know you another world?"

"I am lost. My world is far."

"Where is your world?"

Guillaume the Monster points only at the ceiling.

"Are you an angel?"

"Angel? … Oh." He seems perplexed. He looks as though he is searching through some store of information to retrieve the word. "Oh. You mean Αγγελος." Then he says in French, "Messenger. Yes. I messenger."

"So you claim to be a member of the heavenly host."

"I fall from sky."

Brother Paolo cries out, "Listen! He condemns himself from his own lips. He is a fallen angel."

This was an outlandish claim; why would such an apparition not appear in some royal court, or before His Holiness himself? Why would a fallen angel choose an obscure village to bring his message to the world? But the answer was obvious when I thought about it. It was clear that the foul rites practices by Gilles de Rais had left a sort of spiritual chasm here. When a man murders hundreds of children to satiate his sexual appetites, all the while invoking the names of the Dark Powers, there are surely consequences to the natural order. For the tiniest sin is a hideous affront to God, and these were monstrous. It was as though Bluebeard had dug a well straight through to the heart of hell. Why not, then, a fiend shooting forth from the infernal depths, cloaked in fiery brimstone, to tempt the mind of an innocent?

Still, there were some elementary tests. "Can you say the Lord's Prayer?" I asked him.

The monster said, "How can I know these things? I come from the sky."

Jean the Torturer said, "I'm afraid that there's very little we can do about this." I knew he was not anxious to get out all his instruments, but like all of us he understood the meaning of duty.

I said, "Let's not be in a rush to be cruel. I suggest we try an exorcism first."

As was the custom, I declared, and entered into the record, that the session was adjourned; and we took our midday break, after leaving the prisoner more securely chained up in the council chamber, and well guarded.

The innkeeper sent up a brace of duck to the chateau; it was my son who brought the food, for though we had dismissed him after the morning mass, he had begged for some excuse to return.

We ate quickly and prepared our vestments as well as an aspergillum and a large cauldron of holy water. I asked the Chevalier to send a swift rider to Nantes; I suspected that reinforcements were going to be needed; not more soldiers, but more expert demonologists. Reverently, I kissed the violet stola before placing it over my surplice. I have never taken exorcism lightly.

But when I returned to the council chamber, I found the two Guillaumes alone together.

"What are you doing?" I shouted.

My Guillaume backed away. He had been bent over the prisoner; he had a cup in his hand.

"I'm sorry, mon père. I was giving him water."

I said, "You, of all people, need to stay away from him. He has invaded your mind more than anyone. He has plucked things out and will use them against us—against you in particular. Your immortal soul is in grave peril."

He looked at me and I could sense—defiance. And then, with bowed head, my Guillaume slunk away.

"Do you know what I am going to do?" I asked the monster.

For normally, when one is about to perform an exorcism, the demon has foreknowledge. When the holy water is brought into the room, he begins to howl. He hurls obscenities at the priest, and malodorous fumes begin to rise, which are best counteracted by the liberal use of frankincense. To that end I had already prepared two censers and the sweet fragrance was already seeping into the room. But Guillaume the monster did not respond at all.

I began the asperging, dipping the aspergillum and calling on the Father, the Son and the Holy Ghost, the Blessed Virgin, St. Peter, St. Michael, St. Denis and all the company of heaven to witness. Brother Paolo held up the crucifix to the prisoner's face, but the creature did not flinch; he merely stared at it curiously, blinking.

I started the preparatory incantations and then, summoning up all my inner strength, I bellowed out the words of exorcism: *Exorcizo te, immundissime spiritus, omnis incusio adversarii, omne phantasma, omnis legio, in nomini domini nostri Jesu Christi eradicare ...* and with each sign of the cross I swung the aspergillum, knowing full well that the power that resided in the water would burn the devil from the being's flesh ...

But Guillaume the monster sat there.

And when the ritual was done, he spoke to me. "That was an interesting ceremony, Father Lenclud. What does it mean? May I see a repetition, so that I can play back the recorded memory to my companions in the sky?"

There arose in me a terrible anger. He was mocking me. He was mocking the Almighty. I knew that this blind fury was a sin. I went outside to get some fresh air. I was panting and my heart was beating fast. In the courtyard, I saw my Guillaume, sitting by a well.

My son pulled a fresh bucket of water, and gave me to drink. Though the noonday sun was brilliant, there were still piles of snow among the cobblestones. He held out the bowl for me, and the sun was behind him and the wind stirred his hair and I saw in his face all that I once wished to be, but could no longer, for that I had long descended into tainted ways of sin. I wanted to tell him right then and there, but perhaps it was not the moment. I drank deeply and the water cooled my choler.

"How is he?" my son said. "Is he in pain?"

I saw in his face a profound compassion and I thought to myself, "Guillaume, my son, you are good to feel such Christian love for even such a creature as this." I wanted so much to embrace him. But we are taught to avoid the warmth of human closeness, for darker dangers may lurk behind an innocuous caress. The mere touch of a boy's hand has aroused unnatural passion in many a cleric. It were better not to risk it. Love is best experienced solely in the spirit. I cursed myself for a hypocrite to think such things when only last night Alice had flung herself at me and I had released myself only with reluctance from temptation. I only said, "We are not torturing him at the moment, my son. It is possible that he will reveal all without recourse to the second stage of the Question. And we will all be spared much grief."

All afternoon, I wielded the aspergillum with a will. I shouted out the words of the ritual. Three times we commanded the devil to depart. Three times I flung the water and shouted out those puissant words, words composed to make Satan himself quake in the bowels in hell; yet the prisoner did not yield, did not even show fear; if he evinced any emotion at all, it was curiosity. Exhausted and exasperated beyond all measure, I finally hurled the entire basin at him. It struck him in the head. The water scattered and clouds of steam rose up. And at this unexpected turn, he slumped over and I was immediately concerned, for it is not a priest's duty to inflict pain. But then, when I looked about him, I saw that the pools of water were all boiling, and that there poured from a gash in his forehead a thick green rheum; and the creature began to vibrate as though he had the falling sickness, so that the chains clanked and made a racket that should have woken the very dead. A blast of heat emanated from him, and unearthly sounds poured from his throat; at last, I could see the symptoms of possession.

And, as I gaped, the wound in his brow knit itself together, and the pools of water ceased seething, and the room was as icy cold as before.

And he sat there, unperturbed.

I sank back on my inquisitorial chair. I was sweating. I called for wine. Slowly, the creature seemed to regain his senses, and sat up as before.

I folded my palms and began to pray. "God," I whispered, "I am already worn out. The demon will not budge. Oh God, give me strength. My faith is sorely tested." These words I spoke for myself alone.

So I was surprised when an answer seemed to come, not from heaven, but from my green-skinned adversary. "You know, Father," he said, "there is another possibility."

We are warned never to engage in conversation with the devil, for it leads only to despair. But before I could think of that, I had already said, "And that is?"

"Is it not possible," he said, "that I am *not* in fact possessed, and that I am simply what I say I am?"

I dared not respond for fear of further temptation. For I knew then that we were in the presence of a very powerful force indeed; that this was a stubborn being and that the light of truth would reach him only with the utmost difficulty. If the creature were not inhabited by a demon, he must be making those impious statements out of his own free will; which meant that he must be a heretic.

I took another gulp of the wine, and I commanded that he be removed to the dungeon. This investigation was inexorably moving down a path I did not wish for. Nonetheless, I reflected, *thy will be done.*

***

I rode down to the village because I could not bear to sleep in the vicinity of that being. Of course, in the village I faced demons as well, but at least they were my own.

At the inn, I supped on boiled leeks and a bit of pigeon meat. I sat alone, long after the others had retired, nursing a warm ale. Perhaps I dozed a little. I was startled awake, perhaps by the sound of the embers collapsing, for the fire was dying. I saw that my Guillaume was in the room, and that he was standing over me, gazing down at my face.

"My son," I said. A priest would say that to any boy. Yet I immediately feared to have revealed to much.

"Mon père, I would speak to you alone."

"Shall I take your confession?"

"It's not that. Mon père, Brother Paolo has been speaking to me. He says I should leave the village and seek my fortune as a singer. He told me that a voice like mine could gladden the hearts of prelates and of kings. He told me about cities and places I'll never see if I'm stuck here minding the pigs until I die. My mother told me the same thing. But they also say I will have to give up something. I don't want that."

"Did they explain it to you?"

"Yes. They said that if I undergo the cutting, I'll never become a man. But I'll never lose this voice, either. They say it's a sacrifice I must make. Otherwise I'll always be a peasant, and I'll always be a bastard. But I know it'll hurt and I know people die, sometimes."

"What did you say to your mother?" I asked him.

"I said, I really don't want to do it. I'm scared. I don't like pain. The innkeeper …" He hesitated. "Well, I am a bastard," he said. He turned his back to me and lowered his tunic a little, and I could see scars in the firelight. And I burned with anger, but I held back that anger, for anger is one of the seven deadly sins. Truly, my sin was being visited on the next generation. If my son was willing to be cut, I reflected, at least the cycle of penance would end. "It's all right, really. I don't mind pain that much. I get it often enough. It's like I can't do anything right for him."

"Sit here beside me, Guillaume of Tiffauges," I said. He obeyed. His closeness terrified me. "Did your mother say that you should undergo this operation?"

"She said that it was entirely my decision."

"And what is your decision?" I dared to caress his hair for a brief moment.

"I told her that I will do it if you command it, mon père."

"Why me?"

"Because you are my father," he said.

And I saw that he knew, he knew it with utter certitude, as I knew of the existence of heaven and hell. "Who told you this?" I said. "Your mother swore to me she would never speak of our—"

"She didn't betray you, mon père. I found out for myself."

"But how?

"He told me, mon père."

Should I now say that the boy wept, and told me how he had dreamed for so many years of knowing his father, that he had imagined him a crusader, a warrior, a hunter, a prince, a troubadour, a sorceror, but never in his wildest dreams a priest? Should I tell how his tears broke down my reserve at last, and how I embraced him and felt at long last the joy of an untainted love?

But I may not say these things. Because, at that time, they did not happen. Rather I answered him very simply, "Then I do command it."

And he said, "I will do what you tell me, father." And he got up, and planted a single dry kiss upon my tearless cheek, and he left me.

I thought of the pain I was about to inflict upon him. But I thought also of God the Father, who must have known full well what pain our Lord his Son would have to undergo; I thought also of Isaac, consenting to the knife with joy because it was his father's will; and only then, only when there was no one to see me, did I give way to tears. I cried myself to oblivion, and before dawn they found me there, and woke me for the trek back up to the chateau, so I could say mass.

***

As the "gentle persuasion" portion of the investigation was now over, it seemed more appropriate to continue in the dungeons. The use of torture is never to be undertaken without proper reflection. After all, anxious as they were to obtain a conviction, the Inquisition did not torture Joan of Arc.

The dungeons were the dark heart of Tiffauges. It was there that Bluebeard once made a pile of the decapitated heads of the children he had murdered, so that he could compare them to see which was the most beautiful. It was here that the Marshall of France kept his captives, lured to the castle by the promise of a place in the chapel choir or a position as page in the great lord's estate. It was here that he sated his lusts with all manner of vice, culminating always in erotically charged slaughter.

No torture unto death would of course, be practiced by us. Indeed, the papal instructions are very specific, for we may not even shed one drop of blood during the Question. Bloodletting is the domain of the secular arm; our concern is only with the soul.

Only a single session of torture is permitted by church law, though one can extend that session over many periods if need be.

I entered the dungeon they had selected, one with no light but torchlight, and an odious damp, with vermin underfoot—for it is important to produce in the Questioned person the feeling of utter hopelessness, so as to hasten his confession. Jean the Torturer had already set up the strappado. The Inquisitorial chair had been brought down, and a rich rug placed to receive it and the desk, at which Brother Paolo already sat, with his notebook and quill at hand, making the initial entry by candlelight.

Guillaume the Monster had been stripped of his clothing, for the shame of public nakedness is often enough to induce a confession. Naturally, I averted my eyes, for it is not seemly for a spiritual man to behold such things; but curiosity made me look anyway, and when I did I could not help but stare.

The greenish cast of the skin was of made more reptilian in the dungeon's smoky light. They had already tied the cords to the shoulders, and attached the weights to his feet, but the torturer was waiting for my signal before beginning the actual excruciation.

As I grew used to the dimness, I stood up to examine him more closely, hoping for some sign that would allow me to avoid torture. For example, a clear supernumerary nipple could indicate his involvement in witchcraft; a circumcised *membrum virile* would signify that he was a Jew. We could have proceeded straight to the conviction.

But this monstrosity possessed no nipples at all, nor anything resembling the organ in question. His chest was a pattern of scales. Below his waist, his legs began. The scale pattern continued straight down.

He said, "You seem surprised, mon père."

"You are … you are a natural eunuch! And without even vestigial nipples … you are neither male nor female … were you female, you could not suckle a child … were you male, you could not engender a child … you are an abomination!" The horror of it was unbearable. It was a prodigy.

"Perhaps my kind does not require this type of reproduction," said Guillaume the monster.

"So you claim to be without original sin?" I said.

"What is sin?" said the monster.

"Do you not honor God?"

"Who is God?" he asked me.

I could listen no more. I gave Jean the signal to hoist him up. As the weights left the ground I could hear the crack of the shoulder joints dislocating. "You deny God?" I shouted. "You claim to be in a state of grace?"

He writhed, and a serpentine hissing escaped his lips.

"More weights!" I screamed. "You will confess!"

"To what shall I confess?"

"That you are a heretic! That you claim to be free of sin, a state the Church alone is empowered to bestow through the holy rite of confession and absolution! Confess!"

"I am not a heretic. I am from another world. I am lost. Send me home."

"And how shall that be, when you claim that your home is in heaven?"

"I have already told your son how I may go home! There are two ways; the first is for me to communicate with the mother ship. The device is under the ice! You have but to wait until the spring thaw is complete and—"

At the mention of my Guillaume, I became more furious. With what corruptions had he been feeding my son? I commanded the torturer to add more weights, while every croak, every hiss was carefully noted down by Brother Paolo. The arms were already quite out of their sockets; the muscles were tearing; the monster's eyes bulged and he appeared to gasp. But what I did not hear were cries of pain. And so I hardened my heart and told Jean the Torturer to add weights until there were far more weights than any human could bear, which proved that Satan was behind his unnatural resistance, and which inflamed my rage still more.

"Confess that you have denied the sacraments! That

you're a Jew! A witch! That you have had carnal knowledge of Satan! That you're a Cathar! A Waldensian! You have but to admit to a single heresy and I will cease tormenting you!"

It was at that moment, with my emotions aroused to fever pitch, that our captive's arms tore loose and he fell to the floor with a crash. It was horrible. A greenish sap began to ooze from sockets. The arms flailed back and forth as though independently alive.

"We're spilling blood!" I gasped, horrified that we had broken the papal regulations. "Jean, you must stanch it quickly!"

"I don't understand," said the torturer. "I haven't applied enough pressure to rip off any limbs." He was upset; a professional should know his craft better than to make such a bungle of things; I could tell that he was utterly appalled at himself. Quickly he found some rags so that he could prevent too much blood from touching the ground, which is the actual letter of the law we were violating. There was some straw in the dungeon—it was the prisoner's bedding—and he threw it over the heretic to try to absorb some of the gore.

But Brother Paolo said, "It is green, Father Lenclud. It is not blood."

The severed arms swung back and forth and now began to sizzle and chair, and an acrid green smoke began to fill the dungeon. I ordered more torches to be lit. We had to see what we were doing. A foul green fluid was spurting over our faces. I saw that Brother Paolo was right. This was not blood. It had neither the stickiness nor the characteristic scent. Jean the Torturer had not broken the law.

Meanwhile, Jean the Monster was writhing on the stone floor. A cacophonous babble issued from his lips. Doubtless it was some appalling witchery such as the Lord's prayer backwards. Indeed, clearly there was necromancy afoot, because the creature's shoulder sockets were quivering, vibrating, and small green stalks were pushing their way out through the flesh … he was growing a new pair of arms, as though they were the tails of a lizard! I simply stared. The babble resolved itself once more into words:

"I am not a heretic. I am from another world. I beg you, send me home. I can wait until the spring thaw is complete. Or you can set off my internal monitor to signal the ship… ."

Words they may have been, but it was still nonsense.

"His body magically repairs itself," said Jean the Torturer, and I was reminded of the tale of the hydra, who grew more heads whenever one was chopped off.

"But," said Brother Paolo as he finished a sentence of his trial transcript with a flourish of his quill, "the regeneration the flesh, and the fact that his body contains no blood to be spilled, opens up, by the legal constraints imposed by the papacy, a loophole in the process of excruciation… ."

I understood at once. Without blood, without any permanent destruction of the flesh, there was no legal limit to the violence that could be inflicted upon this monster in the interests of perhaps saving his immortal soul.

Jean immediately strung him up again and, secure in the knowledge that he was committing no excommunicable crime, brought out more extreme instruments of pain. The scourgings, lashings, and burnings made us all wince, but the creature's stubbornness continued to inflame me, and by late afternoon I had almost taken complete leave of my senses. His stubbornness caused almost a reversal in our roles; for where normally the accused would be pleading for mercy after a few hours' torment, it was Brother Paolo and I who were so worn out by the monster's equanimity that we were beginning, pleading, cajoling the creature to try to get even the vaguest confession.

Half a dozen pairs of arms hang from the rafters. Straw

on the floor was soaking up puddles of greenish phlegm.

Jean's art had punctured the monster's skin in several places. There were holes through which we could see the foul workings of his innards, and now, as he lay, his skin pulsating, yet another pair of arms pushing forth out of his sockets, his words were hoarse and accompanied by a bizarre whistling as breath passed through the many extra channels through his flesh. And he continued his talk of coming from the sky, and returning there, and incomprehensible mumbo-jumbo about his mission and about his internal sensors. We must have made some kind of an impression, surely! For his voice wheezed, and it seemed to me that I saw some weariness in his eyes.

I was about to declare an official continuation of the session until the next day, when the door of the dungeon creaked open, and my son Guillaume entered the tortured chamber.

"Church business is not to be interrupted!" Brother Paolo shouted, and threw a cape over the monster. But I knew that Guillaume had already seen.

"Mon père," he said, "I have come as you commanded, to receive the operation."

There was a dead silence. Under the cloak, the monster twitched and fibrillated. Guillaume looked up at the ceiling, where the creature's many pairs of severed arms still dangled. The cloak slid off the monster's face and we could all see his eyes, peering back and forth with a discomfiting watchfulness.

Guillaume looked at me and raised his arms in a gesture of remonstrance, and I said simply, "What can I do, Guillaume? He won't confess."

"Mon père," Guillaume said, "You could have asked me. I know what will make him confess."

"Child, there is a manual of instruction composed by His

Holiness himself about these matters. We deviate from it on pain of eternal damnation. Leave these things to us. Come upstairs, now, into the light. We'll talk of your operation and of your future. Forget what you've seen."

"But mon père," he said, "my mother tells you have an expert, who will wield the knife deftly and who will give me as little pain as he can. Who is he?"

"I," said Jean the Torturer, who in an ideal world would have preferred to be known only as Jean the Barber.

And he held out hands of welcome, hands oozing with the monster's green rheum.

\#

The torturer had not, of course, brought a gelding knife. He had to do with an instrument that had that same day sliced leeks in the castle kitchens. But I wanted the cutting to occur in a room as distant as possible from the squalor of Guillaume's former life. The peasants looked askance when I requisitioned the Marshall's own bedchamber, and commanded that clean linens be set out, and a goose-down pillow; but they could not argue with me, for I represented the Church, and the Church had jurisdiction over the chateau for the present.

I had them gather plenty of wood for the fireplace. I even went so far as to order Jean the Barber to bathe, so that my son would not see the traces of the monster's excruciation upon his hands. And I had extra candles brought in so that he would not wake up in the dark, and be frightened. The finest silver basins were brought in to catch the blood and to hold water to lave the wound.

Guillaume was terribly afraid. We held him down, I by the arms and Brother Paolo by the legs. I gave him a twig to bite on. I could not look into his eyes, could not gaze on the terror which was being inflicted by my will alone. The barber lifted the boy's tunic and sliced and Guillaume started screaming almost before the knife touched flesh, and he went on screaming. We held him fast. I did not realize there would be this much blood. I squeezed my eyes shut as the boy screamed and the torturer turned barber sliced, steadily and methodically, until the boy's scrotum was completely severed. Then, working as swiftly as he could, he applied linen bandages and a salve, wrapping as Guillaume screamed himself into a frenzy and, at last, exhausted from it all, sunk back onto the bloody sheets.

"You can let go of him," said the barber. "It is done."

I realized I was still gripping the lad's arms tight. I relaxed, but he clung to my wrists and murmured, "Papa, papa." And then he fainted.

The others looked away. I knew then that they must have already known. "I will sit with him," I said.

"Yes, you must," said Jean. "The first hours are critical. He is in so much pain that his soul cannot decide whether to depart his body. It isn't only the physical pain, mon père; it's the feeling of eternal loss. He doesn't even *want* to come back … but you can give him something to hope for, to live for."

And all of them left me, and I sat alone, by the side of the bed, listening to him moan. I could not sleep. I did not know whether Guillaume slept; he twisted and turned, and sometimes his eyes opened; he never let go of my hand. The one Guillaume I had meant to hurt, and not the other; somehow I had reversed them. I prayed; how I did pray. "I'll give my immortal soul," I whispered, "if he will only pull through."

Towards midnight, he seemed to quieten. I wiped the sweat from his brow. He stirred. At last, he opened his eyes. He said, very softly, "Don't you want to know how to get him to confess?"

I said, "Don't think of it, my son."

"You hurt me," he said.

"I know," I said. And squeezed his hand.

"I don't mind," he said. "It's what you wanted."

I said, "The pain will go away."

He said, "I did what you wanted. So now, I'm going to ask you to do something I want."

"Anything," I said softly.

"He will confess if you promise that you will burn him at the stake," Guillaume said.

"Don't say such things," I said. "There's no need for you to become involved in—"

"No, Papa, please listen. I will tell it to you exactly as I heard it, because I don't understand it, but he's made me memorize it many times. He doesn't appear to be in pain, but he is desperate. He can wait until the thaw to retrieve his communication device, but there is another way for him to go home, another, more desperate way. He has a transmitter embedded deep inside him. It's not a machine, it's a part of him because he's connected to all the others. If his vital signs suggest that he's in imminent danger of death, it will start to transmit … he told me they're cold-blooded. Extreme heat will set it off."

"You are delirious," I said. "You're speaking nonsense."

"But promise me that you will tell him you'll burn him at the stake."

The boy was clearly maddened by his agony, but I knew I had to promise. I did so. He squeezed my hand again, and finally drifted into slumber.

***

In the morning, I did what my Guillaume had asked me, and the monster immediately, to my astonishment, confessed to an entire litany of heresies. I fell to my knees and thanked God that I no longer needed to have recourse to torture. I swore then that, though I had promised to burn the creature, I would give him a final chance to repent and accept the mercy of strangulation; I owed him that much at least, for it was because of him that I had learned what it is to love a child.

And in the afternoon, we put the heretic's cap and robes on our prisoner and shut him up in a cage, as one would a circus animal, and hitched the cage to an ox; and I wrapped my son up in many layers of blankets and loaded his pallet onto my cart for the drive back to Nantes.

Alice and the innkeeper came to see us off; but I did not say a word to them.

And for the burning itself, Guillaume would not leave the house, though he was hale enough to have started his singing lessons.

There are not so many heretic burnings as there used to be; and so it was that by the time enough heretics had been delivered to the secular arm that a reasonable spectacle could be had on market day, the days had lengthened and there was no more snow to be seen. And each day, my son grew stronger, and we never spoke of the night of his delirium.

But I had made a vow to God that I would personally try to urge Guillaume the Monster towards an eleventh hour repentance. And thus it was I found myself standing beside him at the stake, holding up a cross to him and urging him to turn to God.

"Who is God?" he asked me.

Around us, they were already burning. The crowd was festive; they laughed, they sang, music played, sausages were being grilled; church bells rang. But it all seemed irrelevant. What transpired now was between the two of us alone.

In my whole life, I have made love only once, and that was in shame. And yet I have heard, in the confessional, enough to know what it is like for laypersons. Lovemaking is not permitted to men who have given themselves wholly to Christ, and yet, to us inquisitors, there is an alternative. For the process of the Question is not unlike carnal knowledge of a woman. That may seem twisted, even obscene, but there is truth in it.

First, you see, there comes the foreplay, the teasing, the flirting; that is the first stage, where we try to extract the confession swiftly; yet if we succeed, it is somehow not entirely fulfilling. Then there is the physical part; the writhing, the flailing; that, you see, is the torture, and that can lead only to one thing: the final explosion of passion, the spurting of the seed; that is the confession, you see. And at least, with the violent emotions spent, comes the afterglow, the gentle conversation, the quiet descent into slumber.

And this was the manner of conversation now, at the ultimate hour. There was no going back. He had asked me who God is, and I was bound to tell him: "God is the one who made us all, who loves us, who knows us inside out; and he dwells in Heaven. He who does not seek God is bound forever to the darkness."

"If that is true," said Guillaume the Monster, his scaly face utterly serene, "then I already know God. And I am going to him now. For the being of which I am a part does dwell in the sky, and when I am cut off from him I am utterly desolate."

"You have rejected him," I said.

"And what sane sentient being," said the monster, "would *not* reject your God? You have made a mockery of compassion. You have twisted the truth in a thousand ways."

"Repent," I cried out, and I held the cross right up to his face. It cast a cruciform shadow on his alien features.

"It is because you humans are all islands, because you

are not part of some greater consciousness, that you have invented these fanciful stories about gods and demons," he said. "If you only knew how alone each one of you was, how incapable you are of the weakest psychic communion, you would despair. You would not care to live."

A soldier of the Secular Arm called up to me. "Come down, Father Lenclud! We need to get going, this is the last one."

"For the last time," I cried out. "You can be saved if you only say a few words of repentance. You can become a dwell in Him, in the unity of the holy spirit—"

"Then I am already God, for I already dwell in Him," he said.

And the fire began to blaze. I knew that I myself would be consumed if I did not leave. The piles of kindling crackled. The flames hissed. Already, the creature's extremities were beginning to char.

At that moment, the sky abruptly darkened. A monstrous dark *thing* descended and blotted out the sun. A shaft of brilliant blue light hit shot out of the heaves and struck the heretic, and he immediately vaporized. And then it was over, and the sun shone as before.

I looked wildly about. The revelers in the streets still danced and sang. Hawkers sold wine and food. Had no one seen what I had seen? And was the creature not gone? There were only the chains. Had my eyes played tricks on me?

I was troubled that night. I could not reconcile what I had seen with all that I knew and believed. And yet, as time passed, I grew to believe that it may have only been an illusion. For to believe the alternative made me far too uneasy. And I had to be steadfast in faith, for I had a child to raise.

***

In the bedchamber of the new King Louis XI of France, my son Guillaume is singing. I am not permitted to enter; it is a performance for the most intimate circle of the King's friends.

But as I wait for my son behind the arras, I realize that the song is another by that Burgundian, Dufay, whose song to the Blessed Virgin once moved Brother Paolo to demand the boy's emasculation. This is a secular song, *Donnes l'Assault,* in which the poet compares his lady to an impregnable castle to which he has lain siege. He speaks of battering down the gate to enjoy the treasure within. It is a bawdy song, turning images of war into double entendres. There is laughter in the bedroom; men's laughter, the high-pitched silvery laugh of a loose woman.

I wait for the song to end. It is a tawdry song, but haunting, too. And the wounded innocence of my son's voice transforms the song from a jest to a thing of vaunting beauty.

Was it for this that my Guillaume gave up becoming a man?

He will be wealthy, I know; he will be a courtier. But he did not do it to become rich. He did it as a proof his love. He did it because I demanded it of him.

Yet who was I to play God?

I too have become powerful. I too have become rich. But something in me has died. Or perhaps was plucked from my soul and has ascended into the sky along with the body of my heretical monster.

I too have been transformed by that fire. I have sent many more to the flames since that day. I have signed many death-warrants. I have consented to innumerable sessions of savage torture, and always with the knowledge that my scruples have ineluctably eroded until the act of condemning a man to an agonizing death has become but a figment of bureaucracy. I have come to believe that I am evil. I have come to accept that, because my becoming evil is the price of being allowed to love my son.

For though the heretic from another world has incontrovertibly proved to me that Satan exists, I am no longer certain of the existence of God.

An Appeal to My Readers

This novel was made possible because a few dozen people became my supporters by joining this website: www.patreon.com/spsomtow.

I'm no longer doing these books with the backing of a vast New York publishing conglomerate. It's pretty much do-it-yourself, with all the labor-intensiveness, snatching time away from money-making activities, and sloppy trying to proofread one's own copy that all that implies.

If a few dozen more people would sign up—or a few hundred—my ability to resume my science fiction career would be much enhanced. So, please consider it.

Supporters get to read all my books chapter by chapter—in their unenhanced, inaccurately proofred and yet-to-be refined incarnations—right as they come out of my head. They get Christmas presents (though I am habitually late with them). You can join for as little a $2 a month—though hopefully you will be able to do a higher level.

About the Author

The most well-known expatriate Thai in the world —
International Herald Tribune

Once referred to by the International Herald Tribune as
"the most well-known expatriate Thai in the world,"
Somtow Sucharitkul is no longer an expatriate, since he has
returned to Thailand after five decades of wandering the
world. He is best known as an award winning novelist and a
composer of operas.

Born in Bangkok, Somtow grew up in Europe and was
educated at Eton and Cambridge. His first career was in
music and in the 1970s he acquired a reputation as a
revolutionary composer, the first to combine Thai and
Western instruments in radical new sonorities. Conditions in
the arts in the region at the time proved so traumatic for the
young composer that he suffered a major burnout, emigrated
to the United States, and reinvented himself as a novelist.

His earliest novels were in the science fiction field but he
soon began to cross into other genres. In his 1984 novel
Vampire Junction, he injected a new literary inventiveness
into the horror genre, in the words of Robert Bloch, author of
Psycho, "skillfully combining the styles of Stephen King,
William Burroughs, and the author of the Revelation to
John." *Vampire Junction* was voted one of the forty all-time

greatest horror books by the Horror Writers' Association, joining established classics like *Frankenstein* and *Dracula*.

In the 1990s Somtow became increasingly identified as a uniquely Asian writer with novels such as the semi-autobiographical *Jasmine Nights*. He won the World Fantasy Award, the highest accolade given in the world of fantastic literature, for his novella *The Bird Catcher*. His seventy-seven books have sold about two million copies world-wide.

After becoming a Buddhist monk for a period in 2001, Somtow decided to refocus his attention on the country of his birth, founding Bangkok's first international opera company and returning to music, where he again reinvented himself, this time as a neo-Asian neo-Romantic composer. The Norwegian government commissioned his song cycle Songs Before Dawn for the 100th Anniversary of the Nobel Peace Prize, and he composed at the request of the government of Thailand his *Requiem: In Memoriam 9/11* which was dedicated to the victims of the 9/11 tragedy.

According to London's Opera magazine, "in just five years, Somtow has made Bangkok into the operatic hub of Southeast Asia." His operas on Thai themes, *Madana, Mae Naak,* and *Ayodhya,* have been well received by international critics. His opera, *The Silent Prince,* was premiered in 2010 in Houston, and, *Dan no Ura,* premiered in Thailand in the 2013 season. Since then he has composed many more stage works including the acclaimed fantasy-based opera *The Snow Dragon* (premiered in Milwaukee in 2015) and seven operas in the *DasJati* sequence which aims to put all ten of the iconic *Ten Lives of the Buddha* into music drama form.

He is increasingly in demand as a conductor specializing in opera and in the late-romantic composers like Mahler. His repertoire runs the entire gamut from Monteverdi to Wagner. His work has been especially lauded for its stylistic authenticity and its lyricism. The orchestra he founded in Bangkok, the Siam Philharmonic, has mounted the first complete Mahler cycle in the region.

He was the first recipient of Thailand's "Distinguished Silpathorn" award, given for an artist who has made and continues to make a major impact on the region's culture, from Thailand's Ministry of Culture.

In 2017 he was awarded the European Cultural Achievement Award by the Europa KulturForm, citing his building of bridges between Asian and Western cultures.

Books by S.P. Somtow

General Fiction
The Shattered Horse
Jasmine Nights
Forgetting Places
The Other City of Angels (aka *Bluebeard's Castle)*
The Stone Buddha's Tears

Dark Fantasy
The Timmy Valentine Series:
     Vampire Junction
     Valentine
     Vanitas
Vampire Junction Special Edition
Moon Dance
Darker Angels
The Vampire's Beautiful Daughter

Science Fiction
Starship & Haiku
Mallworld
The Ultimate Mallworld
The Ultimate, Ultimate, Ultimate Mallworld
Chronicles of the High Inquest:
     Light on the Sound
     The Darkling Wind
     The Throne of Madness
     Utopia Hunters
     Homeworld of the Heart
Chroniques de l'Inquisition - Volume 1 (omnibus)
Chroniques de l'Inquisition - Volume 2 (omnibus)
Inquestor Tales One: The Singing Moons

Inquestor Tales Two: A Woman Cloaked in Shadow
Inquestor Tales Three: The Child Collector
Inquestor Tales Four: The Space Between Spaces

The Aquiliad Series:
 Aquila in the New World
 Aquila and the Iron Horse
 Aquila and the Sphinx

Fantasy
The Riverrun Trilogy:
 Riverrun
 Armorica
 Yestern
The Riverrun Trilogy (omnibus)
The Fallen Country
Wizard's Apprentice
The Snow Dragon (omnibus)

Media Tie-in
The Alien Swordmaster
Symphony of Terror
The Crow - Temple of Night
Star Trek: Do Comets Dream?

Chapbooks
Fiddling for Waterbuffaloes
I Wake from a Dream of a Drowned Star City
A Lap Dance with the Lobster Lady
Compassion — Two Perspectives
The Bird Catcher

Libretti
Mae Naak
Ayodhya
Madana
Dan no Ura
Helena Citronova

The Snow Dragon
Dasjati:
>   *Temiya - The Silent Prince*
>   *Sama - The Faithful Son*
>   *Bhuridat - The Dragon Lord*
>   *Mahosadha - Architect of Dreams*
>   *Nemiraj - Chariot of Heaven*
>   *Prince Vessantara*

Collections
My Cold Mad Father
Fire from the Wine Dark Sea
Chui Chai (Thai)
Nova (Thai)
The Pavilion of Frozen Women
Dragon's Fin Soup
Tagging the Moon
Face of Death (Thai)
Other Edens
S.P. Somtow's The Great Tales (Thai)
Terror Nova (in press)
Terror Antiqua (in press)
Alien Heresies (in press)

Essays, Poetry and Miscellanies
Opus Fifty
A Certain Slant of "I" (in press)
Sonnets about Serial Killers
Opera East
Victory in Vienna (ed.)
Three Continents (ed.)
Nirvana Express
Caravaggio x 2
The Maestro's Noctuary
Nox: The Second Book of Dreams